The Heavens Within Our Grasp
A Medieval Anthology

The Heavens Within Our Grasp

A Medieval Anthology

NightEyes DaySpring • J.F.R. Coates • Alex T. Dragonson • Fopfox • Erik Televasi • Valduin • Rob Macwolf • Domus Vocis • J.S. Hawthorne • Utunu Casimir Laski • Rose LaCroix • Thomas "Faux" Steele • Cedric G! Bacon Ziegenbock • Faolan • Pascal Farful

ISBN: 978-1-948743-39-6

The Heavens Within Our Grasp: A Medieval Anthology
A project from The Furry Historical Fiction Society.

Cover by Hunter © 2024 — bluehunterart.com
Title page illustration and section divider by Itoma.

This book uses the fonts Gentium Book Plus, Gotische Initialen, Pfeffer Mediæval and Coelacanth.

Contents

The Furry Historical Fiction Society

The Heavens Within Our Grasp is a collaborative project by the authors of the stories, with each of us chipping in to help with the process of editing, organizing, and decision-making. Thanks is given to each author in turn for their contributions, and we all hope that you enjoy the fruits of our labor.

Learn more at fhfs.ink

Content warnings: Several stories contain religious conflict, violence (including blood, gore, and wound dressing), and death. "Midway in the Journey of Our Lives", "One Book to Burn", "The Seekers of Winter", Spring and Autumn of North and South", and "Houses of Stone" mention or imply sex. "One Book to Burn" and "The Seekers of Winter" include kidnapping. "Heaven Will Weigh the Heart of Stone" involves homophobia as a plot point.

Early

A Final Offering

NightEyes DaySpring

t was in the third year of Sten's rule as jarl when the gods finally sent the one foretold. The sky was gray, and the sun was hidden by thick clouds when the longship came into sight of the island. There was no one on shore looking for the boat, not that her arrival had not been foretold, but no one on the island believed the ship would ever come. It was a fool's errand this time of year to make the voyage, and while the vision had been given, the high priestess thought it was a lie. Their visions no longer came true anymore, so why should this one?

Yet when Sten first saw the longship, sail high, making toward his shores, he knew this was the boat from the vision. This was the end of everything for him, and the beginning of an age without. Without what, though, he did not know.

The wolf went to his small sod-covered home and picked up the sword his forefathers had given him and the shield his ancestors had survived behind. He marched down to the shore ready to face the boat and whomever it disgorged onto his shore. The others of the settlement saw his purpose, and having seen the sail, they too came, a soft murmur of voices behind him.

They were thirty strong when they reached the desolate shore, and Sten got a good look at the coming longship, the oars rhythmically dipping into the water. He was worried these would be Christians, followers of the shepherd, but no cross adorned the sail. Instead, the sail was blank, and whom it bore to their shore a mystery, except to Sten and the high priestesses.

As the ship approached, he realized the crew were wolves, foxes, lynxes, and bears, hearty northern folk, and they waved. Catching sight of a friendly lupine face, he relaxed. This boat looked to be carrying late season traders. Perhaps they had been blown off course and were seeking shelter. The first snows were soon to come, and no one wanted to brave the water when the ice froze to the lines.

The crew put their back into it, and the longship slipped to a halt up on the beach. Ropes were thrown, and villagers greeted the new arrivals. They were from the mainland, he knew that by looking at them, but when they called out a blessing to the gods for letting them make this journey and the ravens for having guided them, Sten knew they still clung to the old ways like him. With a nod, he directed his people to grab the ropes and pull the longship up so she could be unloaded and secured on the beach. There would be no conflict with this crew. None needed to fall and journey to Valhalla today.

Over the side of the boat came a figure in a long cloak, who landed with a splash in the shallows of the cold sea. His fur was not gray or brown like those on the boat. Instead, his fur was sandy colored, and it was thinner, the frame less furred. Immediately Sten was drawn to the stranger as he had obviously traveled quite a distance to get here, and he wondered why. A jackal? It was very rare to see one of them this far north. Maybe he was a trader from the south who was willing to trade with the northerners, seeking to exchange coin for goods. Or maybe his ancestors were from the south and he'd simply grown up further north than most jackals seemed to live.

The stranger glanced around, and the wolf headed toward him. Then the jackal turned to look at Sten, and Sten froze.

The jackal's eyes were bright, even in the dull gray light of the cold and gray day. His eyes shone, as if they gathered light that was not there, and Sten felt his chest tighten.

This one knew. This one saw.

Sten realized immediately he had not made the journey to trade. The sword Sten's ancestors had passed to him could do nothing against a threat like this, for this would not be a battle of strength. The jackal had come to the edge of the world to pray with some of the last holdouts of the old faith, even if his own faith was different.

The vision that Sten had seen was true, and the instrument of the god's bane had arrived. The fire he'd seen would soon follow.

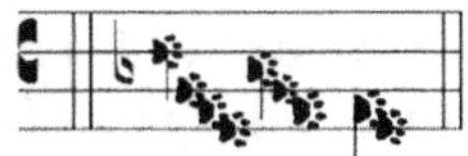

They went up the hill, and Sten welcomed the traveler into his small home. The fire was low, and Sten stoked it briefly while his new acquaintance happily warmed himself by it, trying to get feeling into his paws. "What do they call you, friend?" Sten asked.

"Tamir," said the jackal. "You?"

"Sten. I am jarl of this little island like my father was before me. My mother Bodil is the high priestess of the hof here." He paused. "Winter comes soon. It is dangerous to make a trip like this during this time of year. You are also a long way from home."

"I know," said the jackal, "but I have needed to come here and pay my respects for a long time." His pronunciation was different, but he spoke well, as one who had spent a lot of time learning a different tongue.

"The gods of this land are different from your gods. They might not speak to you."

The jackal looked up, ears lowered. "My gods are gone, erased. They do not answer us anymore, not that there are many believers of the old faith left. The people of my land have forgotten the old ways."

"As they will here someday it seems," said Sten. "Each year, the missionaries seem to creep closer, and more take up the faith of the shepherd. Where do you come from?"

"A hot land by a great river that floods frequently. It is called Kemet. It means black land, named after the soil the river gives us."

The wolf nodded. It made sense if his ancestors had lived for generations in a dry, hot land why the jackal had sandy colored fur. His fur was thinner too than the grizzled gray and black fur Sten had. "You came a long way to get here, it sounds like."

The jackal sighed. "I did indeed. My countrymen once believed in the shepherd, but now most seem drawn to the prophet. The children of the god of Abraham fight, and yet no quarter is given for the pagans there, or anywhere. I have traveled through their holy land, and I felt the questions upon me. Even in the shade of the great dome of Constantinople, there is no peace for a man like me. The old faiths still hold sway among the Rus, but it is probably only a matter of time."

Sten realized the jackal was barely older than him, and yet he seemed tired beyond his years from his long journey. "A pilgrimage to the Allfather is noble, but why?"

The jackal had turned back to the fire, but he looked up at Sten with eyes bright. "Because I saw myself here, and I knew I had to come. I would like to make an offering of incense and pray. If the gods are willing, I might see more of what fate lies ahead for the old faiths."

The wolf felt his ears dip.

"You're afraid," said the jackal. "Don't be."

"I am," replied Sten, "because my visions come to naught. Nothing comes to me to save the faith I love. Yet the only vision I have had in years that has had a remote bit of truth is of you."

"I can show you the old ways of seeing I was taught, passed down from time immemorial," replied the jackal. "It might help."

Sten was silent for a moment, thinking before he spoke. "I saw the altar to Odin burning, and you and I standing before it. I thought it was my foolish pride, but now that you have come, and you are real flesh and blood, what is there for me to do but make this real, and let my gods be forgotten?"

The jackal was quiet for a while. "Perhaps you don't understand the vision, or perhaps I am to be your ruin."

The wolf had unbuckled the sword of his ancestors when he'd brought the jackal into his home and placed it back where it normally rested. He glanced toward it now. "We'll see, it seems."

The jackal followed his gaze toward the sheathed sword. "Do you think my death will bring them back?"

"I would say hope is all I have at this point, but my ancestors fought and died to push back the coming of the cross. They saw some success, but slowly those around them were seduced by its promises. I lack the conviction to believe such bloodshed would change things."

The jackal's bright eyes looked him over as he thought for a moment. "The faithful march to slaughter, hoping to kill the faithful they believe unworthy in a land they call holy, and yet here we are, holdouts of a dying era with dying beliefs," he said. "My great ancestors once ruled a land of sand in a nation built of stone, and yet their works lie broken by time now. I came here because I heard rumor that the old gods are still strong here, and I could offer my vision. When I saw myself here, I knew I must make the journey as soon as I could. Before the ancient beliefs of my people are lost to time, let me see with you what is to be."

Sten dipped his muzzle. "You have come a long way, and I would not deny you the right to pray here, Tamir, but I must consult with the others first. Your arrival heralds something I do not understand."

"I am happy to wait a few days, but the boat must leave in the morning. They did not make this journey without trepidation."

The wolf looked at the jackal, meeting his gaze. There was power in those eyes he had only glimpsed briefly before. He knew then whatever happened, it would happen here. It was his fate to see to it, and yet in those eyes there was warmth, and a soul who had followed a long road to get here. "I have room here in my household, if you are willing to stay through the winter."

The jackal wagged his tail. "I would like that."

The old hof on the island had a peaked wood frame with a sod roof. It had a simple altar, and a small fire was kept burning before it. It was swept daily, and prayers given to the gods. The hof was surrounded by a low stone wall covered in moss that marked the building and the grounds as sacred to the gods.

Sten sat in the hof and studied the low fire.

"What do you see?" his mother, Bodil, asked. When she was young, her fur was brown with only a bit of gray. He'd taken after his father's coloration, but he'd inherited his mother's abilities. Now her fur was whitening due to age.

He said nothing, looking at the way the flames licked at the charcoal, before he looked up. "Nothing," he said to the other wolf.

"Did you throw the bones?" she asked him.

"I did, as you taught me."

Bodil nodded. "You are the most talented seer we've had in a generation, and yet you do not see."

"I try hard to, Mother."

She raised her paws. "It is not you. The gods speak to us less and less. I too have tried, and I see very little myself. In my dreams, you are there, and someone else."

Sten looked at the flames, licking the charcoal. "You think we should grant his request?"

"Your vision showed you this stranger. You would be foolish not to grant him what he asks."

"But the consequences..."

"Our faith is old, but it is fading. The gods do not speak to us, I fear, for too many of us have lost our way."

Sten was quiet, thinking about this.

"It is not your burden to carry," she responded softly. "Here, we are strong. Here we still sing in the old ways, and for as long as we can, we will. Our songs and our beliefs will outlast us here."

"I will have the priests prepare to make an offering then," said Sten.

"No," she said softly. "Only you and the stranger shall make this offering."

Sten looked at his mother and frowned. "Why?"

"Because that's what your vision showed you. That much is clear."

"The fire–"

Her reply was sharp. "Would you not do what the gods asked of you?"

There was no need for Sten to respond, and she got up then and left him with the low fire before the altar. The fire crackled softly, but in the dancing flames, he saw what he must do. Maybe all that was left to him was fire.

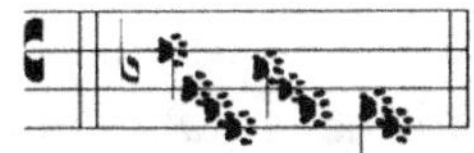

Before they could do the ritual and make the offering though, they needed to prepare. Sten brought Tamir to the hof the next day to commune with the gods. While Bodil would not participate in the ritual, she began the preparations for Sten.

The fall harvest was already complete. Sten had already collected herbs for the winter and dried them. His mother packed the bundle as Sten sat in silence, letting her prepare the sacred herbs. The jackal, for his part, took to writing his thoughts in a book, using a script far different than the runes Sten knew. He'd asked the jackal about it, and he'd blushed, surprised Sten had noticed.

"This is Coptic. It's what I learned growing up. I still record my personal thoughts in it."

"I have never heard of it before."

"It is not as oft spoken as it once was," said the jackal. "Things change."

"Indeed," said the wolf. "I have spoken to Bodil and the other acolytes. We can do the ritual tomorrow."

"Do you have another seer, or am I the only one here?" asked Tamir.

"Only Bodil and I can see," said Sten. "The others do not have the power of vision."

Tamir nodded and looked over the carved runes of the altar. "This place is very sacred to your people. I can feel the power here."

"You are wise," Bodil said, looking up from the careful twining of rope she was doing.

"Indeed," responded Sten. "This is but a remnant of the old ways. The great temples of our faith have been burned, replaced by the churches of the nonbelievers. Our kings no longer worship the Æsir. Soon they will come and demand tribute from us and expect us to bend the knee before their God, and who am I to say their ways are wrong? My gods no longer give us visions of glory, but visions of death. Ragnarök has come for them, but not in the way they ever feared."

"My faith is gone,' said the jackal. "Only a few still believe, and the Roman Emperors destroyed much of it when they converted. Only the old stones remain, our sacred writings lost. Now even Rome has fallen and only the east holds on."

"Many of my ancestors served the emperors of the east, but the faith did not flourish there. At best it was tolerated among the heathens. If so much of your faith is lost though, why make such a long journey?"

"I have long wanted to make a real offering, and to pray to my gods in a place sacred that understands the world has not one face but many. A place that we are many, and yet in our many, we are one. Where the old stories still live, even if the gods no longer walk the earth like they once did. Finally, I saw where I would do that."

The wolf was silent for a moment, thinking. He looked over at Bodil carefully knotting the bundle of herbs, and he made a deci- sion. "We will do the ritual in a week's time. First, let us show you the old ways of our people and celebrate your arrival, not with trep- idation, but with joy. The old hall still stands, and it has been a while since we've celebrated in it. We will feast, and tell you our tales like my ancestors. There are still those among my people who have the tongue of a skald. Let us give them a chance to speak the old stories."

Sten's sleep was disturbed, but the vision had come back to him, clearer and stronger than before. He was there before the hof as it burned, his sandy-colored paws covered in blood. A bloody dagger was in one paw, and a heart was in another. The heretic who believed in the other gods was dead. The heretic was gone. The ravens called out the loss to Odin, and in his dream he knew that the Allfather could hear them.

Off in the distance, he could see the seas shaking. The serpent was pleased. The storm was coming. Unearthly howls echoed in the distance as the roots of the world tree shook. Sten knew then that the gods would fall. High in the sky, a wolf was closing in on the sun, jaws ready to strike.

Sten sat bolt upright with a gasp. Ragnarök! He'd seen it. Was what he was about to do going to start the end of the world?

The gods gifted him his visions, though. That was what Bodil had always told him. They knew what they were telling him. Perhaps this all was a trick by Loki, but why would he want to bring about Ragnarök? His death, like Odin's, was foretold.

Sten sighed. He looked over at the sleeping form of Tamir and shook his head. His mother had warned him not to deny the gods, but he had been delaying. Hoping to buy time to understand his own fate.

He looked down at his gray-colored paws. They shook nervously. The time had come. He would do what they wanted. The vision seemed wrong, but finally, the vision was clear.

Sten lay back down and watched the form of the sleeping jackal, and closed his eyes, wet with tears. Soon, he told himself. The time was coming, and Tamir would complete his journey.

The old mead hall was swept clean, and fresh straw laid down on the earthen floor. Firewood was brought in and stacked inside for the hearth. At dawn, on the day of the festival, the fire in the hall was stoked and a feral pig was slaughtered for its meat. Dried cod and herring caught earlier in the season were prepared into hearty porridges.

The promise of snow was in the air, and the villagers came into the old hall to warm up. Even shepherds from the far side of the island were there, ready to celebrate the old songs. As beer was poured and more people arrived, the space became lively, reminiscent of the days of old when raiders had come back to the island with their rewards. Sten led Tamir to the dais at one end of the hall and poured mead for the jackal. He gave the jackal a blanket of wool to drape over his shoulders because even in the shelter of the hall, he shivered a little due to the cold.

After a while, a fox with white fur stood up and went to the center of the room before the lit hearth. The voices died down.

"Oh, dear friends," he started, "we have gathered today to tell tales and remember ourselves. Today we sing for we must sing, and we sing because we can sing. We howl because we can howl, and we feast because we must eat. Because we are!"

"Because we are!" called back many in the room.

"We live because we live. We love because we can. We fish because we hunger, and we hunger because we live. And why do we do all this?" he asked the crowd.

"Because we are!"

"Yes, because we are. Because we always were, and because we will always be for as long as we can be, because we remember our gods, and our faith. We remember the old stories, we remember the past, and we honor it as surely as the skalds of old did, for here, the skalds still sing!" said the fox, finishing with a flourish.

The crowd cheered, and the fox walked back to where he was seated. A drum and horn were brought out, and a young wolf stepped forward and began to howl a wordless tune to the beat of the drummer along with the horn blower. It was both haunting and beautiful what she did with her voice, letting it follow the horn.

Tamir leaned over to whisper to Sten. "Your people sing beautifully."

"We sing as we always have, or at least as far back the skalds can remember. The tradition has been passed down to each generation," responded the wolf softly, so as not to disturb the singer. "What songs do they sing where you come from?"

The jackal took a sip of his mead. "We do not recite the great poems of your skalds, but we do sing and dance. The wind in the desert where I was born blows incessantly, and one of the favorite instruments from my home village is the ney. It is a flute made from a hollow reed plucked from the banks of the Nile. It is said you can sing to the dunes with one, and the old god Seth will still call back to you. The desert is his domain, but very few still know how to read the signs. I am the last that I know of. The sight had not been seen in a generation before I was born. I was lucky one of the village elders remembered what the old seers used to do, and could teach me a little. The rest I learned from an old codex given to me."

The wolf nodded. "And it brought you here."

The jackal sighed. "That is fate and fear. I wandered for a while. I don't know if I would be welcome home anymore, and few probably would remember me there. My talents always brought me suspicion, but there were those who sought to use them."

"To see beyond is a blessing."

The jackal turned. "Do you really think so? I have wondered long about that. Perhaps the world is better off without it, for we are to meet our fates on our own merits."

Sten shifted uncomfortably. "Perhaps. Yet do we not long to know?"

"We do, but do we not trust our gods?" he asked.

The wolf turned back to the singer who was finishing up her first song. "I do know what fate they have for me, and I trust whatever the ravens of the Allfather see and tell him. Perhaps these are the last days of my people and the three wolves who will bring the end of the world will finally come."

"Three wolves?"

"Yes. One is large and monstrous, and goes by the name of Fenris. It is said he will bring about the final battle, Ragnarök. While he fights Odin and kills him, his children Skoll and Hati will devour the sun and moon. Afterward, the world will be reclaimed, but many will die before that."

The singer started another song.

"My people do not believe the world will end," said Tamir, "at least not in the old faith. Our gods fought a struggle to maintain the order of the world every day, but it was never said they would fail in their daily trials. If they must keep the world moving, then so must I keep myself moving."

"You are a strange man, but I respect you for that," responded Sten.

The jackal shrugged. "It is not strange to me, but I can only hope that this journey was wise. I came here to pray to your gods, but I do not know if they would be willing to hear my voice."

Sten watched the singer lift her muzzle to the rooftops and hit a particularly high note with her wordless howl before he responded in a whisper. "Perhaps not, but tell them about your gods, and they will listen. The Allfather has always favored poetry and enjoyed a good story. Odin went to great lengths to acquire the mead of poetry, and the Æsir treasure it so. Someone will at least listen if you speak well."

They lapsed into silence, and the wolf sang for two more songs before she stepped away. A bear stepped up, and the room focused on her. "I wish to speak of our guest," she called out.

Tamir's ears went up and he turned to Sten. The gray wolf spread his paws out, unsure what she'd say. The bear walked over toward them. "I have been running these lines in my head since you arrived. Please, let me honor your journey."

"Of course," said Tamir.

The bear spoke.

"Oh sandy furred one,
I see you have come far,
And with purpose,
With desire and hunger,
With wisdom,
And with need.

Oh sandy furred one,
What do you seek,
For what purpose did you come,
What can the gods say to you,
That brought you so far,
To sate your desires?

Oh sandy furred one,
What do you seek in this winter,
In this cold land,
So far from your home,
What can you hope to find here,
Here with us on this island?

Oh sandy furred one,
With eyes so bright and clear,
With fur so soft and thin,
With cold seeking out your bones,
Why come here,
To the edge of the earth?

Oh sandy furred one,
With dreams so long,

With so much unknown,
With sight to guide you,
What can you tell us,
What can you say?

Oh sandy furred one,
With tail here in the cold,
What you must have seen,
What you must have heard,
What you must have known,
What you must still do?

Oh sandy furred one,
With ears tall and pointed,
With fur unlike our own,
With bones tired from the journey,
Please accept this verse,
To help warm your heart.

Oh sandy furred one,
Of faith not our own,
But just as old,
Let our gods speak to you,
Let you show us your truth,
Let the dawn light your way.

Oh sandy furred one,
Let not the harsh winter freeze you,
Let not the cold chill you,
But let the mead warm you,
Let the fire light your night,
Let the ravens guide you.

Oh sandy furred one
Whose vision is strong,

Let us welcome you,
And let you welcome us,
And let the gods show you,
Whatever you came to seek."

The bear stopped then and bowed. "May my words please you," she said.

Tamir smiled and his tail thumped. "They do! I hope I can answer you back soon."

"Excellent. Then let us pour you some more mead, and let us sing another song, for there are more songs to sing."

Sten got up and stepped forward. "Indeed, a cheer for our guest!"

The room responded in a raucous cheer, and the wolf who had sung earlier stepped back up. Sten seated himself again next to the jackal.

"We will go tonight," responded Tamir.

Sten glanced at him and felt the ice in his stomach grip him. He nodded. "I had a feeling it would be after this."

"Yes, when the others are asleep. I feel that is the right time."

The crowd roared with laughter over something the singer said and she started a new song, but Sten's attention was focused completely on Tamir. "So, at dawn?"

The jackal flicked his ears, and then nodded. Sten took a deep breath and nodded back. The time had been set. The time of the fire had come.

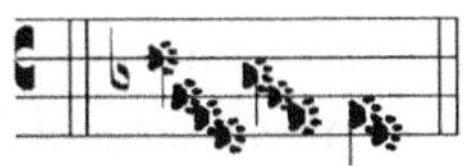

They left the mead hall when the last of the songs had been sung, and the last of the stories told. The day was just starting to brighten, as their paws crunched across the icy earth. Their breath frosted in the air. To Sten the cold was more an annoyance, but to Tamir, it ate at him. He still had the wool blanket over his cloak and had not taken it off all night.

"With the boat gone, I will need thicker clothing for the winter," he remarked.

"As my guest, you are welcome to any cloak of mine."

"I do not wish to impose. How will I repay you?"

Sten felt his heart twist, but it was almost time. "What we are about to do is payment enough. My visions are cloudy. Yours are clear. That will be enough."

The jackal exhaled, looking at the cloud of his breath. "My visions do not always show me great truths. I've seen things that seemed of little importance before."

Sten stopped and turned to him. "But you've seen."

"Yes." Tamir tiled his head. "Have you not?"

Sten's ears fell and he turned to continue toward the hof. "Frustratingly little. The only thing I've really seen is a boat, your boat, and the fire. I thought the vision useless until you came."

Tamir followed. "You said you saw a fire?"

"Yes."

"What type of fire?"

The wolf didn't say anything.

"I hate to ask you this, but what will you do if the gods show me nothing?" asked Tamir.

Sten stopped again and turned around, tail bristling. "You think they brought you all this way here for some cruel joke?"

Tamir shook his head. "No, I know they wanted me to come here. I just worry that what they'll show me is that there is nothing more to show me."

Sten didn't say anything for a minute. He just looked at his paws. "They have shown me what must happen," he said after a minute. "I've worried since you arrived that the Allfather brought a powerful seer to this island because I have failed my people, but two nights ago, I saw the truth of what must happen."

"What did you see?" asked Tamir.

Sten looked down, tears in his eyes. "For long I worried that my gods are truly dead to me. I have done everything they have asked of me, yet they abandoned me. But now I have seen what must happen. I will show you how to speak to them."

Tamir's ears went back. "Gods are fickle. The desert is a harsh place, and when you travel through you pray to the gods you have enough water, and you packed enough food. If Seth wished me dead, he would have spun up a sandstorm and blinded me in the middle of the desert and waited until I ran out of water and food. Instead, I made those journeys safely, perhaps because Seth needed me alive or my actions pleased him. I came here because I believed whatever the gods needed me to do, I could do. There would be no one else who would undertake this journey."

"For how long have you traveled?"

"Ten years, if you count the time I spent in the court of the emperors on the Golden Horn."

The wolf took a deep breath and clenched his paws. His tail bristled. "Come then, let us finish this journey for you. The end has come."

They walked in silence the rest of the way to the hof and entered the sacred space. Sten directed his guest to sit at one side of the altar. The fire still burned before it, the charcoal fresh. One of the priests must have refilled it overnight. He picked up the bundle of herbs Bodil had prepared and tossed them on the fire. Then he reached behind the altar and pulled out the dagger he had placed behind it. He laid it in front of the fire. Then he sat down in front of the altar and silently asked for Odin to give him the strength to go through with this, no matter what terrible thing it unleashed.

Tamir looked at the dagger. "What is this?"

Sten turned to face the jackal. "My final vision showed me what you must do. The most sacred thing you can offer the Allfather is a life. I will be that life. My body will be buried in a well so that you can gain the blessing and wisdom of my gods."

The jackal took in a sharp breath. "I will not kill you for this."

"You must."

"No," said Tamir strongly. "I came to pray to the gods, but my own gods do not ask such brutality of us."

The wolf growled. "Perhaps your gods are weak then."

The jackal's ears flicked. "Perhaps you have given up your faith."

Sten looked at the jackal, and in that moment, he realized that while one of them had to die, which one didn't matter. He reached for the dagger. "If that is your choice, then I must make the offering."

Tamir's ears went back. His hackles went up. "What do you mean?" he asked softly.

Sten's hand closed around the hilt of the dagger. "Odin drank from the well of Mimir to gain great knowledge, but only after he sacrificed one of his eyes to do so. An offering must be made."

Tamir shrunk back from the wolf, but the wolf pounced. Sten was heavier, he was a little younger, and he was stronger. He pinned Tamir down easily.

"Wait, this is not right!" screamed the jackal.

"One of us must die," growled Sten grabbing the jackal and lifting him up, and then slamming him down in the dirt to stun him. "You know it to be true."

"You don't understand," coughed Tamir, desperately trying to claw at Sten to get him off him. The blunted claws couldn't break through the cloak Sten wore.

The wolf lowered himself down to stare into the amber eyes, noses almost touching. "You have powers I can only dream of. The Allfather sent you to kill me. If you are not willing to use the blade, then I will do what the gods ask of us." He pressed down on Tamir's chest with his weight. "One of us must die. It is what brings us closer to the end of all things." He pressed the edge of the dagger against the jackal's throat, into the fur. "I'm sorry it comes to this."

"I saw..." Tamir grimaced as the tip of the blade cut his throat, "your vision."

Sten's resolve faltered, and he pulled back the dagger slightly. "And?"

"We were together. The fire was a bonfire."

Sten growled. "You lie!"

"I can show you."

Sten looked at the jackal with the bright eyes and he snarled. "I saw your paws with my heart in them, I saw the coming of Ragnarök. What can you tell me that I have not seen?"

"We have two eyes to see with. Two seers can see much further than one."

The blade in his hand was heavy. The paws in his vision had been stained with his own blood.

"Please... I came here for you."

"By the Allfather... Fine!" Sten sat up and lifted the dagger to his paw and slit the pad so it bled. He then grabbed Tamir's paw and slit it open also. The jackal yelped, and he pressed his bloody paw to Tamir's bloody paw.

"My blood to your blood. My life to your life," intoned the wolf. "I bind my fate to you by binding my blood to yours. Show me what you see, Tamir, and we will make the gods' fate manifest."

"By the Dark Jackal, you are blind."

"Show me!"

Tamir sighed. "Get off me, and I will show you."

The wolf got off the jackal and threw the dagger aside. Tamir picked himself off the ground and resumed a seated position while Sten stood over him. He looked at his cut paw. "You do not wish to share my fate."

"I wish to help my people. I wish to keep the gods in this world. I wish to make them happy."

The jackal sighed tiredly. "So be it then. Sit," he ordered.

Tamir waited and Sten got in a seated position in front of him. "Your fear blinds you," remarked Tamir.

"My fear is what I have left," responded the wolf.

The jackal huffed. "Look into my eyes, and what do you see?"

Sten looked. "A light that shouldn't be there."

"Look further."

"That's all."

Tamir sighed and closed his eyes. "You have to want to see things you don't want to see."

"But I do."

Tamir opened his eyes and clasped his bloody paw to Sten's bloody paw. "Do you truly?"

"Yes?" offered Sten, with a bit of hesitation.

"Ah, there it is. The doubt, the fear. Look at me, Sten!"

"I am..."

"Deeper."

"I..." he faltered. There was fire in the jackal's eyes. Fire that had not been there before.

Tamir tightened his grip, their bloody paws intertwined. "No, you will see. You swore your fate to me. You will see then, even if it hurts, even if it burns every last strand of your fur. You will see!"

Sten wanted to protest, wanted to say something, but the fire reached into his sky, and he saw. He saw first a bonfire and he stood before it. And then he saw fire reaching into the sky in a land devoid of trees. He heard sounds and words he could not understand.

"Focus on what you see."

He tried to, but there was so much, so much swirling.

"Focus!"

Everything was coming apart, and everything was coming together. His vision was blinded, and he stood before the fire, and with him was Tamir, but everything didn't make sense and...

Tamir let go of Sten's paw and the wolf fell to the side, gasping, mind running.

The jackal shook his paw out and sighed again, letting himself settle. "And now you have seen. Your visions are confusing, but with time they might offer clarity."

"And what does my vision mean?"

"I do not know. That's what I am here to explore."

He felt his paws shaking. "Was that Ragnarök?"

The jackal smiled softly. "My gods do not believe in an end like that," said Tamir, "so I do not believe it to be the end. A moment of something. A noise perhaps? Echoes of past visions or futures we can only glimpse at? Time tells all, but we may not live to see the story. You will rest now, Sten, and tomorrow we will repeat this."

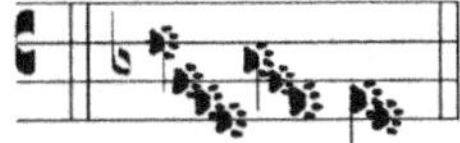

The fires, the visions, none of it made sense. There were more things he couldn't understand. Things Tamir couldn't understand. The only thing he saw frequently that he did understand was a bonfire, so on the shortest day of the year, they built one.

"What does it mean?" asked Sten, watching over the flames of the bonfire.

"Do you think it has to mean something?" responded Tamir.

He turned to look at the fire. "It has to mean something. I keep searching for what it all means."

"What does your mother think it means?"

"I asked. She cannot say. She says she is too old to make a judgment like that," responded Sten.

"I think Bodil cannot say because it doesn't mean anything. It's at least not something we can understand."

The wolf frowned. "But the visions have to mean something."

"I thought so too for a long time, but I don't know. The gods are fickle. Who knows if what they show us has to have a meaning."

"You said the technique you use is ancient."

The jackal pulled the wool cloak closer to himself in the cold. "It is."

"Surely it would not have been preserved if it didn't show some truth."

The jackal chuckled. "I think there is truth in them, but my ability to understand it is lacking. I am not the seer who spoke to the Allfather and saw what was to be his fate. I am not the god Shai from my homeland who knows the span of each life and is there to observe the weighing of their heart, satisfied in their knowledge. The gods are fickle. What they show us are only glimpses of things."

Sten turned back to the fire. "I worry the followers of the cross will one day supplant us."

"Perhaps they will. Perhaps when spring comes, they will be here. All we can do is tell the stories of our gods to those who will listen."

The wolf tilted his head. "How well do you write our language?"

"Not well, but I know how to prepare ink."

"There is still a lot of winter left. If you are willing to help me, I'd like to write some of the old poems down. Maybe we can write some of yours down."

"That's not in the visions," remarked the jackal.

"And are we bound to them? You've said yourself you cannot figure out their meaning. They've shown us places that were, and places that will be."

Tamir considered for a minute. "With my blood to yours, with my life to yours, we will share our fate. I could not leave after a bond like that was forged in a temple. You've practically married us before multiple gods. So, if you wish to write, we will write."

The wolf dipped his muzzle. "I... it's a bit more than that."

The jackal stamped a paw to get some more feeling into it. "It's a bond forged in blood due to visions sent from the gods. With such powerful signs, I would be incredibly foolish not to accept you as my mate."

"We're just very good friends," protested the wolf.

Tamir chuckled. "For now. I've had some visions that suggest otherwise."

The Purple Rose

J.F.R. Coates

hillip paced impatiently at the base of the great walls that surrounded the palace, the austere and smooth walls impossible to climb, should anyone dare consider such a thing. There was no movement around the walls, the muffled sounds of palace life beyond barely audible.

The badger clicked his tongue several times as he kept his eye on the low sun, casting copper and bronze hues across the rooftops of the surrounding buildings. Those who lived this close to the palace were mostly nobles and wealthy merchants, leaving someone like Phillip quite out of place, but no one had confronted him about his presence just yet. It was only a matter of time, though.

Church bells pealed their tune almost all at once. Ochre light radiated against the imposing walls of the palace as sound and light greeted the coming of the night. Hurried footsteps pattered through the shadows, coming from the narrow alley that ran between the walls and the closest row of houses.

A wolf hurried from the darkness, hastily adjusting a royal servant's garb. He carried a bundle of spare clothes and rags in his arms, hunched over slightly to keep it partially hidden from any potential onlookers. He was right on time.

"Where are we going?" the wolf asked, the moment he got within hearing range of the badger.

Phillip lifted his nose to scent the air. He could not detect any evidence of someone chasing after the wolf. Justin had made it from the palace undetected.

"This way," Phillip said, turning and gesturing to one of the narrow roads that led downhill, away from the palace. "I've been able to find a new one."

Justin said nothing. He merely grunted in acknowledgement and followed the badger down the narrow street, towards the lower part of the city and the poorer districts squeezed between the hills of the royal precinct and the coast.

As the twilight deepened, more lights began to flicker on inside the many homes that lined the narrow streets, the scent of smoke strengthening to clear away some of the other, less savoury smells that filled the city. Their destination was a small, plain building not far from the main road, just one of the thousands of near identical houses that made up this part of the city.

Phillip knocked on the heavy oak door a couple of times and waited for a response from within. A deep growl rumbled out. The badger took a step back a moment before the door opened, almost wrenched from its hinges by a powerful lynx with fearsome yellow eyes that glared at the newcomers. Multiple lines of white fur crisscrossed the lynx's arms, evidence of the scars that lay beneath.

"Yes?" the feline snarled. Even from such a curt and abrupt statement, Phillip could hear the accent of a northerner.

"Kristoff?" Phillip asked, struggling not to stutter at the sight of the powerful warrior.

The lynx grunted. "Come in."

Trying not to let his intimidation show, Phillip followed the lynx inside. There was a moment of intense darkness as Justin pulled the door closed behind them, a heavy latch falling into place with a resounding clunk. Another door opened, further down the narrow corridor, and firelight from another room washed into the gloom.

Phillip quickly glanced around the room, taking in the stone walls and the sparse, cheap furnishings. There was only one occupant to the room, a small rat sat by a table in the middle of the room, much of his head shrouded in shadow cast by his oversized hood.

"Leave us, Sigurd," the rat said, flicking his hand towards the door.

Phillip blinked and stared as the lynx shuffled out into the dark corridor, closing the door behind him. There was no further sound from out there. A bodyguard, then. Not the contact. Which meant...

"You are developing quite the reputation, badger," Kristoff said. The rat pulled off his hood, his grey fur well groomed and his prominent front teeth showing as he grinned coldly. "Someone might be inclined to think you were working with the city guard to expose the fences. Were it not for the fact that none of them have gone missing, I might have instructed Sigurd to turn you away at the door."

Phillip licked his lips nervously and spared a quick glance to Justin, but the wolf didn't seem to notice. He stood by the fireplace, staring into the flickering flames.

"I can assure you, we're not working with the city guard," Phillip said slowly. This was what he had feared, switching fence with every sale. Trust was an important and rare commodity when trading in stolen goods, especially when they came from the palace. "We've simply been trying to establish contacts."

Kristoff chittered with laughter, but that amusement did not show in his eyes. "Loyalty is everything in this business, kid. It's clear you're new to this, so consider that some advice before you get yourself arrested or killed. Take heed of it, because it's the only advice I will give for free."

"Understood, thank you," Phillip said. He dipped his head, averting his eyes away from the rat's leering grin.

The rodent clicked his fingers. "But come. Time is money, and you must be eager to share your wares. What do you have for me?"

Phillip had to clear his throat to get Justin's attention. The wolf jerked into awareness, tearing his eyes away from the fire, before he approached the rat. He placed the bundle of rags and spare robes on the table, then reverently pulled back the layers to reveal the treasures within.

A dazzling array of gold, silver, and gemstones was revealed, shimmering in the soft firelight. Justin had swiped an impressive collection, mainly from the kitchens it appeared, as much of it was gold and silver cutlery and plateware, with a couple of gem-laded brooches and necklaces for additional glamour.

Phillip struggled to contain his wonder. Before this arrangement with Justin, he had never come across so much precious metal before, and he still wondered at the wolf's secrets in being able to obtain so much.

Kristoff showed no such awe. The rat leaned forward, fingers twitching, as he peered at the treasures on his table. "A fascinating collection," he mused. Without asking permission, he started to sift through the precious metals, testing each piece carefully between his fingers, even biting the end of one fork and wrinkling his nose at the taste.

"How much do you think it's worth?" Justin asked. His ear flicked back a couple of times, nose twitching.

The rat looked up sharply. His bright eyes darted around, taking in every feature of the wolf. Justin lowered his gaze and turned away. "Eager to make a deal, are you? Why? Does someone know you took it?"

Justin didn't answer, seemingly distressed at the rat's attention. He stuttered a few times, but no words managed to emerge.

"No one knows," Phillip said. Though he could not be certain, Justin had never failed him. He had never been captured or followed. However the wolf managed to smuggle such a steady stream of treasure from the palace, it had proven effective. "Please, if you would. How much for this?"

The rat clicked his tongue. It did not take him long to decide. "Ten solidi for it all."

Mere months ago, such an offer would have been a price beyond anything Phillip could imagine. Before he had known about the sheer wealth within the palace walls, ten solidi would have been an amount of absurd wealth. Even with the experience since then, he struggled to contain his awe.

The badger opened his mouth to accept the offer, but Justin spoke first. "Fifteen."

Kristoff laughed. This time, there was genuine mirth as he shook his head. "You're bold. I may not know you, but I think I like you, pup. You might have something ahead of you, after all. But that doesn't mean I'm going to let you rob me like you robbed those rich pricks in the palace. I'll give you twelve and no more."

Justin held out his hand to seal the deal. A few moments later, a dozen golden coins exchanged hands, the wolf tucking them into a specially made pouch sewn into the inside of his tunic.

The rat bundled up the treasure but left it on the table. Justin's eyes lingered on the bundle of cloth, a tiny whimper escaping his mouth, almost imperceptible to hear.

"Was there anything else?" Kristoff asked.

Justin shook his head. "No. Thank you. That was all." He bowed his head and took a step back. He turned with a seemingly great effort.

The door opened before he reached it, the towering lynx stepping inside to clear room inside the corridor. The great cat's lips parted in a snarl. "On your way," he growled, gesturing with one meaty paw into the darkness.

Phillip hurried after Justin, not wanting to linger too long on the rat's patience. He had no doubt that Sigurd would provide a powerful physical deterrent to anyone testing Kristoff longer than the rat desired.

Despite his fear, Phillip couldn't help but feel a surge of excitement. Twelve solidi would more than cover their plans. This could be it, the day they escaped the tired city and went to live the life they truly desired, out in the great beyond. Not even Sigurd's presence, looming behind his shoulder, could fully dampen that joy.

The door slammed closed behind them, the locks audibly latching shut even through the heavy oak. The streets had started to become busier with the growing dusk, the evening masses finishing, with bells ringing throughout the city. This was one of the few times in the day when the city truly felt dynamic, full of activity and life.

It was like the city put on a mask, desperate to hide its true identity for a short time each night.

Phillip couldn't wait to be rid of it.

The wolf and badger said nothing as they left the fence's home far behind them. They both knew where they were going. As always, they headed further down the hill, towards the rotting and partially abandoned ports, where half the berths were always empty and the piers were at risk of falling into the sea.

The district closest to the water had once been grand and rich, and the buildings still showed shadows of this old wealth. Chipped and cracked columns held aloft balconies that overlooked the shore, while the cobbled roads underfoot were of a quality only matched by those around the palace. But where there were fading memories of wealth, there was an ever-present squalor. Dung and muck filled the nose, while those unarmed soon found themselves feeling the prick of a dagger.

This was a part of the city that set Phillip's nerves on edge, especially when his companion carried such a wealth of coin in his pouch. But the wolf carried an air of quiet confidence about him, strong enough to deter potential attackers, while still appearing uninteresting and without threat. It was a difficult balance to strike, but Justin had always managed to walk that line.

Their destination was a tavern close to the decrepit port. The *Old Gold* was close enough to the main roads to draw in unsuspecting clientele seeking a cheap room and cheaper beer, but just far enough away to avoid the main patrol routes of the city watch. It had been a regular haunt of Phillip's since before he had come of age, and where he had met Justin on one of the wolf's escapades from his duties at the palace.

The door was wedged open with a block of cracked masonry, letting out some of the smoke and noise from within. Phillip warily glanced around to see if anyone watched them, only slipping into the dark interior of the tavern when he was confident no one paid any attention to the comings and goings of a wolf and badger.

A smouldering fireplace and a dozen lanterns provided light that shimmered off the smoke lingering near the ceiling. Behind the bar, a tan-furred jackal barely reacted to their presence, with little more than a flick of an ear to indicate she had even seen her regular customers arrive. Almost every table was occupied, largely with workers from the port, but there was also a pair of mustelid merchants sat in the corner, warily eying the newcomers with their hands protectively resting on bulging packs.

Justin ignored the merchants entirely, and Phillip's eyes quickly slid from them. They were of little interest. Instead, the badger hurried after his lupine companion to the far side of the room, bumping through the boisterous crowd, to take their usual seat by the stairs to the upper levels, where there were rooms for hire. In that dark corner was an old wooden bench, likely a pew from a church in a former life. The firm cushions were never quite enough to ease the hardness of the pew, but it was Justin's favourite seat as it gave him a good view of the entire tavern. The shadows were also a little deeper there, providing some obscurity from prying eyes.

Phillip opened his mouth to speak. He was silenced by a small shake of the head from Justin. The wolf's lips pursed as he flicked his ears back. He tilted his head towards the bar.

The badger glanced around. They were not alone for much longer. A hare approached, a flagon of beer in each hand. "Good timing boys," Irene said, grinning widely as her long ears twitched to the sounds of the tavern. "I just finished my shift, so thought I'd share with you."

Justin's hand rested over his chest, about where the pouch of precious coins sat. He said nothing to chase away Irene.

Phillip's smile was weak. "That's why we're here. Why don't you get yourself a drink? On me?" He held out a small copper coin for the hare to take.

"Too generous, thank you." Irene spilled some of the beer across the table as she placed down the two flagons, before snatching up the offered coin and bounding back towards the bar.

The badger took advantage of the final moments of isolation he bought them. He leaned across the table. "Do we leave tonight?"

Again, Justin shook his head. "No. Not tonight. There's still one thing I need from the palace. Tomorrow, though. After sunset."

"What else is there?" Phillip hissed, barely audible over the noise of the tavern. "We have everything, surely."

Justin chewed his lip. "Not this. Just... I can't tell you what it is yet. You just need to trust me on this. Tomorrow, I promise."

There was no more time to say anything else as Irene bundled her way back across the busy tavern, managing only to get a couple of splashes of beer into her fur. She collapsed onto the pew beside Phillip. "What's the celebration for tonight?"

"Celebration?" Phillip growled. "I survived another day in this city. There doesn't need to be anything else."

Irene scoffed. "Is that really all? Surviving one day at a time? Where's your sense of adventure? Your appreciation for life?"

The badger's eyes flicked up to Justin. They shared a quick, almost imperceptible shake of the head. He then furrowed his brow and stared down into his beer. "There's no adventure or life here. Just a long, slow death, especially for us outside the palace."

"Nonsense," Irene said, slamming her beer down on the table with enough strength to send splashes across the stained wood. "Just because we don't have the privilege of the nobles doesn't mean we can't live a good life. Sure, they're better us, but we can still be happy."

"They're not better," Justin whispered, barely audible over the raucous noise of the tavern. He held his flagon high, covering his muzzle, but he did not drink. He simply gazed into the amber liquid, as though he sought some fortune within it. "Everyone is always taught that those born in the palace are better than those who are not, as though the location of your birth has any bearing on that. Both the nobles and the commoners are taught this and seem to believe it as though it is some great truth of the world."

Irene's ears pinned back as she glanced around the tavern, as though fearful of being overheard, but the noise continued unabated. "I don't know how you've survived this long at the palace if you blurt out things like that. Such talk will get you killed."

Justin shrugged and leaned back on the pew. He finally started to drink, gulping down several large mouthfuls of the bitter and strong beer. He belched and wiped his mouth with the back of his hand, clear droplets sticking to his fur and dangling from his whiskers. "The station of our birth is determined by luck and chance. There is no other difference between us. No difference in quality. No divine intervention. Just the fortune of being born in the purple or born on the street. That's all there is to it."

"Christ have mercy, I have not had enough beer for this," Irene muttered. She managed a nervous laugh. "I dread to ask how you came to believe this."

The wolf smirked. He rested his head against the wall, shadows cast by the nearest sconce dancing across his face. "No one expects me to see as much as I do. My position in the palace gives me access to so many people, but everyone looks at me and doesn't see who or what I am. I'm little more than a shadow to them, serving a specific purpose but having no will of my own."

"And what exactly is it you do?"

"Whatever people instruct me to do." Justin drained the dregs of his beer, showing no ill-effects for downing the entire flagon so quickly. "Like I said, the nobles think I have no will of my own. They see me as a tool to wield. They are not good people, and they certainly are not better than you."

"What's next? The emperor's marriage is just an excuse to strip the city of all its wealth?" Irene said, hushing her voice so it didn't carry far. "I've heard nonsense like that spread at the docks, from people who have spent too long abroad. Not from people like us."

Justin scoffed. "The emperor. If only you knew what really happened in the palace. If everyone knew. They'd see who really runs the empire."

Irene tapped her foot against the floor beneath the table. Her fingers drummed on the wood, grasping her beer with just one hand. "Something is bothering you tonight. Did you need another beer?"

Justin stood up. He flicked his ears back. "No, thank you. I should get back to the palace before someone notices I'm gone." He inclined his head respectfully towards the hare, then locked eyes with Phillip. "I'll see you tomorrow."

Tomorrow. When everything would finally happen, and they could be free of this place. Phillip tried to keep his body language neutral as he waved goodbye to the wolf, who quickly disappeared amongst the crowd, the hood of his cloak pulled up over his ears. No one paid him any attention, but for the mustelid merchants by the door, who whispered to each other and pointed, but they caused no troubles.

"I think I could use that extra drink," the badger said. He started to rise to his feet so he could request one from the barkeep, but Irene put her hand on his shoulder and pushed him back down.

"My treat tonight."

Phillip stared after the hare as she went to get a couple more beers. Perhaps there was one thing about the city that he would miss, but he didn't let himself think about that too much. Nothing could get in the way of their plans for tomorrow. The city had a habit of putting out tendrils and hooks into those who took too long to escape. If they didn't take this chance, then they ran the risk of never being able to get away.

One final night of drinking away his memories. Dawn would bring with it the promises of a new life.

Darkness had fallen once more, shrouding the city in deeper shadow. With the failing light, the city fell from the careful watch of the guards and became the domain of those more upfront about their failing morals. Though his vision was keen in the low light, Phillip kept his senses alert, hand resting on the pommel of his hidden dagger, while he waited for Justin to come from the palace.

The wolf, however, was late. Muffled sounds of celebrations and revelry came from beyond the palace walls, with the nobles gathering for some party or feast as they lived their own lives completely separated from the struggles in the rest of the city. Sometimes, when the wind was right, Phillip could hear small fragments of conversation, allowing him to put together a small picture of the events taking place over there.

The emperor had apparently made a rare appearance before them, sharing a few words and briefly mingling amongst the invited guests of the palace. Those nobles who had come close to the walls to whisper their gossip had speculated there might have been a marriage announcement between the emperor and an eligible foreign princess, but it appeared like they had been disappointed in that regard.

Phillip soon grew bored with the snippets of conversation he picked up from the other side of the wall, but he didn't leave. Not yet. No matter what caused Justin's delay, the two had an agreement of how long to wait should one or the other be delayed. The badger cast wary glances towards the moonlit sky, clouds streaming across the stars.

Finally, someone approached. The badger tightened his grip on his dagger, loosening it only when he recognised the distinctive scent of Justin, unusually refined and fresh for a servant, but then he knew little about how the palace treated even the lowliest of workers.

The wolf carried a leather sack over one shoulder, which would contain their supplies and the spoils of their thefts. Phillip's own sack was much smaller, carrying the few belongings he couldn't bear to leave behind, including the only mementos he had left of his parents. There was nothing else to tie him down, to prevent him from leaving.

"Sorry I'm late," the wolf whispered. He shuffled his feet and seemed unable to meet Phillip's eye. "There was something I needed to do first. One last thing I had to get. I had to wait for a good opportunity…"

Phillip lifted his muzzle and sniffed the air. "What did you get?"

"I, uh... probably best not to say just yet. Can you trust me?"

The badger chewed on his answer for a few moments. "It's too late now to say I don't. We're both committed to this now. But I want you to tell me what delayed you the moment you can."

"Of course." The wolf adjusted his sack as they started to walk. Metal clinked. A bright gemstone flashed in the starlight briefly before Justin tucked some fabric over the top to cover it. "Did you manage to get everything prepared?"

"It's all organised. The ship will leave at the next tide, which will be just before dawn. We're welcome to embark whenever we like, so unless there's something else you wanted to do first..."

"No, we can go right down there now," Justin growled. He kept glanced over his shoulder, ears twitching.

No matter how hard he strained his senses, Phillip couldn't detect anyone following them. Hardly anything moved in the shadows, not even the cut-throats and guards. Down these old and winding streets, the badger and wolf might as well have been the last two left in the decaying city.

Their destination was the port, where a merchant ship awaited them. It had not taken Phillip long to find a captain willing to take them to the distant lands of the west. Few cargo holds were ever full when leaving the city, and so many were eager to earn some extra coin by utilising that extra space with living cargo. It would not be a comfortable journey, but it would get them away as quickly as possible.

Though the port no longer flourished like it once had, it still stank of fish and the rot of seaweed. The scent was easy to follow even from a great distance.

Excitement grew within Phillip. This was it, the culmination of the great plan hatched one summer's evening in the *Old Gold*. It didn't quite feel real yet, and likely wouldn't until they had set sail at long last. If the wolf shared that excitement, then it didn't show. Given his hunched shoulders and quivering tail, Justin was more nervous than excited.

The first sign anything was amiss came from a clash of steel and an angry shout that tore through the relative calm of the night. Justin threw his arm out to stop Phillip from pushing past.

"Wait. That doesn't sound like the city guard," the wolf whispered. They were just a single street away from the port, close enough that Phillip could hear the waves lapping against the stone docks. There wasn't usually a hundred marching feet on the quay at this time of night. Something had gone wrong with the plan.

Slowly, the pair crept towards the port, padding carefully so they didn't make a sound. Those already at the docks showed none of the same caution to limiting their noise. Massive wooden crates of cargo crashed to the quay, spilling their contents across the stone, to both the shouts of fury from the merchants and the barked orders of the armed guards.

Phillip got his first glimpse of those causing the chaos. They were all strong and powerful, with several lynxes, reindeer, elk, and even a muskox amongst their number. They were heavily armoured, and all carried at least one immense weapon: a broadsword or a battle-axe. Justin was right. This was not the city guard.

"Varangians," the badger whispered, awe and terror in equal measure keeping his voice quiet. These were the elite bodyguard of the emperor himself. They rarely set foot beyond the palace except when the need was critical. Something had happened at the palace, and it was linked to something in the docks.

"They can't know. Not already. We were meant to have more time," Justin whined. He crouched low, cowering into the shadows just as the muskox turned in their direction. In the darkness, Phillip couldn't tell if the lumbering Varangian could see him.

The badger gestured to the chaos in the port. "This is because of you? What you took?"

"Yes," Justin whispered. He held his head in his hands. "This is all wrong. They weren't meant to be out here so soon. We have to find another way out. They can't see us or we're worse than dead."

Phillip locked eyes with the muskox. There was no doubting it this time. The Varangian saw him. The elite warrior pointed in his direction and bellowed out an order.

"I think it's too late for that," the badger said, taking a step back from the ferocity of the muskox, even from the other side of the port.

Justin glanced up. "Run." He scrambled to his feet. "Run!"

Phillip needed no further encouragement. He turned to flee, catching sight of the Varangians start the chase. At least a dozen of the elite warriors broke away from their companions, including the great muskox.

The badger quickly took the lead, taking over from the faltering and uncertain steps of the wolf. Fear gave speed to his legs, short in length but quick in their movement. He barged past those few on the streets who did not step aside, ignoring the distant bellows of the Varangians to hold up their quarry.

Phillip turned quickly, a destination already in mind he hoped would offer refuge. Better still, there was the chance of losing the elite guards in the narrow and winding streets. Behind him, the panting from Justin was an ever-present, the wolf keeping pace. Further back, the Varangians slowly gained.

Familiar landmarks passed by in a blur. Phillip's focus was always several paces ahead of where he was, what was around the next corner. Where to turn next. Away from the port and slowly up the gentle slopes. At the summit of the hill, the palace loomed like a dark beacon. But they did not need to go that far.

They reached a small plaza, where once there may have been markets. Now it was simply an open cobbled square surrounded on all sides by overhanging buildings. Four roads branched off from the plaza. It gave them a chance to gain a little time.

"Left here, left!" Phillip barked, hoping to project his voice to echo back off the close buildings and towards the chasing Varangians. He then grabbed Justin's hand and yanked him right. The wolf wisely kept his mouth shut, but for a brief yelp of surprise. They fled down the road to the right.

The badger didn't wait to see if his trick worked. He didn't even glance over his shoulder, lest he lose his footing and fall.

His destination finally came into sight. A tall stone building that rose over everything else around it, a single spire rising above the domed roof. The Church of the Thorned Crown. The old church was largely abandoned now, with even the weekly mass rarely attended.

Phillip didn't bother with the main doors at the front of the church. They were likely swollen shut and couldn't be opened without force and time. Instead, he grabbed hold of Justin's hand again and pulled him down the narrow alley to the side of the church, then leaped over the low fence that surrounded the small cemetery at the back.

Only then did Phillip allow himself to look back. There was no sign of the Varangians, but he did not linger to see if they had truly given them the slip. The badger hurried forward to push open the side door that was always unlocked, partially hidden in deep shadow.

The sounds of the city faded into calm, contemplative silence as the door closed behind them. Phillip felt like he could finally breathe again. He closed his eyes and leaned his head against the wall, the cool from the stone soothing as much as the silence and the scent of the old building.

It couldn't last for long, though. Reluctantly, the badger hauled himself away from the wall and padded around the rows of dusty pews, towards the raised altar at the far end of the church, directly opposite the closed main doors.

Justin moved silent as a ghost, a shadow in the darkness. His attention was raised higher, to the chipped and cracked mosaics and the paintings, once resplendent around the eaves of the church. Now they were defaced and broken, faces scrubbed away and shattered. The wolf whimpered. "Christ forgive me, I should have been stronger."

"Stronger how?"

The unexpected voice almost drew a terrified scream from Phillip. He managed to clamp his mouth shut in time.

Justin reacted by grabbing an iron candlestick and brandishing it in the direction of the voice.

From out of the shadows emerged a familiar hare.

"Irene?" Phillip hissed. "What are you doing here?"

The hare rested her hand on her hip. "I could ask you the same question. Why are you running as though the city guard is after you?"

"It's the Varangian guard, actually," Justin said, before Phillip could stop him.

"What did you do to anger them?" Irene whispered. Phillip wasn't sure if it was shock or decorum that lowered her voice, but he was glad for it.

The badger turned to his lupine companion. "I think Justin was about to explain that already."

Justin lowered his gaze. He whimpered softly. "It's because I took this," he said, reaching into his pack and pulling out a bundle of cloth wrapped around a circular object about the width of his head.

Nothing could have prepared Phillip for what he uncovered. A circlet of pure gold, decorated with extravagant carvings of roses, their petals all massive purple gemstones.

"That's... that's..." Phillip couldn't even finish his sentence.

Irene had no such issues. "The Purple Rose. You stole the imperial crown," she hissed. "Are you absolutely mad?"

The wolf quickly tucked the crown away, as though even mentioning it could summon the Varangian guard through the door. "Yes, I think I must be. I have my reasons for taking it, but it shouldn't be our worry for the moment. For now, we need to worry about getting out of the city without being caught."

"Then you are trying to get away," Irene said, shaking her head slowly. "I thought you might. I can help you get out, but on one condition. I come with you."

Phillip briefly locked eyes with Justin. No matter the shock or confusion over the revelation of the crown, there was still a plan and an expectation for what happened once they were free from the city. There hadn't been an intention for anyone else to be a part of that, but in that brief glance they both recognised that right now, they needed all the help they could get. A hare like Irene would be of great benefit. The fact that she was one of the few anchors left keeping Phillip in the city eased the pain of intending to leave her behind.

There could be no other answer. The badger turned back to her. "How can you help?"

Irene took a moment to think. "The city will be locked down tighter than the emperor's jewelled backside. Every port, every gate. They'll be guarded with everyone they can muster, so we won't be able to get out any of the usual ways. Thankfully for you, my people know ways around the city walls that not even the guards know. Our only challenge will be getting there without being seen, since someone was dumb enough to steal the crown."

"That's one way to put it," Justin muttered. He scuffed his foot against the bare floor, kicking up a small cloud of dust.

The hare smirked. "It's the only way to put it. You sit tight in here, while I go and make sure the way is clear."

"The Varangians are still out there," Phillip said. His eyes flicked towards the main doors.

Irene patted him on the shoulder. "And they're not looking for me. Relax, I've got this part."

The badger nodded and stepped back. The quiet calm of the church did little to soothe his racing heart and the frantic thoughts of his mind. Not knowing what happened outside allowed his imagination to fill in all the gaps. The Varangians could have circled the church and he would know nothing about it. But he forced himself to relax. Irene would not set out blindly into danger. She would be cautious and alert.

She slipped outside through the small side door. For a brief moment, the sounds of the city returned. In the distance was the shouts and commotion from the Varangians as they searched for the imperial crown, but none of it sounded too close. Then the door closed and the sound silenced once more. For the moment at least, they were safe.

Phillip met Justin's eyes. The wolf couldn't meet his gaze for long, looking away and staring at the defaced mosaic above the altar, his eyes drooped low and tail tucked between his legs. There was something more he wasn't saying, but Phillip's throat was dry, tongue thick like it was several sizes too large. The dozen or more questions all remained unsaid while his imagination ran wild.

What had Justin gotten them involved with?

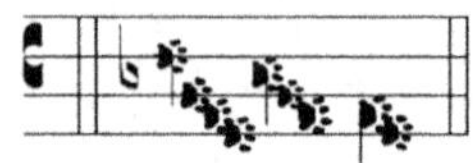

Justin walked around the church, putting his hand on every defaced mosaic and mural he could reach, muttering a quiet prayer beneath his breath for each one. Phillip didn't interrupt the wolf. He remained sitting on a pew, staring at the altar while remaining perfectly still, but for the nervous twitch of his leg.

No one disturbed them. No one even tried to open the swollen main doors. If the Varangians were still out there, then they did not yet suspect the church. Or they were patiently waiting for their quarry to emerge. Until Irene returned, there was no way of knowing. If she returned. There was always the possibility she had been captured and had given away all their secrets already.

He had to believe that wasn't true. If it was, then they were worse than dead. Stealing the imperial crown would not have a small punishment. The emperor himself would likely get involved.

Would the palace try to hush any mention of it and make them disappear? Or would there be a public example made of them? A deterrent for anyone else who might have thoughts of stealing from the palace.

A click of a latch caught his attention. His shoulders ached as he sharply turned his head, a crick in his neck from staying still for so long.

"It's just me," Irene whispered, her voice echoing through the empty church. "Come on, we have a chance now."

Justin's hand dropped from the mural. He whispered out a final conclusion to his prayer, before turning to face his companions. "I promise to explain everything once we're out of the city, but just trust me now. This is all necessary."

Phillip furrowed his brow and said nothing. It was not the time to press for answers, not when they needed to concern themselves more with getting safely out of the city.

Heart pounding, the badger peeked out the side door. The city was quieter now, with the darkness almost absolute with clouds rolling over to block out the moon and stars. A hushed stillness had fallen, with even the Varangian search ended until dawn. Perhaps that was the opportunity Irene hoped to exploit.

The scent of muskox and lynx lingered on the air, but it was not a recent smell. Already it faded amongst the muck and filth that pervaded the streets, making Phillip wrinkle his nose in disgust.

"This way. Quietly," Irene whispered.

The hare led the way, leaving the church behind them. The narrow streets were silent and still. Even the wind was hushed, barely a breath blowing.

Irene led them through the centre of the city, away from the port and towards the city walls that rose around the northern reaches, beyond the palace. There was still a lot of movement beyond the palace walls, with shadows constantly moving and flickering as guards carried torchlight with them on their patrols.

Phillip took up the rear of the group, with Justin between himself and Irene. The wolf carried the precious supplies, the gold and gems that would create their new life beyond the city walls. And the stolen icon that defined a ruling dynasty. The purple roses were symbolic of generations of emperors. The crown was a reminder of past glories and a promise of a great future. A promise that had withered with constant failure and neglect.

Keeping to the shadows, the trio made their slow way across the city. Each moving shadow melted into a guard in Phillip's mind, clouds scudding past the moon creating dappled patterns of pale light and deep dark.

These familiar streets, never to be seen again. No matter the result of the night, Phillip knew he would either escape the city or get locked in a dungeon never to feel free again. This would be his last time. He couldn't bring himself to regret that, not even slightly.

Irene threw out her arm. She stepped back into an alcove and crouched. Justin and Phillip hurried to do the same.

A dozen paces ahead, emerging from a side street, a shadow became solid and resolved into the heavy bulk of the muskox. The monstrous beast of a Varangian grunted and growled as he padded across the street. Phillip could almost imagine the cobbles cracking beneath that great weight.

Feeling exposed with nothing but the darkness to hide them, the badger froze completely. He barely dared to breathe. Surely the muskox would hear the pounding of his heart.

The Varangian snorted and continued on his way.

No one moved, but the muskox did not return.

Irene was the first to gather her courage. She slowly rose to stand, ears perked up and twitching. Silently, she gestured back to the others and crept forward.

Phillip reluctantly followed after Justin. Every sense strained for movement.

They hurried forward as quietly as possible, crossing over the side street the Varangian had gone down. Despite his better judgement, Phillip glanced down to see the silhouette of the muskox prowling away. Fear threatened to paralyse him, before realising that Irene and Justin had not stopped.

Desperation not to get left behind restored movement to the badger's legs. He scampered on before the muskox could turn and see him.

Three more times, Irene flung out an arm to warn them of someone approaching. Twice a Varangian padded by, with once being a regular city guard. Each time they threw themselves into the shadows, with little more than darkness to hide them.

The imposing walls that circled the city loomed large, towering over the surrounding homes as a black void on an already dark horizon. There was no gate at this part of the city, away from the primary trade routes and market lanes closest to the shoreline. That also meant there were fewer guards, and the nervous encounters soon ceased.

That did nothing to soothe the tension. Phillip jumped at every flutter of fabric, of every cloud that drifted across the moonlight. His heart pounded right up at his throat.

The streets wound to the very edge of the space within the walls, some homes so close that they leaned onto the ancient defences of the city. It was to one of these buildings, silent and still, that Irene led them. The hare furtively looked around, but there was no movement on the narrow street. She then pushed open the door. The creak was surely loud enough to hear in the palace, halfway across the city.

The smell of hare filled Phillip's nose. His muzzle twitched as he peered inside. He could see nothing, but from the scent he was sure it was home to a family or two of hares.

A flicker of movement caught his attention, further down the street. Torchlight glowed, smoke rising into the night sky. Someone battered their hand against a door. Distant shouts broke the silence.

The city guard were here after all, at least one Varangian with them. They were searching the houses. There could only be one thing they sought: the Purple Rose.

Phillip stepped inside before anyone could see him. They did not have much time if they wanted to get away undetected.

Through the walls inside came the murmur of quiet voices. They were not alone, but no one came out to meet them. Irene led them into a storage room deep inside the house, where it backed directly onto the thick city walls. Over a dozen amphorae stood throughout the room, the pungent aroma of spice making it clear what they contained.

Irene hissed in annoyance. "We need to move these. Our way out is down there," she said, pointing towards the back corner of the room.

"We'd better hurry," Phillip said. He briefly locked eyes with Irene, and then Justin. They didn't need to say anything to each other. They were all aware of the disturbances close by.

They wasted no time. The amphorae were heavy enough that each of them needed two of them to move. The massive containers came up almost to Phillip's sternum, and they scraped and grated against the ground with each movement. The badger grimaced at the noise. They moved them as little as possible, clearing the required path through to the dark corner, though he could not yet see any way out.

Eyeshine glinted in the low light from the doorway. Multiple people watched their progress. Gloomy silhouettes of two hares and a trio of rats shifted, squeaking and whispering to each other, but none approaching or interfering. A sixth, this one a weasel, peered out the front door, whiskers shining in the moonlight as they twitched.

One by one, the amphorae were shifted across the floor just far enough to make space for the next. Though Phillip was tempted to look outside each time they finished moving one, he stayed put and trusted the unknown weasel to keep watch. Besides, he could hear their progress. The slam of fists against a door got ever closer, and soon they were near enough to hear everyone barked word and command.

"Last one. Hurry," Irene whispered.

Phillip stepped forward to help. His foot scuffed against an uneven ridge on the floor as stone turned to wood. A trap door. There was an underground passage.

The last amphora was pulled into position. A door crashed in. Very close by. The next house along.

Irene pulled up the trap door and gently rested it against the bare wall. She silently gestured for Justin to descend first, which he quickly did without question. Phillip hesitated. His eyes flicked back to the door, then to the hole in the floor. There was no way they could hide that in time to avoid pursuit.

"They'll deal with it. Hurry," Irene hissed.

The badger had no choice. He found the first rung of a wooden ladder and descended into an even deeper darkness. Barely had he gone down enough for his head to sink beneath the floor did he reach the bottom, his foot finding solid stone again. He quickly moved aside to allow Irene the space to follow.

What little moonlight remained was partly blocked as a rat looked down at them. Then the trapdoor closed silently and sealed them in. Light feet pattered against the floor above their heads, then the deep grating of an amphora pushed into place. A sprinkling of cinnamon and spice dusted down through the cracks in the floor.

Irene's hand gripped hold of his elbow. Whether for reassurance or to keep him still, Phillip couldn't be sure. He could see nothing. But he could hear everything.

The front door slammed open. Heavy footsteps thundered in. Torchlight flickered through the floor. A soft, chittering voice squeaked something indistinct.

"Palace business," a deep voice growled. "Keep your nose out of it."

The small voice squeaked again.

"That isn't for you to know. Step aside and let us search."

Another tiny squeak, submissive and meek. The torchlight moved. More trickles of spice dusted Phillip's fur, dislodged by the weighty footsteps of the guard.

Grunts and growls punctuated the heavy thuds. There were even a few scrapes as amphorae were moved around, but there was never any movement towards the trapdoor. The spilled spice hid their scent. The darkness obscured everything else.

Phillip didn't breathe. He didn't dare move, lest the guards above hear him. His companions were likewise frozen to the spot.

"He's not here."

Someone snarled. "The emperor must not be allowed to leave the city. We must find him."

"Then let us keep searching. He has not come this way."

The badger didn't dare move, even as the footsteps pounded out of the small building, back towards the street. His breath came back in a deep gasp, heart racing faster than ever. It wasn't just the Purple Rose that the guards sought. The emperor himself was missing.

A tug on his arm got him moving. There was no time to think about such things. Not yet. They needed to escape the city first.

Even though he could see nothing, he did not feel uncertain. The close walls were like a comforting blanket wrapped around his body. Only down there did he begin to feel safe, his heart rate slowing and his breathing getting back under control. He no longer felt on the cusp of discovery and capture and, as the sounds behind him also began to fade, he began to believe again that this might be about to end.

The compact dirt changed to loose gravel and stone beneath his feet. The feel of the air shifted. He lifted his hand to brush against the ceiling, which was solid stone. The foundations of the great defensive walls that ringed the city. This passage sunk directly beneath them.

Stone returned to dirt, but still the passage did not rise. It remained roughly level, a few bumps and ridges that unsettled the two in front of the badger. He could hear them stumble a few times, but he remained sure-footed. He looked over his shoulder a couple of times, making sure there was never a tell-tale glimmer of light in the distance that warned they were being followed. The darkness remained blissfully total.

Finally, the passage began to angle up towards the surface. At almost the same moment a twinkle of light began to cast shadows down the passage from ahead. Two silhouettes in front of the badger blocked much of the light, but he could see the way out. He could see the freedom outside the city.

The tunnel emerged on the edge of a forest. The hare, wolf, and badger hauled themselves into the free air and stood in awed silence for a few moments. Phillip looked back towards the city, pinpricks of light visible here and there beyond the imposing walls.

A brief sense of joy flooded the badger, but his curiosity and irritation soon overwhelmed him. Before the wolf could react, Phillip had hold of Justin's shirt and pressed him against the nearest tree.

Leaves rustled and fell amongst them, settling on their spice-stained fur and clothes.

"Start talking. Why do you have the crown?"

Justin made no attempt to resist or push the badger away. He merely slumped and looked down at his feet. "I have not been entirely truthful with you since the day we met, and for that I can only apologise and beg for your forgiveness." He pulled the crown out of his sack and unwrapped it. Even in the low light, the purple roses glittered with an ethereal glow. "This has been a symbol of power and control for generations. It is the promise that our great empire will be ruled by one man, unquestionable and infallible. I have known this to be a lie ever since the day I first had this crown put onto my head."

The wolf slowly lifted his head. Tears streaked down his furred cheeks. "I am Emperor Justinian the Third."

Phillip's fist tightened around Justin's shirt. Then his eyes widened and he leaped back, bile in his throat and fear coursing through his veins with a greater strength than anything the muskox and the Varangians had summoned. "You... you..."

Justin lifted his hands, the crown sliding back to his elbow as it looped around his arm. "I beg your forgiveness that I did not tell you sooner. I simply wanted a normal life, but most of all, I wished for a friend who did not know me for my name and title."

"But why throw that all away?" Irene said, finding her voice before the badger. "You were the most powerful person in the empire, and you decide to run away with Phillip?"

The wolf shook his head sadly. "You say I was powerful, but that is the greatest lie of them all. I couldn't even wipe my own ass without getting approval from the council for someone else to do it for me. I was utterly powerless in every way. The council ruled through me, using me as their puppet, and they serve only themselves.

"There was so much I wanted to do for the empire. So many ways I could improve things, but I was never given that opportunity. I could never overthrow their hold over me. I then began to realise that I was making things worse. Because of the power people perceived when they saw me, they would not question my words when the council spoke through me. Every awful decision they made was turned into my own and it was all enacted without question. Without hesitation.

"I watched the empire die of sickness while I could do nothing. So I realised that the best thing for the empire was to take myself out of it. To remove the figurehead and the symbol of that false power. That is why I had to steal the crown. That is why I needed to escape."

Phillip licked his lips, trying to bring some moisture to them. His throat was parched. "Haven't you just given the council the right to rule by themselves?"

Justin smiled bitterly. "Yes, but I also took their justification." He held up the crown in both hands. "Without this, there can be no emperor. And with no emperor, there is no figure of authority the people will respect. They will no longer listen to the council's commands."

"There will be bloodshed," Irene whispered. "A lot of people may die."

Again, Justin hung his head low. "Yes. This could burn the empire to the ground. But if something better can rise from the ashes, then I will have done more than I ever could by staying."

Phillip took a deep breath and tried to clear his mind. So many more questions still swirled around his head, but they all seemed small and insignificant to the truths he had just learned. He opened his mouth to speak. No words came out. He shook his head and tried again. "Then. Where do we go now?"

Justin choked back a sob and leaned in and hugged Phillip. His tear-soaked cheeks wetted the badger's fur. A moment later, Irene added her arms to their shared hug. The crown pressed uncomfortable against Phillip's shoulder, but he didn't dare move to dislodge it.

"I was scared you wouldn't want to stay if you know who I really was," Justin said, when they broke away from the hug. He laughed nervously and wiped his eyes with the back of his hand.

"How can I turn down an adventure with an emperor?" Phillip said, managing a laugh of his own.

Justin smiled and looked up to the sky. Phillip's eyes followed. The clouds had mostly cleared to reveal a brilliant display of the heavens, with countless thousands of stars twinkling in the deep and mysterious unknown tapestry. "We should go west, like we originally planned," the wolf said. He tucked the crown away, hiding it within its bundle of fabric. "We can find another port and get a ship until we find somewhere to settle and start life again, however we choose it."

Phillip grinned. "Of course, your majesty. Whatever you decide."

Justin's breath caught in his throat. His eyes were wide enough to reflect the starlight. Then, realising Phillip's intentions, he lightly shoved the badger in the chest. "I'm glad to have you with me. I'd rather have you than anyone at the palace."

Irene put her hands on their shoulders. The hare smiled. "I know a place. They're smugglers, but they'll be able to get us to safety. Any trade port you want, they'll get us there."

"Then let's not wait around for the Varangians to find us again," Phillip said. Though he looked to the city, all was quiet and still from this distance. Then he turned his back on the only home he had ever known.

The badger, the hare, and the emperor melted away into the night. They left behind an empire ready to fall.

The Seekers of Winter

Alex T. Dragonson

nce, long ago, when the river of time was merely a stream that babbled at the feet of the smooth stones of Eternity, there were two lionfolk, brother and sister, who hunted together across the plains, until the morning Eufraitis woke to find her brother gone. There was no sign of a struggle, no track to follow; but the strangest thing of all was that he'd left his bow and quiver behind.

From that day forth, it was her lost brother Eufraitis hunted, first along the trails they had walked countless times, and then to their family's old hunting grounds, and then farther and farther out, to the rivers and forests that bounded the plains. Nowhere could she find even a pawprint nor a hair from his tail, and soon despair became her new companion.

One night, as she sat before her campfire wondering if her brother were truly lost and if it were time to send his memory West and return alone to her mothers' household, she noticed a human sitting across the fire, watching her from under the hood of his cloak. She'd never seen him before, but all at once she knew in the depths of her heart who he was.

"My lord!" she cried out as she scrambled to her feet.

And Amruoc, Lord of the Hunt, the god she'd called on all her life for strength and patience, both with and without her brother, motioned for her to sit and be at ease. Once she'd sat down again, He spoke: "What is it that you hunt for?"

"I'm hunting for my brother," Eufraitis said. "He disappeared from our campsite nearly a month ago, and I've sought him ever since, on our hunting grounds, in the home of our mothers, and in fields and forests I've never before seen. He must be somewhere, but he is nowhere."

Amruoc nodded. "Perhaps we may be of help to each other," He said. "What is your brother's name?"

"Tigris, my lord."

"And he is lionfolk, like yourself?"

"He is."

Amruoc fell silent, and seemed lost in thought for a very long time, as the fire waned and the moon began to set into distant tree-tops. At last he spoke: "The Lord of the Hunt can find any track, no matter how slight. Your brother's trail is faint, but I know where he must be. But before I can aid you, you must do something for me."

"Anything," Eufraitis said, "if it helps me find him."

Amruoc laughed to himself. "The task is a simple one, and yet among the most difficult known to hunter or quarry. I ask you to swear to me that, in the days to come, you put aside your hunt to aid any who seek what escapes their grasp."

"But if I stop seeking him," Eufraitis asked, "how will I ever find him?"

"Even the mightiest hunter must rest," Amruoc said. "Now, will you swear it?"

There was no other path to take. "I swear to you, Amruoc, Lord of the Hunt, that I will aid any who seek what escapes their grasp."

"Very well," Amruoc said. "Your brother Tigris can be found in the halls of Coreas."

"Coreas! The Lord of Winter has taken him."

"The very same. The journey to the Halls of Winter is not a kindly one, and much of it must be made alone. My familiar can guide you as far as His town below the glacier, but you must find your own way above and beyond it to His home." Amruoc raised one arm, and a ferret emerged from His sleeve to circle the fire and curl up at Eufraitis' feet. She looked down at it, and back up, and found the god had gone.

In the morning, when it came time to break camp, the ferret leapt onto her back, clambered up her coat, and made himself comfortable on her shoulder.

"So," she said. "North?" The ferret squeaked approvingly, and they set off northward.

On the third morning after Amruoc visited her camp, Eufraitis found the wind had grown cold, and a great wall almost the color of the sky began to separate itself from the horizon—the glacier that marked the edge of the world. Seeing it, Eufraitis hesitated, afraid for the first time since she'd sworn her oath to Amruoc, but the ferret on her shoulder chattered at her and nipped at her collar until she got moving again.

By midday the glacier loomed across half the northern sky, wafting its chill across the plains, and Eufraitis found herself on a track full of old wagon ruts. She passed a farm, and then another, and soon the track settled down into cobblestones and became a road, and that road led into a town, and by the time she noticed the ferret was gone from her shoulder she found herself in a market square bustling with folk of all sorts, and all, down to the beggars, dressed in woolens finer than she'd ever seen. This could only be the town of Coreas, which was then as now known for its weavers, its tailors, and its sharply dressed young men.

It was a great deal to take in for a woman used to hunting alongside only her brother. Eufraitis collected herself, squared her shoulders, and set off to find someone who could sell her a cloak.

She was certain she'd given away far too many of her trade furs for it, but the second shop she'd tried had given her a cloak thick enough to keep her warm in the unaccustomed cold of the glacier, yet lighter than the furs she'd paid—surely a magical thing, perhaps even with the god's own favor upon it. The shopkeeper had also given her a wary look when she mentioned she was seeking Coreas, and a word of caution against mentioning to strangers that she planned to challenge Him in His own home.

"They'll think you're mad at best," they said. "There's always been stories of a path up the glacier, but nobody who goes there ever comes back. We don't know if it's the wind and the ice that take 'em, or the god Himself, and there's few enough already who'd know the difference."

"But if no one who goes that way returns," said Eufraitis, "does anyone still know the way?"

The shopkeeper shrugged. "Every few winters someone's fool enough to try it, so someone must."

On her way out of the shop, Eufraitis nearly tripped over a young jay-man crouched in the doorway, feathers trailing in the dirt as he searched for something between the cobbles. She was about to be angry with him—hunters getting in each other's way could be more dangerous even than a frenzied bison—but she remembered her vow to Amruoc, and held her tongue.

The jay looked up. "Sorry," he said, craning his neck to meet her eyes. "Lost something."

"It would seem so." Eufraitis sat back on her heels, carefully out of the path, and watched him. "What sort of something?"

The jay-man shook his head. "Doesn't matter."

"It might matter very much. I am Eufraitis, and I seek the god of the glacier, who has stolen my brother from me."

"Lucky bastard."

Eufraitis' ears went flat. "My brother did not choose to be stolen, and I have sworn to the Lord of the Hunt that I will steal him back."

The jay-man considered this, then suddenly stood, brushed the dust from his knees, and offered Eufraitis a hand. "Perhaps we can help each other. I'm called Sky Blackwood, and I've been trying to get to the top of the glacier for a few winters now."

Eufraitis stood up without taking his hand. "You know the way?"

"More or less. What I mean is, if you've got Amruoc's blessing, then maybe you can find what I've lost. And in return, I'll tell you what I know about climbing the glacier."

"I suppose," Eufraitis said slowly, "that that's the best I'm going to find here." She clasped his hand as she'd seen others do in the market. "You have a bargain."

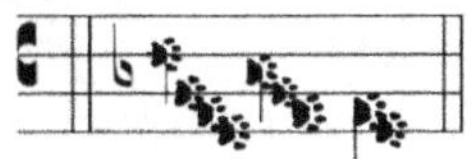

It was a bracelet he'd lost, a silver bangle with the three-pronged sign of Coreas inlaid in tiny blue stones, made by the town's master silversmith as an offering to the god. Sky gave no explanation of how he'd lost it, only that it had been somewhere in this quarter of the market square. Eufraitis agreed to meet him in the nearest inn at dusk and set out to search.

Nothing sparkled at her from the dust between the cobbles, or from under the horse troughs, and Eufraitis could feel the eyes of every merchant she passed following her. After a full circuit of the quarter, it occurred to her that something so fine and valuable must have been picked up by the first person who noticed it, and given how full the town of Coreas was of young men trying to impress each other, gambled away or perhaps even sold again. So she began to search for stalls and shops selling such finery, certain that Sky would have more luck with the gamblers.

She found it at last under the sign of a brass candlestick, in a shop that bought fine clothing and heirlooms from those desperate for money, with the intention to sell them back someday, or so the shopkeeper's apprentice explained it to her. The shopkeeper herself had little interest in Eufraitis' remaining trade furs, and after what felt like endless haggling, her own desperation growing, she pulled a ring from her ear, a loop of jade traded all the way from the western forests and given to her by her mothers when she came of age, and offered it in exchange. The earring seemed to impress the shopkeeper less than the story of its origin, but it was still enough to let her leave with the bangle on her wrist as the sun descended into Mistelin's embrace.

When she reached the inn, she found Sky sitting in the back corner of the tavern, with food and beer already on the way. Eufraitis offered him the bracelet, but he waved it away. "Keep it," he said. "If you're going up the glacier, you can give it to Him in my name."

"And how am I to get there?" she asked. "Hold your end of the bargain."

And so he told her as they ate, under his breath as if he feared someone were listening, of the path north out of town that became steeper and steeper as it went; of the places where previous generations had carved clawholds into the ice; of the hidden doors and passages that were said to run beneath the halls of Winter; and of prayers and spells passed down from older boys to younger over the generations, to guide and preserve travelers in Coreas' domain.

"But how do you know all this?" Eufraitis asked the third or fourth time he paused to catch his breath. "I was told that none who seek Coreas return."

"Oh, He returns them sometimes," Sky said almost absentmindedly. "He'll keep a lover for ten, twenty, fifty years, then tire of him and send him back to town, youthful as the day he left. My great-uncle was one of the lucky few."

Lucky! For the Lord of Winter to tear you on a whim from everything you know, and thrust you back just as suddenly into a world that had given you up for dead? "And you want this to happen to you," was all she said.

He nodded. "Worth every second of it."

"The cloak seller was right," she said. "Only madmen seek Him out."

"Says the woman who walked for days to find Him." His eyes smiled wider than his beak ever could.

She sighed. "I suppose I'll set out in the morning."

She left the inn as Barolin's song faded into memory, setting the sun on its slow climb into a sky as blue and empty as the glacier itself, a new walking stick from the market in her hand, Sky's bracelet chilling her wrist, and Tigris' bow weighing down her new cloak. The path to the glacier was not quite as Sky had described, hidden by snow in some places, completely blocked in others by great cracks in the shifting ice, but always just enough like the stories he'd told that the next step was never hard for a skilled hunter to find.

Until one such crack opened before her as she watched, a great crevasse that spread faster than she could run and seemed to stretch down to the center of the earth itself. Eufraitis leapt backward out of the way, and when it seemed to have stopped, crept back to peer over the edge and perhaps measure the gap against her walking stick to see if she could jump it.

As she lowered the walking stick, it grew warm in her hand. Startled, she let go, and it grew longer and flatter until one end reached the far side of the crevasse and it came to rest in the shape of a sturdy bridge. Eufraitis reached out cautiously to test it, and when she was certain it would bear her weight she hurried across, never quite feeling secure until she stepped off it at the other end.

As soon as she was safe on something like solid ground, the ice behind her gave one last shudder, shaking the bridge until it came loose and fell into the depths.

She supposed she'd figure out how to get back when the time came.

As she came to the first place where the trail turned sharply upward, a breeze began to blow down the face of the glacier, cutting through her fur and chilling her to the bone. She shuddered and pulled the cloak tighter around her, and found herself reciting one of Sky's prayers as she found the first clawhold and began to climb.

Some time later—she had no idea how much, with thick clouds between her and the sun—she had stopped to rest on a ledge, and suddenly felt eyes following her. The wind had brought flurries with it, and peering through the snow she could only just make out four faintly glowing spots against the ice. Two of them blinked at her. The other two rose into the air, making no sound that could be heard above the wind, and soared over her head across the ledge. Perhaps they were just the owls that lived in this place.

Nothing lived in this place, save that which belonged to Coreas.

Sky had spoken of guardians, but not of any way beyond his prayers to appease or avoid them. But if they were owls…. Eufraitis reached into her pouch and took out a few sticks of dried meat from the provisions Sky had given her. She laid them on the ground, just out of reach from where she'd rested, and returned to the climb.

She felt a whisper of wings behind her, and when she next looked down, she thought she saw two owls there, barely hidden by the snow, investigating her gift.

The snow grew thicker the farther she went, until she felt that the spells she whispered into the wind were all that kept her pressed to the cliff face and let her fingers keep finding clawhold after clawhold, and she knew Coreas was testing her.

But she had passed each of His tests so far, and she could not abandon Tigris now. So she climbed on, calling forth memories of her brother and their childhood to lead herself ever upward.

At last she found a clawhold that moved when she pressed on it, swinging a pane of ice upward and outward to reveal something like a burrow in the ice, not dug or carved, but melted, as far as she could tell, by some magic. She pulled herself inside and found herself in pitch darkness as the trapdoor swung shut behind her. At least she was out of the wind and snow now, and wrapping her cloak as tight as she could let her crawl along the passage without freezing her fur to its floor. She wasn't sure if Sky's prayers were still necessary, but she kept whispering them anyway as she pulled herself through the darkness, searching with eyes, ears, and nose for any sign of the god or of her brother.

What she sensed first was movement in the ice. Not the shaking that accompanied the opening of the crevasse, but something softer and deeper, like a great fish disturbing the surface of a placid river. She felt it pass below her once, twice, again, closer every time, until she could almost see a fishlike shape rising toward her out of the endless lightless depths.

She pressed back against the wall and held as still as she knew how, reaching deep into her memory for spells her mothers had taught her as a child, prayers to Amruoc to hide her scent and her warmth from deer in the tall grass, and now from this great fish-thing that rose through the ice, and paused at the peak of its arc to exhale a spray of snow into the corridor and look past Eufraitis with one massive eye.

After what felt like an eternity, it dove again, leaving nothing but scattered snow in its wake. Eufraitis waited, nearly frozen to the wall, counting shallow breaths until the ice fell still and she felt safe enough to press on.

At long last, she felt the air stir against her face, and followed the draft until a flicker of light appeared, and followed that light as the tunnel slowly grew until she could stand. She found herself in an endless-seeming corridor lit by torches placed along the walls in triple sconces in the shape of Coreas' own name, matching the sigil on Sky's bracelet. They burned with a blue flame, so hot that as she approached one she began to feel even colder, but without smoke and without melting the ice that held them.

This, then, could only be the halls of Coreas.

Sky's stories had spoken of towers, with windows that looked out over the glacier but never quite to the edge. Eufraitis set off down the corridor, examining every side passage she encountered for a way up and praying for Amruoc to guide her. She knew not how long she walked before she found a passage that led upward in steps and began to climb it, first meeting a grand staircase, richly carpeted over the ice of the floor, that extended downward into a vast hall, then breaking away and spiraling upward, led by a feeling she could not explain that Tigris awaited her at the top.

And it was there that she found him, fast asleep in a bed carved magnificently from pale blue ice, in a small round room furnished all in the finest cloth of silver with a window overlooking the glacier in exactly the way Sky had told her.

She ran to the bed and shook him awake. His eyes were slow to open, and his face puzzled from the moment he saw her. "Fraity? What are you doing here?"

"We need to get out of here," Eufraitis said.

"What? Why?" Tigris sat up and looked around. "There's no hurry. Let's at least stay for breakfast..."

He moved and spoke as if he were still half asleep. Something was very wrong. "No, we have to leave now. It's too cold here, I don't know what he's done to you–"

"You needn't worry. He's been very kind. I should introduce you."

The weight of the bows on her back shifted, and suddenly Eufraitis had half an idea of what to do. She pulled Tigris' bow free and pressed it into his hands. "You left this behind. I had to bring it to you."

He looked down at his hands, and suddenly he seemed more alert, more like she remembered him. "Oh," he said. "Oh, no. You're right, we need to go."

He had no cloak, so she wrapped him up in blankets as best she could, and turned to lead him to the stairs, only to find the god standing in her way.

You can't mistake Coreas for a human, or lionfolk, or birdfolk, or anything else in this world that speaks. He stands head and shoulders above even some other gods, His skin as dark as a moonless night, His fur a brilliant white that catches the faintest light and turns it to snow-blindness, His eyes the bottomless blue of meltwater. No man can look away from Him, no man can deny Him.

Fortunately for Eufraitis, He has no real power over anyone but men. But she was still in His domain, and He stood between her and the path that would bring Tigris home.

"So you're my uninvited guest," He said. The very air seemed to freeze around him, and ring with silent laughter. "You should know I don't take kindly to trespassers."

Eufraitis tried to not look intimidated. "I've come to take my brother home."

"Well, I can't just let you do that, now can I? He's mine now."

Eufraitis fought the temptation to look back, to see whether the god had cast again whatever spell had kept Tigris here. There had to be a way past him. She couldn't have come all this way, sold her most precious possessions, clawed her way up the glacier by Sky's secret paths, only to give up now.

The thought of Sky reminded her of the weight of the silver bracelet on her arm. She slipped it off and held it before her. "Coreas!" she said, and the god looked down at her. "I bring you a gift from a man of the town beneath your halls. His name is Sky Blackwood, and he wishes to join you here in my brother's place."

"Then you're here on his behalf as well? Could he not have come to me, with or without you?"

"You'll have plenty of time to ask him that," Eufraitis said. "It seemed to me that he dreams of you bringing him here yourself."

The cold cut through her cloak as Coreas thought. She reminded herself to breathe.

At last, Coreas laughed to Himself, and the chill disappeared. "Very well." He took the bracelet from Eufraitis, and it grew to fit His arm as He put it on. "I accept your terms, as long as you both are gone before I return." He stepped out onto the stairs, and when Eufraitis looked again, He was no longer there.

His voice echoed in her ears. "Do go through the great hall, won't you? It wouldn't do to lose yourselves on the way down."

Tigris took her hand, and Eufraitis led him down the spiral stairs to where they rejoined the grand staircase, and down again across the great hall and out through double doors three times her height onto a road that had not been there when Eufraitis left the town of Coreas, along a gentle incline that did not belong to the glacier as Eufraitis remembered it. Indeed, when they reached the edge of town and turned back to look at the road, it had gone, and only the sheer cliff face Eufraitis had climbed remained.

The sun had returned to Mistelin's domain by the time Tigris and Eufraitis reached the inn on the market square. It was exactly as Eufraitis had left it, though everyone there seemed older than they should, save the innkeeper, who was much younger. It didn't take her long to find out why: the older folk cheered for her arrival as if she were a hero of legend, and the innkeeper explained that his parent had seen her off twenty years before, and Sky Blackwood had disappeared mere days after that. "The Lord of Winter works in his own way," he said, "and the rest of us learn to live with it."

In the days that followed, neither Tigris nor Eufraitis found themselves ready to return to their old hunting grounds, nor to their mothers' home. Tigris found friends among those Coreas had left behind, and learned that he had much to tell the young men of the town about his dealings with the god. Soon he'd made up his mind to stay, to learn the ways the winter folk hunted, and provide for these people who had so quickly become his people.

Eufraitis was simply restless, and it took her some time to realize why. The sight of a ferret sleeping by the side of the south road reminded her of her vow to Amruoc, and it occurred to her that that vow had not ended with her bringing Tigris down from the glacier. Amruoc had followers, or so the stories said; an eternal hunting party whose quarry had always been a mystery to mortals. Perhaps it was time she found out what it was.

She hoped He wouldn't begrudge her the time it took to say goodbye to her brother; after all, that was part of what she'd asked of Him in the first place.

When she did leave town, the ferret went with her.

Spring and Autumn of North and South

Fopfox and Erik

 he world under heaven, after a long period of division, tends to unite; after a long period of union, tends to divide. This has been so since antiquity.

All under heaven was unified. The Lord of Ba in the southwest basin, son of the warrior of fortune, Fang Bei, was now a duke in the capital and so too was the sadistic Lord of Yue, Wu Qian. The noble pomeranian clan of Ssu'ma presided over newfound unity after years of their clan's scheming in the service of the Qi dynasty until the grandson of Chow T'sao was compelled to give up the sacred seal of the first Emperor to the Martial Emperor, founder of the Great Zhou, who went on at last to unify the middle kingdom with the aid of skilled horse barbarians hired from the north, who in reward were settled within the borders of the Zhou.

But now the Martial Emperor lay on his deathbed surrounded by officials and pomeranian clan princes. His fur flat and graying all around, he moved with bated breath knowing what was to come: the heir was a puppy and would need a regent. One sly pomeranian prince seeking power spoke into the delirious dying dog's ear, taking advantage of his weakened state of mind.

"We should kill the heir's mother, she seeks to rule the state, do you agree?" The canine nodded in agreement and soon an order was sent out. Before the eyes of the heir, the lady was hung by the neck with force when the order to commit suicide was given.

She was the first violent death, of an age of many more to come, that was birthed when the Martial Emperor's last breaths escaped his stout muzzle. Peace died with the Emperor. From the first day of the puppy's reign, the prince who maneuvered to end his mother, his regency lasted only a week, for he was killed by his brother who joined with the clan of the enthroned pup's murdered mother, to avenge her death. He in turn became regent, but only for a short while and then he too was violently killed, being sold out by his own hounds after a rout at the capital's walls led by an uncle.

Arrows fell like raindrops, it was a march of a million hounds, as if the Three Kingdoms Era never ended. Governors had no armies, but princes and their fiefs did. This would be titled the War of the Princes by the scholars, for they came and went, all fighting over control of the imperial puppy as a possession. When Prince Yi was encircled, he took the child in paw and took to a tower in desperate bidding that his mere holding of the yapping emperor would ensure his power despite all odds. The troops of his nephew poured in and ripped the crying pup from his arms. A sword fell upon the doomed prince regent and blood sprayed across the muzzle of the toddler emperor who wailed. The entire clan of the emperor's dead mother were put to the sword for treason.

Rather than thunder during the stormy season, the sound of war drums filled the northern plains. Instead of rain, scarlet blood dampened the soil, and thus crops were grown with the countless dead.

Chaos was the watchword and farms became abandoned when all able bodies were called to fall upon the swords of others in the name of a Ssu'ma prince with ambitions of power.

As chaos reigned in the plains, a carefree princeling, Prince of the South, Ssu'ma Jen dwelled in his fief the former capital of the vanquest Yue, its walls torn down in symbolism at the unification.

There he hoped for a nice life away from the north where uncles and cousins fought.

Months prior he fled to his hereditary birthright after his uncle, whose city he previously was living in, made war against the regent and he desired not to be there. But now the pampered pomeranian was reclining in his bamboo grove, playing wéiqí with a lady of his princely harem, within a chamber abounded with gilt bamboo with gossamer silk leaves.

"Do you like the setting?" Jen said to the lady, an Afghan hound, while daintily moving a crystal game piece with his manicured claws.

"Oh yes, my prince, it is lovely," she forced enthusiasm as Jen saw a chance to expound on his cultured tastes.

"Ah yes, it's based on the lord of the bamboo grove. Those artistic rebels would play their zithers in the bamboo groves and compose poetry. I was very much inspired by them and commissioned this chamber to be made in their honor."

Jen then pointed to a zither and asked if she could play, the poor houndess not thinking and seeking to get favor jumped to do so, fully aware she did not know how to play at all.

Minutes into her clumsy attempt at the strings with her claws he cried out "A migraine! I have a migraine! Get me the doctor, I shall be ill for days from such inauspicious sounds!"

This was the character of Prince Jen. It was said a solid dish made him faint and clothing with holes made him nauseous. Though others mockingly said his nausea was due to the fur of his breed which he swallowed by accident.

When messengers came bearing news he dismissed them without thought, saying news was bad for his health and would ruin his day. "You envoys always come when I am eating or relaxing, can you not come forth when I'm better suited to hearing them!? Begone!"

The bitter envoy whispered under his panting muzzle "Since when are you ever able, you puffed up furball?"

If Jen had heard this surely he would have been agasp.

Woe unto those forced to listen or look upon Jen's poems or a painting he thought himself talented enough to do. And ill fortune upon those to falsely praise a clumsy painting too much, lest the canine leave behind a landscape dotted with stick figures.

"I am sure this shall look well hanging in your main hall!" Thus a poor dog was made to display it openly, lest the prince come for a friendly visit and find nowhere his *masterpiece* in a place of pride in the domicile.

Jen would be asked to send forth his armies to aid the various princes in the war of regency. The Pommeranian would say to the messengers, "Of course I will make ready!" But everytime he saw the horses and armor he was expected to ride and wear in leading the army, he changed his mind, and left those who called upon his aid with nothing. "The horse, it smells! I cannot ride this walking producer of fertilizer! Take it away from me, I'm becoming ill! The smelling salts, bring me the smelling salts!" That was the first and last time he took requests for aid seriously; all subsequent would be waved off with promises and sweet words but nothing more.

An envoy rushed the prince's chamber late one night much to Jen's ire, who berated the mut for daring to interrupt his sleep.

"But the Prince Regent is dead! He's been murdered by our August Lord with a declaration he is of age and needs no regent!"

Jen rolled his eyes and pathetically growed as if he was able to intimidate anyone, considering all his fluff, "Is that all? That's nothing, begone, I must sleep."

Events went on while he played. The Prince Regent's son rose up in arms and laid siege to the capital. A request for aid to Jen met the same outcome; nothing came. The Emperor, witty and clever, made a gamble by firing an arrow with a message into his cousin's camp with a reward that whoever delivers the rebel prince's head will get the post of chancellor. That night, a mob rushed the prince's tent and over hundred and twenty died over the possession of his head.

"Majesty, I have the head of the rebel prince!" the battered and wounded winner of the contest proclaimed, expecting full-well a rich reward and beamed with pride before the imperial throne.

There and then, the Emperor intentionally forgot his promise, withdrawing the reward and had the poor wretch put to death for spilling the sacred blood of the imperial clan.

When news of this spread to the nomadic horsemen employed by the army reserves, they stormed the palace, burned the capital and skinned the Emperor.

Jen's elder brother, the favored of their mother, was in the Western city of Peace when news arrived of the fall of the capitol. Their mother, a shrewd powerful lady, enthroned Jen's brother as legitimate successor, all while the nomads of the north grew discontent with being used as fodder in the decades-long Princes War and began rising up. They killed their commanders and slew their lords, no matter who they were.

A new age of chaos began.

A wolf fled across the plains on a midnight black stallion, his pale-white muzzle occasionally peering back behind him and his calves clenched tight against his mount's belly.

How long had he been riding, he did not truly know. All Modun Tabgach knew was that he had to flee, his father was dead now and his dear Uncle was Khan.

Modun learned of his Uncle's right to the title far too personally when he was out hunting and an arrow had landed by the hoof of his steed. The nomad's horse panicked and fled just as another arrow flashed past the wolf's ear, saving his life.

Though Modun had only gotten a brief glance at his assassins, the smell of sandalwood wafted through the air. His dear Uncle's favorite perfume, no doubt if there was a chance Modun would survive, a message was to be made clear to the young nomad just who is Khan now.

And who was just another loose end to be tied up.

There was not even the smell of another wolf for over a mile in any direction. Modun and his steed alike both wanted to keep on going forever, but it was impossible. Though Modun was young, fit, and the picture of health, he could not keep going forever.

Modun blinked and one moment later he found himself resting behind a crop of rocks atop a hill next to his horse, feeding him a carrot. The wolf panted, drooling onto the ground uncontrollably despite his thirst, and reached into the saddlebags for the fresh cheese he had prepared earlier, before the hunt which his Uncle ruined. The white curds tasted of salt and rice vinegar imported from the south as he shoved them into his maw and chewed. The last luxury he'd have from his life as a Khan's son, no doubt.

With that in mind, he shoved his muzzle into the bag and lapped up the last curds, leaving the whey to rest below the porous cloth. He'd need the whey sooner or later, he didn't cherish it, but there was no telling when he'd get fresh food again, or water for that matter.

The moon, a thin crescent right now, hung over the night sky and he opened his mouth but stopped himself from howling.

There was no one to answer, no one friendly at least.

Not anymore.

With no friends up north, his homeland, where else would one go? To the west, the vast endless desert? To the east and brave the sea?

There was only really one choice.

Modun went south, having heard of the dogs of the south and their land. The Middle Kingdom was what it was called, where they farmed, and lived and died in the same place. Modun thought it foolish to imagine trying to eke out a fortune in the same spot and not move on when it grew dry, but...

After much war their Khaganate broke in three and for a century their Khans fought, till one united the country. Modun heard it was a land of much gain, having heard others had moved south and got much wealth in service to the lords there

Riding across a merchant on camelback, Modun hesitated before approaching. The merchant did not display any token of protection from any clan or lord atop his steed, he was a free merchant, alone and vulnerable. Even by himself, Modun knew he could have waylaid him, taken his cargo and the merchant captive.

But that would be too impulsive, too short-sighted. Times had changed. It was far more important to approach things cautiously and this mere peddler had some things to tell Modun, he could tell as much. The merchant's legs were rested in a strange device hanging from the saddle and nestled in his feet and as much as Modun was convinced the merchant might fall off at the slightest alarm, he did not.

Modun rode up and spoke with him after convincing him he was no raider. He was a sand dog from the western cities of the oases, a stripe of black fur running along his scalp and down his back. He was slim compared to the wolves of Modun's clan, almost frail looking, but it gave the merchant's appearance some charm to Modun's eyes.

Had he not smelled of camel, Modun would have considered flirting with the merchant a little.

"You know they have fallen into calamity again? Their princes are waging war over each other."

"I thought the land was unified?"

"Well it was, then the founder died and left a puppy and now all the others began fighting over it. Last I heard some nomad took the capital and in the west they put up some prince as another, the last I heard this Nomad Emperor was going to sack the western capital."

"What would happen after that?"

"Who knows? I think there is a prince in the south, he'd likely be the next, he happens to be the brother of the prince, now emperor, in the west. But with the Khagan staring at his holdings, who can say for how long?"

Wealth, luxury, battle…and perhaps romance? Modun felt like a cub again despite everything that had happened. Perhaps his Uncle had unwittingly pushed him towards an opportunity. He was told once that the Southern folk had the same word for "Crisis," as they did for "Opportunity." He didn't think much of it at the time, but perhaps they had some wisdom there.

At the very least, it would be a chance to make their crisis his own opportunity.

Modun edged his horse close to the side of the sand dog's camel, soothing his steed as it grew fearful of the strange beast and leaned forward, whispering intimately.

"You're a merchant, of course?" Modun asked, sniffing in the sand dog's direction. Without the smell of camel masking it, he had a scent of clean sand on his fur.

"Aye," the dog sniffed back, "at least I try to be. The Princes don't make it easy."

"How so?"

"They're not a fan of merchants, especially not ones from abroad," the jackal curled his snout. "Or tributaries as they like to call us. It's a hard field to break into and there's a lot of risks. Supplies, weather, bandits..." The jackal looked Modun in the eyes, "...Nomads."

Modun laughed heartily, "The clans aren't much friendlier to merchants I must admit!"

Pausing, Modun ran a paw through his white fur and thought.

"But we have some admiration for an industrious spirit, you know. Back in my clan, the wool-spinners...they're all descended from the same branch of the clan. Every last one of them, going back to the very first person who thought to grab some slaves and go up to the herders and tell them that they'd take care of the spinning business and let them not worry about it. They saw an opportunity and took it, and once they were in they got all the riches from it."

"Back in my parts, out west, we prefer to keep matters of business brief and to the point."

Modun smiled, "How would you like to get in on the start of a new opportunity?"

Great changes, sudden jolts of shock often begin with small sparks. Such a spark was in the form of a haggard envoy bearing the most alarming news to the Southern City. With ripped and torn armor, he showed the imperial tally to the gatekeeper. Unofficial whispers began of the dreaded news it came with him. The fall of the capital, the capture of the Emperor, Prince Jen's brother.

In an instant, the whole government was gone! The central government was wiped from existence and the Zhou Dynasty was headless. Governors, and princes were left hanging, far to the north-west the governor near the corridor to the west sat unsure who to call superior. Was the Zhou extinguished? The barbarians were sending demands to pay homage. Many were like this, and all feared for their necks if they made the wrong move and so delayed any and all.

The palace of the prince was a flurry. Even before the messenger arrived, hints of the news were well-spread. Taking his place in his princely hall, Jen was mobbed, as he took his place in his princely hall, by everyone discussing what to do even before the extent of the disaster was known in full.

A shout came out, "We must have a Son of Heaven, we must acclaim our prince as Emperor, we cannot go without for heaven will forsake us all!" all the canines agreed and turned to their nervous lord. All the ministers fell to their knees and began bashing the snouts against the floor, whining and whimpering theatrically.

"SIRE! Assume the throne! For the sake of the Zhou, take the throne!"

The Pomeranian, petrified as once again the mantra was repeated, while all crawled closer to him. An old hound grabbed at his sleeve and howled painfully at him. Jen snapped back his paw and yelped. Unable to handle this, Jen ran out as all clambered after him, shouting to save them and the state.

Rushing to his chambers, he barred the door behind him and tried to collect himself.

"What has become of the world!?" thoughts rushed through him and hesitation overcame him. Soon, all were at his door pounding at it, shouting again and again their pleas. It went on for hours and attempts to wait it out failed. No amount of pillows could block out the cries and, unable to take it anymore he shouted out, "I will! I will! Please leave me alone!"

Thus was the inauspicious beginning of Jen's reign. Still more inauspicious was the enthronement. Lacking the trappings of the court, they made do with what was available. A throne was made from a bench and the twelve emblems of rulership were merely painted on imperial robes, and beads from the Empresses' necklace were used for the beaded strands of the imperial cap.

What the envoy had brought was a decree from his brother himself, naming Jen as successor, it was read aloud during the hasty rites

"Faced with the twists and turns of fate, the imperial principles are not upheld. I, with limited virtue, have inherited the great lineage but failed to pray to heaven for eternal blessings, leading to the audacity of the hostile barbarians who dare herd their sheep into our lands and assault the imperial carriage. I am currently in a state of anxiety within the remote borders, fearing the collapse at any moment. You, my brother, are entrusted with the mandate and shall take charge of all affairs. I beseech you to return to the old capital. Restore and repair the ancestral shrines to wipe away this great shame."

The Era Name was proclaimed...

Preserving Harmony.

Times of chaos always made the folks of the South, those farmers and slaves to those who would hide away in palaces of stone, act quite unusual to Modun's eyes.

In times past when one would wander too close to their settlements, there would be alarms, the guard would be summoned and they would politely inform you that they had many dogs waiting at a garrison nearby who would hunt you down. A deal would then be struck, some gold went one way along with a few captives, and the imperial authorities need not know about it.

But now Modun found he could practically gallop into town squares with his saber or bow drawn and not only would the villagers give him tribute, some were even volunteering to join him!

At first, Modun doubted their resolve to be nothing more than desperation, so he got off his horse and looked one square in the eye, a brown wolf-dog mix, and demanded to know if he knew exactly what kind of life he intended them to lead.

"We've already had our possessions stolen by our own lords," the wolf-dog replied back without hesitation. "Figure we're just stealing them back with interest."

Tashkent, the Western merchant Modun counted as the first and greatest member of his still-growing horde, laughed heartily. The jackal couldn't so much as string a bow and he had a nasty habit of fleeing when trouble came, but Modun could not deny he had a way with coin and the locals.

Especially when Modun and his burgeoning band had gotten a bit out of hand and raided towns beyond reason. Tashkent always had a gold coin somewhere up his sleeve that tended to make people calm down or even invite Modun to dinner.

In one such village, Modun sat next to the jackal beside a blazing bonfire, having successfully recruited not only more fighters and horses from the village, but a good deal of gold, and asked the question.

"What's your secret?" Modun wrapped his arm around the shoulder of Tashkent and pressed him against his chest. It was both a display of his physical power and affection.

"These folk," Tashkent sniffed, "between the lack of protection from the local authorities, the range, and the general chaos engulfing the lands...most of them have not seen my kind in ages."

"I can see why they might miss your kind," Modun squeezed Tashkent once more.

Lowering his muzzle, Tashkent chuckled, "My people are the gateway between East and West. We're called tributaries but in reality if we can't do as we please, nothing travels between us. Glass to the East and Silk to the West, it is the way of things."

"I haven't seen a whole lot of either."

"No, no you haven't," Tashkent slipped out of Modun's grasp and unraveled a bag lying at his feet, rolling out a bundle of robes of varying degree of quality, all of which were clearly made of silk. "During good times even a commoner could purchase a silk robe if they saved up. Silk is strong, lasts a long time, and–"

"A raider like me would uncover a lot of folk's hidden robes."

Shrugging, Tashkent leaned back into the wolf's embrace, "When silk thread vanishes from the market, the Westerners will accept old, used robes. I'm sure they can figure out how to dethread them. And with no one else managing the market-"

"You'll make a killing."

"We'll make a merchant out of you yet, my nomad."

Of course, like all good times, they did not last. Modun knew in his heart that he couldn't have fun forever in the chaotic North, sooner or later someone bigger than him would take notice.

While leading his horde, now two hundred strong, he halted his horse and raised his muzzle. Sniffing into the air across the plains, he caught wind of at least a thousand horses.

"Khan Modun?" Tashkent edged up beside the wolf on his camel. Modun's black stallion had learned great restraint around the strange creature Tashkent rode over time. "What's the matter?"

Sighing, Modun lowered his head, "You'd best stop calling me Khan."

Tashkent tilted his head, "What should I call you?"

Dust-clouds rose on the horizon followed by the sound of earth pounding.

"Whatever this asshole says I can be called..."

Modun felt a gentle paw stroke his muzzle and he raised his face. Tashkent had a smile draped across his face.

"Vassalage need not be the end, only the beginning."

"What do you mean?"

Peering over at the gradually approaching horde, Tashkent's grin did not fade for a moment, "Let me tell you about my past life as a slave."

While Modun knew that his life as an independent warlord was coming to an end, he couldn't have expected the style with which it came to him.

Holding a banner of truce, Modun rode forward with Tashkent toward the halted mass of mounted wolves while they sent one of their own to meet him.

Before Modun could so much as greet the enjoy, a white wolf much like himself, he was ordered to dismount his horse and follow the envoy on foot behind his own horse. There was to be no negotiation it seemed.

Obeying and tucking his tail behind him in a sign of submission, Modun suppressed his ego as he slowly marched towards his new overlord's army, leaving his horse behind with Tashkent. At least they didn't bind his arms and tether him to the envoy's horse.

Modun expected jeers and mockery when he entered the pack of wolves, but they were remarkably restrained, holding their formation with only a slight glance in his direction.

Things only got more unexpected when he was finally brought to the center of the camp and gazed upon its commander.

The Emperor...or Khaganate, for the sovereign often switched freely between the titles, sat atop a portable throne backed by a screen with gold carvings of the visages of dragons atop them. The wolven Emperor, his fur as black as night, sat atop the throne with a burning gaze in his orange eyes. A yellow, silk robe was wrapped around his powerful chest, but he wore a mantle of heavy furs and a matching cap. A confusing mix of nomad and city-dweller fashion.

He was introduced as Yuan Di of the Greater Liang Dynasty and Modun was ordered to supplicate himself. Modun was taken aback by the nomad's adoption of a Southern name and title, so much so that he froze in place before being barked at to bow once more by a dog eunuch nearly half his size.

Engaging in the ritual humiliation, Modun pressed his snout to the rug and declared Yuan Di his sovereign.

"My army is yours."

The dog presented a series of documents made of bamboo slats tied together on behalf of his Emperor which Modun could not read but was assured they were declarations of amnesty for every act of banditry he engaged in and promises of fealty. Modun had no seal with which to sign the document, but dipped his thumbpad in the ink and pressed it on the bamboo where he was instructed.

With the last document signed, Yuan Di rose and clapped his paws together. Cups of yogurt were presented to the Emperor and his new vassal. A sheep was slaughtered and grilled mutton was served with flatbread to honor the occasion.

Modun was still not sure what exactly he had gotten himself into, but he was told his new title was to be the Duke of Han, whatever that meant.

Jen's Empire, the last bastion of the Zhou in the south, was reduced to a near rump state. The only thing in its favor was the north was disunited and fighting amongst each other. Khan against Khan, Proclaimed Emperor against Proclaimed Emperor. Khan-Emperors ran riot taking the northern capital in succession and found themselves with the same issues as when the Zhou controlled the north civil war and treachery. The faults of the Zhou were not its own alone.

Horsemen with new stirrups changed everything, no longer was balance needed to ride and fight upon a steed. New dogs and seasoned generals of the Zhou would be the first to realize the potential and implement it in the south.

"The South is well guarded by the river. It is thankful the heavens made it so horses could not tread upon the waters lest we all be doomed."

Supreme Commander Ping memorialized Emperor Jen during the first day of the month's audience before the imperial palace's gate.

"I, your humble servant, give thanks to your august majesty for this task you have placed upon my unworthy shoulders! I bow and prostrate myself to your majesty and shall take up the sacred banner of the Dynasty against these hordes. I shall lead forth and vanquish them!" Ping continued on with his memorial. "The nomads have taken the north, that is known, but their character is weak, I shall strike through, shake them and send them flying! Now, I ask for your decision on this lowly one's memorial? Shall your majesty consent to an expedition force?"

Sitting atop his throne before the lacquered gate, the Pommeranian looked drained, it had been nearly a year since he rose to the throne due to the will of heaven and it weighed on him heavily. The once rich fur that bounced and puffed up was now flat and dull. One could argue the lack of luxuries made in the north was the real reason, but that would not account for his lack of decent sleep affecting him.

"Since you have made me Supreme Commander the northern barbarians have been turned back time and time again at the banks of the river!"

A rival came forth, a civil official posed and dignified in silks opposed to scaly armor.

"That has less to do with yourself than the land itself and the river that protects us! No barbarian Khan is foolish enough to seek to cross the Pearl River and any forces fought off are only small raiding parties!"

Ping growled and marched over and shoved the insolent official, "Ha, and now he disregards protocol! Even Chow T'sao treated his Emperor with protocol in his dictatorship"

Jen became nervous, the mention of Chow T'sao deeply worried him. Memories of Chow T'sao's use of the last Zheng Emperor as a virtual prisoner puppet for his own legitimacy came forth and he worried the same. Funny, normally Jen would have moves of Weiqi in his mind but no longer. The board was laid with dust now in a corner of the palace...

The bell rang out the next hour and seeing a chance, Jen dismissed the court and retired deep within the palace as if he hoped the further he got inside the further away the issues of the world would be as well.

Jen soothed himself with some liquor and a mild narcotic: the cold food powder. The Pommeranian was boiling hot, even though he was fully nude. His body fur was just as flat as his head and only his tail was close to that of his old fur's volume.

"The longest one can hope to live when taking the drug is ten years or so; for some, it is only five or six," famed scholar Huangfu Mi said of the drug and Ssu'ma Jen knew this, but felt forced to indulge for his own nerve's sake. It made his weak form feel as if floating like a lotus upon a calm pond.

Once settled into his system, when reclined upon a jade couch, blocks of ice in golden trays beneath it gave him the cold his body demanded from the powder. There, Jen dozed and dazed, reading the works of Zhuangzi.

"Is a man dreaming of being a butterfly or a butterfly dreaming of being a man"

"Ha, what butterfly would dream of living my life!" Jen murmured.

A vision! A horror! A spear tipped in blood waved in the blood red sky! No! No not a spear; it's now inverted facing the ground! It's not a spear, it's a brush; it's not blood, it's ink; the sky is not sky, it's paper! A book, a title came into view and was read...

"Annals of the Last Emperor of Zhou...personal name is Ssu'ma Jen...armies of the nomads surrounded his capital and all he did was partake in the cold food powder as all died around him and so took his own life."

The Pomeranian awoke with a jolt. His head laid in a puddle of sweat from his nose and on the floor twin puddles from his paw pads. His heart racing, he cried out in response to his horrifying vision of the future.

"No more! I am done! I will not be the bad last Emperor like so many before!" Names, names came forth examples of the past marched by. King Jie of Xia, King Di Xin of Shang, King You of the Ancient Zhou. The Lake of wine, the laughing Baosi and the feudal armies! No! He will not be them, no! He would not allow his spirit to be cast down like that.

He got up, grabbed the jar of cold food powder and dashed it against the floor. He would not be ruined like them, he would endure, even if pathetically he would endure it not for his own sake but his ancestors. To have his great-grandfather's work end in him would draw down the ire of heaven and earth and he would be nothing but a hungry ghost roaming the earth. Jen ordered the head palace eunuch to remove all of the powder from the palace and capital itself.

But Jen was not without issues, he needed to counterbalance Supreme Commander Ping with another before removing him. Ping did have his own staff, surely a hound of his could be raised to rival his former master or a commander on the frontlines could be found. There had been a young hound in his retinue during one meeting named Chu, perhaps him?

The influx of émigrés from the north had been causing much disquiet among the southern canines. The only thing in Jen's mind about that plan was learning to tolerate the dialect common in these regions, it was so inelegant but then again elegance died in the loss of the central plains.

His thoughts then turned to his own sons, seven in total and many were soon to come of age. He would keep his eldest in the capital and send out the younger pups to the provinces with military staff. Garrisons should be made across what was left of the Zhou and this would be a good excuse to keep control of them through his issue. Even if that meant sending a child as nominal head of a garrison force.

It might do good, the clan is long in need of military spirit and if the dynasty was to endure, princes with martial experience are for the best of the state.

"Unlike me..." perhaps if Jen had known better sooner in his life, instead of trusting the bravado of his commanders, who knew what to do in battle, he might have been able to contribute himself to the war. But all he could do was wait in the capital praying to heaven and earth that he chose the right hound for battle. Later, he would pray to that eastern god, that Buddha. Many had said he gives many blessings despite being of the western barbarians.

Being a member of an imperial army was not quite so different from Modun's life before. He had to travel around to different towns as the army marched South with the eventual goal of destroying the last remnants of the Southern dynasty; collecting tribute and demanding fealty. Modun got to keep a cut of the tribute of course.

Really, it was just the pretenses that changed. One had to declare themselves an officer of the Most Serene Emperor and perform a bunch of very specific rituals before having to resort to blades and spears being drawn if necessary. The latter was rarely employed and when it was, most were more than willing to submit.

During one such incident, Modun found himself exceptionally bored and began chatting with a peasant, a brown and black dog, who had the misfortune of passing by his horse.

"Why do you submit so easily?" Modun asked. "Is it not humiliating to prostrate towards wolves such as us?"

"We humiliate ourselves towards the Southern Dynasty every day," the dog shrugged. "It hasn't gotten us much, so why not humiliate ourselves towards someone else?"

Laughing, Modun tossed the dog a silver necklace he had looted from a town that had been less submissive.

Another thing Modun found himself displeased with was when sharing drinks with the vassals he had pressed into servitude. It had been custom to break bread and share yogurt among his people, including the nobles of the Greater Liang, but the further south they had gotten the more villages politely requested tea instead. The brew was invigorating, though it burned Modun's lips and tasted of leaves to him.

As a compromise to his tastes, he mixed yogurt in with it and much to his surprise, the dogs were fascinated by this combination and began to take it up.

The job was fun, Modun supposed, and safer than what he had been used to, but it did not have quite the same degree of glory.

Emperor Yuan Di was beginning to build up a large harem of dogs and wolves alike but was failing to produce healthy issue. Whispers about his fertility began to spread, an embarrassment at best among the southerners, but an unthinkable weakness among the northerners.

The Emperor had expressed his wish to follow in the southern inheritance tradition of primogeniture to consolidate his influence over the entire land. But the Emperor was only one wolf and others might have their own opinion on how one should inherit.

Of which Modun was beginning to develop his own opinion on the matter.

And gradually he had begun to introduce himself as the Duke of Han, rather than a mere representative of the Emperor; who he also began to forget to mention entirely.

And so Supreme Commander Ping did seek to grab power. Feeling himself slowly isolated, he rose up one fateful day on march to quell an uprising in the southern mountains. Half-way there he stopped.

The Imperial envoys were publicly beheaded before Ping's army and he ordered the whole mass of canines to turn around and march back.

News of this threw the entire court into chaos; the entire department fled on their own accord and as the warships made their way back, Emperor Jen was in all ways acting as a debauched Emperor. Drinking and throwing banquets within the palace gardens, having seemingly forgotten his moment of clarity and any scheme to put Chu in power in favor of wine and concubines.

"Ping is no match for me, he is but nothing to my might!" Jen said as siege equipment was put up along the walls of the capitol. Those who had long wavered, switched sides en masse leaving only those who truly were loyal to the falling Jen behind in a desolate palace as it became more and more devoid of life.

"The foolish dog has doomed himself! The Mandate is lost and belongs to me!" Ping bellowed to his makeshift court made up of military men and turncoat ministers. All fell over each other to give praise higher than the others.

"A true Son of Heaven!" One shouted.

"A dragon among us!" Another claimed.

"The mandate is with you! Down with Jen and his fallen dynasty!"

When the walls were breached, Ping, in full shining armor upon a white horse, rode in and made way to the palace. He took Jen and was filled with the fullest of pride and confidence. It was his, all of it was his now. Jen yelled and howled with righteous indignity shouting, "I AM EMPEROR, HOW DARE YOU!?"

"For now, you still are, dear Pomeranian, but soon you shall relinquish it."

Jen threw a goblet of wine at the impetuous dog, "OUTRAGE!" he shouted at Ping, who only laughed in response.

"Take the pampered pup away and confine him to his chambers." He ordered as he turned to his adjunct, asking, "Also, what about the palace guards?"

The dog responded, "On our side, corps lead Chu is now loyal to us."

In came the dog Chu, whose fur was as brown as dirt, who greeted Ping with respect as Jen was led away, the two shared a glance. Jen seemingly gave a nod as he left.

That evening, full of confidence, Ping paid a visit to Jen seeking that which he truly desired.

"You will abdicate to me, you understand?"

By now, Jen was despondent, "Oh, my Ancestors, what have I done to shame you!?" He wept and tore at his fur and clothes. "I brought ruin to your shines, how can I ever face you, even in death?"

"Cease this, it is over, your Majesty."

Jen pulled himself together just enough, "You shall have it, but shall I be able to live?"

"Yes, you shall, as a Duke of the former dynasty you shall remain to tend to the shrines of your ancestors and do whatever debauched thing you like."

"Agreed."

"Now, where is the seal!? I must see it!"

"As you wish."

Jen led the eager dog to the place where the seal was hidden under his bed, crumpled under a pile of rags.

When Jen unveiled it before the eyes of the bullish dog, Ping's eyes lit up as if they were building the will of Heaven. Plucking it from Jen's paws, he turned around and cradled it, muttering to himself of how it was finally happening. With his back turned, he placed it on a table and gazed at it. Ping lost all sense of his environment looking at it.

A blade!

A swift motion!

Flesh tearing!

The Jadeite seal showered with crimson!

Jen standing behind, dagger in paw, sleeve red with blood!

"Dear Commander, this is your prize..."

The form of the General fell forward onto the very seal he sought and then to the side bleeding out, his eye glazed over.

"Chu, get in here, it's done!"

From the outside, Chu marched in and nodded at the corpse.

"You know what to do now? Right?"

"Yes your majesty!"

"Spare no quarter, all must die, save for the rank and file troops; but those who supported this traitor, especially those who switched sides...none must be spared."

Chu nodded and went out to perform his task, but before leaving Jen reminded him "Do not forget to distribute the treasury to the masses of troops, that must be done first and under my name!"

"Understood!"

As Chu left, Jen was rightfully proud of himself. Just like that he not only removed one who sought to overthrow him but also removed all unloyal parties in his court.

"Heaven decides if I have the mandate or not! Not anyone else!"

The fun could not last forever. Modun knew that they could not merely knock on village's doors and demand tribute forever, eventually someone big would knock back.

That day came when the Greater Liang's horde reached the Pearl River and saw the banners of the Zhou fluttering in the wind beyond it.

This put everyone at pause. The Greater Liang had very few boats and the currents of the river were known to be deceptively treacherous for horses. Even if the environment had been more ideal, it would have been better to find an alternative location for the assault.

Modun was beginning to doubt Yuan Di's grand plan.

In public, the Emperor was as cool and collected as ever. As strong as the mightiest nomadic warrior and as sharp as a scholar.

However, in private, Modun began to notice concerning behavior. His obsession with siring an heir had begun to wear at him even more and was getting more and more fantastical with his solutions. One of which involved cinnabar pills and the other was that by somehow capturing the young Zhou Emperor and adding him to his harem, that would somehow solve his fertility problems now that he had the unquestioned Mandate of Heaven.

Which would normally not be a problem, had not such private matters begun to whisper out into the army. The horde was only as good as its cohesiveness and strange habits from the Khagan was enough to wear at it.

Tashkent was the first to notice, bringing Modun aside one evening.

"The soldiers and their horses are spooked," he whispered.

"The horses must just be scared of your camel!" Modun laughed, hugging the jackal tight. "Don't worry so much!"

"I wrinkled my muzzle at one of the fiercest war-horses in the army and its rider could not control the beast's panic. It reared up and bucked," Tashkent lowered his voice even more. "The soldiers are panicked, despite our fortified position. They are losing trust in the Emperor."

"Duke Modun!" a voice barked and Modun broke from his embrace to find a soldier with a paper lantern bowing before him. "A messenger from Commander Chu wishes to speak to the Emperor!"

Modun looked past the wolf and at first did not notice the small, black dog in the shadows wielding a scroll of bamboo slats as if it were a blade.

"Go on then," Modun nodded his muzzle towards the Emperor's yurt.

Wolf and dog alike were silent as they passed Modun. Modun sniffed at the air behind the dog, detecting no fear or apprehension from the messenger.

"I have a bad feeling about this," Tashkent whispered.

Modun growled silently.

"But if things go badly...there are other options..." the jackal narrowed his eyes.

When word of the plan had spread from the Emperor to his generals, the camp practically reeked of fear and even the shortest-muzzled of dogs could smell it.

Modun himself was practically paralytic when hearing it, wishing to remain in his bedroll long after the first daylight with Tashkent at his side.

The Zhou had requested the Emperor to allow them to cross the river so as to solve this little matter in one decisive battle.

The Emperor had accepted without hesitation.

On the one hand, Modun recognized that this would put the Zhou in an exceptionally bad position with their backs to the Pearl River, but on the other hand it was still a position that they wanted and the Greater Liang had accepted without delay in granting them it.

Never give the enemy the position they want.

Modun had bowed his head and as politely as he could muster, asked Yuan Di if he planned on doing some treachery, such as attacking them in the middle of the river.

Yuan Di laughed and shook his head, sipping a cup of tea.

"We're not savages anymore, Duke Modun, we can't abide by such treachery in an honorable battle."

Modun kept his muzzle shut and refused to point out that it was neither honorable nor treacherous to let the enemy take a position they wanted, merely stupid.

Eventually, Modun had to rise from his bed, put on his armor, and mount his horse.

The Zhou were already beginning to cross. The Greater Liang army was standing firm but any canine from here to Tashkent's homeland could sense the unease wracking every soldier's nerves.

Whispers noting the array of equipment on the ships crossing the river were abound. Even something as innocuous as a cart were pointed out as if they were secret weapons.

Which it turned out they were. The moment the first ships landed, a crew of dogs shoved the carts they were carrying across the land and formed makeshift walls with them while another crew planted stakes in front of them.

Now would have been the time to charge and end this, to hell with honor! But Yuan Di did not give the word.

Even a fool could see that their cavalry would be halted from making a successful charge.

Modun growled, not even hiding his displeasure in the ranks for all to hear. Yuan Di's ear flicked for a second, atop his horse barded with gold and lacquered armor. He heard, but made no show of noticing it.

A sudden crash ran out to the far right of Modun's unit. Twitching his eyes over to it, Modun saw a large warhorse, far bigger than the ones he would have used up in the far north, crashing into a group of mounted warriors and knocking them to the ground.

An attack? No...not even the mightiest of the south's crossbows could reach that far...probably an undisciplined fool...

"Emperor!" another wolven general called out. "They're attacking us!"

"No!" Yuan Di raised his palm. "Have the commander of that unit disciplined! The Zhou have not attacked us, they gave their word!"

He's right, Modun could see the enemy were marching into position and nothing more. They held to their word.

Yuan Di's words were loud enough and spoken with just the right lack of confidence that uncertainty spilled through the army. Wolf and dog, on horse or foot, were starting to look around for an escape route despite the fact that the enemy were nowhere even close to reaching them.

The battle is lost from a sheer lack of courage. There is no victory here. Only what I can gain.

"They're firing on us!" Modun bellowed as loud as he could, his first and last lie to his lord.

"What!?" Yuan Di barked. "Are you blind, Duke Modun!?"

The moment Yuan Di took to argue with Modun was a key second that had him lose track of the army. The refusal to order any sort of reprisal against, Modun admitted, a non-existent attack was the deathblow to the already fragile morale.

Some generals ordered a retreat, while others were trying to muster an assault on the Zhou. The latter quickly faced their soldiers unseating them from their horses while one particularly brave soldier promoted themselves to general atop their former lord's horse and ordered a retreat.

Yuan Di only was able to no longer deny reality when a parade of panicked light cavalry smashed through the pavilion behind him.

"Retreat!" he ordered, though no one was truly listening.

Everyone had already given themselves the order at this point or faced the consequences.

Despite the sheer disaster faced at Pearl River, there were remarkably few casualties, save for pride. Plenty of deserters however; though plenty of soldiers arrived at the camp the army had rapidly shrunk.

Morale reeked. The moment Yuan Di made himself present, his yellow robes now tattered and covered in dirt, countless hungry eyes would be upon him before he would vanish to his yurt.

"It's time," Tashkent whispered to Modun. They were both resting by a campfire together, Tashkent laying against Modun's chest.

Snorting, Modun looked over at Yuan Di's yurt, "Do you think so?"

"The Emperor has attempted to play by Southern culture and has failed," Tashkent whispered back. "He has failed to take the Zhou, he hides away in his yurt, and he has sired no heir."

"When the ways of the South fail..." Modun grumbled, "...perhaps we should return to our Northern roots."

Standing up, Modun placed his hand on the hilt of his saber and sauntered over to the entrance of the Emperor's yurt. Two particularly large dogs stood in front of it, resting on their polearms.

"Yuan Di!" Modun barked. "I challenge you for leadership by right of combat!"

The two dogs blinked before one of them poked his muzzle into the yurt and whispered audibly. Modun's ear twitched as he heard Yuan Di speak back.

The eunuch Yuan Di kept at his side must have deserted, Modun figured. He was talking with his guards directly, a poor sign for him.

Modun had to give Yuan Di credit. The wolf, still dressed in his elaborate robes, emerged from the yurt with his saber drawn. His lips were peeled back, baring his slightly yellowed fangs. For one the Emperor looked like a true warrior and not someone putting on airs.

"We don't do this anymore," Yuan Di snapped his jaws. "My son will-"

"Your son will never exist," Modun drew his blade and punched his fist to his chest. "You have shamed heaven and your ancestors with your defeat. Show courage and die on your feet like a true wolf."

The Emperor charged forward, saliva trailing past his maw as if he was rabid. His blade flashed and Modun caught it with the hand-guard of his own.

Yuan Di was courageous, that couldn't be doubted, but he was foolish, headstrong.

Perhaps he wished to die. It would only make sense.

Growling, Modun shoved the Emperor back and slashed at his side. Yuan Di parried and sent Modun spinning two steps to the side.

Yuan Di paused, clutching at his side in pain. Modun hadn't hit him, he was certain of that; it almost looked like the Emperor was suffering from something unrelated to the battle, such as indigestion or a chronic disease.

Modun never got a chance to ask him. His blade met Yuan Di's neck and in mere seconds it was dislodged from his shoulders and on the ground. His body soon followed.

The very same hungry eyes that looked upon Yuan Di earlier were now on Modun. The rules of the game had changed and no one was certain what might happen.

Not until Modun sheathed his blade, still covered in blood, stood tall before them.

"I am Emperor Modun of Han!" Modun proclaimed boldly.

Tashkent filed through the crowd, nodding at Modun with a smile.

Modun looked at the ground. Just before his boot was a tiny pink peony peeking up from the dirt, looking out of place among the smoke and dust of the camp. Spring was returning again.

"I will honor the heavens and earth!"

"I will not make the same mistakes Yuan Di did!"

"I will lead us to victory and prosperity! I will bring the so-called Emperor of Zhou before us in chains!"

The crowd cheered and dog and wolf alike bowed.

Secretly, in Modun's head, he knew he was in no shape to wage war on the South. The army was in bad shape and he had no idea how many soldiers he could muster up.

Most likely he'd have to retreat north and reinforce his domains up there, especially now that many would have to swear fealty to a new Emperor.

But that didn't matter now. Right now it was all about puffing out his chest and promising the world to his vassals.

Reality would set in later and Modun hoped Tashkent would still be by his side to help.

The victory was spectacular; cunning Chu drove back the hordes of the north, sending them scattering like dust in the wind of galloping horses! Their heavy cavalry's armor littered the river banks like sprigs of grass, all of them pulling them off in their flight. It filled Jen's heart with joy and ease.

"Quickly: a brush and paper! I shall make Chu the Barbarian Ruining Duke of Zhao with a tax income of 10,000 households!" Jen commanded in his imperial writ to be dispatched immediately to the front.

"Furthermore, let there be a holiday declared! Let grain and silk from the palace warehouses be distributed to the capital!" Emperor Jen and all his officials drank in celebration in full regalia and court attire. Elegant court music was played and the colors of the dynastic element, that of metal's white hue, decorated the halls and chambers of the palace.

In the grand shrine of the Ssu'ma Clan, the news of victory was announced before their memorial tablets. Though omens began to arise, a black bird flew into the temple and perched on the tablet of the Martial Emperor and Venus was seen in the daytime.

"Black is the color of the element of water and Venus challenging the power of the sun means a usurper is in the world and will challenge the Imperial Clan..."

As if answering his fears, a letter came from Commander Chu.

As Jen opened up the letter following the victory it showed him the one the omens pointed to. It was a gentle but firm request for the Nine Bestowments to be given to him. Had not Chow T'sao asked for the same, had not his great grandfather also asked the same before dethroning the last Qi Emperor!?

Supreme Commander Chu was threatening him.

He holds in his heart usurpation!

Had not his own dynasty asked for the same before taking the throne from the Chow's? It was clear intent for it. Chu wanted his throne, maybe not in his own time but perhaps in the time of his son's. A plot formed in his mind.

When Chu arrived, Emperor Jen held the audience. The banners of the Liang, mud-soaked and stained with river water, were thrown before his throne as Chu, in full armor, soaked in the court's cries of praise. The now-wisened Jen stood up and held aloft a cup of rice wine "To you, my Supreme Commander, Victor of the Pearl River, thanks unto you the ancestral temples of the Zhou stand firm!"

Chu bowed down and gave a knowing look to his lord, expecting what he had firmly asked for.

"Ah, yes, my Supreme Commander, but patience is a virtue, we have much time to celebrate first and I wish you to join me in a banquet this evening. I shall have you given the bestowments on an appropriate date, for to give you it on a date that lacks auspicious signs would not befit you and your great achievements."

The hound looked satisfied, it would not be long...

Evening came and his alchemists presented Jen with their tonic prepared for the commander's *health*. A test of it was performed on a murderer and it was to his expectation. Turning to a trusted eunuch, Jen spoke, "You will make sure this is put in the Supreme Commander's drink, will you?"

"Yes Imperial Majesty"

When all was read, the dining hall was decked in brazen candelabras in the form of long-necked birds that illuminated and perfumed the air in warm spices and wood. Musicians and dancing borzois spun and sang, lulling the commander with songs of praise and glory. A poetic rhapsody on the battle was read aloud, "Commander Chu soared over the barbarians like a dragon and he was like a tiger in battle," it rang.

"Come, a drink to your health, my *dear* commander. I have offered you this wine especially for this moment," the hound's mien betrayed total trust, he was no longer going to endanger him or his dynasty.

The jade cups were arrayed before them all and all stood for the toast, "To the everlasting health of the Supreme Commander!" All downed the contents and returned to their sitting mats, Jen's eyes fully focused on the head of Chu, waiting for it to happen. Like all things, it came slowly...

A few pounds on his chest with his paw, complaints of the food not sitting right, then knocking over a cup with clumsy movements, and dropping his spoon as he tasted some meat broth.

Then suddenly...

Spasms in the gut, he clutched his belly and his eyes went wide as his muzzle hung open with increasingly sustained panting. He stood up, stumbled and tripped over his dining tray. Shouts and cries of "Commander Chu, what's wrong?!" all were in a state of panic, all baring Jen, who watched silently, circling the rim of his bronze goblet with his manicured claw.

He should have known his place... he should have not dared to seek MY throne, the throne my clan had schemed and fought for. Jen would not be another last Emperor dethroned by an upstart, nor would his son or any of his successors.

As the savior of the Zhou breathed his last, Jen only thought how it was a pity he overstepped his boundaries. He was a skilled hound and could have taken the north but due to his own greed and ambition the north would have to be forfeited for the sake of the Ssu'ma's. Though it did not matter that the barbarians could have the north for now, their dynasty could claim the mandate but *they* were the only legitimate dynasty.

News would soon come that a certain Modun now claimed to be "Emperor," in the north. He had betrayed his former lord and killed him after the battle of the Pearl River and then unified the north again under his horsemen. Later afterwards he sent to the south ambassadors bearing gifts and came not as a tributary but an equal.

Jen was outraged by their audacity "How dare they come to me as if I was equal! Burn their gifts and cast them back to whence they came. I shall only entreat them if they give me back the north!"

As the gifts were thrown onto a pile and set ablaze, Jen watched from atop a pagoda. He brought a shallow cup of wine to his muzzle and was shocked to find a dried-up leaf had landed atop it. He picked up the dreadful omen of autumn and tossed it off of the balcony.

In the middle-aged pomeranian's mind it was he who was the true and only Son of Heaven, no other could share in such as long as his august throne stood. Even with the north gone, he and he alone would stand alone as the true Lord of Ten Thousand Years.

"It was I and I alone who fought and struggled to near exhaustion to ensure tablets of spirits of the Ssu'ma's remains standing in the ancestral temples, who maintained the altars of grain and soil of the Empire. The Zhou unified all under heaven, and though it lost the north, it still had unified it first and will always be preeminent."

Alas, maybe some future emperor would reunite the middle kingdom once more, but now things had settled into their divisions.
One became three.
Three became one.
One became two.
North and South.
Spring and Autumn.

High

Doomsday

Televassi

November, 1069
Yorkshire, The Kingdom of England

erhaps the heathens were right." Karli paused, poking the fire. "Right about winter. About it heralding the end of the world."

I said nothing as the old stag stared across the flames at me, waiting for me to challenge his blasphemy. I wouldn't admit it, but I felt the chill in his words. Despite the fire, the shadows leapt and flickered behind us like baleful spirits, delighted by the power the dark days gave them.

It had been three years of ever harsher winters. The snow drifted far and deep from the hills, burying the roads and all other traces of civilization. On the rare, clear days where the winds paused to take a breath before howling once more, York seemed an ocean away, across the gulf of an impassible, wild white sea. The weather was harsh enough that even Karli had become earnest in his prayers, but the nights remained testing: long, dark, unrelenting.

"I know it's heathen nonsense," the old deer rumbled, his eyes focused back on the hearth. "But, events do make me wonder. Even heathens can be right about something."

Karli grunted and tossed another block of wood into the fire. We didn't need the additional burst of warmth - he just wanted to see something burn.

I didn't bother to protest further. Karli had sixteen points to his magnificent antlers. He had weathered many winters; raised the walls and roof of the farmstead. He had turned a forsaken patch of wilderness: remote, cut off, and on the northern border of England, into eight bountiful fields. And all I had to my name was a set of antlers with a single point each, and not even an alluring scar from a famous battle that I could flaunt in lieu of such achievements.

"If Father Beorhtsige could hear us now," I murmured.

"I'd have told him to pray much harder," Karli retorted.

He grunted and shuffled closer to the fire, stopping only before the heat would singe his fur. He took a deep breath and bared his thigh, glistening in the flames. It had been three years since the battle at Stamford Bridge, but here he was, still fighting, as lame as the day he limped back home.

"For your leg?" I asked.

Karli shook his head and spat into the fire.

"For when King Harold marched south to face the Normans."

He seemed stoic, but his lip twitched, betraying the discomfort beneath his stillness.

"Do me a favour, and go and fetch some water."

I nodded and grabbed an empty bucket, stepping outside hastily. The fresh, cold air hit me as soon as I closed the door, adding urgency to my hoofsteps.

The heavens put on quite the show above me. The afternoon's dying rays found some strength in the faltering day; painting the ends of my dappled russet fur an airy bronze that rippled weightlessly in the breeze. The golden rays burst through the dark clouds, painting their underbellies a brilliant, rosy crimson. Perhaps the day would not have been so bitter, had they not saved their strength for these final moments. For, no matter how striking the display, the sight was over as quickly as it started, smothering the world under the dark, grey clouds, and the growing tyranny of the night.

The sharp bite of the cold as it wormed through my fur focused my mind on the task at hand.

Rascill got cold easily. Wedged between the rolling fen-hills that loomed to both the east and west, the lay of the land funnelled the freezing winds down from the heights. In the summer this was a welcome reprieve when working the fields, but now it brought a bitter edge to winter that seemed almost spiteful.

I cast the bucket down the well, grateful that the heavy wood was enough to shatter the ice on the first throw. But that small mercy didn't change the larger, uncertain future looming before us.

Things had slowly fallen apart since the Norman, William, took the throne. The fact the Witan elected him king meant nothing; isolated rebellions grew in size and severity, while the nobles of Northumbria resorted to outright murder for the title of Earl. Fortunately those troubles had not yet reached us, but every day the peace felt more fragile.

"God, things are fucked," I breathed, pulling up the bucket and trudging backinside.

Back inside, I knelt next to Karli, pouring the clear spring water into a large claw jug. When I finished, a long, rolling sigh rattled from Karli's muzzle.

"I'm sorry," he whispered. "I don't mean to argue." The old deer shrugged. "But the future has always been out of our hands. We just have to survive what's to come."

"How?"

Karli shrugged, stroking his chin.

"I bled for Harold at the bridge fighting off the vikings, and you - you were much too young to have gone to either battle." Karli winced and moved his thigh back towards the fire. "Technically, neither of us have raised arms against the king, so surely he will see the difference." He swallowed. "I am sure of it."

"Or... we don't leave it to chance."

"And go where?"

"I don't know. Somewhere, anywhere."

"And leave this work behind?" Karli sighed. "I went to the battle to protect our home, our land - you. That's what the *Fyrd* does." Karli grunted. "There's nothing treasonous in that."

I tried to swallow the tremble in my voice.

"It's been three years, and still we don't know anything about William."

Karli shrugged, exhaling the instinctual fighting spirit. I did the same, lowering my head, willing to meet the older stag halfway rather than keep clashing horns.

"Please, listen," he murmured, his words rumbling in his throat like the moving earth. "You are all the family I have left, and I need you to trust me. Kings come and go, just like the seasons, Canute. Their wars are winters of our own making," he sighed. "Our struggle with the land remains constant. But it will always look after us, if we water it with our sweat and blood-"

"You're sounding more like the pagans with each passing day," I grumbled, folding my arms.

"Maybe God is in the earth, rather than the heavens?" Karli laughed. "Don't you think it miraculous how such bounty springs from the barren soil year after year, so long as we faithfully tend to it? It really is a wonderful act of creation-"

"You really *are* a terrible Christian."

"You're not the first to call me that," the old stag laughed, leaning forward from his seat and towards the flames once more. "In my time I've been called a terrible Dane, a terrible Saxon, and a terrible warrior." He pointed at his leg as firm evidence of the latter. "But I have always put food in our bellies. That's got to be worth something?"

I chose to ignore him as I snatched a loaf of bread, a wedge of cheese, and a stick of cured, salted meat to chew on. It was tough, dense, and bland like most winter stores, but its abundance meant even in these years of hardship, we haven't yet had to worry about going hungry.

"Did I ever tell you how our line got our Danish names?" Karli asked, changing topic.

"Mother always was tight-lipped about that."

I closed my eyes, trying to remember her smell.

"Well, when Canute the Great dethroned the Saxons and became King of England all those years ago, your grandfather took up a more viking-sounding name to smooth things over - in a not entirely different situation to us I recall," Karli smirked. "It's surprising what people will do to keep their estates. Ealdorman, thegns, even the lowest of the common-folk."

"Are you suggesting we take up Norman names?"

Karli shrugged, gazing back into the fire as if it might give him some sort of sign clearer than the silent reply of prayer.

"Maybe. Nothing remains the same in the world, Canute. There is always change. Slowly. Suddenly. But always change." Karli smiled, reaching out to ruffle the tuft of fur on my head. His breath steamed out from his muzzle like smoke. "Don't dwell on the troubles of the world. Kings come and go, but good kings recognise the struggle the people have with the land, and leave us in peace to wage it. After all, the Lord made it so we must all eat, rich and poor alike - and I doubt we'll ever see William stoop so low to tend the fields himself. "

Perhaps it was his words, or a combination of the warm fire and a full belly, but the darkness seemed to shrink back.

"Now... I want you to be up early tomorrow to finish the north field, before the snow comes in earnest." Karli ignored my protests. "See if we can break up the last of the damn roots, then wait to sow it in spring."

"You always give me the worst jobs," I grunted.

"You know I would join you. You still have much to learn about toiling the earth." Karli sighed, not bothering to finish the sentence. "But the cold does not agree with my leg, and I would only slow you down."

Karli smiled, patting me gently on the shoulder. There was a weight to his arm that felt beyond its mere physical weight. There was something tangible, or his pride, or his legacy, a desire to pass on the weight of his mantle.

"It'll be worth the work, trust me. If you don't wish to starve, you never gamble and sow your fields with only one crop."

The next morning, the air smelt of blood.

I scrambled to my hooves, instinct compressing thought into a blur. My head pulsed; my heart beat harder still. I tried in vain to find my assailant in the darkness, but the seconds crawled by without a shout or unsheathed blade.

My breathing steadied. Detail returned to the world with every breath, and as I sieved through my thoughts, I spotted the two white spurs of bone among my bedding. That was the source of the scent - my antlers had shed in the night.

I stared. I'd always felt anxious with how small they were, even though they were my first set, but now they'd left me I felt only loss and disgust.

I swallowed and left the hut to deal with my blood-caked head-fur. It was still before dawn outside, the air bitter and crisp, the birds beginning their cautious dawn song. Thankfully, the cold numbed my bleeding stumps before I drew fresh water and submerged my head.

I was glad it was not light enough to see my reflection on the surface of the water. I gripped the edges of the bucket with my hooves, wishing not to be reminded. What deficiency made them fall from my head months earlier than they should? And if the reason didn't matter, I was a fawn again - useless, defenceless, weak.

I pulled my head from beneath the water, gasping and shivering, but the blood was stubborn. Massaging my scalp, I doused my head while the sun rose from its slumber. The soft, pink light combined with the sanguine water turned my wet, russet fur a deep shade of crimson - a bloody trick of the light that felt ominous enough, until the water started to run clear from my fur.

Satisfied, I returned indoors and stoked the hearth, my fur steaming as it dried. My stomach grumbled for a hearty meal, but I thought of the looming winter and made do with some old bread and a chunk of bitter, salty cheese.

I wished Mother was still here.

Sometime later, Karli appeared beside me, stealing a bite from the remnants of my breakfast.

"Even when nature disarms you," Karli murmured, "always keep your weapon close." He handed me a set of small, single-pointed antlers. They were clean and tidy, sharpened to a curved point, with strips of leather wrapped around the base and faint norse runes etched all the way along them.

"Old habits die hard," Karli shrugged. "And before you start, you should also have this," he finished, handing me a sturdy axe. It looked to me more like a farming tool than a weapon of war, but it felt sturdy as I held it in my hand.

"Thanks," I murmured.

The old stag nodded.

"Remember the roots in the far fields today. Then it should be good enough for some barley to shoot up next year."

"Barley? Are you looking to brew some ale?"

"If you'd like?" Karli smiled. "I'm sure we can do better than the piss Aldwark brews for us." He muttered some choice curse, some odd mix of Norse and Saxon.

"Doesn't stop us from downing it so fast."

"What else is there to do in winter?" Karli laughed. "And don't say pray," he complained.

I frowned and flicked an ear in annoyance.

"Fine! When you're done in the field, see if you can haggle Leofwine for something better."

"Are you going to give me some coin to sweeten the deal?"

"Like you need that in winter." Karli shook his head. "Take a sack of planting seed - none of the milled stuff. That should be enough," the stag finished, waving his hand towards our burgeoning store.

Still munching on his bread, he limped back to bed, leaving me to dress for the day.

I turned the decorated antlers over in my hand. I knew they were Karli's, but for his first shed, they were more slender and shorter than I expected. I wanted to think that mine were more impressive, but instead I found comfort knowing my father had begun humbly too.

I suppose a single point is all it really takes.

I held onto that hope as I threw on my clothes and a thick fur cloak to keep the cold at bay. Looping my axe to my belt and shouldering the tools and bag of seed, I set out into the cold morning. The field's thick mud clung to my hooves as I trudged up the trail to the topmost field, no thanks to my heavy load. By the time I arrived I was panting, so I paused to rest on the crumbling stone wall for a moment, observing the odd boundary where our lands touched the wilderness beyond.

Even in the late autumn, the tangled wilderness still had a primal beauty. The air swirling down from the hills was crisp and clean, while the tangled mass of trees communed together among the currents, their boughs thick and gnarled with age. But instead of the usual frenzy of winter preparation - jays fluttering between the boughs, squirrels dashing through the undergrowth - there was silence.

Deer may not have the noses of wolves, but we pick up on the scent of fear better than anyone else. Call it a relic of the distant past, a lingering blessing of the herd, but as I caught my breath, the smell floated in like a waveless tide.

Something was wrong.

I set my tools down and clambered on top of the wall, trying to find the source of it between the gaps in the trees. To the southeast, the thin wisps of smoke about York seemed normal. I turned about in all directions, but my feeble nose was not enough to pick up anything further. Still, it set my fur on edge, and I knew I couldn't shake it until I figured out the source.

I grabbed the sack of grain and set off towards Aldwark, hoping Leofwine and the others might have some news, along with some decent beer. As I wandered down the overgrown trail towards the village, the smell on the wind rose, thick on the cloying, damp air that blew off from the river. Without even thinking of it, I began to crouch low, fur blending in with the tangled undergrowth, placing my feet carefully among the treacherous leaf litter.

The air beneath the trees felt dense and heavy, as if a single sound would shatter the silence as the woods held their breath. Then, finally, a break in the trees let me catch sight of the river, and the few huts on the banks that Leofwine's folks called home.

Two longships floated on the water, their draught shallow. Their sides were clad in brightly coloured shields, while their bows were decorated each with a snarling wooden figure that reared up from the water. Thanks to Karli's insistence on our traditions, I could tell from the green flecks of paint and serpentine form that they resembled Jormungandr - perhaps the writhing spawn of the world-serpent - but either way confirming them as vikings.

I lay flat on the wet leaves, thankful that my antlers were not there to get caught as I crawled through the undergrowth. The banks were filled with strangers. I could make out the glint of their mail and helms, their laughter, the sounds of their language, but I couldn't spot Leofwine or any of his family among the abandoned buildings.

At least I couldn't smell any blood...

My head throbbed painfully, just like when I woke this morning.

Shit.

I backed up, crawling as best I could, knowing my open wound would betray me.

Shit. Shit. Shit.

They had already smelt me. The sounds of bodies crashing through the bushes swiftly followed, and they caught me even before I'd managed to get to my feet.

"*Létta! Létta!*" they jeered, pointing their spears at me while they held me down, grabbing my axe and antler-bone daggers before pulling me to my feet and parading me towards their camp.

I tried to avoid the humiliation of my capture by making my eyes useful, drinking in all the details. About fifty crew, men and women, hurriedly gathered dried food, salt, and just about anything that would preserve at sea. There were a few signs of violence between the few buildings clustered between the bank: the brewing vats were empty, the fires long burnt out, and the building's doors were pulled or smashed off their hinges, but fortunately no bodies or blood. The Norsemen didn't even hesitate to toss my sack of barley onto their ship.

My captors brought me to the centre of the clearing, where a small grey-furred wolf sat clad in leather and mail, counting a pile of coins and other useful metals, and dividing them into discrete piles.

"*What is it now?*" she growled, snapping her jaws and restarting her count. My Norse was patchy, but what words I didn't know I found I could either guess or infer.

"*We found another spy skulking about the woods.*"

"*Looks more like a farmer to me,*" the wolf sniffed, her nose twitching as she drank in the smell of my blood.

"*Wouldn't that be the point?*"

"True," the she-wolf said, switching to Saxon. "But they'd have to be stupid to come within even a mile of me." She grinned, pulling her black lips back to reveal her pink gums, and brighter fangs still.

"Leave us," she commanded, shooing away her minions. Instead of questioning me, she sat there in silence, finishing her counting.

She was lithe, even from what her winter pelt concealed, and the coat of metal plates covered her chest and legs. A fearsome dane-axe was slung over her shoulder, and a fine sword with a golden hilt hung from her hip - well off for a raider, but still tattered and rugged at the edges from a hard life at sea. When she finished her count, she spent a few moments staring hard at me, as if her narrowed eyes could cut through any conceit before them.

"Well, at least you're entirely Saxon," she spat, eyes glinting as she caught sight of the rune etched bones. "Who gave you these?"

"My father."

"A stag of tradition I see," she nodded. "Do you know what the runes say?"

I shook my head.

"So not as much a Dane as I thought," she shrugged, taking a tip from her wineskin and swishing around her muzzle. "Pity, there's a powerful spell carved in those."

"I don't believe in such heathen nonsense," I replied, but I was surprised to find my rebuttal met with a look of indifference.

"Fair, but I suppose it always helps to have more than one god watching your back," she finished, as if it was a purely practical affair. "Not that they are helping you," she grunted, rising to her paws and barking orders at her subordinates to divide up the spoils. "Why should I spare you?"

"I'm not a spy," I replied. "I've spent my entire life working the fields."

She recoiled and blinked rapidly, as if I was thick.

"No... I mean, why should I take you aboard my ship?"

My blank look only ceased to amaze her further.

"What rock did my crew find you hiding under? Haven't you heard William has come to crush the rebels, and since they won't fight fair and square, he's going to burn them out from the land, one settlement at a time. I've never had people beg and offer so much for a spot on my ships!" She laughed.

It was news to me, and it made me shiver, thinking of Karli stuck back at the farm. If this was true, I needed to let him know, now. This had to be the source of that fear I smelled.

"We're not rebels," I said firmly. "We've only ever taken up arms against the vikings."

"That's a cute sentiment," she chuckled. "What's your name?"

"Canute."

"So... you are a half-dane?"

"On my mother's side."

"We'll see," she mused, eying me up, and tossing me my weapons. "Prove yourself a *warrior*."

The rest of the band sniggered. For which word it was for, I was uncertain, but one of them returned my weapons with a knowing wink. It became clear enough when the she-wolf gave a shrill cry in norse, pulling her sword from its scabbard and letting it shine in the brilliant autumn sunshine. Lifting her shield up to cover her chest, she crowded low and pointed the blade at me, advancing slowly.

She paused, hackles bristling, before thrusting her sword forward. Panicked, I dodged to the side and gripped my axe, trying to push her away with the blunt top of the weapon, but it just bounced off her shield harmlessly.

"Aren't you going to even the odds?" I panted, dodging the wolf's heavy movements with graceful ease. I tried stepping around her, instinctively trying to get past her guard - use the hook of my axe to pry open her shield and go for her neck with the antler bone.

"Your foes will not show you such luxury on the battlefield," she snarled, taking another swing. The blade hummed through the air impatiently. She covered her flanks well.

"Show me you're a *real* Dane!!"

I tried dodging around her again, but the she-wolf read my move and thrust her shield out - smacking me square in the chest with the metal guard. It knocked the breath out of me, and I scrambled about on the ground, struggling to breathe. She stamped her hind-paw on my arm, snarling and pointing her sword at my neck.

I don't know why, but facing the edge of that sharp steel, I bared my teeth and refused to yield.

"Well," the she-wolf spat, tongue lolling out of her mouth as she panted - breath steaming out in the chill air. "Half-dane? More like a quarter," she laughed. "But like any warrior, you don't beg for mercy, as if I'd somehow feel bad killing you." She laughed, sheathing her sword. Extending her now free paw, she grabbed hold of my tunic and lifted me to my feet.

"Is your name really Canute, antlers?" she asked. I nodded in reply. "Mine is Rune," she said, patting me on the back. "Now, help the rest of the crew load up the boats before we cast off."

"What?" I tilted my head to the side.

"Sorry?" She mirrored my movement, before shaking her head and explaining. "Ah, I forget deer can't smell. "The scouring has already begun - the Normans are coming in a net, from the north, south, and west all at once. They plan to trap the fleeing rebels against the coast-"

"How do you know this?" I snapped, looking back in the way of Rascill, hoping I could race back in time.

"Because William paid us to switch sides?" She shook her head, remembering how I clearly knew nothing. "Where on earth have you been living? At first our king decided to set sail to help the rebels, but it turns out he was much happier to be paid to leave than to fight a losing battle."

"What do you mean?" I growled.

"We heard about what happened at Hastings - how the Normans rode down your king and his huscarls-"

"It was the Wessex *fyrd* who broke first, leaving the real warriors outnumbered to fight to the end."

"Exactly, so, you can see why we have little reason to fight for a lost cause."

"Funny, you seem to forget that it was the Northumbrian *fyrd* that killed your old king at Stamford Bridge..."

"A good death for old Hardrada; a warrior can ask for little better. They say he was busy composing poems as he fought - evidently not quite to your kind's taste," she laughed, patting me on the back. "But the point is, we came away empty handed from that affair, so it's certainly a good deal for us to get a good haul for not having to fight a single battle." Rune shrugged, kicking the heavy strongbox at her paws. "You've got to learn to take what's in front of you, deer."

She motioned for one of her crew to take the box and load it onto her ship, along with the remaining sacks of grain. Over on the horizon, the dark smoke thickened. I swear I could even see the occasional greasy flame lick up over the trees, until it was certain the woods behind our farm were ablaze too.

"I'm sorry," the she-wolf sighed, her touch softer than I expected. Her shoulders sank, and her tone lost its sharp edge, becoming softer, maternal even. "It won't do you any good going back there. He'd want you to remember him well, not rush back to join him before your time."

"What do *you* know about that?" I screamed.

"Why do you think I don't have a home?" she replied, her ears folding. "I did say I would not kill you, did I not?" By now the last of the provisions were aboard, and it was all she could do but look about idly, searching for anything that might be missed, until her yellow eyes fell squarely on my shoulders.

"You can stay, if you want. But you won't find peace or mercy here," she sighed, tilting her muzzle away from the wind and breathing lightly. The smell of smoke must have stank to her - it was already starting to burn my throat and make my eyes water.

I knew there would be nothing left by the time I got back. The smoke would obliterate all the scents, destroying any chance of revenge and leaving me with nothing but empty grief.

It felt sick, deep inside my heart, but I had no choice.

I didn't really remember getting aboard the ship. It all felt hazy, surreal. Everything I had known was suddenly gone. Ash.

"Sit here," Rune commanded, pointing to a sheltered nook at the rear of the boat. "I can spare you some time while we navigate down the river, but once we reach the sea, I'll need you to be ready to work. Okay?"

I nodded, watching as the afternoon blended into evening. Night came while we still sailed downstream, but the darkness revealed the true scale of the devastation. I could see the fires, some glowing embers, others burning bright - a wave of flame bringing destruction across the North. Nothing was spared; even York had turned into a blazing inferno.

"Why?" I whispered. "What could possibly justify such destruction?"

Rune's ears flicked, picking up my words.

"Among the rebels, there was the last royal claimant of the house of Wessex." She tilted her head to look at me. "Do you really think your king will rest until his corpse is speared on a stake somewhere?"

By the time we reached the sea dusk was falling, but I felt so numb I thought I would never sleep.

"Go, take Rjanolf off the oars," Rune said. "Focus on matching their stroke and technique," she paused. "It's the only way you'll find sleep without dreams tonight."

The she-wolf's muzzle wrinkled visibly in dim light.

"Good thing the gods cut your antlers. Can't have you skewering the crew on the bench behind you."

As the longship slid across the dark, rolling sea, I shed a single tear for Karli. I grabbed the oar and *pulled*.

Soon England slipped beneath the horizon, leaving me alone among the crashing waves inside me.

August, 1072
Constantinople, The Empire of the Romans

"Canute! You'll want to see this."

The she-wolf's claws scratched my chest as she kicked me awake. The tang of the sea breeze brought me back from my rolling dreams. Rune towered above me, grinning, her scraggy tail wagging as she pointed across the water.

The great city appeared, serene in the morning light. Towering buildings rose from the darkness, the white stone and graceful, sloping domes catching the morning light. It was unlike anything I had ever seen in both size, scale, and beauty. Suffice to say that it seemed beyond the ability of mortals to build: enough that its reflection on the calm waters of the Mamara seemed more real.

"People... made this?" I croaked.

"A thousand years ago, too," she chuckled. "*Miklagarðr* - our name for Constantinople, gets newcomers every time. I still remember the first time I saw it. It felt like... everything else shrunk, both in size and grandeur." She paused, fur fluffing up as a beam of sunlight warmed her. "Worth the years I made you wait for it, huh?"

"I was starting to wonder about your navigation..."

"Cheeky pup!" She grinned, batting my ears with her paw. "Take Astrid off the oars. I don't want her so tired that her tongue won't work, and I want to get the last bit of strength I can from you before I let you go."

I sat down on the bench and grabbed an oar, relieving the wiry stoat who served as Rune's translator. I quickly settled into the familiar rhythm of the oars without skipping a stroke, excitement bubbling inside me as the longship slid towards the city.

My ears flicked instinctively to the helmsman's commands, then Rune took over as we approached the tall harbour walls. The wolf bellowed for us to be sharp in our movements - that we were soon entering the busiest harbour in the world, and she would personally dock the pay of anyone responsible for a collision.

I tried to keep my attention focused on the task, but the commotion of the waterway was an alluring mix of sights, smells, and sounds. Behind the impressive sea walls, the azure waters bustled with ships of every shape, size, and nation. Smaller craft and punts darted between the sprawling jetties and berths, hawking all manner of wonderfully smelling goods to frustrated crews, while their captains clamoured with each other as they waited for a free berth.

Closing in for a spot to dock proved more tricky than any assault, but it was a fine testament to Rune's seafaring as she guided us in, slipping between two bulky dromons having some argument over who hit who. As soon as the fine stroke brought us up to the jetty the crew sprung to work, lashing the mooring lines together, throwing down sturdy planks, and swiftly unloading all the raw materials of our haul that would find market here.

"You'll want to find the *Akolouthos*," Rune panted, recovering from the exertion. "That's the Roman official in command of the varangians - you know, the ones who made old Hardrada rich."

"I know, you've told me a thousand times," I breathed, bending over to take a deep breath.

"You'll swear an oath to the Emperor, and then, who knows? In the years to come you might just become as rich and famous a guardsman as him, and maybe even have the wealth, money, and following to return home?" She laughed, her eyes distant as she regarded the future.

"Or I could just stay with you?"

Rune's ears drooped and she shook her head.

"I took you on because you were desperate, and didn't have any choice. You're a decent sailor, I can tell in breath that this life's not in your heart." She sighed, shoulders sagging. "You can keep searching for it here. And whatever it is you find, I'll be proud that I let it be of your own choosing."

"But my ancestors were Danes-" I began, as if that was reason enough to stay.

"And you're still a half-Dane. No good comes from looking to the past for answers." Rune smiled. "Besides, you'd have to keep cutting your antlers." Rune smiled bleakly.

"I'm starting to think you might have gone soft."

"I'm *this* close to throwing you in the sea," Rune grunted, her fur fluffing up in indignity. "You don't keep the helm of a ship without knowing what's best for your crew."

"Sounds like you're not giving me a choice after all."

"So you think," she smiled, "but, if this doesn't work out, I'd always welcome you back." The she-wolf paused, her hackles bristling. "I imagine we'll stop by to trade every autumn here, given the Danes have given up any designs on England." For a moment I thought she was going to say something kind, maternal even, but instead she merely nodded and walked away, receding into the crowd.

I sighed and tried not to linger on it.

"So… find the *Akolouthos*," I repeated, the unfamiliar word tripping up my tongue as I stared at the writhing crowd and the winding city streets beyond. "Sounds easy." I grunted and set off down the wooden jetty, following the milling crowd as they shuffled towards the city gate.

Jostled and shoved by all manner of elbows, knees, tails and hooves, I was glad that I didn't have a particularly strong sense of smell. When we finally trickled through the gate, I was dismayed to find the small, winding streets equally crowded. Resisting the urge to lower my head and butt my way through the crowd, I shoved through the mess of scents, diving towards the less crowded space, until the masses finally dispersed and I could see down the street ahead of me.

Beyond the busy docks the great city gave way to a maze of ancient, narrow streets winding up from sea walls. At first the buildings were small and austere, weathered by time, the flurry of trade, and the salty spray of the sea. But as the streets led me away from the docks, a gaudy edge crept into the growing opulence. My fur itched as my hooves clacked on the ancient flagstones. The masonry of antiquity threw back the sound of my footsteps, as if the place refused to acknowledge my step. Doubt wormed through my gut - the feeling that many forgotten names before me had passed this way, and, unlike the wet clay of the fields at home, here I left no impression.

The feeling only grew as I walked under the gilded arches, through the fountained squares and verdant gardens encroaching from over their enclosures. The more I saw, the more my awe took on a bitter taste. The storied buildings, the overflowing markets, it all felt saturated with the weight of the past, and a feeling that no matter what I did, it all would be pressed to nothing under the weight of history. I even began to doubt whether I'd find this *Akolouthos*. Perhaps Rune just wanted rid of me?

"I suppose it'd be much easier if I could just ask for directions. Not like I can even speak Greek," I muttered.

Perhaps my sour mood was down to the hot sun beating on my back, and the sensory assault of the new setting. After all the walking around, I definitely needed a drink. I let my ears and nose guide me. Despite the clear water in some of the fountains looking alluring enough, I eventually found some promising establishment round several corners and through a set of bronze-embossed wooden doors.

It felt like heaven, wandering into that secluded courtyard. Nothing but the silence of trickling water, the sweet, shy sound of birdsong from the walls covered in creeping vines. The conversation was low, quiet, and muted.

Next thing I knew, I was tackled to the floor, muzzle jammed in between the flagstones, while a fox and a wolf competed with each other to see who could bark orders loudest. As a bony knee crushed my head, my crumbled ears picked out some fleeting lines of Saxon.

"Who left the gate unbarred? I'll have you thrown out of the guard for such incompetence-"

Guard?

"Wait! Wait!" I wheezed, trying to pick out more.

The adrenaline made me realise the sword first, and my speech second.

"Who sent you?" The black wolf snarled, half-feral and all spittle in his anger. He towered over me, clade in fine mail and lorikon of Roman make. A gold edged cloak fell over his shoulders, the rest of it filled with a luxurious crimson that certainly was beyond any ordinary soldier.

"No one sent-"

"*Lies!*"

His snarl barely even sounded like a word. Grabbing me by my neck, he pulled me out from his guard's embrace and dragged me to my feet.

"Don't play dumb, *who sent you?*"

"That's enough, Wulf!" the fox snapped. The lupine's ears twitched, but his grip did not slacken. "*Nambites!* Stop!"

At that word the wolf lifted my crumpled body up from the ground, and dragged me over to the fox. Drunk on several gulps of air, I barely took in the details while I focused on recovering.

"Why did you use my name, *Alexios?*" He growled with barely contained rage. "You were the one who called this meeting!"

"And you picked the location," the fox smirked, amber eyes settling on me. "I have to punish you somehow with your failure."

"Like anyone could."

"Whatever," he waved a dainty paw as if toying with a butterfly. "The boy's clearly not a threat. Of course you missed it, but did you not see his blank expression when you screamed at him in Greek?"

"What makes you so sure?" Wulf, or Nambites (I wasn't sure which it was or why) growled.

"He stinks just like a trader fresh off the boat," the fox laughed. "Surely a wolf with a nose like yours could snuff that out - or has standing guard in the Emperor's perfumed halls ruined your nose?"

"Scents don't give as much security as the dead do," he grunted.

"How unimaginative. That's why you're just a guard, and I'm an eminent general," the fox groaned, grabbing a crystal glass from the table and pouring a cup. "Here, deer," he said, snapping his fingers. "You've earned a drink at least."

The fox crossed the courtyard, hissing at the other guards, and knelt down to pass me the cup. I didn't even consider the flattery of being offered such a princely drink, but the rich, burgundy liquid slid down my throat like soothing velvet, calming my burning skin.

Fuck me, wine was good.

"My Norse friend over there is quite a wild breed." Alexios turned to look over his shoulder. "You still believe in your heathen gods, don't you?"

Wulf snarled even fiercer than when he held me.

"I really must get him baptised at some point," the fox tutted.

"You can bathe me when I'm dead!" Wulf grunted, grabbing a cup of wine and throwing it down his maw, before stalking over to the door and slamming it shut behind him.

"I wish he'd learn a little subtlety," the fox groaned. "I can't convince you the wine was poisoned now that he's gone ahead and downed it too"

I gulped but the fox just laughed, tapping me on the shoulder.

"It's not. But, if you really were a court spy, you wouldn't have drunk it."

The fox's Saxon was workable, but rusty. It lacked the worn edges a born speaker had - his accents too sharp, and some of his phrases at times more lyrical than practical.

"Where are you from then, newcomer?"

"Rascill," I began, before expanding, "a smallholding near York."

"I've heard of it," one of the guards rumbled from further back. "Some of the other varangians fled from there."

"Before, or after Hastings?" the fox asked. His eyes burned curiously, tail swishing. "Sorry, touchy subject they don't like talking about," Alexious shrugged. "When did you leave though?"

"Three years after the battle. Before William began torching the north."

"I see..." The fox flicked an ear. "Well, take it from me there's no love here for those bastard Normans either. The Empire's been fighting them over Italy for decades now, and as you can see from these varangians, the Emperor is remarkably sympathetic to your misfortune, even if he is an incompetent fool."

"Having a big axe and a grudge always helps," I replied, taking the natural pause in our conversation to run my eye over the fox before me. He was advanced in years, grizzled from years in the saddle. He wore a fine cloak and brazen scaled armour that matched his fiery fur, but I was surprised at how short he was, and how shrewd his gaze - eyes so sharp they seemed to cut through everything.

"Are you the commander of the guard? The *Akolouthos*?"

The fox winced.

"You *definitely* can't speak Greek," he chuckled, pouring some more wine. "It's **Akolouthos**, and no, I'm not him. That's Nambites, who as you know made a wonderful first impression."

"You mean... Wulf?" I titled my head to the side.

"Others find Nambites more palatable, but yes. It still prickles their fur that an outsider got the post," he laughed, licking his lips. "Even after Manzikert, we'll take almost anyone."

I half-smiled, thinking back to Karli and home. "That's why a Saxon like me came to have the name Canute. What was Manzikert?"

The fox smiled, nodding.

"Quite the fuck up, that got the Empire into quite the fucking mess," Alexios sighed, rubbing his temples with a paw. "But I have a plan to turn things around, so long as Wulf's carelessness doesn't fuck us over."

As if called by his name, the tall black wolf burst through the door, grunting as he drew the bolt shut.

"The deer came alone," he snapped. "Either torture him, or kill him."

"That's no way to speak to your latest recruit."

The wolf looked at the fox, then at me, then back to the fox.

"Are you mad? Fuck no!" He laughed for the first time. It seemed more insulting than anything else he'd said. "I can see from his eyes he's never fought a battle, nevermind he's so scrawny he could barely wield an axe."

"I'm not talking about the guard, Wulf," Alexios groaned. "To make it all this way as he is, he must have some resourcefulness, and that may make him suitable for our other problem?"

"Sometimes you've got to learn to take what's in front of you," I retorted.

Wulf half-raised an eyebrow, drawing another smirk from Alexios.

"See?" The fox laughed.

"I'm not taking him on."

"Of course not. I can't have that pesky oath of yours trying his hands when I need them," Alexios shook his head. He leaned over to me and explained. "The varangian guard's oath is legendary. In that brave, barbarian fashion, they swear to serve the Emperor loyally, to the death if necessary. That reputation for loyalty, some would say blind loyalty, is what gets Wulf here paid so well, but unfortunately it has its weaknesses. The disaster that was Manzikert has shown us you can't just blindly follow a fool's orders, and unfortunately, we're stuck with another on the throne now."

The fox waved for Wulf to be off, turning to me with a frown toying at his brow.

"By answering directly to me, you can be far more flexible." Alexios nodded.

I froze in my chair, taking another hearty gulp of wine.

What the hell have I managed to walk into?

"Don't look so alarmed, Canute, I'm not asking you to do anything drastic. It's quite the offer actually - you can stay here and guard my estate, enjoy the luxuries, wine, and wonders this city has to offer. But when the time comes, I want you to do exactly what I say, without delay or hesitation." The fox leaned closer still. "Serve me as loyally as your kinsman in the guard."

"Why me?"

"Because you're not another Roman," he shrugged, as if the very mention of my kinsman irritated him. "It's a fabulous deal, one that others wouldn't hesitate to leap-"

"When it's done, make me one of the guards."

"If that is what you wish? So be it." Alexios nodded. "Now, I'm off to clean up the mess in Anatolia. One of my servants will see that you're taken care of."

I caught Alexios as he left the table.

"Thank you." I wished I could speak Greek. The old fox smiled and patted me on the shoulder, a grin across his muzzle.

"Thank me later," he said in sufficient Saxon. "Nothing in this city is free."

With that the red tail slipped away, chuckling to himself.

The fur on the back of my neck prickled. Despite my best attempts to smooth it down, it felt like it was being pulled by an invisible string.

March, 1081
Constantinople, The Empire of the Romans

"Get up, and don't make a sound." Wulf growled, his fur blending with the surrounding night. "Your benefactor wants his dues."

"The fox?" I grumbled, picking the sleep out of my eyes. I grabbed hold of a cup of water to wash the sour taste of the evening's wine from my muzzle.

Time passed in a haze of litanic dirges, hot summers, and freezing winters. It had an unreal quality in the ancient city. Behind the towering Theodosian walls, the world and its troubles seemed a lifetime away, while guard duty remained a constant, unsung witness to the passing intrigues of the purple-robed court.

Greek had proved hard to pick up, but my ignorance proved some insulation from the palace intrigues that seemed to engulf the less fortunate members of the court. Still, it was impossible to escape the unfolding reality - the names of troublemakers abroad sounded less foreign, more Norman. But at least I had plenty of warm baths, silk clothes, and rich, fruity wine to keep me pliant.

"Don't tell me you've been making other friends," Wulf growled, watching as I laced up my cotton breeches.

"With ones like you, I try my hardest not to," I sighed, grabbing a fine silk shirt and a thick, dark cloak to see out both the night's cold, and watching eyes.

"So I've noted," Wulf replied, tapping his footpaw impatiently.

"Are you going to enlighten me then what this is all about?"

"No," Wulf snorted. "That's the whole point."

I raised an eyebrow and sniffed, wishing to glean even a sliver of a useful scent.

"Go to the gate of St Theodosia. A priest will be waiting. Follow him and keep your mouth shut."

Without saying anything more Wulf ducked out the door and disappeared into the night. I grabbed my sword and belted it onto my hip, pulling the black wool cloak over my chest.

Even at night, Constantinople thrummed with activity. Lanterns bobbed and swayed along the old streets, hooves and claws skittered and clattered against the stone. The old forums and markets hummed with the gentle buzz of wine and laughter. People, rich and poor alike streamed out from the bathhouses, or drunkenly sang songs about their team's victory at the hippodrome even less tune-lessly than wolves howling.

The city varangians patrolled street to street, eyes sharp and ears sharper, betraying the only sign of tension. It was easy enough to make my way through the now familiar streets, picking the an-cient sideways and narrow alleys to avoid sight. Vaulting two walls later, and through several midnight gardens, I scrambled through a breach in the decaying walls of Constantine. Long defunct since the famed Theodosian walls and slowly picked apart for stone and mortar, they were largely unmanned.

My meeting point, the Gate of St. Theodosia lay on the north-east side of the city, close to the golden horn. Among the quiet fields and fruit gardens that lay behind the main city walls, I abandoned any winding route and moved north, then east over the fifth hill, until the rounded domes of the church loomed out from beneath the stars and guided me home.

Getting through the gate itself, being on the seaward side, was easy enough. A few *histamenon* opened the way, even though the golden coins were much lighter and thinner than years before. As the door opened and closed swiftly behind me, the priest, a lion I guessed from further in Anatolia, said nothing and offered me the reins of a bay warhorse.

We rode along the narrow strip of land between the golden horn and the city walls, heading north until we cleared the city, and then due west if the stars partially obscured by the clouds did not lie. Af-ter three hours riding with little but the moon's pale light to guide us, we came to a forested outlook, tall enough that looking back, I could make out the faint outline of the city in the clear night, and the twinkling outline of the watch fires along the walls and hilltops.

"My, you have grown," the fox smiled, embracing me. His touch was warm, a welcome greeting after the cold hours of riding. "I could almost not recognise you for the lost deer that stumbled into my meeting."

"The years and the city have been kind to me."

"Which is a relief to hear. Constantinople, the jewel of civilization, always nurtures those who have such talent to rise. Do you still think of home?" Alexios asked me, his Saxon markedly better than mine after the years I had spent away.

"Sometimes, but it has been so long, I no longer think of it as home."

"Ah, a true cosmopolitan!" Alexios beamed. "You have no idea how it warms a Roman's heart like mine to hear that. But clearly, you have spent too much time idle in the city." The fox sighed and shook his head, pushing past me to stand at the lip of the hill. "Have you forgotten the injustice inflicted upon you that led to your passage here?"

I flicked my ears in the same, nonchalant way they would bat the intrigues of court aside. Not because I had forgotten, but because I'd learned it paid in the city to betray nothing of yourself, just as much as the people I served.

"I have a feeling you will tell me anyway."

"Normans, Canute. The people who butchered your father, and set your country ablaze. They are coming for this city."

"Good thing the Emperor entrusted you with an army then," I raised an eyebrow, looking at assembled campfires in the darkness behind the fox.

"It'll take more to defeat the Normans, certainly not this paltry force that the Emperor has granted." The fox sighed, shaking his head. "When he deposed his predecessor Michael, the Emperor made one fatal mistake in letting his rival go free. Now Robert Guiscard, leader of the Normans in Sicily and Italy, whom we have long struggled with, has taken up his cause - claiming not just to champion that fool's return, but to defend the succession of the Empire to Michael's son, Constantine..."

"...who was engaged to his daughter, Helena."

I remained silent for a while, my gaze flicking back between the city beyond and the sleeping army. It all seemed quite familiar,

"They are making their preparations for war, and I am afraid that many do not know the danger we face, unless we act swiftly, and now."

That being said, despite all my intentions the mere mention of that name set my jaw.

"It's simple, Canute. Someone needs to steer the Empire through this coming war - someone strong, not a withered relic of the past like Botaneiates."

"And who is that?"

Alexios chewed his lip, as if the decision still pained him.

"This army is not enough to stand up to Robert's knights, but if the Emperor marched with his varangians-"

"Spit it out fox," I grumbled. "You have no idea how refreshing it is to me after all these years in the city to just hear the plain truth."

"Me," he shrugged. "I have won battles against Normans and Turks alike in Anatolia with far fewer men. The last few Emperors; Romanos, Michael, Botaneiates - have led us to nothing but ruin. I would push Robert back into the sea and liberate southern Italy from his grip."

"And what would you have me do?"

"Open the city gates for me. There will be no fighting - Wulf has seen to that. With that pressure, the old Emperor will relinquish the throne, just like Michael did before him. Better he surrenders to me, rather than the Normans."

"You know, you could have paid anyone to do that. You didn't need to put me up guarding your estate and drinking all your wine."

"You're wrong," Alexios sighed. "I knew it had to be you. I saw it in your eyes when we first met. You have seen what the Normans do."

"Fine," I sighed, kicking the earth with my hooves. It had been a while since I'd touched anything but the finely cut flagstones paving the city, but I was surprised how familiar the mud felt. "But you know it's going to take some gold to convince the guards to open the gates."

"Don't be surprised," Alexios grunted. "You managed to pay them to let you out, so we know they can be bought. Now it's just a matter of price."

"I think they'll charge a lot more for an army."

"True," the fox nodded. "And you will offer that to them, of course." He pointed towards a fresh horse brought up from the camp, saddlebags weighed down. I could tell it was plenty of gold.

"Canute," Alexios said coldly. "When they crowd around to divide up their payment, they will be distracted," he hissed, showing his teeth.

I understood the message, but I still did not understand.

"Why do they have to die?"

"Walls are only as strong as their defenders. There may come a time when I have to rely on the Theodosian walls, and I cannot have them undermined by purchasable men. Imagine if we were the Normans?"

I snorted in contempt. It wasn't worth thinking about. Still, as I saddled up and rode back towards the city, saddlebags heavy, I didn't know what to think. Alexios was really trusting me with such a princely sum. I could easily take a different path, off to the north towards the Khanate, or flee overseas or buy some land...

I shook my head, wind whipping through my headfur.

Alexios was right, and after all, I had given him my word.

October, 1081
Dyrrhachium, The Empire of the Romans

Even in a time of crisis, and with the swiftness of a coup, the Roman state moved with a lethargic, sluggish pace. At first I thought it was the breakdown of control; three days where the Roman army terrorised and sacked their own capitol. But even those troublesome days burned quicker than the byzantine affairs of court.

A month after I opened the gates - the thing that gave that fox his throne - Alexios deigned to meet with me - the wait some political calculation to test my resolve no doubt. The fox fulfilled his promise, granting me a Greek title that felt sour in my mouth, and a set of armour that fit my cervine body awkwardly, pinning all its weight on my shoulders.

"When will we march against the Normans?" I croaked, taking another sip of wine - the only thing I found that helped blur the ghostly faces that came for me in the night.

"Soon enough," he nodded, tail swishing behind him, disappearing back to court as if my words buzzed unpleasantly in his ear.

Summer passed slowly, with a sickly heat that made even the wine sour. When I bumped into Wulf by chance, coming by his own wine from the only vintner able to procure something half-drinkable, even he was tellingly short with his words.

"He's the Emperor. Just do as you're told," the black wolf muttered, but his ears twitched all the same when the other soldiers joked about his accomplished string of defeats when in command against the Norman rebels in Anatolia.

"That's the problem," I snapped. "I've been told *nothing*."

"Well I'm telling you to wait. You don't win wars by racing off to the first battle your enemy's picked for you," he cursed, trying to stalk free of my questions.

"At least tell me something."

"Will you shut up and let me drink in fucking peace?"

I nodded.

"They're besieging Dyrrachium," he growled, stalking off with a barrel slung over his shoulder. It was an impressive show of strength, eclipsed only by the play he'd ensnared me with: I didn't even know where that was.

Mercifully, August brought a change in the weather, and by September we were ordered on the march, the dirt roads of Thracia turning to mud underneath the paws, hooves, and wagon wheels. As the leaves burned with the colourful throes of the dying season, we finally laid eyes on the Adriatic sea, and the walls of Dyrrachium.

The sea-fortress was a dour sight, its stone walls blackened by scorched pitch and half-burnt tar. Sickly clouds billowed up from fires behind the walls, equally as bleak as the ones twisting up from the desolation before them: a mess of snapped arrows, broken siege ladders, wheeling crows and rotting corpses. I was glad the wind blew away from us, and glad again to not have a nose like a wolf's.

The walls still held, but for how much longer seemed doubtful. The ominous thud of catapults and ballistae pounded the eastern walls, while a great siege tower inched closer to the crumbling battlements.

My fur bristled. Perhaps now was the time for the glories I'd heard in songs and stories - a swift, aggressive charge to break the enemy lines, break the siege, and push the Normans back into the sea.

"Wait here until dawn. Your legs are blown from a day's march - your charge won't even make it to their lines before running out of steam," Wulf grunted. "And the rest of the army is yet to make it, so who'd have your back if your charge stalled?"

"That's a risk we'd have to take. We certainly won't take them by surprise now," I said, remembering the vague story Karli once told about his victory at Stamford Bridge.

"Good thing the Emperor didn't put you in charge," he muttered, shaking his head, walking back from our vanguard towards the fluttering banners marking the Emperor's tent, notably at the very rear of the deployment.

"Get some fucking sleep," the wolf growled, stalking off into the sunset, his hackles raised like sharp daggers.

That night there were orders to light no fires, making it a cold, miserable wait. No one wanted to speak. We were all lost in our own thoughts, dark silhouettes underneath the wheeling stars.

Dawn came with an intensity I'd never experienced. Despite the lack of sleep my eyes were sharp to every detail, even if my body trembled at the end of every breath. I'd never noticed how the sun seemed to shiver like liquid as it rose from beneath the horizon, or appreciated the miracle of how those first cold rays strengthened, warmed, and brunt dew that clung to grass and fur alike.

Wulf had not joined us by the time the runners passed around full wineskins around the front ranks for courage. I took a gulp, then several more, copying the lead of the biggest varangians around me, but all it did was make my eyes feel perversely heavy - threatening to droop shut, as if they didn't know that by the end of the day it might be forever.

"Wake up," a familiar, gruff voice snapped at my ears. "I told you to sleep when you had the chance," Wulf muttered. He didn't exactly look any better.

"Right, you mean, ugly fuckers," he bellowed. "Alexios has ordered us to break the Norman right. We'll advance first, and archers will screen our approach. Let's show those arseholes what real Saxons can do." His growl was met with snarls from the largely Saxon varangians, bordering on

The speech was premature. It took until noon for the rest of the army to manoeuvre, while the Normans opposite seemed to suffer the same issues.

"Right," Wulf grinned. "Time to get even after Hastings."

I tried to dig up the memories of the fire, the farm, Karli. But it was all just distant and without shape, like walking through a thick fog. Even when I did manage to picture something, it was only a fleeting glimpse of him smiling cheerfully as he tended to spring's first green shoots - hardly a sight that would fill me with rage.

I cursed Rune's intervention and hoped the wine would do the rest of the work. Instead I missed the order to advance, stumbling as the rank behind shoved into me. I abruptly found my step, focusing more on placing my hooves securely on the uneven ground. The front rank obstructed my view, and my ears rang from the din of steel, metal, and a thousand feet marching forward. I processed things only in fragments, my senses overwhelmed by the unnatural spectacle.

Bizarrely, I remember the soft whoosh of the first volley of arrows, white feathers gleaming in the light as they arced over head and fell to the earth with deadly grace. Loud cries followed, from both sides. Curses and insults rougher than any from the roughest of streets. Then they faded only to groans, sobs, and the most pitiful of sounds. Following behind the front rank, I stepped over the broken, blooded, mutilated bodies - some of them still clinging to life, reeking of fear, their diming eyes full of tears as their grip loosened.

Everything just seemed to slow down; the weapon in my hands weighing me down, the churned up, mud and blood pulling at my hooves, staining my fur, pulling me back, telling me to stop.

The faces on the earth were there behind my eyes. How could they be the people who took everything from me? But they were the same faces, the same white eyes, the same terrible cries. It all seemed too familiar.

Next thing I knew, I was bent over heaving my guts out, until not even a dry fleck of spittle was left. I still felt sick.

Then there was roar, like a crashing wave, louder and louder until it broke with a piercing cry. The press lessened suddenly, exhausted and startled enough that I fell to the ground.

It took me a moment to realise the front rank had broken the enemy, now fleeing, tails flapping in the air behind them as their main line buckled before our might.

"After them!" Wulf roared over the din, his eyes seeming more alive than ever. Revulsion turned my stomach again, but I only followed through herd instinct, knowing the danger would only be worse if I stayed behind.

I lagged behind as we pursued, the ground becoming flat, open, the salty whiff of the ocean the only sign our enemies' flight must soon come to an end. The familiar cries of battle began ahead, except this time underscored by the muffled thud of a crossbow bolt punching into flesh.

The front rank fell, then those to the left and to right, their chests riddled with the stubby fletching of crossbow quarrels. I crouched and fell to the floor as a crossbow bolt shot past me, then another, and I stayed there until the dreadful sound ceased. When I looked up, the same men who had fled from us now turned about to finish us off, laughing about the trap they had sprung.

Just like Hastings!

I looked around, trying to find the archers that had supported us, but they had not followed. They were much further back, barely visible, unable to reach us or reply with a punitive volley.

Panic setting in, I tried to spot some cover, somewhere we could regroup and shelter from the next volley.

"The church!" I bellowed, hoping my cry was louder than the misery all around me. As the crossbowmen began their long reload, the few varangians who heard me and could still run struggled over the boggy ground, our arms and armour weighing us down.

It was a small building, barely enough to fit fifty among its rustic structure, but as we barreled through the doors, the stone walls and strong wooden door offered protection enough.

"What the hell?" Wulf cursed, spitting on the floor and unleashing a further litany of curses I never thought could be uttered on holy ground. "The archers were supposed to follow us - the entire army was *ordered* to follow us."

"Fucking Romans," another varangian snarled. "They'd always rather someone else fight their fucking battles."

"What the fuck did Alexios tell you to do?"

"He told me they would. He *ordered* me to," Wulf snapped, his eyes wide and pupils sharp.

"They left us to die! What the fuck did we do to deserve this?"

I didn't bother to even look at Wulf while the terrible realisation clawed its way up my spine. My fur bristled and stood on end, tough and coarse against my armour.

It made perfect, callous sense. That was the look in the fox's eyes. That was why he was reluctant to meet. He didn't trust us. He never had - and why should he? We'd been useful tools in his coup, and now it made perfect sense for the evidence of the whole sordid affair to die with us. It felt naive to cling to the idea that no, it couldn't be possible - as a general in Anatolia he'd lost several armies and still emerged victorious, so there was no doubt in my mind that he was unafraid of defeat.

It all felt futile now anyway.

The sharp tang of smoke cut through everything else, and any remaining shred of loyalty between us. Not content to leave our shattered remnants barricaded inside the church, the Normans would either burn us alive, or smoke us out into their clutches.

"Fuck this," Wulf snarled, grabbing his axe as the conflagration spread quickly through the rafters. "I'm not going to die cowering inside some fucking church."

In the manner of his old kinsmen, he didn't even bother to ask who was with him. He gripped his dane axe in both hands and roared in defiance, taking one deep breath before the smoke tainted the air. The other survivors were either pulled by his magnetism, or followed reluctantly, unable to see any other choice.

I did not join them. I'd cast aside my weapon long before in disgust, and all I wished was for the violence to end. I felt hollow. I should have stayed on the ship with Rune, or found some small patch of land away from the rest of the world to tend to.

My eyes just slide across the details of the church, resignation settling in. Perhaps there was something wrong with us all. It felt pointless to pray - no wonder God never answered our prayers.

Perhaps it was the fire, the stress, but as I stared at the flames enveloping the rafters, I heard a familiar voice from long ago.

Perhaps God is in the earth?

I frowned, thinking back to Karli's words. Perhaps I was already delirious from the heat, and the growing smoke, but as I crawled about on the floor, I spotted a loose slab that wobbled to the touch. Moving closer, I could smell a damp, earthy smell, and when I tapped it, it gave a hollow sound unlike the others.

I didn't question my good fortune as I heaved aside the heavy stone slab and ducked into the darkness below.

The tunnel as small and dark, but the air inside was damp, fresh, and most importantly free of smoke. I paused for a few moments, breathing deeply, giddy from my deliverance. Following the scents of the earth around me, I crawled through the darkness, until the ground delivered me from its clutches, far away from the din of battle. I found myself on a remote cove, facing the sun as it set over the calm Adriatic. It was strange; the cool sea breeze, the rustle of the wind in the leaves, but I felt I finally understood what Karli had tried to tell me, all those years ago. I stayed on my knees, thanking the god in the earth and the smugglers who'd built the tunnel in equal measure.

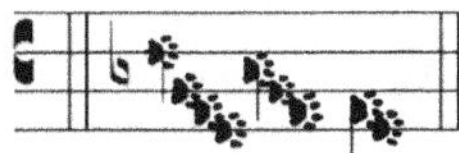

Winter, 1086
Yorkshire, The Kingdom of England

The chronicler arrived sometime in February, his fur blending into one of the many grey winter days. I could tell the wolf was Norman-French, not because he rode a horse, or because he had the same short cropped mane they favoured. It was his paws: they were smooth and uncalloused - a mark of luxury few could afford here.

He went about my farmstead, smaller than I would have liked, counting the people and livestock with the same indifference. His nose didn't even twitch as his quill scratched away, solidifying everything he smelled and saw.

When he finished writing, he snapped his fingers and saddled up onto his horse.

He didn't bother to show me, or anyone what he'd written down.

"In the name of His Majesty, William the First of England: the settlement Rascill in the hundred of Bulford and the county of Yorkshire." He took a breath, bored of his unwieldy script and why he was even addressing the peasants.

"The lands formerly of Lord Canute, son of Karli, are declared waste, and rightful lordship transferred to the Crown as the Tenant-In-Chief."

The wolf closed his ledger with a muffled thud.

"Be about your business."

Doomsday

I paid no attention to the diminishing figure as he sped up the north road. He could say what he wanted. My blood was in this earth, and as long as I'd continue caring for it, the earth would return the favour.

Siegewalkers

Valduin

eavy paws crashed down the long, narrow corridor, its high stone walls ringing with snarled orders. Through the window of his cell door, a lone figure watched the torchlight vanish, then swell, then vanish again with the bodies of soldiers as they ran. As soon as the clamour faded away the prisoner's ears swiveled. He listened closely to the soft sounds of moisture coming from around his cell, the crackle of a dying torch in its sconce, and somewhere in the distance a muffled hiss of pain.

He closed his eye, the sheen of its reflective surface winking out amidst the dark.

Somewhere high above there came a great and terrible boom. The fortress shivered to its very roots; dust fell from hidden timbers as they smarted from that distant blow. A sizzled screech followed: the sound of cannons spewing liquid flame into the valley and the narrow pass beside it. Arrows melted, warriors cried in retreat, and ponies neighed in panic. Siege towers splintered against inviolable walls.

The cannons shot flame for a long time.

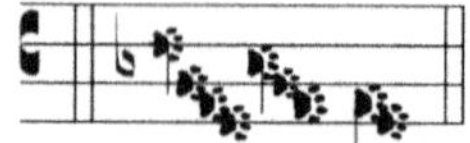

Breathe in, breathe out.

The prisoner sat on the cold stone floor. In the barest trickle of the light, his feline eye traced faint claw marks on each wall. A tapestry of panic and pain much like his own. New wounds crisscrossed his body as they overlapped old scars; they all stung in the cold.

Then a whisper came from overhead: faint, familiar, relieved.

"There you are. I've been looking all over for you."

The prisoner spun round and craned his neck, whiskers primed to sense the air. A shaft of light had appeared, briefly illuminating his sharply striped cheeks before it was blocked by an aquiline head. Rubbing his good eye with surprise, the prisoner — a manul cat — could barely utter a croak. "Sogaai? Can it be?"

The visitor pushed his way in through that narrow opening. Great wings and scrabbling claws worked on cold, unyielding stone as Sogaai descended to the floor, until finally the prisoner could make out the polished beak and dusty feathers of his steppe eagle friend.

"I thought you were dead," he managed.

Sogaai chuckled and crouched against the far wall of the cell. "Shiban, please. It was only an arrow."

"You fell," Shiban continued, his salt-and-pepper coat still bristling with surprise. "I saw you fall."

"Well, here I am," the eagle replied. "And here you are."

Shiban sat back on his haunches across from a friend he never thought he would see again. Not since...no, he was here, that was what mattered. He survived. The manul trembled, half with relief as it rose up from his bowed shoulders, half with pain both old and new.

Silence stretched out between them. Shiban felt it physically, a ball of raw tension in his gut that refused to shake loose. Words —

accusations — rose up in his throat and died on the tip of his tongue. Sogaai, however, was not so restrained.

"They're trapped, you know. The whole Horde. Was this the plan? For your team to get caught, while the Khan's army broke on the walls like wind on a mountain's face?" The eagle shook his head and slapped a wing on his thigh. "It was impossible from the start. She was foolish, and you too, by the way."

"The Khan is no fool!" the grizzled feline hissed. "As for me, that's not up for debate."

"Well, it sure looks like it to me." Sogaai shrugged, nibbling a loose feather with his wickedly curved beak. It broke and drifted to the ground, then melted away in the dark. "Sokhor? Her uncle? He is dead. Died when outriders broke his position on the ridge, he never stood a chance. The valley is surrounded, Shiban! The only way out is through this pass. Bah. If I didn't get shot I'd be flying over the steppes by now. I'd find General Qoge's gers by the blue river. Hundreds of mounted bows would be charging up from the pass. He would have torn an opening in these fortifications like marmot-flesh…"

"The Three Talons are impenetrable," Shiban replied, paw waving dismissively. "The Öndur'at tribe made certain of that. Manul, like them, belong to snow and stone, not the plains. But I know all of this already, old friend. Tell me what I do not know, what I cannot see — agh!"

Shiban bit back a snarl. Gaping wounds tensed with a sudden spasm, and agony shot up his body like a thunderbolt from Tengri himself. With a startled cry Sogaai rushed up to his friend, stopping just short as the feline steadied himself on his own. "No, I am fine," Shiban growled through a mist of pain.

"You are not fine," Sogaai said tersely, pinions frozen mid-furl. A heartbeat later he sighed. "Fine. I will tell you what I can find out, but stay alive for me. It is not your time, understand?"

Shiban watched Sogaai leap up and clamber along the wall as deftly as a mountain goat. Briefly that shaft of light came into view up above, then vanished at the same time as the eagle did. And just like that, the prisoner was alone in his prison once more.

He dreamed of the open plains.

Hills rose and fell, felted gers with richly painted doors nestled in their midst. Herds of dappled ponies ran across the landscape, while rivers wound their serpentine lengths towards the horizon and into eternity beyond. He felt the wind stream though his cheek fur, he smelled the fresh crispness of steppe grass as its nightly coat of frost succumbed to the sun and became dew. Shiban tucked his paws into his warm, padded deel. For that one moment, both eyes were open, eyes that were much younger than he looked. The scarred tissue across his face and body didn't feel so taut and he felt the morning warmth soak into his bones. For that one moment, Shiban felt peace again.

"Take it, wretch."

Dragged out of his reverie, Shiban blinked himself awake. A huge manul in lacquered armour stood over him, sneering as he levered the tip of his sword to snag and flick a bag at the prisoner. It opened midflight and spilled its contents across his paws: curds. Despite the provocation, Shiban refused to move, instead he watched as the other unhooked a waterskin from his belt and gulped it down in greedy draughts, precious drops darkening the stones underfoot. Only a mouthful remained when the soldier wiped a sleeve across his muzzle and threw the rest into the dust. "The only reason you are alive is because the master wants you alive," he growled.

Shiban remained seated, calm and unmoving to the other cat's chagrin: if hoping for a reaction the soldier found himself bereft. Tail lashing with annoyance, he whirled around and slammed the door behind him. Shiban waited until those heavy steps had faded into the bowels of the fortress and a distant door thudded shut. Only then did he reach for one of the hard, small morsels and the waterskin.

"I still don't know how your kind can eat something like that," muttered Sogaai from up above.

Shiban took a bite of curd followed by a small sip of water, with each chew he felt the sour cheese soften and release its juices across his tongue. He had not eaten since his capture and his stomach groaned in protest, but the manul found some relish to the meal. After a moment of silence the prisoner shot a glance at his companion.

"How long was I asleep?" Shiban asked as the eagle swung from the rafters, landing deftly in the dust behind him.

"I don't know about you, but it's been a few hours for me," Sogaai replied.

"What did you find out? Is Ogene alive — and the others?"

Sogaai could only shrug as he leaned back into his seat. "Last I saw she was. They were going up the mountain with their equipment. The fog was heavy, it got too hard to make out where they were, even for my eyes." Feathers shifted to show a sharply cut face with eyes of polished jet. "So much could have gone wrong, I told you this was too risky."

"Hrmph," Shiban agreed, holding a stick of curd loosely in his dark furred paw. "We all have a duty to our Khan, old friend. We knew the risks. I trust her to complete the mission."

After a moment of contemplation the eagle began to chuckle. "Hey, do you remember when she nearly blasted her tail off? What was it again, oh yes. The clay pot with gunpowder inside."

"I do." The manul smiled faintly.

"And she kicked it away before it could burn down the gers. Her father was furious! I had to help everyone wrangle ponies after they broke down the fence in a panic. Me!" Sogaai cheerfully flapped a wing to stress the point, laughing. "And you said" — at this moment the eagle's voice changed pitch — 'she needs to burn her whiskers off before she can make grenades.' Ha! In the span of a year she's your second in command. Tengri's Talons, that was ten years ago? I can't believe it."

After a moment of mirth, the eagle's eyes became gentle. "Ogene is a good successor, Shiban. She's smart, curious. A great engineer, a true Siegewalker. She learned from the best."

"Not the best," the manul replied gruffly. "But she will become the best, in time. And she will teach others the art."

"If she and the others don't die on the mountain," Sogaai retorted.

Shiban flicked his tail reproachfully but did not respond. Deep in his belly he feared the worst, not for lack of faith in his second. Enemy soldiers could have gone on patrol and caught them on the mountainside. Heavy snowfall could have impeded them even with their dense manul coats, cats of the steppes could only survive. The Öndur'at at least had walked the mountains since the moon was young, manul like them were made for such a place.

If the plan failed the entire Horde would be wiped out, the Siegewalkers along with them. There was simply no other choice.

"You had no choice." The eagle echoed his thoughts.

The pain had subsided to throbbing for the moment. Shiban looked at Sogaai, his best friend, the one he had rescued so many years ago when his wing was broken in a storm. Who had saved Shiban in turn when he blew off part of his paw in an accident that left his body webbed with scars. Who had risked his life to get the Khan's message over the mountains, despite Shiban's pleading.

"There is another way." Shiban remembered with anguish. "Not if I can help it," Sogaai had replied. But his friend did not return from the mountains. Not in time. And now Shiban was here.

"Where did the arrow hit you, Sogaai?" he asked quietly.

"Hm? Oh. Just my leg," the eagle replied, twisting his body round to show the wound. It was black with blood and the arrow shaft was broken. "It doesn't hurt," he insisted, "but I wish I had been quicker, it would have been better for both of us."

Boom.

The stones trembled beneath their feet. Shiban threw out his one good paw against the floor to steady himself while Sogaai glanced around with alarm. "What was that?" the eagle hissed.

"Recoil," Shiban said, "didn't you see the ball cannon on the tower? Between that, the fire launchers, and the ramparts, the Three Talons are unbreakable."

Sogaai leveled a gaze at the manul. "Built by the best?"

The feline felt his ears flatten against his head in a momentary lapse of control. Raw emotions welled up as sharp and bitter as the edge of a broken knife.

But he did not respond.

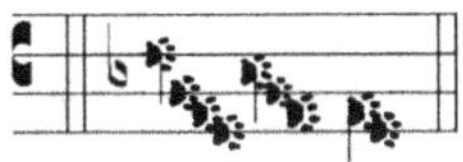

The blasts were coming regularly now. Every so often soldiers would run through the corridor beyond his cell, steadily becoming an afterthought to the growing pain in his side. Soon his breath had become a whistled rasp, while an occasional cough yielded dark red spittle. Shiban imagined the red threads holding his body unraveling with each tremor.

Sogaai sat against the wall still, flicking a stone between his talons like he always did. Liquid-black eyes watched his best friend's struggle with gentle and silent sympathy.

A period of respite fell between the shots and muffled cries somewhere far away. Shiban tensed, ears raised, desperately trying to catch even a sliver of sound to follow the course of battle. It was some while until the distant door swung open but this time there were no footfalls of running paws. Instead he heard the heavy clack of lamellar; measured, calm and ful of intent. Shiban gritted his teeth and lashed his tail up behind him — 'get out!' the gesture silently exclaimed.

Moments later the cell's latch released and two manul came inside.

The first crouched without taking his pale golden eyes off the prisoner. His broad, rufous face was fierce with jagged black marks, and one ear was ripped to ribbons. The armour he wore was distinctly Öndur'at: maroon cloth fronted with laced leather plaques; they rustled softly at the motion. *Tap* — he had placed a lacquered wooden stand on the floor. On it were two little bowls and a steaming brass jug besides; from the coiling steam Shiban caught the tang of milky salt tea. Immediately behind her comrade was a second soldier; she holstered a torch in a stone sconce carved out of the wall itself. The light from the brand threw dancing shadows on every wall and seared the back of his eye. Shiban used his wince as an opportunity to glance at the wall where Sogaai had been, why did the Öndur'at not react to his presence? To his surprise however the eagle had vanished. Shiban blinked, confused, then watched as his captors waved their companion in and slipped outside to stand watch.

A third manul padded into the cell. Unbidden, unwanted, a scent from a distant time filled the prisoner's nose.

"Shiban, look at me," she said.

Fighting against a body screaming from pain, the Khan's Chief Siegewalker took a breath and stilled himself. A manul unlike any other sat across from him, her back straight with authority. Her fur, once auburn and brown, was now speckled with silver hairs, and her thick striped tail rested loosely around her paws. She was armoured like the others, but her harness was strapped around an embroidered silk deel and a sheathed sword lay strapped by her side. With a fluid motion the newcomer took up the jug and poured a stream of pale liquid into each of the little bowls. Taking one in her paws, she extended it towards him.

Shiban took it, scrutinized the contents, then raised the proffered bowl to his lips.

His host nodded with satisfaction and sipped from her own.

"I appreciate that you still trust me," she said.

"I do not, Belgütün," Shiban replied evenly. "However, you would not have killed me with poison where a sword would have sufficed."

The other dipped her ears in agreement and took another sip. Her eyes never left the chief Siegewalker's own. The air grew as tense as sinew — for a moment Shiban wondered if Sogaai had escaped outside or if he was hidden in the rafters above, watching.

"I see the Khan has failed you." Belgütün paused as Shiban trembled again, a brief look of concern flashed across her eyes while her prisoner struggled to bring his failing body under control. "Shiban. Her Horde has attacked our walls several times to no success. Her enemies surround her from the west while she tries to break out through the mountains. *Our* mountains. They will be crushed at the walls of this fortress of my design, you know this. You've always known that this would happen." Belgütün paused, drawing her pale whiskers through equally milky claws. "What I want to know is...why? Why did you come here?"

Shiban coughed wetly. Motes of red began to swirl in the steaming milk tea.

"You should know," he hissed. "I was doing my duty to my Khan."

"Is that what Qarqali had said? Altan? Your finest engineers? They are dead, Shiban. The sky holds their bodies now. Is the Khan so wealthy, or their lives so cheap, that they are easy to throw away for fruitless conquests?" Belgütün's previously measured voice grew louder as she spoke, pitiless stone walls echoing each syllable.

Shiban felt Sogaai's stone-cut eyes watching him.

"We do not throw away our lives needlessly. We never have. The pass is the only way to the plains and the survival of our brothers and sisters. For our unified people to survive, the Three Talons must be destroyed."

Belgütün's green eyes sharpened into knives. "Unified by force. Families split apart at the tip of the sword to fulfill her battlefield fantasies."

The injured manul growled, tail lashing. "Or split apart by choice," he spat. "You abandoned us. *Me!* You taught me everything and you abandoned *me* to hide in the mountains!"

Boom.

The cell rocked violently against the burst from up above. Belgütün stiffened but not from the motion, slanted ears flat against her head and a low growl in her throat. Despite it all, the two sat a pony's leap from each other, unmoving as the tense thread of Shiban's fate stretched thinner between them. He felt the pitter-patter of dust across his shoulders like a soft grey rain.

"How dare you. I did not hide, Shiban. I refused to be the Khan's hammer. I saw death and defied it." The older manul gripped her bowl with unsheathed claws before putting it down on the stone floor. "I refused to lose my family to her vision of the future, one that now stands in jeopardy thanks to her pride and zeal. She is a fool, Shiban, always has been. Nothing has changed!"

"Was I not your family?" Shiban asked, voice tinged with manifold pain.

"You still are, you never stopped being so," Belgütün replied.

The sounds of the living world had faded into a buzzing white silence.

"Why are you here?" repeated the master of Three Talons, her slitted pupils running over the prisoner's ruined fur. "Why were the cream of the Khan's Siegewalkers here, if they knew they would be caught?"

Boom.

Stricken, a rush of understanding seared Belgütün like a thunderbolt to her core. Somewhere outside the two soldiers had rushed away, their howls vague and so very far away. The red manul leaped to her feet where Shiban could only slump, a fresh spurt of wetness painting his fur. He could only just make out the feathers across his shoulders as a familiar voice called him home.

The ground itself shook beneath their paws as both master and pupil relaxed, eyes glistening with words unspoken. Anger, bitterness, betrayal, unfathomable pain...then peace. Belgütün bowed her head and smiled; she was wrong. The Khan was no fool.

A blinding nova of white fire pierced the air. For a heartbeat there was nothing, weightlessness suspended in a gasp of silence, and the world around them shattered with a catastrophic roar.

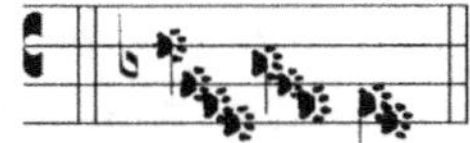

Surrounded by snow and sloping rock, five manul in padded deels stood still on a ledge that overlooked the pass. The whole range trembled from the explosion below and they tensed, waiting, watching, as fires leaped from one tower to the next. Cannons, their bellies full of liquid fire groaned from the heat and burst, sending an avalanche of blackened masonry down into the heart of the fortress; hidden magazines were laid bare in consecutive blasts that shook the heart of every mountain in sight to their deepest roots. Remains of the rolling bomb that the Siegewalkers had delivered and assembled lay broken at the base of the ruined northern wall, while acrid smoke from the blasted guts of the fortress billowed high into the grey mountain skies.

Somewhere higher still, unseen and untethered from mortal concerns, an eagle cried mournfully into the wind.

Farthest from the opening of the pass into the valley these treacherous screes had protected the flank of the fortress for many years. No Öndur'at patrol had seen their ponies struggling up the slopes, nor caught the scent of the Khan's Siegewalkers working tirelessly in the cold and wind to prepare their payload with frozen paws.

The foremost manul, her dark yet frost-kissed fur protruding from between pale wool wrappings, focused intently on the scene below. A great mass of horse and cat had begun to move from the valley into the mountain pass that now lay littered with smoking rubble, undefended by arrows and cannon fire. To the east, far, far away she could just make out the dun smudge of the steppes, her home. Their home. The Horde was free but she felt no joy. None of them did.

"Ogene?" One of the engineers touched her shoulder gently. "We must go."

The young manul, now Chief Siegewalker of her team, stood a moment longer in silent contemplation as she collected her thoughts. There was nothing more to do here, and every second longer in the cold put them all at risk. As much as her limbs refused to move there was one more choice left to make.

"Move out!" she cried.

The others turned to gather what they could, leaving much among the rocks like the bones of a long forgotten battle left to moulder with time. Ogene spared one more glance at the wreckage that they had made, bowing her head in the memory of her teacher.

Then, as one, they melted into the mountainside.

Midway in the Journey of Our Lives

Rob MacWolf

uch has been said of the perils of vice. Many are the parables of honorable knights undone by hubris, of august clergy betrayed by unchastity, of good folk led to ruin by usury or gluttony or sloth. But let us too spare a word—you faithful, you devout—for the perils of virtue. Let us speak too of outlaws, heretics, and all the stout-hearted reprobate throng whom god-fearing folk must spurn—brought to dire danger through straying too far into the daylight of righteousness. Let the Good Messiah content us, we who are outsiders, to look in through a lighted window and depart again into the night. For peril may come wearing an honorable surcoat as well as a highwayman's hood, as my tale shall prove and as you shall hear.

In the days of the saintly King Hugues the Ninth, may he find rest from grieving, there was a crossroads. Beside it stood a tavern. This was true of many a place. This was but an isolated crossroad, and an unremarkable tavern to fit to it. If the tavernkeeper found such isolation and unremarkability not to his liking, then it was long past the days when something ought to have been done about it. Yet within the fortnight of the feast of St. Coueren, when days are gentle and idleness is rewarded, there came to his door a collection of scoundrels and knaves. Though which are the scoundrels and which are the knaves, goodfolk, you must wait ere you venture to discern.

Let us begin with the tavernkeeper himself, one Parcevaul Perforse, for begin with someone we must. The leopard had been well favored and handsome, once, but time had dulled his spots and loosened his jowls. His clothes had been fine, once, but late nights of wine, long road, and overmuch familiarity with the pawnbroker had already exacted a piteous toll on them ere the road washed him up in this place. He had been a citizen of splendid Versinne de Touris once—which place was not yet the greatest city in the world for Maxentiople still stood, if only barely—but now the poor fellow was a citizen of nowhere at all.

Once he'd purposed to take his spotted hide south, toward the sea, in the footsteps of the bygone troubadours, to lands where a disgraced poet may make a living as a drunkard and a wastrel in relative peace. But more than his soul desired peace and poetry, his belly desired daily bread and cheap wine. He had been weary, as all travelers must sometime be, and sick at heart, as all poets must sometime be, and as ever the cure for both of these was to be found at a tavern bench. So the young leopard had thought it wise to take a seat in the yard of a place called The Huntsman's Judgement. He had no money, of course, but he was offered work in exchange for a meal. Such had been the trap.

What had once been meant to be a single winter of tavernwork, for the sake of a warm place to lay his head, had taken root in him, and sprouted into a spring and a summer. Autumn bore the bitter fruit of a plague to carry away the innkeeper for whom he had labored, as well as the son who might have succeeded the same. Their absence sent the barmaid, a genial and charitable harlot of irreproachable character, off to repentance in a nunnery, for she had oft mused on such a retirement when she tired of a life of dissolution. When the snows of winter came again they found a leopard alone at the tavern where he had bound himself with that most insidious of snares: familiarity.

Be not mistaken, it was not the sort of tavern to which you may be accustomed in your prosperous city: a throng within, a torrent of voices from every window, mugs and pitchers carried high overhead like ships upon a rough sea of hands and faces. Not was it the smaller, more homely place you might find in a quiet village, where the keeper knows every man by name and the plowmen drowse over their cheese and ale. No, the Huntsman's Judgement was a lean and hungry place, for beggers to duck for a moment from the rain, for vagabonds to sulk in ill-lit corners, for highwaymen to snatch a breath after their deeds of infamy, and to which those who visited it did not return. Still, the leopard told himself, each morning when he arose to neglect his prayers, and each sunset when he lay down in a lonely bed, and each midnight when unnamable beasts of this uncivil place worried round the back corners seeking whomsoever they might devour, a tavern is a tavern. And better than nothing. I pray you, good folk: be not fooled, as he was!

"Hail, traveler! You had a safe journey I pray?" Parcevaul called on the morning of which we speak. "They say there are fell beasts in these woods, you know, who devour those who wander from the straight path!" The traveler, a dog, brooded over his bread and wine like a priest fallen asleep mid-sacrament. Like all tavernkeepers, Parcevaul had a vice, and his was gossip. Never could he resist conversing with the few who tasted his hospitality, sometimes for hours. "And what is it you call yourself?" Indeed, his fellows in the tavernkeepers' guild, from inns in villages a half-day's journey north, or a day's journey east, had told him it was why he had so few guests to talk to.

The dog raised his head, studied him for a moment, and apparently decided to answer, "I am called Thaldeau."

"Thaldeau of where?"

"Thaldeau of This Tavern, for now."

Which was an intriguing answer enough, to be sure, that the leopard had no choice but to respond. "Well, I call myself Parcevaul."

"Parcevaul of where?" the dog immediately riposted.

"Of nowhere at all, anymore." Parcevaul looked across the fence, at the crossroads which no longer threatened to take him any direction at all so long as it was not to the city he still loved. "Once, many years ago, it was Parcevaul of Touris. Alas, no more.

Ah, city where our lady's glance once fell
So thou did put on every luxury
Of music for the ear, perfume for smell,
And every gladsome elegantery
That once mine youthful eyes could long to see.
Now evermore wilt thou be lost to view.
Now you must live within my memory,
And I must somehow live apart from you."

Thaldeau's face was an unreadable mask. "How many years have you been away, then?"

"Why, not so many goodsir. Ten, it may be? Nay, twelve."

"And have you been composing this all the while?" The dog regarded him levelly.

The leopard sputtered long enough that the dog was able to finish his cup of wine, then of course hospitality required it be refilled, so Parcevaul had no opportunity to protest there were at least two more verses, not to mention an envoi, which he would no doubt get around to composing any day now. Just as soon as the work let up!

But the leopard was a long-studied expert in that genus of debate which is to be found on a tavern bench. So what if the dog had gotten the best of him in the first salvo, once he returned with more wine, and something to eat himself, he'd show him the kind of arguing one who has been a student at the University of Touris never wholly forgets!

Before this battle plan could be put into practice there came a thing unheard of—a second guest. The wolf who rode from the east on a dappled mare—nothing so fine as a palfrey, but it would be ungallant to notice—wore linen dyed with lavender and a pendant of obsidian, why, she must be welcomed. Her kerchief was hung with silver bells in the shape of pomegranates, and she desired sweet mead, or brandywine if such a thing was to be had, and Parcevaul silently thanked St. Nannette that she asked not for hippocras. The man leading her horse by the bridle, another wolf, older, of much darker pelt and grim visage, disappeared round the back toward the stables as Parcevaul attended to his mistress. He had to be searched out and tempted back with small beer, subtly asked if his mistress would have him seated in the front benches with the gentlefolk—or the closest the Huntsman's Judgement had seen to gentlefolk in Parcevaul's days there—or will she be aggrieved if he is not kept out of sight? And then a warm loaf must be fetched, to give him to take out front, as a pretext for sending him back to her side where he insists, with the vehemence of a Roland, it is his duty to stay.

So by the time Parcevaul again had leisure to converse, his argument with the churlish dog was quite forgotten. Thaldeau made no attempt to remind the tavernkeeper of it.

The good lady proved much more companionable. "I am lately," Parcevaul said, with as much flair as he could summon, "of the city of Versinne de Touris, of splendid fame! You have seen it for yourself, I hope?"

"Alas," the slender sad-eyed lady beside him at the bench said, "I have not."

"It is a wonder of the world," the leopard let himself flourish the remnants of his urban accent a little. "And alas, mine to behold no longer!"

"A piteous fate, t'would seem." The she-wolf fingered the obsidian teardrop at her throat. "How came you by it?"

"*A heart may prove a most unheedful thing,*" Parcevaul did not hesitate to take the invitation,

"That acts without its master's by-your-leave.
That yearns above its station. That will cling,
As if pierced with a pin, upon thy sleeve.
I failed to rule it. To this day I grieve.
Take heed of me, and better may you do:

Rule well your heart, ere it learn how to thieve.
And I will somehow live apart from you."

"Elegantly said, goodsir!" the wolf's smile was patient. "But it leaves me yet uncertain what happened."

"Ah."

The old wolf glowering behind her and the dog in the corner—what had his name been again?—were both content to be ignored.

"But if you have such a thing as a hot meal, then I should be delighted to hear of your fondest memories of that splendid city. From one who will never behold it again, to one who will never behold it at all."

"I would be honored to share the tales, madam-?"

"Demoiselle. The Demoiselle Gevaudienne."

The leopard was being as friendly as it was in his power to be. He fetched pigeon pie, which he had meant for his own supper, and the best wine the inn could provide. And perhaps his intentions were mercenary, for it had been months ere the Huntsman's Judgment had seen so noble a guest. And perhaps this was vanity, for it had been long since the sight of another had made him feel as if he could desire to be desired. But I think, good folk, it was loneliness. Poor Parcevaul, I hold, wanted more than aught else to feel as if he were back at the taverns of Touris, of his youth, among noble folk, speaking noble reminiscence of noble things. If talking to this good lady would do it, why, a pie was a small price to pay.

The Demoiselle Gevaudienne declined to partake of pigeon pie.

Alas, before any of the companionable speech Parcevaul hoped for, he was called upon to play tavernkeeper yet again. There came such a party as a place like the Huntsman's Judgement had seldom seen. Five men at arms, strong and well-favored in the colors of the Martial Order of Pilgrimage Guards. A young novice, a vole, loop of parchment-edge note-scraps on his belt, leading a donkey with all the solemnity of the ambitious apprentice, and mounted thereon a lion. Paws folded within the ash-grey and pine green habit of the Barlinican Scholars: sworn to discover lore of physic and chirurgery and provide same to those in need, mane disarranged with tonsure as if invisible secrets from the higher angelic spheres pressed down always upon his head, eyes near closed yet ever watchful, peering through the lashes like a stalking predator through the high grass of far Presterionaeia, beyond the torrid heats, under the mountains of purgation.

But most extraordinary was that, of all the introductions or benedictions possible, instead the lion said "By the good faith, Parcevaul? Is it you?"

"Bartolomeu?" The leopard swallowed a mouthful of the kind of shock which knows not yet whether it is joyful or horrified. "Bartolomeu of Flanders?"

"So you once knew me, it seems." One of the men at arms helped the lion dismount, which was wholly unnecessary. "Though it is now Frater Bartolomeu, Doctoral Master of Natural Philosophy and Alchemy, and Lector with the University of Touris."

The leopard's memories groped backward until they found a young lion, underfed, hungry cheekbones without yet enough mane to hide them, somberly disapproving at the dormitory door whenever another went out drinking. "I can understand how you came to it, Frater," Parcevaul said.

"Yet I am quite at a loss," Bartolomeu needed no invitation to take a seat, after his attendant novice brushed it clean, "to suppose how came you here. Once these good men have their refreshment, I shall be most eager for your tale, old friend."

So as the Demoiselle Gevaudienne introduced herself, and confessed that she too awaited just such a tale, Parcevaul was sent scrambling back into his kitchens in search of enough food and drink for five men at arms, a novice scribe, and a renowned scholar.

If what he returned with was poorer than they hoped, well, what did they expect from a place like the Huntsman's Judgement?

"Why does any scholar emerge from our dusty libraries?" Frater Bartolomeu was amid explanation when the leopard returned, puffing gently, from distribution of bacon and turnip stew and the rosemary loaves meant to be his meals tomorrow. "I am seeking some secret. Of late I delivered a lecture, you see, on divine predestination and immortality. I could summarize if the subject will not weary you?"

"Oh, by all means, good frater." Gevaudienne's smile did not reach her eyes.

"By your good grace then, lady." Neither did Bartolomeu's. "For it is said Divine Being is all-knowing. Then it follows that it must know what is to come. This is supported by prophecy recorded in holy scripture, as well as a great many arguments from sense and reason, of a certainty much too tedious for a summer's evening amusement. Given that Divine Being knows what is to come, it follows that each man's death is likewise foreknown. It would likewise follow, then, that by departing from the course of life which Divine Foreknowledge ordains before one, it may be possible also to avoid one's ordained hour of death. Which is to say, if there is a time and place when a man is meant to die, and he is not there, then death may disregard him. Just as the yeoman leaves behind a patch of stunted wheat, come Hallowsmas, which he deems not worth the labor of harvesting."

"Would not such departure from Divine Foreknowledge," Demoiselle Gevaudienne's smile had not moved since Parcevaul had returned, "be a sin?"

"And a grave one, doubtless," the lion answered, "but this is not to be wondered at. Any departure from Divine Foreknowledge is sinful, and any sin may be considered as a departure from Divine Foreknowledge. But to the man impious enough to commit such a sin, it may erroneously seem practical. For to the impious the only cause for the avoidance of sin is the fear of damnation, which absent death they may fondly think to be no longer a danger."

"Is this a worthy subject for discourse, Frater Bartolomeu?" Gevaudienne raised an eyebrow.

"The guiltinesses of the impious may yet serve as a lesson to the wise without partaking in their guilt," the lion looked down the length of his muzzle at the leopard, "is that not so, Parcevaul?"

The leopard's laugh was of the kind used to mean 'I am not your enemy, there is no need to attack me.'

"I could never," the wolf spoke up, perhaps to save him, "countenance such a course. My mother and father, may their spirits find rest from grieving, they were as the very saints. Though I say it myself, they were indeed. Before they left some little land and incomes, they raised me to live always in peace and kindness and to have nothing to do with unholy things. Can you imagine living forever? The very weariness of it would be a curse unto itself!"

"Your parents sound good and wise folk, madam!"

"Ah, I thank you Frater! Would that all clerics could have seen as much!"

"And I shall pray their sins be forgiven them."

"Now there you sound as I would have expected from a cleric." And if her eyes glittered like the obsidian jewels she wore, then, it may very well be none but the tavernkeeper marked it.

"I remember the University," muttered Parcevaul, a trace of poetic flourish still doggedly holding fast in his voice. "Know you what the life of a student is, amid the magnificence of Touris?"

"Of course," Bartolomeu folded his hands in his sleeves. "I remember it well."

"Why, you could have deceived me there, Frater!" Parcevaul drained a tankard of hearty wine in a single gulp, and why not? It was his wine, was it not? "I do recall many dear companions... Ramses de Setroivre, Louis le Jongleur, Antione who we called 'the Generous.' Pierre St. l'Origine, refusing wine in favor of cider and laughing at our frustration. Petit Georges, forever complaining he had not slept enough to countenance whatever we proposed but doing it nonetheless. Ettiene of Aquireine, singing at sunset on the steps of Pont d'les Neiges d'Anten, and if one claimed his voice echoed yet over the glittering river I would gainsay them not. Yet nowhere," the leopard snapped, "in my memory can I see the face of Bartolomeu of Flanders among them! If ever you tasted the delights of Touris, my old friend, then failed I to witness it!"

"And which of us may return to behold Versinne de Touris, old friend," the lion's tone was like unto a confessor, "and which may not?"

Parcevaul wished heartily there were something left in his tankard.

"Goodsirs, must we?" Gevaudienne said gently.

"I too," Bartolomeu ignored her, "recall places where I ought to have seen the face of a fellow student, yet the face of Parcevaul Perforse is nowhere to be remembered. At lauds prayer, for he is still abed. At breakfast, for last night's wine has turned his stomach. In the scriptorium, leaving others to cramp their paws over the pages he neglects. In the lecture hall, or at debate, which gives one to wonder, if a man will not bother to attend lectures then what is the purpose to his being a student?"

"I attended lectures! I do recall well, Father Alberecht's lectures on the Angelic Principles of... something! Something alchemical!"

"Rotation and Refinement." The lion shook his tonsured mane gravely. "I see, poor Parcevaul, you remain as you were." He turned smoothly to Gevaudienne, as if this had been a rhetorical flourish deliberately arranged, "Yet all things bear a lesson for the wise man. Even I daresay a failure of a student who cannot remember the Angelic Principles of Rotation and Refinement."

"Bears this on the matter of your journey, Frater?" the Demoiselle's tone had cooled somewhat.

"Ah, I thank you for the reminder," Bartolomeu continued. "Sources on the matter of Divine Foreknowledge and Immortality are, alas, scarce. Accounts in books are doubtful, many heretical, and many more clearly mere fables. One must base philosophy on very unfirm foundations, sometimes, for the accounts that could prove a surer foundation are lost. But I had the good fortune, after my lecture, to receive a rumor of one such account, thought to be only a legend."

"I do not know, Frater, if you ought credit such a rumor." Gevaudienne stared across her goblet like a prince watching the siege engines across the moat. "We have no libraries in this rough country. Wisdom, in these lands, has long been in the form of good men and women, wise and pious, who forsake worldly things and go from town to town, speaking of the consolation of the Good Messiah as once did the Holy Apostles."

"Oh yes, it is well known the Cathartic Brethren once infested these lands," the lion waved a dismissive paw. "They did disdain written scripture, it was one of their many heresies. Only a fool would expect to find a text worth the reading in wake of such heretics, hedge sorcerers, and disgraced wastrels," his eyes turned toward Parcevaul and hardened, like those of an unmerciful archangel, "banished from respectable society for a senseless death in a drunken brawl. But by the Good Messiah's grace, I am not a fool. It is not a book I seek. It is a man."

There came a cry, and the sound of a stool being overturned, from within the tavern. Presently two of the men at arms emerged. One with a drawn sword, the other dragging the sullen looking dog who last Parcevaul had noticed had been sitting at a bench in the far corner of the yard, minding his own business.

"Here now," the leopard said. "This man is a guest of my tavern, just as much as you! Is this any way for ordained brothers of the martial pilgrim's guards to behave toward a pilgrim?"

"But goodsir," Gevaudienne growled and pulled the leopard back into his seat, "these men are no more of the order of pilgrim's guards than you or I."

"We caught this one," the pheasant held the dog by a wrist twisted behind his back, "trying to steal out the back into the woods."

"As I said you would," Bartolomeu nodded, then turned to another man at arms, a goose. "Captain, I believe it is time to assert your authority."

"By order of the Royal House Henriac, the throne Carolingian, and the Duke de Manteau," the goose raised the pommel of his sword, wrought in a heraldic insignia unfamiliar to Parcevaul, "I must order that none may leave this place until the prisoner in my charge is safely delivered to captivity."

Parcevaul and Gevaudienne looked in astonishment at the furious brindle dog then at one another.

"Well, old friend," said Frater Bartolomeu. "Have you such a thing as another glass of wine? It seems we may all be here some time yet."

"Is your friend the monk quite mad?" It was past sunset before Gevaudienne had sufficient privacy to whisper a question to Parcevaul.

"Lady, I know nothing of his wits," the leopard sighed. "Indeed, I begin to wonder if ever I knew aught of him at all."

The novice had been dispatched, upon the donkey, back to the last town, to return with 'the rest of the soldiers' who apparently had 'waited behind at the abbey.' He had been right willing to be gone, and Parcevaul could not blame the lad. The moment they were free of any pretense of holy orders the soldiers had been at once discourteous, threatening, and if possible even haughtier. So eager to sneer and brandish their swords had they become that Gevaudienne had been obliged to order her attendant to retire to the stables lest he challenge all five of them to avenge the insult to her honor.

"Before I put questions to you a third time, knave," Bartolomeu spoke not like a captor to a prisoner, but like a solicitous attendant at a feast, concerned a man might need a bowl and cloth to wipe his fingers, "I would urge you to consider. Should we reach the Castle of Manteau with my questions unanswered, then you must know the dungeons therein will have much direr implements of inquiry than polite discourse."

The dog, bound hand and foot, glared at him.

The Frater seemed not to mind. "Very well—I ask again, what are the means by which you have extended your lifespan so far beyond what Divine Being has allotted to man?"

The prisoner's glare did not waver.

"Were they alchemical?" Bartolomeu tried, "Or by ritual?"

The dog glared.

"Was it by the aid of, or covenant to, or congress with any unholy spirit?"

The glare was nigh severe enough to be tasted in the air.

"Or was it as the learned have reasoned, that it was by such extraordinary depravities that Divine Providence itself rejected you, and death itself refuses to touch you?"

"Our Lady's sake, Man!" Parcevaul got to his feet, quickly at first, then more slowly when he saw the pheasant's hand leap to his hilt. "Surely this is but another homeless and outcast vagabond! Wretches throughout this whole province, since the plague swept through some years ago, have been reduced to such! He knows no more of immortality than I do!"

"I must contradict you, old friend," Bartolomeu did not turn away from the dog to answer. "Though accounts are rare, some yet survive. This man is mentioned in some of the earliest histories of Albalonga, before the Emperors. The hermit monks of far Hibernia record of him in passing. He is mentioned again in accounts from the golden age of Maxentiople. Many thought these but legend, yet new texts from the east, among translations of philosophers long thought entirely lost, place him in Passanidia and Zamurkanda, beyond the Holy Lands. By these accounts, then, he must be twelve centuries old, at least!"

The dog's jaw tightened. His head was lowered, Parcevaul had not marked when he ceased to glare at Bartolomeu.

"Even if these were not mere legends," Gevaudienne spoke cautiously, "what have they to do with a poor man taking a meager meal alone at a tavern? How claim you to have found him?"

"But that is the surest proof of all," Bartolomeu smiled. "I did not find him. He found me." Now the lion did turn. "You had not the chance to know, alas Parcevaul, but King Hugues, patron of the University, decreed lectures be open to all who are willing to make the attempt at understanding, that wisdom become more general among the populace. A worthy monarch, indeed!"

The goose captain scowled, but if he had any objections they were set aside when another soldier, a cockerel, approached to whisper in his ear.

"In attendance of the lecture I spoke of before, on Divine Foreknowledge and Immortality, was a seeming mendicant wanderer who asked questions too insightful, too experienced by half. Questions my own studies had spoken nothing of. What was it you asked, good sir?" He turned again to the dog. "How might it be if old age, too, ignored a man? And I answered that, should this be the case, then it might indeed follow, as some of the old philosophers held, that old age and death are one, as dusk is merely the first part of night, and that senescence is merely the first greeting which death gives as it approaches."

"In thanks for which," the dog growled, "you tried to set the guards on me."

"So you will own you were there?"

"You are determined, plainly, to treat me as if I were."

"Then you confess your immortality, and you will," for the first time Frater Bartolomeu's countenance was less than perfectly placid, "deliver to me the answers I seek?"

"Does a man who knows secrets," sneered the dog, "attend a lecture in hopes of learning them? I have no answers for you."

But if the scholar had a ready retort to that, he had not yet the opportunity to give it, for in stormed the captain, neck tense, thick bill scowling. "Frater," he said darkly, "something is without."

"What mean you, captain?" Parcevaul said.

"I do not answer to you, Ale-Swiller," snapped the goose.

"His question is worthy nonetheless," Bartolomeu rumbled disapprovingly. "What do you mean something is without?"

"Perhaps he credits peasant's tales," Gevaudienne snorted, "of a wicked beast, summoned up from hell by the last of the heretics, to wreak revenge upon servants of Apereostic Church and Carolingian Crown. Such as himself."

"I went to post Thibault in the stable, to watch lest yon beldame's servant attempt to abscond." The goose hissed at the wolf's apparent mockery, "Ere we arrived there was a crash and strangled cry, I deem from him. We found the fellow gone, and the stable gate broken."

"My Abelard is gone?!" Gevaudienne gasped.

"I left Thibault to keep watch, but when I returned he too was gone. I know not where." As the captain spoke, one could not help but feel how dark the Huntsman's Judgement was, how meager the lamps, how many dark corners in which the Good Messiah alone might know what concealed itself. "And now Gilles too, posted in the inn yard, is gone. And in his place is only spilled blood!"

Parcevaul crossed himself. Beside him could be heard Gevaudienne's whispered prayers. But Bartolomeu continued unconcerned. "Wisdom," the lion said, "suggests one need not plumb the unknown for what the known is able to explain. These secluded taverns are oft the haunts of bandits and outlaws. Parcevaul, know you of any such lawless men?"

"If I did, I'd not be such a fool as to say so in front of him," the leopard glared at the goose.

"Curb your tongue, you wastrel-"

"Captain, I beg of you," Bartolomeu sighed, "rule your temper."

"But an outlaw," Parcevaul continued, "does not kill armed men, one by one, to no purpose. If my tavern were a haunt for outlaws, then they would know there is nothing worth stealing within, and know better than to make an enemy of the only tavern within leagues!"

"What then, if not bandits?"

"Well... they do say, in these parts, fell beasts roam the dark woods, seeking to devour those who lose their way."

As if in reply, from outside there came a cry of pain, suddenly cut off. Parcevaul and the captain, allies for a moment, ran to the window, but of course outside nothing could be seen but the night.

"That sounded like Jean," the pheasant at the front door cursed. "Gaillard, we are all that is left!"

"We must leave this evil place, Frater!" The goose, for all his vices, was a man of boldness and determination. "While yet we can!"

"Nonsense, captain."

"The Duke will not brook-"

"It is hardly whatever Duke you serve," the dog laughed, darkly, from the corner where again he'd been nigh forgotten, "whom you need fear. If all you fools mean to drag me out into the dark woods, so be it. The one among us whom death touches not will have by far the least to fear, I would guess."

There was a powerful silence in the Huntsman's Judgement, for the space of a few breaths.

"Parcevaul," Frater Bartolomeu said, very quietly, "I do recall, in the aftermath of the woeful circumstances of the death of one of our fellow students, there was mention made of a sword."

"Aye."

"Do you have it still?"

"I will need," the tavernkeeper turned to the captain, who looked now much less hostile, "to step into the kitchens for a moment, by your leave."

The only light in the kitchens was the oven fire, now burned down to embers. Without, the clouds had parted, and the moon briefly appeared, but it failed to illuminate anything of the room. It had been years since Parcevaul had touched the scabbard he'd stowed behind the preserved apricots among the rafters, but he needed no light to know exactly where to go to lay hands upon it.

When he stepped back down, there was a bestial shape, sharp ears and wicked muzzle, moonlight behind it, peering in at the window.

Only for a moment. Then, without a sound it vanished.

Parcevaul hurried back to the common room.

"I hope, Frater," Gevaudienne growled bitterly, "whatever secret you think this one will tell you is worth the lives of your men. I know it is not worth poor Abelard's life."

"It would be an error, Demoiselle," Bartolomeu looked perfectly untroubled as he paged through his book of hours by the light of an oil lamp, "to hold any in this tavern accountable for the actions of some fell beast of the wilderness."

"Oh would it indeed?"

The two remaining men at arms had turned the common room into the nearest thing to a keep they could manage. The goose watched the front door, the pheasant the kitchen door. Parcevaul had been told to stand by 'the Prisoner' and he did not know what felt less comfortable: the looming peril without, or the memories that feeling a sword again in his hand summoned from within.

Gevaudienne stalked away from the Frater in disgust. "Tell me, fellow," she approached Parcevaul instead, "for it has been much mentioned but only in hints. How is it you came to be banished from Touris?"

"It is shameful to tell of it, good lady."

"As shameful as it was to commit of it?" the wolf's voice sharpened, "As shameful as the abduction you comply in now?" But then she sighed, and it softened again. "Come now, one need not be an Ordained Frater and Doctoral Lector to know confession is a needful thing. And we must talk of something to pass the time until dawn."

"Very well," Parcevaul rubbed tired eyes. "It was the kind of foolish affair that seems like the wittiest of jokes after enough wine, and we were young, and if any of us knew of the quarrel between crown and archbishopric we had forgotten. Someone, memory wishes to say Etienne but I cannot be certain, proposed that all we students have a mock processional, from tavern to tavern, as if delivering sacraments. And well, a procession must needs have vestments."

On the other side of the room Bartolomeu frowned and gripped his breviary tighter.

"I think the deacon thought we were from the crown, come to rob the church," the leopard continued. "I had only just said 'Good Master, we wish to borrow-' when he struck me on the cheek and swung fast the door. Before we knew what was happening, guardsmen were upon us, spears up. I remember we laughed much at that, for we all had swords—we were well-born students, of course we had swords. We thought fighting back to defend ourselves against what was clearly an unjustified attack sounded a grand adventure. And none were wounded! At first. But the sound of battle opened windows and lit candles in each of them, and brought more guards. Which brought forth more students, who knew not what they were pouring forth to defend. Which meant more guards, and…" He raised his hands, as if some spirit unseen in the darkness might give the explanation he could not. "By morning the chapel roof was in flames, and poor Etienne was dead. I never knew who struck him down, this I swear!"

"Twenty and seven of us were banished." Parcevaul concluded. "The crown's chancellor himself pronounced sentence. Aught we tried to say in our defense only made him the more certain of our guilt. 'Go back to your family lands in the country,' were the terms of the banishment, but only three of us had those. The rest of us might go anywhere so long as it was away, with nothing but the clothes upon our backs."

"You were fortunate, perhaps," Gevaudienne said gravely, "it was not death."

"Aye," sighed Parcevaul, "I deny it not. Yet also do I say, what did we do that was wrong? None did forbid us drink, none did forbid us talk to a churchman, and I should hope none would forbid we defend ourselves against men with spears. Each choice we made was lawful, yet we came to lawlessness nonetheless. A mystery, that, one I have understood not these last twelve years."

"A man who chooses to turn this way, or that, on the whim of the moment," Thaldeau said, "cannot complain if the place he arrives is not what he intended."

Parcevaul started. He had again forgot the dog was listening.

"Nothing is unforgivable," Gevaudienne began.

"Indeed so," Bortolomieu interrupted. His book of hours snapped shut and vanished back into his sleeve pocket. "Do not doubt, old friend, it is providence this man stopped at your tavern, and I accosted him here. Come day, when it is safe to depart, if you will lend your aid, then I shall see this banishment shall be lifted, and your crimes washed clean."

For an instant Parcevaul believed, and hope filled a heart long unused to it, but then he frowned. "How is it, old friend, you can promise such a thing?"

"They do not dispatch men at arms, alas," explained the lion as if it were a point of commentary on Averroës, "merely to satisfy the curiosity of a scholar. You know, of course, of His Majesty's vow of chastity? Praiseworthy, to be sure, but it leaves the question of an heir when he goes to the reward it wins him. Yet his royal cousin the Duke de Manteau has reasoned with me: if the way for a man to avoid death were found, is it not possible that all the woes that attend upon a kingdom when the crown must change brows would be no more? No more assassinations. No more dynastic wars. No more divorces of a blameless queen for bearing of a daughter. No more trusting to fortune that the prince and heir will not be, as the historian puts it, evil, mad, foolish, or all three!"

"Did you not say," Gevaudienne said, baffled, "that to claim immortality was a grave sin?"

"If His Majesty is saintly enough to decline this," the lion shrugged, "then the Duke de Manteau is, alas, content to be as much a sinner as any of us. Given time and patience we shall have a king proof against death, one way or another."

"Never mind the consciences of kings," Parcevaul snapped, "how can a man of holy orders countenance this?"

"I? No blame attaches to me. I act only intending the peace of the realm, and the uncovery of hidden truths. If another man's wickedness be also the effect, then I intend it not and am no more culpable than the fisherman when an old crone chokes on a fishbone!"

Parcevaul knew not what to say.

Gevaudienne had no such difficulty. "Fool!" she spat, "as I looked for in one such as you! As I cannot guess why all the world does not yet see in men such as you! You have a man like this," she stabbed a finger at Thaldeau like a lance, "who has seen all he has, and all you can think to ask of him is how rich and wicked men may keep their riches and their wickedness longer still? Out upon you, fool, and out upon your whole Church of Fools, and its adulterous marriage to the wickedness of the world!"

"It scarcely to be wondered at," Bartolomeu snorted, "that one such as you defies the Holy Apereostic Church. You would be of the Cathartic Brotherhood, then? It is no wonder you despise the precious gift of life, it is all a piece with your heresies! That marriages and births are an abomination! That the taking of one's own life is a sacrament! Blasphemous!"

"You know nothing of what I, or any like me, believe." The Demoiselle Gevaudienne drew herself to an icy height. "As those monks, those knights, who murdered my parents knew nothing, and preferred to make up heresies for which to burn them! But I, thou sanctimonious fool, know better what questions to ask a man such as this!" The wolf bent down, like a concerned mother, before the bound dog. "Goodsir. If all is as has been said, then you lived while the Holy Messiah was on the earth, and dwelt among us! You walked the earth among the first Messianics, who despised not wisdom spoken by a woman, who reviled not the love of chosen brothers, or bond sisters! Who admitted not the rich or the powerful among them, but held all that they had in common! Tell us, I beg you! And bear witness against this corrupt world and its corrupt church, what true Messianic faith is!"

The prisoner raised his eyes at last. What must he have seen looming over him? The lion mustering the power of both church and crown to devour him. The wolf desperate and furious, seeking whom she might be avenged upon. The leopard angry and fearful at his own heartsickness. "I know nothing of the early Messianics, lady." His words were like the scent of an ancient desert monastery, dry with sand and heavy with ages, glimpsed suddenly round a rocky cliff face above inhospitable seas. "I was far from here, in those days, seeking my own business in other regions of the world. When I left these lands none had yet heard of your Messiah. By the time I returned you had already slain him, some centuries ago, and were nigh to war over what he would have had to say if you had slain him not.

From all that I have heard, I would guess these first Messianics were just as much like this monk as they are like you."

He turned his dark-masked face on Parcevaul, and the leopard shrank before whatever excoriations were to come. But for the space of a few breaths, he said nothing.

A crash, muffled amidst the thatch, echoed between the rafters.

The two remaining soldiers climbed cautiously toward the attic, the goose first, the pheasant behind. As they vanished into the darkness, Thaldeau leaned forward. "And now," he said as if Parcevaul and he were alone in the room, "you are the only one with a weapon. To you, and none else, I will promise: free me, and I shall tell you all my story. Any secrets you can glean from it, you may have with my blessing."

"This is nonsense," Gevaudienne scoffed, and though her voice was still all calmness and grace the fury in it had returned, abated not a whit.

"On this point, heretic," Bartolomeu growled, "you are correct."

"The right thing to do, I suppose," the she-wolf seemed neither to speak to, nor hear, any but herself, "would be to put this man to death, that he be released from the foul unnaturalness of unending life, and men such as you and the duke you serve be denied forever his secrets! Perhaps Abelard," and her growl was dark as a midwinter night, "can attend to it when finished with his other work."

Bartolomeu looked as if he should like to question that, but was cut off by Thaldeau's disdainful bark. "Frater, you are among the greatest fools I have ever met. And I have lived longer than you guess, meeting fools all the while. Even if you had any way to compel from me the answers you seek, you could understand them not, and they would profit you nothing. You and I have nothing more to say to one another, save this: I thank you for answering my question. You hold my death is denied me because I was not where I ought to have been, as I ought to have been, to meet it? Then I have no doubt he too failed to keep his appointment. If reunion is but a matter of patience, I have learned to be as patient as death."

If the lion, or the she-wolf, or the leopard felt moved to ask who 'he' was, and what Thaldeau meant, they were given not the chance. For with a heart-stopping crash, through the thatch of the roof and the brittle planks of the loft, came two men locked in combat. Below, like an image of the devil trampled by San Michel, was the man-at-arms, the pheasant, whose name Parcevaul had never a chance to discover. Above, like a trebuchet-stone from the sky, was the grim wolf who had come as Gevaudienne's servant, fangs bared and knife drawn. They reached the ground in a tangle of roofing, broken rafters, smashed table, and broken lamps. From the wreckage, only the wolf arose.

Ere he could advance on any of them, the captain was upon him. Within a moment, they were struggling with his heraldic sword, even as the flames greedily took the spilled lamp oil around them.

Bartolomeu and Gevaudienne both turned wild eyes to Parcevaul, the only one left who held a sword. As had been foretold.

"Help him!" commanded the lion.

"Nay," gainsaid the wolf, "help him!"

"Help yourself," said Thaldeau, quietly. "We must leave unless you wish us all to burn with this place."

How is a man to judge, good folk, amid so dreadful a throng of choices? As flames lick hungrily over home and livelihood? Like the flames of hell, perhaps, or the flames of a chapel burning amid riot broken free and innocent blood drunkenly shed. Be not severe, I beg you, with the frantic leopard who leads forth from the flames a vagabond of a dog, unbound. After a moment, behold, there emerges a fury of a heretic and a furious hierarch in his wake.

You may well think he has chosen poorly. He may well have thought so himself. But chosen he has.

"Well chosen," Thaldeau rubbed the feeling back into his wrists, "I owe you my thanks."

"You owe me your secrets," Parcevaul growled. He raised his sword and planted himself between the purported immortal and the flames swallowing the Huntsman's Judgement. Gevaudienne slumped to her knees, peering back anxiously, but Bartolomeu was risen to his feet and turned his now-somewhat scorched mane toward them.

"It is not too late, Parcevaul," the Frater's eyes were narrow and cold, "to regain a life in the city while yet some of that life remains to you. You need only do what is right!"

Parcevaul's back straightened, his teeth clenched, and he met the lion's eyes, glimmering in the firelight. *"Nostalgia is a prison-house, old friend,"* he said.

Bartolomeu blinked. "What?"

Parcevaul's smile was mocking as he continued, *"What cannot be forgot, an oubliette.*

Thou shalt not tempt me into it again!

I shall not shoulder once again that debt!"

The poet spared a glance up the road, north, toward Versinne de Touris, most magnificent city in the world for those who did not care for Maxentiople. But he swallowed and hardened his heart.

"To what end, city, were we twain once met?

Was love merely the prelude to adieu?

Why then, be thou the love I can't forget,

And I will somehow live apart from you."

Bartolomeu had no chance at a last word, for Gevaudienne gave a cry, and out of the flaming ruin staggered the form of a man. The grim wolf's fur was singed and blackened, and many a wound he bore of sword, and more of fire. But still he managed to walk across the yard and sink to one knee, fully as gallant as any Paladine, ere he collapsed.

"Abelard!" she rushed to him.

"May my deeds completed," the old wolf groaned, "find favor in my lady's sight..."

"Hush, hush, thou good and faithful champion," she cradled his cheeks, though he winced when her fingers touched his burns, and she cried, "Frater! Medicines, quickly!"

"I, lady?"

"You have your vows, do you not?" she snapped. "You have your alchemies? Are either worth anything, when a life stands in need of them? Or must I prove myself the heretic and give him last consolation?"

Bartolomeu gave a last covetous look past Parcevaul at Thaldeau, then surrendered and turned to administer the medicines his order were sworn to provide.

The leopard and the dog agreed without words that this, when all eyes were turned away, was the best moment to steal into the night like the rogues they were.

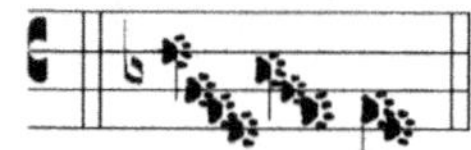

"And now, goodsir," Parcevaul stopped once they had put a good league or two of forest between them and whatever the fire had left of his inn, "what I was promised! What is the secret of life everlasting?"

"That," Thaldeau said, "is not what I promised you. I promised you my story."

The leopard's face fell.

"Be comforted," the dog shrugged. "The one may contain the other, though I can imagine no way for the knowing of it to profit you. But you are a poet, or purport to be? Then if you mean to make yourself a living you will need a story to tell. I daresay your former living is no more."

"...what manner of story is it?" Parcevaul grumbled.

Thaldeau looked south, beyond the horizon. Perhaps to the sea, perhaps at something beyond the leopard's sight, perhaps simply away.

"Prince that was mine when once the world was young,
I loved you. What is more, you loved me too.
We've long abandoned what the fates once spun.
Without you burns a never-setting sun.
On your return my hopes, and life, are hung.
Until then, I will live. Apart from you."

"Very well," Parcevaul, after all, had little in the way of other options. "Let us go, and carefully. They say dangerous beasts are to be found in these woods, that may devour unwary travelers."

"Aye," said Thaldeau, "I have been met with three of them, this day."

The last the moon saw of them, she would report if but we could ask of her, they did continue south together, talking as the night turned to morning, of long distant days in splendid Versinne de Touris and elsewhere.

And if a storyteller, who deprived of both city and inn must earn a living somehow—and is most grateful for your generosity at this, the tale's conclusion—knows more of what passed between the two of them, of the dog's tale told onto the leopard, of the secrets of great antiquity therein? Why I fear, goodfolk, those secrets shall remain ever denied to men such as Frater Bartolomeu and his Duke. They are nothing to the point of the moral I promised: those of us who are outsiders, belong outside. If Frater Bartolomeu had been content with his cloister, he need not have slunk back disgraced in the eyes of royalty. If the Demoiselle Gevaudienne had mourned her heroic heretical parents in seclusion without revenge, she would have had peace all her days. If Parcevaul had been content to be but a rogue and a rascal, he would have been burdened with no inns, and had nothing to lose. If Thaldeau had not longed to know when his long wandering would end, none would have guessed he might have secrets worth grasping at. To each came peril, not as a thief in the night, but like a tavernkeeper offering deceitful welcome to a place at a respectable table.

And so, goodfolk, do I conclude with mine envoi:
Oh wand'ring prince, may you your heart's desire
Find someday. And I pray it finds you too.
Our Lady bless us each, as we require,
While we will live, and die, apart from you.
So saith Parcevaul de Cette Taberne!

Scapegoat

Domus Vocis

They dragged us from our cells into the village road. The twilight sky cast a glow over the taller buildings, with the church's spire burning in an orange haze. As if God Almighty set the cross atop it on fire. Below the heavenly symbol, former friends and neighbors gathered to watch, their jaws frothing and yells echoing in every direction.

Arnolf and I inhaled the stench of refuse piling around the streets. Among them were dead bodies contaminated by the Plague. They openly decayed as a doctor, one who did not decide to partake in our executions, continued trying to remove the corpses. He didn't turn his beak towards the two half-starved goats being dragged to the center of the loud square.

Two rough paws gripped our arms, making us face the path leading into wilderness. Our rabid neighbors and former friends—our own disappointed families—pelted insults upon us like stones, while a few preferred the latter. In fact, one pebble struck me above my forehead, causing blood red liquid to drip over my right eye, clouding my already teary-eyed vision. It covered the wooden buildings and mortar homes in a hellish color. The wolf gripping Arnolf's wrists behind his back kicked him behind his knees, causing him to collapse. The same wolf returned my friend to a kneeling position, clutching a horn to keep his head level.

The hoarse, growling voice of Father Armine carried over their shouts.

"Rejoice, for we shall end this curse they have wrought upon us!" the mad ursine priest proclaimed to his quieting flock. "For too long, the Plague has scorched our land and beyond! It has taken the local lord, taken the archbishop, taken our children, because of these two!"

The large, albeit gangl brown bear glared at us, pointing his claw at Arnolf and me.

"Arnolf, Baldram, you have been committing the highest sin of all!" he bellowed, the sky matching the seething red in his bloodshot eyes. "You are sodomites, sent by Lucifer to bring death and disease, while having the disgusting urge to fornicate! It is not sheer coincidence neither of you have been affected by the Plague! This curse must be purged!"

The villagers surrounding us cheered. None of them questioned the bear as he described how we committed the highest sin, or how we were unaffected by the Plague currently ravaging the known world. He lied though about us being responsible for it. Had any of them listened, they would have known what Arnolf did with me in private happened long before the first recorded death. We'd known the risks of being discovered, but not the volume of consequences.

"Sodomy is the highest sin, dating as far back as the Old Testament, which is why we must purge it with a ritual of the Old Testament," Father Armine told the roused mammals. His words transformed into a deeper, darker mirage of a holy man's speech. "I am talking about the scapegoat ritual, used by the people of Moses to cleanse their cities of hoarded evil. One shall be sacrificed to the Lord and the other driven away into the wilds to carry away our sins. We have prayed, we have fasted, and we have called for a sign. None have arrived until this moment!"

Arnolf and I listened in silent horror. We both attended the father's sermons ever since childhood. Most of our village did. Never had we heard of such a ritual before. Did the father even recite it from Holy Scripture?

The mad priest smiled deliriously, stepping aside next to my friend. He nodded to his wolf captor, announcing to everyone, "Thus, His will shall be done! One of you will be sacrificed, and the other shall carry away our sins, along with your own!"

"Get fucked, you vile excuse for a priest, Armine!" Arnolf, frothing and struggling to break free, shouted, "Your soul will be the one to burn! All of you will still burn! This will not end the Plague! All of you will still burn! *All of you!*"

Pleading for Arnolf to be let go, crying for them to choose me instead, I tried breaking free too. Arnolf shared a final defeated look with me. His blue eyes filled with defiant tears while the wolf behind him drew a hunting knife. Using his other paw to still grip one of the goat's horns, the canine rested it to the shaking throat of my first true love.

In a single motion, he sliced.

Crimson everywhere. Bawling too. Cheers echoed everywhere.

Raw screams bellowed from my throat like a dying animal, yet I didn't feel the cold steel to my throat. Rather, I was pushed to my feet, then struck repeatedly by fists and stones, and instinct drove me to run for my life. The insults intermixed with absolute agony. I could only see the approaching dark trees and the awful tapestry of Arnolf lying in a pool of his own blood.

I ran. I ran. I ran. I ran. I ran until the villagers of my previous home faded into nocturnal shrieks. Branches became the claws of feral beasts. Crunching leaves resonated like enchanting choruses in a cathedral. Glinting moonlight revealed demonic grins and serpentine fangs in the darkness. They transformed into abominations that attacked me, laughed at me, surrounding me, devouring me until—

I let out an anguished gasp. My forehead ached at the memory, as did my limbs.

My crusted eyes stared at the ceiling until sunrise peeked through the shuttered window. I remained on the inn's bed but dared not to move. Harsh memories reenacted continuously at the forefront of my mind, tormenting me. Facing away from the wall, I surveyed the solitary room once I had wiped my eyelids. Daylight reflected from the dirtied, cracked mirror hanging above a wash basin.

I glanced at the foot of my bed, to the window. The sounds of city life trickled in with the day. Then, my eyes widened at seeing him in the mirror.

"Don't worry," he told me. "It's still there. It hasn't been stolen during the night."

Sure enough, I reached underneath my bed to feel the leather satchel and found no sign of anything being emptied from it. A nervous sigh of relief was replaced though by anxiety.

"You cannot stay here for another night, Baldram."

"I know," my lips wanted to whisper. Doing so would acknowledge the past.

"You need to get up," he said when I didn't reply.

I grumbled in agreement, ignoring Arnolf's worried smile reflecting through one of the mirror shards. The clothes he wore were no longer stained in his own blood, nor did he have a jagged scar across his throat, not unless I stared too long at the ghost. If I did, the horrific image of his death would flicker in and out of existence. So, as always, I tried my best to ignore him.

He didn't look away from me, not as I stared at the dark circles beneath my eyelids, nor when I splashed water from the basin all over my face. Not even when I went to empty my bowels into the chamber pot, let alone when I tossed the contents into the closed alleyway where the other guests abandoned their excrement. He only disappeared when I closed the windows' shutters.

Arnolf was right, as always. I needed to find extra money. If not for the innkeeper to let me stay another fortnight, then to save up. I tried not to think of a reason for it.

I stretched my feet and arms, then snatched my satchel and coat from beneath the mattress. The contents—a bag of coins, a map, and a sheathed knife purchased from the Romani merchant wolf who first found me, wandering for months between small towns and sleepy villages. He'd given them to me as payment in exchange for helping him sell his wares along the Rhine, before making my way to Holland. The money was made through various odd jobs performed along the journey.

"Do you think there will be a ship?" Arnolf asked me, to which I didn't reply. Rather, I fished for the bag of coins from inside the satchel. "Will you have enough for a meal?"

I paused, feeling my ears lower until they ached.

The tavern beneath the inn's rooms didn't provide free nourishment, but the lynx innkeeper, a middle-aged man with greying fur named Jon, said I would be allowed to stay in one of his rooms if I was able to help serve drinks in the evenings, as well as pay for half of what a room normally cost. Otherwise, he'd have me stay in the stables with the other travelers and wayward pilgrims. Doing so risked losing everything I had left.

Reaching for the bag of coins with my other paw, I set the satchel back underneath the bed. Without acknowledging Arnolf, I ventured downstairs.

Laughter and chatter and scents overwhelmed my senses. I carefully placed my coin purse into a pocket before stepping in front of the corner fireplace. Two recently chopped logs had been fed to the burning pile of cinders. I held my paws to the hearth until I felt content enough to approach the bar, which was manned by a bored deer.

"What's your poison today, sir?" He spoke in a heavy accent I couldn't recognize.

"It is an hour after sunrise," I informed him, to which the deer shrugged.

"Tell that to them," he motioned to a group of large bears raising their cups. "I take it you would wish for a morning meal then. What can I get for you?"

Hesitantly, I reached into my pocket. "How much will this give me?"

From the tiny purse, my paw pulled out one Heller coin. Within the pouch, I held approximately six schillings, two Heller, and eight pennies, but experience taught me not to reveal one's (lack of) wealth. Weeks previously, the purse had held even more schillings.

"One half of a penny?" The deer mused, then examined the Heller in my fingers. "Half a pound of roast, some cheese, and perhaps a cup of water."

"Perhaps some bread instead of roast?" I requested. "P-Please?"

He relented after thinking it over. I didn't object when he snatched the currency away. Instead, I counted my blessings as minutes later, the cold bread's scent wafted over my nose when I inhaled it. The chunk I'd bitten into was stale, but the cheese helped me ignore the taste in favor of the dried curd's flavor.

Around me, tavern guests talked as I sat in silence at my lone table. Topics of discussion included sultry women as well as current affairs. Among them were hushed whispers of ongoing civil wars and anarchy that filled Holland and the surrounding rural counties of the Holy Roman Empire. Though I did not care for meaningless politics compared to survival, I was aware of the consequences. While William V, Count of Holland, quarreled with his own mother and her allies over the right to the title, the peasantry needed to contend with the Black Death.

Of course, nobody talked of the Black Death. Not in public. Doing so attracted attention. In the east, those who discussed it aloud often met critical gazes. These often led to rumors, which transformed into engulfing paranoia. However, some still discussed the rosy-boiled pestilence in subdued whispers that couldn't be heard by those wanting to blame the wrong mammal. Some spoke of Constantinople being empty. Others said a literal wave of feral rats swarmed Rome. The monstrous creatures dripped and oozed through every crack, flooding every home, devouring their occupants to bone, then evaporating away to other locations when nothing else could sustain the legions of hungry mice. The Pied Piper of Hamelin would sooner die of fright than deal with such infestations!

"Good morning, Baldram," Jon appeared behind me, roughly slapping my shoulder after I finished my last morsel. The urge to grimace at the old lynx was strong, but I hid my disdain. "How did you sleep? I've got something for you!"

"Morning to you too, sir," I spoke up, stiffening in my chair. "What is it you need?"

The first time I met Jon, he almost tossed me out onto the street, but all it took was a well-rested sleep the next morning for the lynx to welcome me into his tavern. At first, I'd wondered if he had a temperamental twin brother, but it wasn't long before I learned from his workers that Jon's mood depended on how well his business did. When not under stress, the feline would be cordial. Any interruptions to his happiness resulted in an angry storm.

"I have a new horseshoe from the blacksmith that needs to be collected, but I cannot leave Henri unattended." He motioned to the deer from before, already providing drinks to the same group of excited brown bears. "Bring it here before mid-afternoon, and I will add another day."

How could I not say yes? Scarfing down the cup of water in a single gulp, in turn ignoring Arnolf in the water's reflection that appeared for two seconds, I happily accepted the offer. Jon provided directions for me, gave me the schilling to pay the blacksmith, then mentioned the possibility of two free nights at the inn if I helped his wife shovel manure out back later. Again, I accepted the proposed offer, then walked out onto the street.

Compared to the rural outlands east of the Rhine River, Amsterdam felt crowded. The red-roofed buildings and claustrophobic structures jutted higher into the sky, and the presence of too many mammals often caused discomfort to my nostrils. Heavy scents and foul smells struck without warning, to the point I preferred covering my mouth with the sleeve of my coat.

On the upside, Amsterdam's diversity of mammals surprised me when I first arrived. I'd been half-starved, hopping from village to village, town to town across the Holy Roman Empire, but it wasn't until I reached the city that I encountered more herbivores than ever seen in the confines of my village. They stood packed in an area of mortar and stone split in half by the river Amstel, with a view of seawater along the riverfront obscured by wooden pillars or docked sailboats.

The sight of a raven flying overhead made me pause. Memories threatened to resurface again. The masked doctor feigning indifference, Armine's growls, Arnolf's gurgling as he choked on blood, our friends' shouts, the pain of being struck on the forehead, and seeing crimson. So much crimson, it hurt.

Slowing my walk, my left paw reached up to caress the healed scar. It throbbed like a bruise, even months later. Somewhere behind me, an impatient mammal grumbled before walking swiftly around me. I didn't open my eyes to see who it was.

Gritting my flat teeth together, I sighed to myself, then held the schilling in my pocket. A selfish thought encircled my head at keeping the wealth on my own.

"Don't consider it, Baldram," Arnolf's gentle voice reminded me. "It won't be worth the consequences. Just go to the blacksmith, pay for the horseshoe, then return."

Guilt replaced the urge once the latter emotion resided. Heaving another sigh, I again ignored the love of my life in the shop window's dusty glass reflection and returned to the day's task. A part of me wanted him to simply go away. Another wished for him to stay, and for me to speak with him.

Yet I didn't. I couldn't.

A few whispers talked of England and Scotland being unaffected by the Death. Due to the pestilence spreading though, no boats ventured across the Channel. None would dare to face the English ships, which made life ever more surprising when I spotted white sails peeking around the corner of a building leading towards the city's harbor. Glimpses of its flag on the tallest mast revealed the standard colors.

My heart went aflutter, while my tail wiggled delightedly at such a sight. Then, both became still. Still gripping the acquired horseshoe in my paw, I strode in the opposite direction back towards the inn.

"You should consider it after delivering the horseshoe," Arnolf's voice echoed from somewhere. "Baldram? Baldram, will you at least consider it?"

A chill shivered up my back, and I gripped the horseshoe harder, almost until the metal dug into my palm. Memories again tried resurfacing, only for them to be quashed when I started walking faster.

"Baldram," Arnolf's voice sliced through the crowd. "Baldram, you cannot keep ignoring this."

I tried imitating a growl, "Shut. Up."

Biting my lower lip, the flat teeth inherited by my species didn't allow me to pierce the skin. Even so, it helped to distract me from giving the ghost another reply. Doing so would not only force me to endure another one of his pointless queries, but consider the possibility—

"Baldram, please! Baldram, you cannot discard this new chance!"

The fast strides transformed into desperate running. I found myself shoving between the shoulders of men going about their day, shouting or swearing at me if I startled them. Quite a few swore at me in foreign languages. The horseshoe in my paw nearly slipped once or twice, then suddenly slipped free, hitting the ground with a loud *CLANG*.

"Oh no," I gasped, whirling around.

The horseshoe skipped over cobblestone and was kicked by a couple of boots until it suddenly disappeared from view. I tried gazing between scurrying legs for the item, only to find nothing. Either somebody within the crowd picked it up, or it fell into one of the many dirty puddles filling the cracked street. Whatever the case, it was lost.

"Where is it?" I quavered madly, eyes darting from one location to the next. "Where is it? Where is it? Where in the name of God is it?!"

Emotions welled to the surface, rising from the depths of my stomach. Hyperventilating as if the air from my chest was being pulled out by a hook, I began coughing. It would not stop no matter what I did. The mammals who didn't care about my plight maintained their distance as I stumbled against a shop's exterior wall, then knelt against it to dry-heave my breakfast.

His visage appeared beside me, apologetically placing a cold paw on my shoulder as I wept. It didn't match the comfort I'd felt when we first kissed in secret, or when I expressed my desires to him in cautious hope. Or after our first coupling, when we held each other in bliss.

"Leave me..." I muttered softly, finally able to breathe again. "Why can't you...leave me be?"

The memories resurfaced, tormenting me. Crimson everywhere, shouting everywhere, and pain everywhere, with the scar on my forehead burning brightly. Only the sensation of Arnolf's phantom paw caressing my shoulder pulled me away from abyssal oblivion.

"Baldram, please," he whispered into my ear, "at least give them a request. One simple request. That...that...that is all I ask for."

A warmer paw suddenly tapped my shoulder. "Young man, are you quite alright?" A concerned vixen's voice stabbed through the other noise surrounding us. "Do you require help?"

I turned wearily to find a middle-aged vixen with an outstretched paw. She smiled in a motherly manner when our eyes locked, and I accepted her offer of assistance. Standing up and thanking her, I didn't have time to hear her say 'you are welcome' before an older fox aggressively murmured for her to be careful, lest I give the plague to them.

"He's also clearly raving mad," he told her, pulling her by the wrist. "Come on, wife!"

Other mammals watched us, or rather me. The walls of Amsterdam in the distance miraculously shifted into a forest's tree line and the cloudy sky became night. Shaking my horns, I covered my mouth with an elbow and coughed, noticing the ghost was nowhere to be seen.

Unable to find the horseshoe, my defeated legs carried me back to the inn. I didn't consider customers leaving the tavern nor if Jon or his workers spotted me during the mid-afternoon rush. I scurried upstairs, sobbing and hysterical, and slammed my door shut before tumbling into the darkened room. Tears flowed freely down my cheek and choked anguish bubbled out of my lips as I collapsed onto the bed.

"Do you enjoy suffering, Baldram?"

Arnolf appeared in the cracked mirror again. He stared at me from across the room, and as soon as I blinked the tears away, he suddenly turned corporeal. The deceased goat wore the dirtied, blood-stained clothes from that night, and I tried to squeeze my eyes shut, hoping the nightmare would end. Why wouldn't he stop tormenting me? Why?

"Baldram, please look at me. You cannot continue torturing yourself."

I whimpered in fear. "You are the one who tortures me, Arnolf," came my reply. "Y-You continue to follow me from beyond the grave..."

Opening my eyes again, I flinched upon seeing Arnolf's phantom kneeling beside the bed, his paw resting beside mine. "I apologize, but it is beyond my control," he murmured, his voice rising. "Even so, I need to understand why you refuse to ever consider leaving the mainland. People are getting desperate and frightened. We both know the Plague is worsening, we have very few prospects in the Empire, and war outside of those walls is going to come any day. If Jon does not kill us for losing that horseshoe, then staying will!"

"You don't think I know that?" I rumbled disbelievingly.

"Don't keep setting these chances aside, Baldram," he admonished me. "Before you came to Holland, you possessed more money and had plenty of chances to leave for England, Scotland, Norway, or Sweden! Even when the Icelandic merchants visited the marketplace, you didn't consider asking for passage! For God's sake, you merely joked about wanting their fish! Fish, Baldram! Why don't you ever take advantage in finding a better life beyond—"

Turning back to the phantom, I spat out, "Because I do not deserve it!"

That suffocating silence echoed around the room following my outburst. A couple of shouts and annoyed rapping from the neighboring wall startled me, and I winced. The other inn guests likely considered me stark-raving mad. Jon would too.

Arnolf held my paw, squeezing his digits around my fingers. Concern and confusion laced his features, the goat's cerulean pools fighting back tears. "It was not your fault…"

"I didn't do anything," my quavering voice came out strained. "I…I just let them kill you, got careless with our rendezvouses, and they killed you with the idea the Lord would help our village." Another lone tear snaked down my chin. "I should have died instead of you…you were always braver, stronger, better than me at living on your own. You didn't deserve to be killed."

"I can agree with your last statement, but not the rest," he squeezed my paw. "There was nothing you could have possibly done, Baldram. If you fought back like I did, we would be sharing a grave together…You too would be dead, Baldram."

"That does not sound—"

Arnolf interrupted, "Finish that thought and I shall haunt you for the rest of your days."

"Is that not what you already do?" I asked, then sat up to stare at Arnolf. He was so deathly pale, even for a German goat. I wiped my tears away, staring down at my fingers. "Is this my punishment from God? To have my fellow sodomite follow me as a ghost forever, reminding me not only of what I have lost but whom? If only…If only I can…"

"Forget?" he finished for me. When I glanced away, he leaned closer until I was left with no other choice but to gaze into those cerulean orbs that first entranced me in our teenage years. "Baldram, do you regret the moments we shared?"

"I regret we were not more careful," I answered, staring back down at the blood on his clothes, as well as returning to his neck. Just faintly under the white fur could be found the scar where his throat had been sliced clean. "But no...I do not regret the moments we shared. Never."

He whimpered. "If you won't live for yourself, then you should at least live for me," my lover pleaded. "I will never feel sunlight or enjoy one's laughter again, but you can. Please, live for me. For us."

"Oh...Arnolf," I sniffled. "Oh Lord, I miss you so much...It hurts."

His paw patted the top of mine. "I know you do, and so do I..."

Arnolf leaned in for a hug I could not feel. Cold air enveloped me, even as I witnessed the ghostly goat rest his head along my shoulder, press his chest to mine, and I enjoyed his comfort. Without another word, I lay myself back down on the bed, next to Arnolf, and fell asleep like we did after our first time.

KNOCK! KNOCK! KNOCK!

I awoke alone in what felt like minutes later. Sunlight continued creeping between the window shutters, indicating little change in the passage of time.

"Baldram, are you in there?" The door shook. "Baldram, one of my boys spotted you earlier running in here! Where the Hell is my horseshoe, lad?!"

KNOCK! KNOCK! KNOCK! KNOCK!

I jumped from the mattress in fright, stammering, "I'm sorry, Jon! I'm so sorry, I had the horseshoe! It was in my paw, and I paid for it, but it got lost during the walk back! Please don't kick me out, I'll...I'll pay you back the schilling!"

He kept pounding on the locked door, growling, "We are far too past compensation, you brat! You're giving me all the money I'm owed, then you're leaving my inn! Now!"

The angry storm outside grew worse. Hissing angrily, the lynx innkeeper didn't cease rapping on the door or shoving his elbow against it. Between his strikes, I eyed the satchel beneath the bed and grabbed it, feeling the weight of my savings within.

"Open the door, or I'll have the city guard put you in the nearest asylum!" Jon hissed, "I've been getting complaints about ya talking to thin air, and now my guests are getting scared. I have been lenient because I felt sorry for you, but now you have the audacity to steal from me?!"

Panicking, I put the satchel along my back, fled for the closed window, then opened the shutters wide. My face wrinkled in disgust. The vapors belonging to months and possibly years of bodily waste wafted over my horns and into my nose as I leaned out the window. Putrid smells belonging to a sewer caused water to form in my eyes, but I dared not to let go of the railing. I recalled the months spent climbing trees in the woods and utilized the structure's uneven bricks to climb downward. Just as I heard the sounds of wood splintering, I dodged the middle-aged lynx's claws as they swiped at me from the window ledge.

"Come back, thief!" he hissed with bloodshot eyes. Whatever kindness had been there earlier ceased to exist. "You mad fool! I will have you rot for stealing from me! Come back up here, you damned goat!"

"Run, Baldram!" Arnolf's voice echoed from somewhere. "Reach the boat!"

Jumping from halfway up the wall onto the opening of the alleyway not filled with feces, I stumbled, then fled from the inn. Jon's rambling shouts caught the attention of a nearby city guard. One who didn't question circumstances or context.

Gripping the satchel for my life, I escaped the situation, running in the opposite direction of the inn. Everywhere, I felt people's eyes bore into me, much like that dreadful night in Spring. Some cursed me for bumping my shoulders into them, others paid no attention at all, while most stared at the odd goat fleeing through the crowds.

"Stop!" one of them shouted. "Stop that thief!"

A couple of paws tried and failed to grab me along the street. By some miracle though, a group of pilgrims appeared on the road. Many of them were sheep and goats, in a procession that exited De Oude Kerk parish church following a Friday mass. Ducking and weaving, apologizing and praising the Lord, I disappeared into Christ's flock and the city guard lost sight of me.

With nowhere else to go, I finally relented. Arnolf was right, as always.

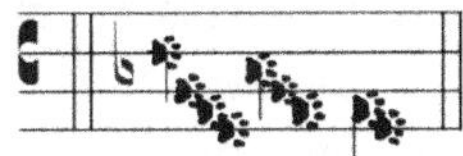

The shipyard contained very few...well, ships. Most were docked within the Amstel and only allowed to leave for fishing within the mouth of the IJ. The once vibrant and thriving area walled off with the rest of Amsterdam used to dock many merchant ships. As well as the Imperial Navy. I held not many memories of city life before the Plague reached Holland, but I heard stories from unemployed traders who frequented the tavern.

As I walked forward to the ship about to set sail, I felt my palms sweat against my satchel. All around me, random reflections and dirty puddles as well as polished armor plating contained him. He didn't speak, but simply watched. He mutely encouraged me to not slow my strides or turn away from the direction of the docked boat.

A wolf loading crates onto the English vessel noticed me approaching. He spoke to me in his native tongue, but I couldn't understand. Setting his crate on the ground, the gray wolf instead told me in broken German, "We do not take passengers."

Some part of me surmised he would refuse, but it didn't prevent me from fishing for the entire bag of coins in my satchel. I handed it to the curious wolf, who examined the purse's contents before tying it up. He then asked in poor German if I held knowledge of working on a ship, or if I knew how to climb.

I feverishly nodded to the second question.

Satisfied, the wolf motioned to the other crate, uttering something in English. Despite the language barrier, I guessed correctly that he wanted me to help bring the rest of the supplies aboard, and sighed in relief when the wolf didn't give an angry shout. Gripping the crate with both paws, I lifted it from the ground, then followed him up the walkway.

My heavy feet started to slow me down, but I did my best to ignore them. The wolf informed his crewmates about the additional hand joining them, and I carried the final crate along the walkway when I paused. Looking back at Amsterdam, to its imposing walls, the skyline, and to Holland beyond, I hesitated.

Arnolf appeared at the foot of the walkway. He smiled up at me, his clothes no longer bloody. Smiling back at the goat nobody else noticed, I gripped the bottom of the crate, then entered the schooner. I felt Arnolf follow closely behind me, then watch me from afar.

As the boat set sail from the docks, I continued feeling Arnolf's presence. Sometimes, he would take form in the reflection of a filled cup. Other times, I'd stare down at the ocean to catch glimpses of the goat standing at the bow of the ship. During which, the crew instructed me how to tie knots properly or assist in rigging. The language barrier didn't help, but I could understand just enough what to do, and none of them appeared to resent my presence.

At some point during sunset, I finished dining with the crew, and chose to venture on the deck. Arnolf was still there, smiling back at me, then returned to staring northward.

I slowly walked up beside him, whispering a hello. Underneath the wooden boards we stood on, I could still pick up slivers of laughter and drunken conversations from below the deck. All it took was an impulse of lust for me to lose him.

"I'm sorry."

He met my eyes. "For what?"

"For ignoring you." I shuddered, ashamed. "I'm sorry for trying to forget...forget you."

He leaned closer to me. "It is fine. I am just happy you are now safe."

We did not speak much. Arnolf and I did hold paws though, caressing our fingers together and silently appreciating the solitude. "Do you still wish for me to go?" he asked, not long before the Sun disappeared.

I sighed, looking out to the horizon with him. Behind us, the mainland vanished along with our pasts. All that could be seen ahead was a clear blue sky turning into purple hues.

"Never," I whispered.

The stars twinkled into appearance, one by one. They would all vanish the next morning, as would the Plague and the world's troubles, one day.

"I still miss you greatly, and one day, I wish for us to be together again."

"Not yet though," Arnolf replied, smiling at me. "Perhaps when you are old."

Offering my own brightened smile, I answered, "No, not yet."

Under the Empty Sky

J.S. Hawthorne

he day that Öljei died, the sky became empty to Min-seon. Nevertheless, she could not help but stop periodically and stare up into its vast expanse whenever her thoughts found their way to her wife, as though Öljei might be visible in the cloudy blue sky that she had so loved. For nineteen years, Min-seon had searched the empty, eternal sky, and seen nothing beyond the sun and moon.

And on that chilly spring day, the fox guided her father's old dray down the ramp from the boat she had taken nearly all the way from Huangzhou as she searched the empty, eternal sky. The cart hitched to the dray had begun this trip filled with her family's celadon pottery, but now the pottery was gone and replaced with what goods had caught her eye as she wended her way to Dàdū. After that, soon, blessedly, she would find her way across the sea and home to Buan, ready to sell the goods she had picked up over the past few months. Next year, she told herself, as she always said as the walls of the great palace of the Yuán Emperor came into view, she would hire someone else to make this trip. This land was too full of Öljei and too empty of Öljei for her to keep coming here, year after year.

And then she let her eyes rise, as they did every year, and look to the sky to the north, over the land from where Öljei and the Emperor had come, the great Steppe that Min-seon had never seen except in the stories that Öljei had told of her homeland.

The empty sky beyond the palace was filled with dark and ominous clouds. Distant lightning flashed, creating weird shapes in the storm. Min-seon squinted. She swore she could see something diving through the thunderhead, the way an eel darted through a kelp forest in search of prey.

"It's a dragon," came a soft voice from the other side of her dray. She followed it to its source, and found a water deer, not quite a teenager, huddled under a roll of heavily embroidered silk. He was covered in short, rough brown fur, gray at the tip of his muzzle and black at the tops of his broad, triangular ears. A dark circle of fur surrounded both of his eyes, a short line of black running, like tear tracks, down his nose. Most notable were the long canine teeth. They were not yet fully grown, reaching down barely past his chin. His eyes, Min-seon noted with some discomfort, were the exact same color of gold-brown that Öljei's had been. Their similarities began and ended in the same place, though. Öljei had been a dhole with tawny skin, short and broad.

Water deer were rare and rarer still since the Sòng Emperor, himself a member of that species, had committed suicide and his grandfather, the last of the Sòng dynasty, had joined a monastery in the distant south. Min-seon had been there, more than a decade before, at the last battle before the Emperor had reigned as undisputed ruler of all of China. She had entered the Emperor's service out of love for Öljei, and had stayed out of obligation to see her beloved's dream become reality. And then, she had put her bow aside and returned home to Goryeo.

"Who are you?" the boy asked, dragging Min-seon back from her remembrance of past campaigns.

"A merchant," she answered him. He raised an eyebrow at her accent, but did not comment on it. "I am Min-seon. Who are you?"

"Míngshuǐ," he said. It had the rote sound of an answer he had practiced. "Is this your dray?"

"My father's. You can pet him, if you want." The boy reached up to rub the creature's scaly, beak-like snout. The dray made a pleased sort of grunting noise and pressed his muzzle into Míngshuǐ's hand. "Where are your parents?"

Míngshuǐ shrugged. He seemed content enough to pet the dray.

"Why did you say it was a dragon?" Min-seon asked, after the silence had stretched for a moment.

"Because it was. You saw it," the boy replied. His attention did not shift from the dray. "They say dragons bring..." Míngshuǐ's voice trailed off and, as subtly as he could, which was not particularly subtly, he hid behind the dray. He lifted his muzzle just enough to peek over the beast's shoulder.

Min-seon followed his gaze and saw a group of Westerners emerging from an unremarkable building. There were a dozen or so in total, a hodge-podge of different creatures, most of which were types for which she had no name. Their leader was a fox, like her, with the same bright red fur, the same black markings on his ears and along his muzzle as she, the same broad, bushy tail. They were all dressed in identical black robes, marking them as clerics of some religious sect of which she had no experience.

And the boy was clearly hiding from them.

Min-seon stepped forward to block Míngshuǐ from their line of sight. They appeared to be arguing, the leader's teeth bared in a snarl as he barked orders at the others. Their expressions were a stone mask, their emotions carefully hidden. Finally, the fox finished his screed and pointed towards the city. Without a word, half of the pack turned and headed in the direction he had pointed. The rest fell into line behind him.

Min-seon stared a moment too long, and the other fox's eyes caught hers. His were a bright blue, like the empty sky, in contrast to her own deep black. Öljei had always told Min-seon that her eyes were the most beautiful the dhole had ever seen. She would have hated the fox's eyes.

He strode towards her with the purpose of a man who believes he is entitled to the world. His followers, still rocky-faced, followed at a more respectful distance.

"You!" he barked at her in a heavily accented version of Öljei's language. She startled, hearing the familiar sounds from so unfamilial a person, "Have you seen a boy, a deer boy? He would be this tall." He held his hand up to Míngshuǐ's height.

Min-seon feigned ignorance and answered in a dialect from the far south, "I am sorry, sir, I do not understand."

The foreign fox clucked his tongue and snapped his fingers under the chin of one of the other clerics, a horse with piebald fur and glacial eyes. He looked as though he had just taken a large bite of a particularly bitter lemon, and his expression only grew more sour at the fox's imperious command. They conversed for a moment in some far-off language, then the horse turned to Min-seon and offered her a perfunctory bow. The fox snapped something at the remainder of his troupe and then moved to interrogate the owner of the cart behind Min-seon.

"Our apologies for bothering you," the horse said in the same dialect she had used. His voice was honey. Had Min-seon not been put off by his leader, the horse's tones and politeness would likely have disposed her favorably to him. "His grace seeks a small boy, a deer, approximately this high." He held his hand up as the fox had. "It is an issue of some sensitivity to the Emperor. Have you seen him?"

Min-seon wavered. The fox was deeply unpleasant, but the horse seemed nice enough, and she had no wish to anger anyone working on behalf of the Imperial family. She knew that the Emperor had adopted a somewhat egalitarian stance towards foreigners, particularly clerics and priests, perhaps they did have a legitimate reason for hunting for Míngshuǐ. On the other hand, it was easy enough to claim the Emperor's authority.

Her hesitation caused a momentary ripple of annoyance to flash across the horse's face, there and gone so fast that she might have convinced herself she had imagined it had not so many other things already had her hackles up. She silently prayed that Míngshuǐ was making good his escape.

"I may have," Min-seon said, her voice filled with doubt and uncertainty. "Though you understand, the boat was moving very swiftly and I was only taking some air as we traveled, so it was only a glimpse. It was two... no... three villages back." She pointed south.

The irritation flashed again, and the horse took a long breath, his overlarge nostrils flaring as he struggled to control himself. "The boy his grace seeks would be in the city, I'm afraid." He offered her another bow. "Thank you for your time, miss. Should you see or hear anything of the child, please let us know. You may leave word with any of the Christian churches in the city, they will know who we are and how to find us." He hesitated, eyeing her with naked suspicion. "What are you selling, if I may ask?"

"I am afraid I'm not selling," she said, in perfect honesty. "My family makes pottery, but I sold the last of that some time ago."

"A large cart to be carrying nothing."

"Art from the lands in which I've traveled, mostly calligraphy." Min-seon lifted up the edge of the canvas draped over her cart, revealing a multitude of tightly rolled scrolls. "I was lucky to find a collector selling a number of works by Mǐ Fú, some others. Such works sell well back home."

"May I?" the horse asked, reaching for one of the scrolls without waiting for Min-seon's nod of assent. He unrolled a beautiful ink-wash landscape of the Great Canal, nearly half the length of the empire away. The horse seemed deeply moved by the scene, and stood, in silence, taking in its every detail. When he finished, he carefully rerolled the painting and handed it back to Min-seon, his actions filled with a kind of reverence.

Another bow, and then the horse stalked off without another word. Min-seon watched him go for a long while, before the noise and bustle of the city reminded her that she was obstructing traffic. She joined the queue to the nearest gate, and was not surprised to find Míngshuǐ popping up beside her as soon as the guard had permitted her to enter the city. The distant storm clouds remained at the horizon, an ominous bulwark in that empty northern sky, as the sun sunk ever slower, nearly grazing the tops of Dàdū's buildings.

"I feel like you are going to get me into trouble," Min-seon told the boy as they inched through the crowded city towards her favorite inn. The shadows were rapidly lengthening, and Min-seon was eager for a warm bed and a cold drink.

"Sorry," Míngshuǐ said, though he did not sound contrite. "And thank you."

"Why are they looking for you?"

"Don't know." The boy shrugged his narrow shoulders. "Don't want to find out, either." There was a finality to his tone that inclined Min-seon to drop the subject. After all, she told herself, eventually the boy would tire of the novelty of yet another merchant in Dàdū and wander back home.

There was a crack of thunder, and Míngshuǐ flinched and pressed a little closer to the wagon. Min-seon eyed the crowd around her, and then tugged her dray to the side, aiming for a dark alley running between two empty stalls.

"I don't think we should go that way," Míngshuǐ said, though he kept pace with the wagon.

"You don't have to follow me," Min-seon replied. "And this is the fastest way to get where I want to go before it starts raining." They cleared the crowd and passed into the alley. It was barely big enough for the wagon, but they were free to move at their own pace.

Min-seon led the way deeper into the city, farther away from the bustle of the main road, keeping to the empty alleys and side streets until they found themselves on a lonely avenue in the shadow of the palace. The sky had darkened to a deep steel grey, and flashes of light on the western horizon warned of incoming lightning.

"Are we almost there?" Míngshuǐ asked, peeking his head around the dray.

A nasty laugh preceded an equally nasty looking lynx as he stepped from a shadow-filled archway. He was burly, bulging muscles stretching the leather jerkin he wore, but his fur was patchy with mange and old scars. Across his shoulders he held a stout iron pole, its numerous dents speaking of long use and dark purposes.

"And where are you headed in such a hurry?" the lynx asked in Öljei's language. Min-seon felt her face flush at hearing her wife's language coming out of the brute's mouth.

"Two lost little lambs," came an answer in the same language from behind them. Min-seon turned to see a black-tailed gazelle, wearing the same leather outfit and carrying an identical iron pole, grinning the same grin as the lynx. The gazelle was missing her left eye, but the right one glittered with greed and menace. "Maybe they need some directions?"

"We'd be happy to show them on their way, wouldn't we?" said the lynx, his grin spreading. "For a small fee, of course. The boy has some silk he doesn't need, that might be a start."

The gazelle nodded in agreement. Min-seon chivvied Míngshuǐ behind her, blocking him from the thugs' sight.

The lynx took a step forward, hefting his pole like a club. The joke died on his lips as a sudden flash of lightning illuminated Míngshuǐ's face in the twilit gloom. He shot the gazelle a look of meaning.

"You think?" she asked. Her words became faster, less enunciated, designed to be harder for someone unused to the language to understand.

"They'll pay us a fortune if we bring him back," the lynx responded with a nod, speaking just as fast. He turned back to Min-seon and switched to the local dialect, though heavily accented. "It's your lucky day, merchant. You give us the boy and we'll see him carefully returned to his family." The gazelle snickered as she and the lynx advanced on Min-seon.

"I strongly advise you to move on," Min-seon told them in Öljei's language, her fingers curling into fists. She settled down into a subtle fighting stance, feeling the tension in her muscles as she prepared herself for a fight. "There's nothing for you."

"Oh, the shopkeep fancies herself a fighter," laughed the gazelle. "Maybe a broken bone will show her who she's dealing with!"

"Your mistake, merchant," the lynx told her, "This is your last chance to give us the boy."

Min-seon shook her head, and the lynx snarled as he rushed forward, swinging the iron pole downward, aiming for her knee. Min-seon took a single step, then brought her foot down on the pole long before it could be a danger to her. The pole snapped out of the lynx's hands and Min-seon kicked it up into the air. She caught it with the grace of an acrobat and, with expert precision, jammed its tip into the lynx, sending him spinning. She cracked the pole over his back and he went down into a heap.

Min-seon turned, bringing the pole up like a sword, and caught the gazelle's attack, whistling down on the fox's head, in a shower of sparks. Unlike the lynx, Min-seon could tell, the gazelle had had at least some training as a fighter, and their poles rang out like bells as they crossed and recrossed the empty street, locked in combat. The gazelle was taller and broader than Min-seon, and each of her strikes crashed with the force of a tidal wave. Min-seon did not try to absorb the attacks, but parried each blow so that it hummed through empty air or cracked nothing more than the stone of the streets beneath them.

Min-seon allowed the gazelle to push her back until she was nearly pressed up against her cart. Scenting an opening, the gazelle rushed forward, intending to flatten Min-seon. Min-seon ducked underneath the attack and brought her pole down on the small of the gazelle's back, just hard enough to throw off her stride. The gazelle tripped and hit the ground, rolling several times before coming to a stop. In an instant, Min-seon was upon her, kicking the gazelle's pole into a gutter before the attacker could react.

The gazelle looked up at the fox with smoldering anger in her eyes. One hand inched towards her waistband.

"Who is looking for the child?" Min-seon demanded. In response the gazelle yanked a knife free and tossed it wildly at Min-seon. The fox stepped easily out of its path, almost casually grazing the gazelle's head with the side of the pole. The thug went limp as she lost consciousness, a second knife slipping from nerveless fingers.

The sounds of marching echoed through the allies, though whether soldiers or robbers, or both, Min-seon did not know. She threw the pole away and dashed back to the dray and Míngshuǐ, and urged them both forward before they could be caught.

The two trotted through the streets of Dàdū in silence until they reached the warm glow of the tavern. The proprietor, Mr. Pān, was sweeping the step as Min-seon approached. Míngshuǐ melted back into the shadows of the cart, his head down and the silk pulled up to cover his burgeoning canines. Thunder rumbled around them, and the first patter of raindrops began to mist the inn.

"Ah, Miss Min-seon!" Mr. Pān said, a bright smile spreading across his round features. He was a tiger only in the sense that his fur was striped in black and orange. He was short and a little doughy, and as fierce as a caterpillar. He fancied himself something of a trend-setter, Min-seon knew, and his unfortunate choice of outfit that evening was an attempt to blend the fashions of the Emperor's northern homeland with traditional Han clothing. The result was a mishmash of clashing colors and incompatible styles, underneath a thick, overly embroidered coat with dense pleats at the waist and topped with a popular, but distinctly unflattering, twin-plaited hairstyle. He reminded Min-seon of a favored uncle—kindly, moderately useless, but a blessing in the world.

"I hope you might have space for me, Mr. Pān?"

"Of course, of course!" His voice was booming, more like a trumpeting elephant than a tiger's roar. "And for your..." He hesitated, taking in the boy still skulking in the shadows of the cart, curiosity burning in his dark, amber eyes. Mr. Pān had been a soldier himself, appearances to the contrary, and had known Öljei and Min-seon about the same time that Míngshuǐ would have been born.

"My companion," Min-seon said, as smoothly as she was able. It was a forceful reminder that she and Öljei had never had the opportunity to decide what family they wanted to have together. "And he can stay in my room for a night, just until we can reunite him with his parents." She put extra emphasis on the final two words, to make clear the answer to Mr. Pān's unspoken question.

"Of course, Miss Min-seon," Mr. Pān said with a bow that belied his size. "Might I offer you a dinner, and your companion, of course, we have several delicious meals tonight, including fresh cooked bāozi, or we've just begun making, from the Emperor's own recipe, as I understand it, a kind of small fried meat cake, very simple, but very fashionable..."

Min-seon offered a small smile to Mr. Pān as he rambled and pulled her along into the tavern, Míngshuǐ trailing in their wake. A swift nod from the innkeeper sent a couple of hands to stable her dray and lock up her cart.

"...And of course you must have some tea after your journey, luckily we took on a new shipment just yesterday, you'll never have fresher tea! Or if you would prefer something new, I had a merchant come all the way from the Ilkhanate who brought a strange, sweet drink, not unlike tea, but made with a variety of syrups that I could try to recreate for you..."

Min-seon cut the innkeeper off with a soft gesture. "We should be glad of whatever is ready to be served, Mr. Pān, and tea for the boy. A mug of äärag for me."

The tiger led the pair over to a table near the back stairs, a small frown on his lips. "Far be it for me to criticize the tastes of a customer, Miss Min-seon," he said, "but tea is a more healthful drink, and better for your constitution. Why, as Lù Yǔ instructs..."

"I am familiar with Master Lù's writing," Min-seon said, her smile taking the sting out of her words. "And I promise I shall drink all of the tea you can brew me whiling away my hours in your pleasant establishment but today, I would like a..." Her words trailed off as she took in the crowded tavern. Each table was filled, not with passing merchants, but uniformed soldiers, all relatively young. She felt Míngshuǐ hide himself behind her back. "Did you become a barracks since last year, Mr. Pān?"

"Hm? Oh!" He laughed heartily. "The Emperor has been spending more time in his capital, and so there are more retainers and soldiers in residence. My humble inn has become something of a favorite. I must say, at least some of that is due to you, Miss Min-seon."

"Me?" Min-seon asked, shock causing her hackles to raise slightly and her tail to lash at the ground behind her seat.

Mr. Pān had the decency to pretend to be embarrassed. "Indeed, yes. It seems someone may have let it be known that a certain hero likes to frequent this tavern whenever she might be passing through the city. When the word leaked out, it seemed that up-and-coming soldiers hoped to, ah, well, meet her." And, indeed, several of the soldiers were whispering to each other behind their hands, shooting glances at her table. Min-seon felt the relief she had been riding upon ever since coming within sight of the tavern fade away.

"Mr. Pān," she said reproachfully. The old innkeeper bowed deeply and pretended not to notice.

"I'll be back shortly with your food and äärag, and a pot of tea for the young master, of course."

Min-seon stewed as Mr. Pān vanished. Öljei would have roared in delight at this turn of events, would have teased Min-seon for days afterward, tail wagging broadly at the ridiculousness of it all. Min-seon could have handled it, had Öljei been at her side. She would have been embarrassed and rueful, but the dhole's presence would have been a fair enough trade for that. Now it was only Min-seon and the emptiness where Öljei had been, and it was unfair of Mr. Pān to make her face this alone.

"Are you really a hero?" asked Míngshuǐ.

"No," said Min-seon. "My wife and I fought in the war to unify the Empire, that's all."

"Oh." Míngshuǐ digested this for a moment as a waiter brought them a small plate of buns and meat cakes, and a pot of tea with two cups. Mr. Pān seemed to have disappeared entirely. "Where's your wife?"

Min-seon felt her stomach drop. "She died. It was a very long time ago."

"I'm sorry," Míngshuǐ said, managing to sound more convincing this time. "I think maybe my parents are, too."

"You don't know?"

The boy shook his head. "They sent me away when I was just a little kid to live with an old servant, Lìjìng, but she…" Emotion choked Míngshuǐ to silence, but Min-seon didn't need to hear his words to understand what happened. She poured him a tea and pushed the cup into his hands.

"And this?" she asked, touching the silk still draped over his shoulders.

"Lìjìng said it was my father's," he admitted, his voice soft. His voice was empty, and she understood that.

Before she could decide how to continue the discussion, three of the young soldiers marched up to her table. They were eager and nervous and simultaneously bold and obsequious as they presented themselves to her. Their leader was a pangolin, natural slate-grey scales covered in the red and black scale armor of the army. His eyes were kind and vaguely familiar to Min-seon, though she couldn't place him. Behind him, in identical armor, was a steppe fox, all pale-blonde fur and green-gold eyes, not at all unattractive, and a bronze-furred mountain lynx with eyes as deep and dark as a well. All three bowed courteously, as though she were some noble lady.

"Mistress Min-seon," the pangolin said, and his voice was familiar, too. "We hope we are not intruding."

"I was just about to have my dinner and then retire," she said cautiously. She considered sending them away, but curiosity, and a desire to postpone the conversation she dreaded having with Míngshuǐ, made her reconsider. "Do I know you from somewhere?"

He shook his head. "No, ma'am, but you knew my grandfather. I am Zhāng Hóngfǎ."

It all clicked together in an instant in Min-seon's mind. "Ah, you mean General Zhāng?"

Zhāng Hóngfǎ flashed a rueful smile. "Yes. Grandfather used to tell me stories about you." He looked a little embarrassed at the admission. "Not just you, you understand, but all of the soldiers he commanded, or the important ones, I mean. That is…"

Min-seon held up a hand to stop him before he dug himself a deeper hole. "I understand what you mean. I was sorry to hear of your grandfather's passing. He was a good man, and a great general." She waved the soldiers into seats and then called one of the servers over. "Please, a round of äärag. I believe Mr. Pān said my next glass would be free, and I'm sure he would be generous enough to extend that to my young friends. Could you ask him? I'm happy to discuss it, either way." It was an act of petty revenge, forcing Mr. Pān to choose between a few wén in free drinks or to subject himself to Min-seon's temper.

The äärag arrived, without the innkeeper, a moment later, and Min-seon passed a pleasant hour drinking and talking about the Sòng war with Zhāng and his friends. They were a good audience, listening attentively while Min-seon talked, and asking incisive questions about strategy and tactics. They were just as pleased to debate the finer points of old battles whenever Min-seon lapsed into contemplative silence. The äärag went quickly, and was followed by two more rounds before, by mutual assent, they switched to tea. Somewhere around the second plate of bāozi, Míngshuǐ nodded off against Min-seon's side. She tucked his silks around him like a blanket.

"Mistress," said the steppe fox, with the accent of the Chagatai Ulus. Her name was Pú Zànměi. "My apologies if I overstep, but, where did you find the boy?"

Min-seon scented danger in the question, and in the way the other two soldiers suddenly went silent, staring down into cups of tea. Pú's ears were erect, though Min-seon saw them tremble as the soldier fought to master her anxiety in the asking.

"He found me," she said, her tone guarded. She laid her hand on his side, feeling the gentle swell of his narrow chest as he breathed the slow and steady rhythm of untroubled sleep. "Why?"

"Forgive us, Mistress," said Zhāng. He rubbed at the plates of scales covering his narrow, pointed nose. "There have been some unsettling rumors of late, involving a lost grandson of the former emperor."

"It's likely nothing," said the lynx, Lǐ Yuèliàng. "In fact, the Emperor has forbidden anyone from acting on these rumors unless there is a clear danger."

"But it hasn't stopped some from hoping to curry favor with the Emperor by finding the boy," said Zhāng. "Er, not that this supposed child is the same as your boy, of course."

Lǐ muttered an echo of Zhāng's reassurance, but Pú looked unconvinced.

"What is it?" Min-seon asked her. Míngshuǐ mumbled something in his sleep and Min-seon became aware that she had tightened her arm around him.

"That silk, did you buy it for the boy?" When Min-seon shook her head, Pú continued. "Does it not have the imperial dragon on it?" The three soldiers craned their necks over the table to squint in the dim light at the sleeping deer. Min-seon herself couldn't resist peering a little closer. It was true that there were serpentine designs along the edge, though whether they were true dragons was difficult to tell with the way the cloth was folded tucked around the deer.

"Three claws," said Lǐ, with satisfaction. "Not a dragon."

Min-seon shook her head. "The symbol of the Sòng emperor was a three-clawed dragon. It was the current Emperor who chose a five-clawed design."

"So he is the grandson of Emperor Dùzōng?" Lǐ asked.

"Not necessarily," said Zhāng. "The old emperor sometimes gave away dragon-worked robes as honors to favored courtiers."

"I think the reality matters not so much as the perception," Pú said, her ears flattening and fangs exposed. All three of the soldiers turned stormy, echoed by a great peal of thunder and the sudden crash of the delayed rainstorm.

"What?" Min-seon prompted.

It was Zhāng who answered. "You know the Emperor's feelings towards worship?" Min-seon nodded. Öljei had told her that Chéngjísī Hán, the Emperor's great-grandfather, had decreed that all religions would be honored equally. The Emperor had followed his grandsire's lead, as had all the children and grandchildren of the Great Hán, and permitted free worship across the Empire. Min-seon was nominally Buddhist—as was the Emperor, to the best of her knowledge—but she was far from a devout worshipper. Öljei had been the believer, though her deity was the Eternal Blue Sky, as had been the Great Hán's.

"The Emperor's tolerance for other religions has created at least the perception of a power vacuum," Pú added. "Some believe they can gain the Emperor's ear and tilt him in their favor by capturing this last heir."

Lǐ shook his head, "It matters not a whit to them that the Emperor appears uninterested in their schemes. They are assured of the righteousness of their cause and expect all else to fall in place."

"I see," said Min-seon. "I believe I met some of them entering the city. Clerics in dark robes."

Lǐ made a soft ah of recognition. "Brother Mǎtiě."

"Mathé," Zhāng corrected.

Lǐ continued as though he hadn't been interrupted. "He leads a group of traveling priests who have been very vocal of late about their beliefs."

"They're not the worst, by far," Zhāng said in a philosophical tone of voice. He gazed towards the ceiling as he spoke, a slight frown on his muzzle. "There are many factions fighting for the Emperor's ear and custom. Those battles happen outside the sight of common soldiers such as we." The conversation lulled then shifted to the Emperor's failed attempts to conquer the islands to the east and whether a third invasion might be attempted.

It was another hour before the three soldiers said their goodbyes and, by then, Min-seon's thoughts were filled with nothing more than a desire for bed. She carried Míngshuǐ, still dozing, upstairs to the rooms that Mr. Pān had prepared for them.

It was a comfortable, if small, space, with a window that overlooked the city. The view was dominated by the Tower of Orderly Administration, a glorious red and green building that marked the center of Dàdū. The rest of the city was obscured by the pounding rain except in the occasional flash of lightning that lit up the buildings like a flare.

"What would you say, Öljei, my love, if you were here?" Min-seon muttered, staring into that tempestuous sky.

"She'd say close the window and go to sleep," Míngshuǐ grumbled, not opening his eyes.

Min-seon pulled the shutters closed with a faint smile. "Yes, I suppose she would."

The rain was still coming down when they awoke. It made a tattoo against the roof, and filled the streets with muddy puddles. Min-seon had Mr. Pān bring their breakfast to the room, and spent most of the morning writing short letters to facilitate her trip home. Míngshuǐ presented something of a problem. She was unwilling to abandon him to the mercies of whatever factions haunted the streets of Dàdū, and Mr. Pān, he told her in his roundabout way, was unwilling to take in a stray for any length of time. In the end, she arranged for the dray and most of the goods to be shipped across the sea to Goryeo, intending to extend her stay slightly until she found a place for the boy. She convinced Míngshuǐ to pack up his silk with the rest of her merchandise, with a promise that it would be safe. What she did not tell him was that the silk too easily marked him for Mathé and others to find.

Around midday, with no sign of the storm lessening, Min-seon took Míngshuǐ to the market. Without his silk, he looked more like a pauper than some lost Sòng heir. Their first stop was a clothier, who outfitted Míngshuǐ in a simple robe and jacket. It was fashionable, but not ostentatious and, most importantly, didn't stick out in a crowd. From there, they walked Min-seon's dray to the docks, where she had to show Míngshuǐ exactly where she was putting his silks, among the carefully packed scrolls of calligraphy.

She also took the opportunity to remove an old wooden case, its cover decorated in a motif of horses and tigers. Inside was a bow, handed down from great-grandfather to grandfather to mother and finally to her, not long before she had accepted an invitation to fight on behalf of the Yuán against the Sòng. Unstrung, in its protective box, it looked like a strange spiral of wood and horn. She showed it to Míngshuǐ when he asked, under an awning where it and the case would be safe from the rain, and strung it, turning it from spiral to sleek, sinuous line, deadly and powerful.

"Will you teach me to shoot it?" Míngshuǐ asked. Min-seon was taken aback at the question, but not displeased. She hadn't expected to be with the boy for an extended period of time, nor had she expected he would want to stay with her.

"If you'd like," she told him, thinking to herself that Öljei would have approved of the boy. She then led him into the city to get a lunch and seek information.

No one seemed to know anything about Míngshuǐ, or his parents. Lìjìng had been known to a handful of people, but the impression they had gotten from her was the dismissed maid of a minor noble family that had found themselves unable to pay her. That Lìjìng had been caring for a child was so far out of the realm of possibility that several of Min-seon's acquaintances laughed when she suggested it.

An hour after lunch, her inquiries began running ahead of her. Shopkeepers, couriers, and old soldiers were waiting for her, the answers to her questions on their lips before she could open her muzzle. Shortly after that, she found herself being asked questions by folks she didn't know, many wearing religious robes.

Through it all, Míngshuǐ trailed dutifully in her wake. Occasionally he would question her about something he had seen or ask if they could go into one shop or another. He never asked her to buy him anything, outside of a honey-sweetened treat at one point, but seemed content enough to just look. Min-seon got the impression he had not had much opportunity to wander Dàdū.

They had ducked into a small shop selling paper when she was approached by an old badger, extremely rare in this part of the Empire, wearing the dark robes of a Christian priest. He offered her an awkward bow and spoke to her in an accented but fluent local dialect, his rheumy eyes meeting her own in a way that made her uncomfortable.

"Peace, child. I am called Brother William. Might I have the honor of speaking with one Min-seon?"

"Yes, sir," she responded politely. Míngshuǐ looked up from the sample of red dyed paper he was examining, and she nodded to let him know she was alright. Even if this Brother William turned out to be a villain of some sort, Min-seon was confident she could escape his ancient clutches.

"Excellent, excellent. I have been looking for you for hours. My whole order has."

"How may I be of assistance?"

"Oh, no, child, it is my hope to be of assistance to you. You see, early this morning, we were approached by several... ah... how do you say it in your language?" He considered for a moment. "Traveling priests. They have been seeking you, by name, and attempted to enlist our aid to find you."

Min-seon scanned the tiny street outside the shop warily.

"They did not say why, but from rumors several of my brethren have heard today, I expect that they are looking for a boy." The priest's old eyes flashed briefly down to Míngshuǐ, who was tugging at the high collar of his new jacket, as though trying to disappear into it. "Unfortunately, my order are rather elderly and our eyes are not so good as they used to be." He chuckled at his own joke. "So, sadly, we have been unable to assist our traveling brothers."

"Why tell me this?" Min-seon asked.

"Because I do not believe my savior would approve of what these," he said a word she did not understand, "are seeking to do, and certainly not the methods they are employing to do so. We are commanded to act with love and compassion, and these..." The priest sighed. "I am sorry to burden you with our petty disagreements. I came only to warn you, and to offer you this." He held out a thin metal object.

At first, she thought it was a simple copper coin, but the weight was off. It was certainly shaped like a coin, round with a square hole in the center, and covered with strange writing on one side, and the animals of the zodiac on the reverse. Min-seon had never learned to read the thousands of Han characters used by scholars in the Empire beyond a handful of common ones, but to her the characters on the strange coin did not seem to be the same script. Related, perhaps, but definitely different.

"Some kind of Western magic?" she asked, a touch of skepticism tinting her words.

William chuckled again. "Far from it. A Daoist monk gave it as payment for a service one of my order performed for him, and she, in turn, wishes it to go to you. I am told it is a charm that invokes a great spirit of lightning to banish evil. My sister swears by its power." He shrugged. "It is not our way to turn to the supernatural for protection, outside of the arms of our Lord, but I would not gainsay the word of a member of my order."

Min-seon examined the coin in her left palm. Perhaps it was her imagination, but she felt a creeping kind of electricity rolling down the nerves of her hand and into her arm.

"Oh," said Brother William, pointing at her wrist. "Perhaps there's something to it after all." When she gave him a quizzical look, he pulled her other hand up so she could see both limbs side by side. The fur on her left arm, from finger tips to the elbow, was standing on end, while the fur on her other arm was groomed as flat as when she had left the inn that morning.

"Ah, one last thing. I have spoken with a magistrate in the Ministry of Justice, a friend of mine. Rumors abound, of course, about the lost heir of the Sòng, and I thought perhaps to convince the Emperor to stop this foolish hunt. Well, it seems that the Emperor already held a convocation in the palace to decree that there should be no reward or favor bestowed on any who present him with any supposed descendants of the former emperor." Brother William gave her a strange smile and bowed again in his awkward way, before hobbling out of the store.

"Is it really magic, do you think?" asked Míngshuǐ, peeking around her at the coin.

Min-seon handed it to him, then attempted to smooth her fur down, feigning disinterest. "Foreign nonsense," she told him with more conviction than she felt. Her thoughts drifted towards the monk's parting words, and a foreboding shiver made her hackles rise. "I think we should head back to the inn for now."

"Alright," said Míngshuǐ. He was staring out at the dark clouds that filled the sky. "But I think the dragon is back."

They fell upon Min-seon and Míngshuǐ in a dark alley only two streets over from Mr. Pān's inn, just as the storm kicked up in earnest again. There were three of them: a tiger, his chest bare and his muzzle covered with a dark rag; a horse with a sleek and shimmering coat; and a bear so thoroughly covered in bandages from their head to their paws that Min-seon wasn't even sure the color of their fur. They had thick staves which they held with the easy posture of those accustomed to their use in violence, and the tiger had a scimitar strapped to his back.

"Give us the boy and leave the city," the bear said in a deep growl. Their accent was from the far western plains of the Golden Horde.

"Stay behind me," Min-seon told Míngshuǐ, "and get my bow out."

The trio advanced on Min-seon as a unit, professionals who had clearly trained together. These were not simple robbers attempting to take advantage of what they saw as weak prey, but warriors. Min-seon raised her fists and crouched slightly, trying to keep an eye on all three at once as they circled.

Nearly too late, she realized that the tiger and bear were merely a distraction while the horse attempted to grab Míngshuǐ.

"Run," she yelled, ducking under the spinning staves, barely more than a dark blur in the rain. Míngshuǐ glanced up from where he was struggling with the case housing Min-seon's bow and caught sight of the horse bearing down on him. With a cry, the deer tossed the case to Min-seon, then sprinted off down the alley. The horse shouted something in what Min-seon took to be Kipchak, and hurried after Míngshuǐ.

Min-seon caught the ancient case and used it to block an overhand blow by the bear. The case groaned under the force of the blow, and she prayed that the bow was undamaged inside. She brandished the case like a shield, fending off strike after strike from the bear, until the tiger struck the back of her knee with his own staff, sending her tumbling to the wet and muddy ground, the case and her bow skidding off into the darkness.

She had no time to worry for it, however, as she twisted and rolled out of the way of the staves that crashed down on the stone hard enough to send up sparks that briefly illuminated the darkness. Neither Míngshuǐ nor the horse were in sight. Min-seon spared a glance to the storm-thick sky and whispered a prayer to Öljei to watch out for the deer.

Min-seon rolled away from the bear to avoid being impaled on their staff, and found herself staring up at the tiger. He grinned down at her, staff raised high. Before he could bring it down on her, she hooked her foot around his thigh and yanked. With an undignified squeal, he fell backwards, while Min-seon used his own momentum to pull her upright. She somersaulted past the tiger, grabbing the handle of his scimitar as she rolled and pulling it from its scabbard.

Turning to face the two attackers, scimitar in hand, Min-Seon offered a grim smile. The bear and tiger glanced at each other, then split, rushing to attack her from two sides simultaneously. Min-seon stepped into the bear's swing, deflecting the staff over head with the scimitar. She ducked down and kicked the bear in the solar plexus, then spun and brought her leg down in an axe kick on the small of their back, pushing them forward into the path of the tiger's own strike. He pulled back at the last minute to avoid hurting his compatriot, dodging around the bear while they buckled backwards in a synchronous movement so fluid that it almost seemed as though they had rehearsed it.

The tiger stabbed at her with the staff, forcing her to parry blow after blow in rapid succession. He clearly intended to keep her on the defensive long enough for the bear to recover and resume their two-pronged assault. Meanwhile, the horse was still on Míngshuǐ's trail, if he hadn't already found the boy.

The staves had too much reach for her to reach the two attackers with her stolen scimitar, and it would do her little good to continue to parry and dodge forever. Min-seon desperately wished for her bow.

A flash of lightning threw the alley into sharp relief, followed by a rumble of thunder loud enough to rattle windows. There was a great shape in the sky, hovering above a building several blocks away, but Min-seon's attention was drawn by a glimpse of orange and brown nearby. The bear was slowly getting to their feet, and the tiger was starting to shuffle sideways to hem Min-seon in against a wall before dispatching her.

She flung the scimitar into his face, causing the tiger to yelp and duck out of the way. While his attention was divided, she turned and ran into the darkness. The bear shouted after her, and both of the assailants were soon on her tail. Min-seon nearly tripped over the case, mercifully undamaged from its use as a make-shift shield. She scooped it up and made an abrupt turn into a maze of narrow alleys running between several stalls. With practiced grace, she retrieved her bow and strung it, barely breaking her stride. She could hear the tiger and bear yelling back and forth as they searched for her.

Min-seon skidded to a halt next to a small garden and raised her bow, too late realizing that she had never thought to purchase any arrows. She cast about desperately, but the only thing remotely appropriate were the garden's tall plant stakes.

"There she is," growled the bear, coming into view. Min-seon pivoted to run again, only to see the tiger emerge from the darkness, scimitar in hand and a nasty look on his face.

"No escape this time," he told her.

Without thought, Min-seon grabbed two of the stakes, shaking the creeping snow pea vines loose. The robbers laughed at her as she nocked one of the stakes as best as she could. She let them saunter close until they were only a few paces away, then loosed her makeshift arrow. It hit the bear between the eyes, snapping their head back and sending them crashing to the ground. Min-seon turned to catch the downward strike of the tiger's saber on the curve of her bow, turning it, and him, away from her. She followed with several swift punches to his back and sides, forcing him to skip away. While he tried to reorient himself, she used the stake like a switch, hitting him along the back and ribs. He covered his face and she drove the end of her bow into his sternum, knocking the wind out of him. As he doubled over, Min-seon swung upward with the bow and knocked him off his feet to crash next to the bear, both of them unconscious.

She stood over them for a long moment, catching her breath, before she remembered Míngshuǐ. With a curse, bow in hand, she ran back into the darkness.

The sound of Míngshuǐ's hooves echoed against the stone streets, mirrored by those of the horse close behind him. He turned at random down the narrow alleys, guided by instinct and the brief flashes of lightning that split the sky. His hooves struggled to find solid purchase against the slick stone and more than once he nearly lost his footing. His only hope was that the horse was finding it equally hard to run through the darkness.

Míngshuǐ rounded a corner and found himself in a large, empty square. Another flash lit the city and revealed, twisting amidst the clouds, the dragon for a brief instant. He stared open-mouthed at the dark sky, blinking rapidly to clear the afterimage of the lightning from his vision, trying to see it again.

The horse's hand clamped down like an iron vice on Míngshuǐ's shoulder, and then the horse was shoving him against a wall while his other hand pulled a long, sturdy rope from his pack. Míngshuǐ struggled but the horse was simply too strong for him.

"Hold still," the horse snarled. His breath was sickly sweet. "You're lucky I'm being paid to keep you alive, but that only goes as long as the money is worth the trouble, boy."

Míngshuǐ swallowed hard, but stopped struggling as the horse spun him around, shoving his face against the rough wooden wall. His arm was wrenched upward and the horse began to tie the rope around his wrist. He shoved his free hand into his pocket, as much to delay being bound as in the vain hope of finding something to help him escape.

His fingers brushed against the strange coin that the foreign monk had given Min-seon. The fur along his arm stood on end as he touched it, and his fingers tingled as he wrapped the coin up in his fist.

Míngshuǐ thought of the dragon, twining across the sky, filling the sky with lightning and thunder.

"Please," he murmured, squeezing the little coin.

A sound like a roar split the air and the tingling sensation spread, like tens of thousands of needles, across his whole body. The horse gave a horrid yelp and jumped back, shaking his hands where they had been holding Míngshuǐ.

"You little wretch," he growled, pulling a knife from under his shirt. It was a wicked looking thing, long and narrow, its edge gleaming even in the darkness of the storm-rent night.

Míngshuǐ, for the second time, turned and ran into the rain. He could hear the horse chasing after him and imagined the dagger slashing at his back. He didn't dare check to see how close the horse was getting. Instead, his gaze raked the heavens, searching for deliverance in a sky full of menace.

A ladder, leaning against a stout building, caught his eye and he swerved towards it. He felt a faint tug as the horse caught his jacket briefly, and then Míngshuǐ was leaping towards the ladder. As though demons were following him, he climbed as quickly as he could until he reached the sloped edge of the roof. He scrambled onto the roof, inadvertently kicking the ladder behind him. It landed with a clatter on the stone street below, followed by the horse's loud cursing.

The sloping sides of the roof ended in a flat plateau, and it only took Míngshuǐ a moment to reach its relative stability. He kept low as he inched to the far edge of the plateau, then slipped down onto the far slope. He kept just his head above the roof's apex, watching for the horse.

Without warning, the wind and thunder died, leaving nothing but the rhythmic percussion of rain on stone and slate. The relative silence was broken by the loud crack of the wooden ladder hitting a roof. Míngshuǐ tensed, ready to slide down and jump to the street below. He squeezed the odd coin in his hand and whispered a silent prayer to whatever god or spirit had blessed him so far that night.

A flash of blue-white lightning split the air and, to Míngshuǐ's amazement, he saw the ladder against a building across the narrow alleyway, the horse climbing unsteadily to the distant roof. Uncertain and unsteady, the horse inched across the far building, his back to Míngshuǐ the entire time.

Míngshuǐ slid quietly down to the gutter and then leapt to the stones below. He landed heavily just as the wind picked up once more, the sound of his landing masked by the howling storm. With one last glance towards the rooftops, Míngshuǐ dashed into the cold and empty streets.

Min-seon searched the whole night without any sign of Míngshuǐ or the horse. She returned, soaked to her bones and exhausted beyond words, to Mr. Pān's inn as the first rays of dawn broke, briefly, through the heavy cloud cover. Inside, she found Mr. Pān, wringing his hands with nervousness, huddled with the three soldiers. They looked up at one as she entered, and relief washed over them.

"Are you alright?" Zhāng asked, rushing forward. She held up a hand to forestall him.

"Is Míngshuǐ back?"

"The boy?" asked Mr. Pān. Min-seon worried he might snap his own fingers off with the force of his handwringing. "No, he hasn't come in. What happened?"

Min-seon summed up the attack, becoming separated from Míngshuǐ, and then searching for him through the night.

"We'll find him, Mistress," promised Pú. "If any have seen him in the city since last night, we will know." She beckoned to Lǐ, and the two made for the door.

"Mr. Pān," Min-seon turned to the innkeeper. "I need you to find me some arrows, as quickly as possible." The innkeeper bowed and was gone. "Zhāng, I don't think they want to turn Míngshuǐ over to the Emperor. There's something else going on. Can you go and..."

Her sentence trailed off as the door slammed open. A hush fell over the crowd like a wave washing outward from the storm outside. The patrons fell back, revealing Brother Mathé and two of his subordinates. One, the piebald horse that had questioned Min-seon previously, stood to Mathé's left, an ornate scroll case in his arms. To Mathé's right was a burly grey wolf, her yellow eyes ablaze with hatred. All three carried long swords with ornate hilts at their hips, wildly incongruous to their religious robes.

"You understand me?" Mathé asked in the Han language, stopping no more than a pace from Min-seon. She nodded. "Good. I want the boy. Bring him to my ship by noon."

"Why should I?"

The horse cleared his throat and removed the scroll from its case. He unrolled the first part to reveal a poem, written in elegant calligraphy. Min-seon couldn't read it, but she recognized it as one of the many she had purchased on her travels. She stared at it for a long moment, then turned her gaze on Mathé.

"The boy, or a small fortune in painting and poetry burns," the foreign fox said, a nasty smirk on his lips.

"You presume that some trinkets are worth more to me than a boy's life?"

"If I may, your grace?" said the horse smoothly. Brother Mathé nodded and the horse stepped forward. "As I said in our earlier conversation, miss, our errand is on behalf of the Emperor himself. It is not just your material goods at risk for this boy, but your very freedom. I am *very* sorry it has come to this, but we must insist. For the good of the Empire." He flashed her a bright and winning smile, a picture of triumph.

"How dare you," Min-seon said, her voice dripping venom. She stepped forward, ready to punch the smile off the horse's lips. In a movement so fast she scarcely had time to register it, Brother Mathé had drawn his sword and swung it so that its tip stopped a hairsbreadth from her throat.

"Brother Milvio speaks only the true nature of your position," said Mathé. His voice was as calm and lifeless as a glacier. The sword was equally steady, longer than Min-seon was used to, with a triangular blade thick near the handle and wickedly pointed at the tip. Combined with the gold-worked hilt, it was a strange but elegant weapon, except that someone had inexpertly cut out a large section of the blade near the base and used wire to fill the resultant hole with a length of ancient, rusted iron. It radiated malice.

They were as still as statues until the door banged open and Mr. Pān entered, his arms laden with arrows. He skidded to a halt, gawping, open-mouthed, at the sword Mathé had pointed at Min-seon's neck.

Mathé followed the old tiger's stare. "A pagan thing," he told them, "The remnants of a dagger used in a deadly trap for the heir to Rome itself." He sheathed the sword with a flourish. "That is the secret of my order, we repurpose the dangers of the past to fight against encroaching heathenism. The boy, by noon." And with that, he turned and led the other two out of the inn, leaving the crowd quiet as the grave.

"Zhāng," Mr. Pān said, shattering the silence. "Go to the Palace, find a way to inform the Emperor." The old tiger turned to see Zhāng standing still, rubbing his armored muzzle with a paw. "Now, lad, go!" With a start, the pangolin fled.

"What will you do, Miss Min-Seon?" asked one of the soldiers in the crowd.

"There's nothing to do," she said, with a pang of regret for the lost art. "As soon as I find Míngshuǐ, we'll leave the city. We should be safe once we're home."

"I hesitate to mention this," said Mr. Pān. His face was creased with worry. "While I doubt they have sway with the Emperor himself, I think they must have some favor in the government to make threats like that. And if they have a patron highly enough placed, even Goryeo won't be safe for you."

Min-seon was spared the necessity of answering by a sudden cry from the doorway. Míngshuǐ, dripping wet, his new clothes slathered with mud, was flanked by Lǐ and Pú. He ran forward and threw himself around Min-seon. She hesitated for a moment, then hugged him back. Their embrace lasted long enough for Mr. Pān to tell Lǐ and Pú what had happened.

"Are you alright?" Min-seon asked Míngshuǐ. He nodded, then pressed something into her hand. She looked down to see the strange coin the monk had given her the day before.

"It really works," he said, quietly so that only she could hear. "It saved me. It can help you, too." She gave him a quizzical look, but stuck the coin into her pocket.

"We have to leave," she told him, "To keep you safe. If you're willing to come with me?" He nodded at her, his eyes bright, trusting.

Unbidden, she thought of Öljei, of what her dhole would have thought about Min-seon's choices. She realized, with considerable surprise, that in that moment, it was Míngshuǐ that mattered to her more than Öljei. Not that she did not miss her wife, nor did she suddenly feel that emptiness that Öljei had left in her any less keenly, but that living, breathing Míngshuǐ required her more than the shade of Öljei. She thought that Öljei would understand.

"Mr. Pān is right," Lǐ said, kneeling down next to Min-seon and Míngshuǐ. "You have to resolve this fight first, or they will hound you to the ends of the earth."

"But you won't be alone," added Pú. She slammed her fist into her palm, pointed muzzle open in an eager smile. "We'll be right beside you. And Zhāng, too, when he returns."

"I can't ask that of you," she said.

"You didn't ask," Lǐ said.

"We offered," added Pú.

Min-seon didn't want to waste time arguing. "In that case, go down to the canal and look around. I want to know what I'm up against before getting into a fight. I'll meet you there shortly. Mr. Pān, will you watch Míngshuǐ?"

"I want to go with you!" the deer protested. She shook her head at him.

"We have to keep you out of their clutches." Min-seon put her hands on Míngshuǐ's shoulders and looked him in the eyes. "I promise I'll do everything I can to make sure that you and I can leave here together, in safety and in peace. I need you to promise me that you'll stay safe, though."

Míngshuǐ hesitated, then finally nodded. "I promise."

"Then stay with Mr. Pān. I'll take care of everything." She gave him a hug and tried not to wonder if it would be their last one, so soon after their first, then stood. "Mr. Pān, do you have a quiver?"

Min-seon, her bow strung and at the ready, found Lǐ and Pú waiting for her at the docks. The rain had not stopped, but it threatened to, and what had been a downpour was now little more than a drizzle. The temperature had warmed slightly, too, resulting in a thin fog that roiled around the canal. Now and then, Min-seon caught a glimpse of sunlight peeking through the clouds.

Pú pointed out the barge Brother Mathé's monks were occupying, but Min-seon hadn't needed it. She recognized it as the ship she had booked to take her wagon and its cargo back to Goryeo. Whether it had been seized or its captain had been convinced to turn it over, she did not know. It was docked not far away, a dozen figures in dark robes standing silently atop it. Min-seon could not see Mathé, but Milvio strutted up and down the deck, shouting orders at the others. A handful of wagons, her own included and still hitched to her dray, were arranged on its deck, a simple oil cloth draped over them against the rain and mist.

"A few of their number patrol the docks every few minutes," Lǐ told her as they did their best to hide in the milling crowds. "Our time is not unlimited. What is your plan, mistress?"

Min-seon brushed a hand over the quiver of arrows at her hip, then the strange coin tied to it with a spare bowstring. It almost seemed to jump as her fingers got close.

"We go for the head," she told them. "Find Mathé and end this. Without him, they will be scattered and disorganized, and Míngshuǐ and I can make our escape without fear."

"We haven't seen him," said Pú.

"I know how to draw him out," said Min-seon with a grim smile. "When the crowd splits, head for the barge."

Lǐ and Pú exchanged a confused look, but Min-seon tuned them out. She drew an arrow and nocked it in one smooth, practiced motion. Excited murmurings spread through the crowd, which swiftly became a panic as she loosed the arrow. It whistled through the air and pierced Milvio's shoulder. It went clean through and buried itself in the wooden deck as the horse, knocked off-balance, tripped and fell into the canal with a splash. A scream from the onlookers shattered the morning and the crowd was soon running for cover.

Min-seon casually nocked another arrow, striding through the panic as though she were the wind. She let loose and one of the guards collapsed, clutching his now-wounded knee. A third arrow followed close behind, and slammed into the broad triangular shield that her target raised at the last minute. The other guards were tossing their robes aside to reveal metal armor made of thousands of interconnected rings. Complicated, expensive, and, Min-seon thought, utterly useless before her arrows. She leapt to a boat inching down the canal, ignoring the protests of the crew, and then to a faster ship with a tall prow. Climbing to the bow, she stood on the railing, firing arrows down onto the barge as the ship bore her along.

The guards had recovered from their initial shock to gather in a tight formation along the side of their barge, several holding up those heavy shields to protect them from her arrows. Two had produced crossbows and were firing back up at her. They were slow, however, and not as skilled as she. Min-seon shot the crossbow bolts out of the sky long before they became a threat to her, though at the cost of slowing her own attacks significantly.

She could see, running along the docks amidst the thinning crowd, Lǐ and Pú. Pú had in her fist a long, slightly curved cavalry saber, more than half her own height in length, while Lǐ carried a heavy metal hand-cannon on a long wooden pole. Brother Mathé was still nowhere to be seen.

Min-seon waited until her commandeered ship was level with the monks' barge, then leapt straight down. One of the guards popped up and took aim with his crossbow, and she fired an arrow down the muzzle, snapping bolt, string, and stock before it pierced the guard's hand. The others ducked beneath the shield phalanx.

She landed hard on two of the shields, knocking all of the warriors to the deck. Min-seon somersaulted free, narrowly dodging an awkward swipe from one of the strange, triangular swords. She spun in place and caught one of the guards, too slow to get his shield up, in the hip, then knocked him unconscious with a well-placed kick. Another, a burly elk with sheets of iron protecting his antlers, rushed her.

She dodged back, ducking under and along his slashing sword. He raised his weapon high and she dashed under his arm, slamming one end of her bow against his helmet and leaving him senseless on the ground.

A crossbow bolt narrowly missed her throat, shearing off a hunk of her fur, and she shot an arrow in the finger-width gap between two shields, shattering the enemy archer's wrist.

The remaining fighters closed on her, forcing Min-seon back, threatening to box her in against the prow of the ship. She fired shot after shot, turning the shields into a mess of quivering arrow hafts, but she was unable to find a break in their defenses. One of the guards swung low and she misjudged the attack, taking a long, deep cut to her thigh that forced her to one knee.

"Mistress!" came a shout from behind the guards, followed by a boom of thunder that made Min-seon's ears ring. A huge chunk of the deck was simply missing, and a black, noxious cloud floated over the barge. As it cleared, Min-seon saw most of the guards scattered, two down and clutching grievous wounds, while Lǐ stood reloading his still-smoking hand-canon. Pú stood in front of him, defending him with her long saber, the steppe fox's fangs bared. The guard closest to Min-seon took a look down at her injured comrades, then pulled off her helmet, revealing the face of the one-eyed gazelle that had accosted Min-Seon and Míngshuǐ on their first day in the city. With a sneer, the gazelle leapt into the water and swam for the far shore.

Chaos reigned on deck, the other guards attempting to flee or regroup as Lǐ leveled his cannon once again. The lynx braced himself to fire, and did not hear the door opening behind him, disgorging three new attackers—not wearing armor, but the same outfits that they had the night before when they had separated Min-seon from Míngshuǐ. She shouted a warning but too late—the horse with the shimmering pelt slammed his shoulder into Lǐ's back, sending him flying. His hand-cannon belching another cloud of black smoke and destroyed a second large segment of the deck. The barge lurched, its inner hull clearly breached. The sudden shift snapped one of the mooring ropes, and it began to swing out towards the center of the canal.

"Min-seon!" came a shout from the shore, and she chanced a quick glimpse over her shoulder to see Míngshuǐ, followed by a panting, out-of-breath Mr. Pān. Before she could react, Míngshuǐ had leapt onto the barge and was pulling on the reins of Min-seon's dray.

"Miss Min-seon," wailed Mr. Pān as he slid to a halt at the edge of the dock. "He ran off as soon as my back was turned! I-I couldn't stop him!"

"Never mind that," Min-seon shouted back, leaping over the holes in the deck and racing towards Míngshuǐ. The barge was listing dangerously and she found herself running uphill, dodging unsecured cargo as it tumbled past and into the water. "Míngshuǐ! Get back!"

"I'm going to help!" the boy cried defiantly. He managed to untie the dray's halter and had it plodding, cart still attached, slowly towards the dock.

And then the bandage-wrapped bear was in front of her, a scimitar in each of their paws. Min-seon ducked under a slash and attempted to dodge past the bear, but found her way blocked by the spinning blades. She drew back an arrow but the bear lunged and shattered the missile before she could release it.

"Mistress, here!" called Lǐ, stepping in front of her. His handcannon was whirling around his head as though it weighed nothing. He brought it crashing down with tremendous force. The bear parried it, but the weight of the cannon shattered their scimitar, sending hot shards of metal in every direction.

Min-seon slipped past the two and caught a glimpse of the horse crossing swords with Lǐ, both moving with a terrible grace as they seemed to almost dance across the deck, sliding between the two massive holes with easy steps, as though they were on solid ground instead of a listing, sinking ship.

Míngshuǐ had just gotten the dray over the gangplank and into Mr. Pān's hands when Min-seon broke free of the fighting. Too late she saw the third of the attackers, the burly tiger, wrap his arms around Míngshuǐ and heft the deer bodily off the deck as though he were no more than a sack of potatoes.

"This was a mistake, child," came a low and dangerous voice. Brother Mathé stepped from the shadows, his sword with its iron contamination held in a ready position. His posture and the liquid way he moved over the tilting, twisting ship proved that he was no stranger to combat. "This is your last chance to leave. If you choose to fight over this boy, then neither of you, nor that fat innkeep or your friends, leave here alive."

Lǐ slammed his cannon into the bear's stomach, sending them sailing off of the barge, then turned and rushed towards Mathé, hissing. With hardly a glance towards the lynx, Mathé sidestepped the hand cannon and brought his sword up. It was so fluid that Min-seon barely saw the point of impact. Lǐ let out a soft howl of pain and then collapsed to the deck. The wound was superficial, barely more than a scratch over his bicep, but it seemed to have drained all of the life from him.

Mathé whipped the sword around and faced Min-seon, his eyes boring into hers, a wordless challenge written across his face.

Min-seon lifted her bow and drew an arrow, then spun at the last minute and placed the arrow in the tiger's shoulder. He snarled in rage and tipped backwards over the ship's railing, still clinging to Míngshuǐ.

"Foolish," Mathé growled, closing the distance between him and her in an instant, his sword whistling through the air as he struck a half-dozen times in the space of a breath. She ducked and parried with her bow, knocking his sword away each time. Too late she saw his feet move as, at the apex of her last parry, he kicked her hard in the stomach, knocking the breath out of her. He spun, ready to bring his knee into her face, and she brought her bow down on his thigh at the last minute, deflecting the strike and forcing him back.

In the space he left her, she drew an arrow and fired, only to see him slice it out of the air as if swatting a fly. He was back on her in an instant, sword singing as he tested her defenses. The barge jumped as part of it broke off, knocking her off her feet, and Mathé leapt forward to deliver the final blow.

Zhāng Hóngfǎ dropped down from the dock, his head tucked down as he landed between the two. Mathé's sword rang out as it struck and bounced off Zhāng's scales, both natural and artificial.

The pangolin nodded at Min-seon, then spun, bringing up his own weapon, a flexible wooden spear, batting away Mathé's attack and forcing the monk back out of range.

"Go, get Míngshuǐ," Zhāng told her. "I have this."

Min-seon took off at a run, leaping over the prow of the sinking barge and landing on a double-masted junk. The bear was dragging a struggling Míngshuǐ to the side of the ship. Another boat was pulling alongside the junk, its deck crammed with dark-robed monks reaching down to take Míngshuǐ from the tiger.

Min-seon checked her quiver—she was down to her last three arrows. She drew one and fired, catching the tiger in the thigh and knocking him off-balance. He seized Míngshuǐ by the cuff and looked ready to toss the boy to the waiting arms of the monks. Míngshuǐ kicked out as hard as he could until he managed to pull free, his coat ripping loudly.

"To the shore!" Min-seon yelled at him, before her attention was drawn to the loud thud of Zhāng landing on the deck behind her. He had a thin gash on his cheek, but looked half alive, his breathing labored and his body unmoving.

Mathé jumped from the barge and landed lightly on his feet, sword in his hand, steel tip flecked with Zhāng's blood. He had barely touched down before he raised the sword and, in terrible silence, dashed forward.

Min-seon caught the sword in the curve of her bow and redirecting its force harmlessly to the side. She was prepared for Mathé's follow-up strike and blocked his kick on her forearm, then returned the attack. He ducked under her kick and then blocked her punches before slashing at her throat and stomach, forcing her to jump back.

"The coin!" Míngshuǐ shouted from the dock where Mr. Pān was helping him onto his feet. "Min-seon, use the coin!"

She snatched the strange coin from where it still dangled from her quiver, and felt electricity shoot up her arm. Mathé thrust at her and, in reflex, forgetting the evil magic of the iron shard, she punched the flat of the sword. To her amazement, a blazing shield of purple lightning sprung up between her hand and the sword, protecting her from its vile touch. Snarling, Mathé swung at her and she ducked inside of his swing, catching him in the chin with an uppercut that cracked like thunder.

Mathé spun backwards and Min-seon drew her second-to-last arrow. Mathé caught the arrow in mid-air with his sword. Where blade and arrowhead met was a sound like the earth cracking, and a release of energy like a bolt of lightning that shot upward, burning away the last of the clouds, revealing a bright blue sky framing the late morning sun.

Mathé was running at Min-seon, sword held to strike. She slipped the coin around her last arrow, then knocked it. The monk was less than two paces away when she fired. He raised his sword to block and the arrow hit the blade in the center of the twisted iron sliver. The whole world seemed to stop and shudder, and then Mathé's sword exploded into a thousand shards, blowing him backwards off of the ship.

A great rumbling grew from the depths of the canal and, before Mathé landed, a dragon more than a lǐ long breached the water. With a roar it snatched Mathé out of the air and then dove back beneath the waves, leaving little more than a ripple behind it.

Arms, strong but gentle, grabbed her by her arm and led her back to the dock, but Min-seon had eyes for no one but Míngshuǐ. He rushed towards her as soon as she reached dry land and she hugged him tightly.

Two hours later, Min-seon and Míngshuǐ were led into the richly appointed throne room of the Imperial Palace. The Emperor himself, a horse as wide as Mr. Pān, his greying mane looking much more elegant in two braids than the innkeeper, lounged on the throne, looking down on Min-seon with interest as he stroked a beard that had significantly more white in it than the last time Min-seon had seen him. Around him were a number of courtiers and ministers, including a dhole that Min-seon recognized as a distant cousin of Öljei. He smiled at her and gave an encouraging nod. Next to the dhole, looking uncomfortable in traditional steppe clothing, was a foreign otter, one eyebrow raised as he, too, regarded Min-seon.

Pú and Mr. Pān, wringing his hands still, followed Min-Seon and Míngshuǐ, and they in turn were followed by Brother Milvio, limping and still damp after being fished from the canal. Milvio was flanked by several of the guards on the barge, including the elegant horse and the one-eyed gazelle.

"Well," said the emperor. No one spoke. The gazelle shuffled her feet uncomfortably.

After the silence had stretched for far too long, Pú cleared her throat. "I'm sorry, Your Majesty, but may I inquire about my friends?"

"Ah, Zhāng Hóngfǎ and Lǐ Yuèliàng?" The emperor gestured at one of the ministers, an officious looking Bankhar dog with dark fur in the robes of a Buddhist monk.

The Bankhar took a step forward and bowed to the Emperor. "Majesty, both are resting comfortably after being attended by the imperial physicians. They are lucky—a dark curse was placed on the weapon used to injure them, but much of the magic was destroyed when, according to witnesses, this woman summoned a dragon."

"A dragon?" asked the Emperor, raising an eyebrow with some skepticism. "Well, I can't be too surprised. I remember stories of your heroics from when you were a soldier in my employ, Min-seon." She was shocked to hear her name come from the Emperor's mouth, and she chanced a peek up at him. His stern features were softened by what she thought might be the slightest of smiles. "Your exploits seem to have done some not insignificant damage to my canal, not to mention the loss of a boat that its owner assures me was an innocent in this, but I am inclined to overlook that in the face of your prior service and ridding my city of what seems to be a very evil artifact."

"Your Majesty," Brother Milvio stepped forward, outrage etched on his handsome face, "My pardon, Your Majesty, but this woman murdered, in cold blood, the head of my order. Any stories spread about Brother Mathé's weapon are lies. I assure you he had no more evil a weapon than my own sword, and I would ask your Majesty to examine the weapon yourself. You will see there is nothing out of the ordinary about it."

Pú and Mr. Pān started to protest, but the Emperor raised his hand and silence fell.

"Go on," he told Milvio.

"Our order is a peaceful one, Your Majesty, as you are well aware. We were preparing to take our leave of the city, when this woman attacked us without provocation. Moreover, as we had previously explained to your Majesty, we believe she is harboring a false heir to the Sòng Emperor, and intending to use him to raise a rebellion against your Majesty!"

"Ah, you mean this boy?" the Emperor asked, leaning forward to peer at Míngshuǐ. "Hm. There is little resemblance to my predecessor. What say you, boy? Who might your parents be?"

Míngshuǐ hesitated. He glanced at Min-seon, and she took the opportunity to whisper into his ear. He nodded a bit, then stood up straight to face the Emperor.

"If it pleases your Majesty," he said, his voice bright and strong. "I would claim Min-seon as my mother."

"Oh?" the Emperor turned to Min-seon.

She bowed deeply. "If the boy is legally my child, your Majesty, his inheritance includes only the bow I used to fight your Majesty's enemies. And I suppose a pottery business."

"Well said," the Emperor told her, then turned back to Brother Milvio. "It is difficult for me to credit your words, Brother Milvio, and I see little truth to the allegation that Min-seon and her son are plotting to overthrow me. Nevertheless," he waved his hand at the Bankhar minister, he began to take notes, "A full inquiry will be held. You may go."

Milvio, swallowing his anger, bowed and then then turned on his heel to storm out of the throne room, followed closely behind by his guards.

"I'm afraid I have only delayed your troubles," the Emperor said in a voice approaching contriteness. He stood with some effort and descended the throne to embrace Min-seon. "I was sorry to hear of your wife's passing."

"I... thank you, your Majesty," Min-seon mumbled. She found her throat constricted by unanticipated emotion. "She would be pleased to know that you remembered her."

"But of course. Now, a question remains of how to deal with your problems. Bóluō, what do you think?"

The foreign otter joined them, offering Min-seon a bright smile. His accent was thick as he responded. "Well, Majesty, Princess Kököchin is preparing to travel to the Ilkhanate for her marriage to Arghun Khan. Surely, she would be pleased to have a guard of such renown as this? And the boy, would he not like to see the Great Empire in all its glory?"

The Emperor nodded and then turned to Min-seon.

She struggled to find words. "I... We would be honored, of course, but my father's pottery concern, Majesty, he is too old to travel and sell his wares."

"Oh, I'm sure Mr. Pān has been wanting to expand into pottery sales, isn't that right?" said the Emperor. Mr. Pān went pale under his stripes but nodded his assent. "And of course while the merger is being worked out, I am sure we can have some Imperial soldiers take your place for a time. And they would be happy to carry whatever messages you want home to your father."

Min-seon bowed deeply. "Yes, Majesty, thank you."

The Emperor placed a hand on her shoulder as she straightened. "It may not seem it, but this is a kindness, child, in more ways than you realize. I can, and I will, in recognition of you and your wife's efforts as my soldiers, stymie these monks you have so unwisely angered, but their brotherhood extends outside even my reach, and I could not protect you forever. Far better that you be where they will not think to follow."

She knew that was only part of the answer, that the Emperor could not suffer to have someone reputed to summon dragons, someone who had assumed guardianship over a child many believed to be the Sòng heir, to have free reign in the very capital. Min-seon found herself not deeply concerned with the Emperor's greater motives, though, as she and Míngshuǐ were led out of the palace and into the sun-soaked streets of Dàdū. The sky opened up before them, and the world seemed full of adventure, adventure which had been missing since Öljei's death. She took Míngshuǐ's hand and offered him a smile before leading the way into the city, to prepare for the next story in both their lives.

Late

Houses of Stone

Utunu

The afternoon sun beat down upon Muvezi as he sat, legs crossed, at the threshold of his hut.

his weight and pulling some loose robe out from beneath him, the painted wolf freed up enough fabric so he could hike it up, a makeshift hood draped over his large, rounded ears in an attempt to ignore Zuva's unwavering strength.

His attention shifted back to the carving in his paws. He turned it, a critical eye upon the shapes he'd formed. A push there, a chip here, a dent there, smooth it here. Better. Wood shavings rested on heat-beaten, dust-covered footpaws.

He sighed then, an exhalation of annoyed acceptance, and fixed his robe back to how it was. Having it draped across his ears was too distracting. Zuva laid his eye upon the hot fur of Muvezi's muzzle once more.

"Hullo!" The voice was distant, accent-tinged, foreign, familiar. Zuva's eye blocked his as he squinted against the sun.

"Hullo over there! Muvezi, it's me!" Closer now, he knew that voice. The heat of affection, of familiarity, added to the sun's unflinching warmth. Quickly, he set the carving and tools down and got to his feet.

"Paru!"

"The same!" He could see him now, a silhouette against the sun, caracal ears up in excitement. And then Paru was beside him, hugging him tightly, and he felt those almost-forgotten feelings once more.

"Paru," Muvezi grinned, teeth white-sharp. He held him at arm's length so he could gaze upon his face, and the caracal smiled back, golden earrings glinting in the sun, kaftan carrying the evidence of long months of travel. "You're filthy."

"Ah, road-dust and age-dust and longing-dust. And maybe some donkey filth. Let me tie up Aisah, then you must tell me where I can bathe." Paru gestured at the donkey standing stoically behind him, saddle-bagged and be-reined, the leads in his paw.

"Ha, she still follows you?"

"I don't give her much choice, to be honest. But she's a good companion, has been all these years."

"The river's where it's always been. You can tie her to the tree, hopefully she'll remember it. There's grass in the shade there too."

"The river? Out here, I suppose that's how things are. Nothing ever changes, eh?" Paru chuckled.

"No, not really. I like it that way. Go. I'll make dinner."

With a nod, Paru set off, dutifully winding the reins in the fork of a tree, checking the saddlebags for fresh clothes, then heading off towards where he knew the river would be.

Brushing the dust and wood shavings from his robe, Muvezi began dinner.

A goat, fresh-killed and with thanks to the gods: that would be perfect. The season had blessed him with many kids, and he hoped the others wouldn't notice the loss. Even so, he hid the knife and there was a minimum of fuss; as he prepared it, several blinked stupidly at him, strange-eyed and ignorant. Into the pot it went, red-cubed, and taro went with it. Some spice from the shelf within the hut, and soon it was comfortably nestled in the firepit, amongst coals glowing orange in the fading light of day.

The caracal returned, newly clothed and damp, eyes bright. "Smells wonderful! Goat?"

"Goat," confirmed Muvezi. "My paws are dirty with its blood, so I must visit the river. Stir the pot, would you? I'll be right back."

Upon his return, Paru was crouching by the stewpot, one eye closed and tongue out in concentration, tapping a claw delicately against the side of a tilted glass vial, powder-full, held over the pot. "New spices! Thought we'd try some. From way up north."

"I would love to."

The taro softened, the goat sizzled, the spice-smell wafted and its pungent notes mingled, as Zuva slowly closed his eye and stars pricked the sky. Bowls were fetched, and wine too, as with an exclamation Paru suddenly remembered some he had brought. "For this occasion! How could I forget," he said, rummaging through the saddlebags and uncorking the bottle. "I brought cups too; I seem to recall yours are in poor shape."

"That they are," acquiesced Muvezi, and held out a cup as Paru poured.

"To my treasured friend," said Paru.

"To my treasured friend," Muvezi stated in return, heartfelt, and wine was sipped in unison. Bowls were filled, and soon stomachs too; it was a star-guested night-silence, comfortable between them, as they ate their fill.

"So," Muvezi said, the word muffled around the wine-cup at his muzzle. "You've done well for yourself."

"Hmm?"

"Look at you! That shirt—are those buttons? And those trousers—silk? I count at least five gold earrings in your ears since last time. They'll be nothing but tufts and gold soon. And no wonder it took you so long to return from the river. You had to do up all those buttons!"

"Ha!" laughed Paru, and stood up, cup in paw wine-sloshed, and twirled with the slide of a footpaw and a twist of his tail. "Do you like it?"

"Hmmm," the painted wolf pondered, slowly tilting his head one way, then the other. "No," he stated, muzzle mock-serious.

"What?" cried Paru in disbelief. "I am insulted!" He held his paw dramatically against his forehead and some wine dribbled down. "Now look what you've done. I've got wine on my shirt."

"Your clothes are fine," Muvezi laughed. "In both ways. They look expensive. I am happy with my simple robe." It was loose now, his chest and stomach open to the fire's warmth, and he held out his arms to the sides. "See? Comfortable. No buttons."

Paru gazed at him a moment, then sat down with a dust-puffed thump. "I would trace your patterns once more," he said, voice husky and wine-brushed.

"And you will," smiled Muvezi. His ears and face were hot and it wasn't just the fire. He took a sip of distracting wine. "But tell me, what have you been selling? Look at you, all the gold in your ears, thick gold at your throat—why not just make a beaten mask of gold at this point."

"Spices, of course. And inks, now! They're much sought after, although at the Houses of Stone I'm not so sure. Those two things fill my saddlebags along with the wine. I wanted to put my banter and my wit in there too, but they wouldn't fit. And I felt safer carrying those on my person since I was visiting you, my friend."

Muvezi laughed. "Is that how you managed to avoid bandits? Banter and wit? After all, with all that gold, you would glint in the sun from miles away! 'O Bandits, here am I, gold-covered and waiting!'"

"See? I knew I had to hold those skills close to me," grinned Paru. "But no. I walked with a trade caravan from far to the north; I met them at a caravanserai a couple months back. They were willing to let me travel with them for, oh, a reasonable price. As long as they could talk to me about their beliefs. Inwardly I rolled my eyes, but I accepted. I've heard that talk a lot in the north; it's getting more prevalent."

"Beliefs?"

"Ach, we can speak of the caravan tomorrow. The night is too pleasant to spoil with world-happenings elsewhere. Anyway! You whine about the gold, but I have a gift! Sit there, my splotchéd friend." Paru rose and walked unsteadily over to the shade-tree and his donkey, who eyed him dolefully. He dug through the saddlebags, muttering to himself, and Muvezi watched curiously from the fire.

"Here it is!" Paru returned, and in his paw was a circle, thick and gold-rich, reddish in the flames. He grasped Muvezi's paw and placed it within.

"This is gold, Paru. Why are you giving me something so... heavy? This must be expensive."

"Oh, extremely," he smiled. "You think I mind? You are important to me."

Muvezi peered at it. "What exactly is it?"

"A tail-ring!"

"A what?"

"A tail-ring. It has a clasp, see here, it opens, then you can snap it around the base of your tail. Tightly enough that it will stay there. It's fashionable! It'll look good on you."

The painted wolf eyed him uncertainly.

"Really! I mean, you have no ornamentation whatsoever. Besides, of course, your fur and your lovely amber eyes. But look at those ears! They are huge. And have nothing! They are round, blank canvases just waiting for some decoration! But I know how you are, so I thought, well, perhaps a tail-ring. It can be hidden under your robe if you are that concerned," Paru grinned.

Muvezi chuckled. "Thank you, Paru. I shall give it a try. It is from you, so of course I will wear it. Let me place it on the shelf inside the hut so I don't lose it. That is where I placed my gift for you, so, give me a moment."

Muvezi returned, paw hidden within the folds of his robe, Paru across from him at the fire, eyes curious and expectant. "What is it?" Paru asked, when he could wait no longer.

Muvezi pulled out the small wooden sculpture he had painstakingly carved, and handed it over.

Paru cradled it in his paws, running a thumb along its smooth-worked surface, following the lines of its form, the elegant legs, the tail, the rounded ears, the strong muzzle. He held it in one paw briefly, so he could rub his eyes with the other. "Thank you," he managed.

"Of course. Now I can be with you on your travels too," said Muvezi.

Paru traced the gentle smile on the figurine's face and looked up at his friend, eyes tear-bright. "I... let me wrap it, I have some silk in my saddlebags, I do not want it to be damaged," he said, and quickly got up to make his way once more over to his long-suffering donkey, who eyed him questioningly. "Oh!" he called, as he made the wooden painted wolf silk-safe. "I'm curious about something." Walking back, he handed a small glass vial to Muvezi, who looked at him, eyebrow raised.

"Ink. I bet you could decorate some of your carvings with it. It's vivid, you could draw some shallow grooves and patterns, allow the ink to rest there. Try it!"

Muvezi stood and went to select a carving from his hut. One of the woodwind gourds, perhaps. They were more utilitarian, undecorated—he could add some patterns. He selected a small metal knife and returned to sit again by the fire. Paru watched with interest. "What's that?"

"A gourd-flute," Muvezi said, and handed it to him.

"Hmm. Where do I... blow? There are several holes."

Muvezi laughed and showed him. "All your riches, and where is your culture! Don't even know which hole to blow on a flute."

"I didn't say I was cultured!" Paru smiled. "I leave that to others. I have inks for artists to create masterpieces, spices for cooks to craft wondrous meals. They can do that, I'll be happy with the gold."

"And what will you do with all that gold?"

"I'm not sure. Have a home built, perhaps. Well north, along the coast—it is beautiful there." Paru was quiet a while, and he watched as Muvezi worked, lining the gourd with grooves in curves and whorls, and carefully allowing ink to seep into the welcoming channels.

Muvezi, for his part, was carving-focused. A long time passed and the sky was black yet brilliant when he realised Paru's eyes were no longer on the gourd, but gazing at him.

"I have missed you, Muvezi. Come lie with me."

Muvezi blushed. "Soon. I cannot leave this unfinished, for it is one of the pieces I plan to sell. But I am almost done."

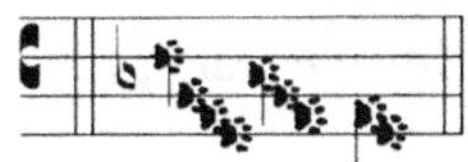

Later, they laid bliss-tired and moon-glistening-naked against each other within the hut, Mwedzi discreetly watching them from the heavens, her eye coating them with soft light that glittered off a tail-ring newly placed.

Paru sleepily traced the patterns in Muvezi's fur, lingering and coaxing.

"Come with me," Paru pleaded. "Back north."

Muvezi smiled, and if there was a touch of sadness there, the caracal did not notice. "You ask me every year, every visit. There are things I still need to do. I have things I need to finish. But as always, I shall accompany you to the Houses of Stone."

"I know. I ask anyway. You know that." His fingers were slow, insistent. "One day you'll listen."

"You have a carved Muvezi to be your companion."

"I want the real one," Paru said, shifting and lowering his head, and Muvezi gasped at the kiss, tufted ears brushing his belly.

The too-soon dawn arrived, and Muvezi set out for the nearby village to find someone to care for his goats in his absence. It would only be a few days, for the Houses of Stone were close by. Paru was busying himself with Aisah's saddlebags when Muvezi returned, and gifted him a broad smile.

"Aisah's got plenty of room for your goods as well, you know."

"Are you certain? I assumed she would be weighted down with yours."

"What, these? They're light. Barely anything in them!"

Muvezi was confused. "Did you not bring goods to sell?"

"Of course I did. I just have samples in the saddlebags. My stock is on the wagon," Paru said with a grin.

"You have a wagon." One ear perked up, the other low and questioning.

"Told you I've been doing well! You think I'd have all that gold from small bags like this?"

"I suppose not."

"But yes, I have a wagon. It continued with the caravan when I split off to find the real reason I make this trip."

Muvezi's ears grew hot again, and he failed to avoid Paru's meaningful gaze, so he smiled shyly in return. "I am glad for that."

"I have two assistants, red jackals both. Brothers, in fact. They're good boys. They'll have set up my stall by the time we get to the Houses of Stone."

"You have assistants." The ears swapped positions.

Paru laughed. "Yes, I do. You seem surprised by all this!"

"I just didn't realise," admitted Muvezi. "I am truly happy for you and your success."

"So, fetch your bags. Aisah awaits!"

Muvezi did so, taking more care than usual to collect all he might need, with a last look around the hut to make certain. "Ready!" he announced, and Paru helped him attach the bags, one large, one small and heavy.

"What's in here?" Paru asked, prodding the small one.

Muvezi opened it. A stylised bird of soapstone, smooth-dark and elegant. "A commission," he explained.

"It is beautiful!" Paru said, and meant it, for it was.

After breaking fast with some leftover stew, they set off, following the path denoted by nothing more than the occasional donkey hoofprint from the day before. It was not long before their path crossed the main caravan trail, dust-packed, hoof-gouged, wheel-rutted, and they turned to follow it. There were other people now, scattered in ones and twos, and more as the day wore on. Zuva's eye was as hot as it was the day before, and it was a relief when finally, atop a rise, they could see the valley and hill of the Houses spread out before them.

"Finally!" said Paru. The city-bustle was evident even from their vantage point, and even though stone walls blocked the view of parts of it, they knew it would be full and chaotic as well. "What is its name again in your tongue?"

"The Houses of Stone, you mean?"

"Yes."

"Dzimba dza Mabwe," said Muvezi.

"What does that mean?"

"Houses of Stone," he replied with a laugh. The caracal rolled his eyes. "Isn't it magnificent?" added Muvezi.

"Yes, it is," said Paru, and Muvezi looked askance at him.

"You managed to sound indulgent. Do you not agree?"

"No, it is. It is an ancient place, is it not? There is much history here."

"But?" Muvezi prompted.

"But the world moves on, my dearest friend. Centuries ago, this would likely have been one of the most marvelous places. It still is," Paru added, at Muvezi's expression. "Yet there are cities now far to the north that would fit dozens of it. And with buildings tall and wondrous."

"Yet it is still full, is it not?" argued Muvezi.

"It is," said Paru. "But...it is harder to find caravans willing to make the journey. And when they do, it seems they bring along fewer goods and more gods."

"Ah, the gods. You were going to tell me of that. I know that there are many from further north that worship but one god—I have seen and spoken to them when I have visited the city here. Is there something more?"

"Yes and no. There are those, yes, and plenty in the caravan. But there are others too who worship one god. Their debates are lively some evenings, but seem well-intentioned enough. I have heard, though, their arguments have flared to violence on many an occasion."

"Doesn't affect me, really," said Muvezi.

"Well, it does in a way. Both these groups have decided that their one god is the only one. They dislike worship of others."

"That seems ignorant. Proclaiming that everyone else's gods do not exist?"

Paru shrugged. "I only say what I have heard. Strangest part is, these two groups seem to worship the same god."

"Then why are they at odds?"

"Apparently, they disagree about which person was sent by the god to tell them all the various rules. So those differ. And they argue it until day turns to night then day again."

"It seems to me I should just avoid them."

"You can, but for how long? With every caravan there are more and more. They wish to spread the truth of their god and the supposed falseness of every other. They have found the Houses of Stone, so they will spread it there too."

"It has stood for hundreds of years, it will stand for hundreds more," declared Muvezi.

"Perhaps."

Paru scanned the valley before them, then pointed to an area outside the walls populated with wagons, people, and burden-beasts. "There. The caravan group I accompanied. Evening is almost here; we can stay in their camp."

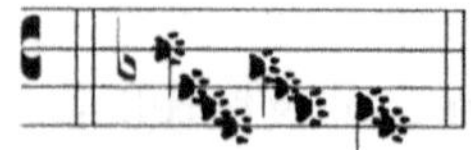

It was a clear night once more. After Paru had acquired some blankets from his wagon, he and Muvezi found a spot, soft-grassed, distant from the chatter and hustle of the camp proper.

"Far enough from them that we're alone," Paru had said. "They would disapprove of us sleeping together. It is against their god's teachings."

"Why is that? Because I am a painted wolf and you are a caracal?" Muvezi had asked.

"Ha, no. Because we are both male."

"Why would a god care about that?"

"I wouldn't know," Paru had admitted.

And so, beneath the black bright-specked sky, they found themselves lying astride each other, as the lilt and murmur of the camp and its shibboleths, strange to Muvezi's ears, wafted and lulled with the breeze.

"It is my turn tonight," whispered Paru, and Muvezi's large ear flicked.

"Is that so?" said Muvezi. Paru could hear the smile on his muzzle. "Won't we be noticed?"

"It's too dark for them to see!" claimed Paru.

"So, you're going to fumble here in the dark with me?"

"No," Paru chuckled. "The moonlight will shine down and reflect off your tail-ring, a beacon such that I know where to go."

"Won't they see it too?" Muvezi asked, his voice thick with amusement.

"I shall cover you with my body. And the night shall blanket us."

"And the blanket?"

"The blanket will blanket us too," laughed Paru, and moved close.

"Then I shall do my best to keep quiet when I cry out your name," said Muvezi, and turned for him.

The morning bustle of people in and out of the Houses of Stone seemed unending. Muvezi carried his bags and Paru nothing as they merged into the foot-traffic and soon found themselves within the high granite walls. The vast marketplace sat at the base of the in-ner hill, and they made their way through the jostling, the ware-hawking, the smells and sounds and sights, until Paru's eye was drawn to a pair of red jackals at a large stall ink-strewn and spice-heaped.

Introductions were made, and Paru took his place. Muvezi began to leave, to find a place to lay out his goods, but Paru stopped him.

"Stay—I have another, smaller stall beside me, it is empty. The boys set it up at my request; it is for you. There is no need for you to find a spot to spread a mat and sit cross-legged on the hard stone, risking the trampling of such wonderful creations as you have made. Please, sell by me," insisted Paru.

So Muvezi did. He set out his wares: the gourd-flutes, the wooden figures, the hearth-gods, the soft-stone carvings with their whorls and curves. Paru would sell his inks and his spices, then immedi-ately insist that the buyer visit his friend and examine the artistry of his creations, for there were few that could match. Muvezi's stock diminished quickly, and his gold grew. It was nothing compared to Paru's earnings, but it was a lot in Muvezi's eyes and would last him quite a while.

Evening arrived before they knew it, and the night was shared in entwined affection.

The next day Muvezi sold his last piece, and Paru smiled, muzzle agape, applauding him. "Well done, my friend! Come, let us wander. My assistants here can watch the stall." And the caracal took his arm, leading him through the winding mass of buyers and sellers, stop-ping to purchase some pastries from a food-vendor, then wandering further, browsing as he went.

He stopped suddenly in front of an immense stall, resplendent with clothes of myriad fashions, from the simple robes and kaftans Muvezi was used to, to the strange garb of some of the folk from far north, the ones carrying the new god. Or same god, whichever.

"You're wanting more buttons?" smiled Muvezi.

"Ha! No. We're getting you a new robe."

"What? Mine's just fine. It's comfy!" Muvezi complained. "Anyway, I didn't make so much gold that I can spend it on fashion."

"Which is why I'm buying it for you."

"Paru, please. That's not necessary!"

"But I want to," Paru insisted, and would hear no more of the painted wolf's protestations. "That kaftan there, my good sir, may I see it?"

It was a rich, dark red, and Muvezi raised an eyebrow. "Red?"

"Isn't it wonderfully coloured? It will match perfectly."

"Match what?" Muvezi was dubious.

"Your colours! The lovely black, tan, and white of your fur. The amber-orange beauty of your eyes. The beckoning pink of your—"

"White will be just fine, I think," interrupted Muvezi, his face hot.

He escaped with a white one, delicately folded, and Paru would listen to none of his effusive gratitude. "You deserve it. You are my dearest friend," Paru said, "and my lover," he added more quietly, so no others would hear. "And I want you to have it."

They arrived back at their stalls, and Muvezi set his new acquisition behind his stall and extricated the small bag, the bird still safe within. "I'll return soon, Paru," he said. "I must deliver this."

Paru raised a paw in acknowledgement, already in the midst of haggling with his newest customer, and so Muvezi set off, his eyes and paws set upon the path up the hill to the centre tower. He spoke of his business, and was ushered swiftly into a room of stone amidst the highest of the Houses of Stone to await the august personage who had commissioned him.

Muvezi knew of him, but little more than that. A priest of the gods of Muvezi's people, and of the gods that had watched over the Houses of Stone since their construction, so long ago. To him he delivered the bird of soapstone, the carved-smooth god-messenger, protector of his people, and in return he was given a heavy pouch, weighted and solid, full of gold, and Muvezi bowed low.

He returned to the marketplace, pouch paw-pressed protectively against his hip.

"The caravan departs on the morrow," said Paru, with a sadness he could not hide. "Even so, sales were good. And we have tonight still."

"We do," agreed Muvezi, and they did.

The jackals were charged with the wagon, and so with the morning Muvezi found himself with Paru and Aisah, freshly saddlebagged and placidly awaiting departure. The caravan rode, and the painted wolf and caracal along with them, though staggered and set apart, where conversation might not be overheard or overconsidered by those with different gods.

"I saw the pouch you held when you returned. The bird was a good sale, I take it!" remarked Paru, as they walked. He had been quiet, and Muvezi had been worried.

"Very much so," laughed Muvezi. "A heavy pouch of gold. I was not expecting it."

"Much deserved," Paru stated. "Why was it so desired, if I may ask?"

"It is a sculpture, a representation, an idol of the messenger-god, protector-god of my tribe and my people and my city of Dzimba dza Mabwe. Properly blessed, he will watch and warn. Even as these new gods breach the lands, he will be there, and he will watch for us."

"I hope so," Paru said, his voice full of sincerity. He was quiet once more, and Muvezi knew why. The day stretched, Zuva watched, and afternoon brought them to the divergence—straight ahead the road continued, but left was the path to Muvezi's hut and home.

Paru stopped, and Aisah halted with an annoyed grunt. His eyes were bright as he looked to Muvezi.

"We do this every year, my friend," Paru said, his voice breaking.

"We do. I have something else for you," Muvezi said, and went to the saddlebags, searching, and pulled out another figurine, woodcarved and delicate and beautiful. A caracal. Paru began to weep.

"Now the painted wolf and caracal will be together," Muvezi added, and Paru could say nothing.

Finally, "Shall we go through the motions, then?" managed Paru. Muvezi just smiled. "Go ahead."

"Come with me, Muvezi. Come north, and see the world I leave to see you. Come see the wonders I've beheld and behold them yourself, with me," he said. He was quiet a moment. "Your turn now. This is where you tell me perhaps next year, perhaps when you are finished doing the things you need to do. Do not make me suffer in waiting."

"I will come with you," said Muvezi, and Paru wasn't sure if he heard the words correctly.

"What?"

"I have done what needs doing. I am finished. I have delivered the last of the birds—the final and eighth—and it, along with its fellows, will protect Dzimba dza Mabwe." Here, Muvezi's ears lowered, and his muzzle dipped slightly. In a voice husky but soft, he continued. "I am getting older, dearest Paru, and I have completed what I have set out to do. So now, the rest of me is for you. Show me what the north is like. Show me where you would build this home upon the coast. For from now on, I will be by your side." He raised his muzzle and met his friend's gaze, ears standing tall.

With a small cry, Paru embraced him tightly, as close as he could, muzzle buried in Muvezi's tear-wet fur.

The Abbey of Saint Vera

Casimir Laski

Though summer flourished in the dales below, winter still held the heights of the mighty Avergne in her talons, dusting their peaks with white. Sister Lucille stood at the terrace overlooking the pass, savoring the crispness of the late evening in her fur, the silence that spoke to the peace of God. It was a welcome reminder after the news borne by the latest couriers: Whatever might befall the world below, there was a power beyond the turmoil, a rock against which no tide could prevail.

Turning, the young weasel took in the sight of the Abbey of Saint Vera, her home and posting for the last three years. The slender central spire rose lonely in the soft moonlight, dwarfed by the mountain beyond, like a knife thrust into the earth by the very hand of God. The Abbey, built nearly four centuries prior by the Blessed Tobias of Auxenne, had weathered fires and blizzards, conquests and heresies; it had seen emperors rise and fall, and kingdoms burnt to ashes. Three Church councils had been held in its lifetime, one of which had been hosted in the once-thriving town of Charrefor that lay in the shadowed valley. King Martín of Sarré had granted the enclave immunity from royal taxes, a status which his apostate grandson had attempted to revoke; two decades later, the armies of the mad pagan Torrik had been broken upon its walls hoping to force the mountain pass. And yet, though it had dwindled to a specter of its former glory, presiding over a scattering of half-emptied villages, now garrisoned only by two priests and a nun, this fortress of the Lord's splendor had, nonetheless, endured.

With the last hints of daylight having fled the far reaches of the land, the rocky trail below lay in pools of darkness too deep even for her sharp eyes—until the flare of a torch amidst the gloom drew her gaze. To see travellers on this path was far from unusual, but to attempt to brave the Avergne pass by nightfall was folly. Which meant they would most likely seek shelter here. The flicker of excitement in her chest at the thought of some novelty was just as quickly dashed by guilt, and a trickle of fear: Who might these newcomers be? If they were heading north, could they be bound for the council in Korraine?

Muttering a silent prayer, the nun closed it by clutching a clawed hand to her heart, then turning the palm up, before hurrying for the arched doorway to the abbey. Bathed in the gentle warmth of candlelight, she repeated the gesture before the altar, bowing her head low, whiskers twitching at the faint, lingering scent of incense. She had said vespers alongside the two priests not an hour earlier, though compline, the hymns to be sung before sleep, would not be due for a while.

Beside the altar, upon which rested ashes still warm from the day's liturgia, stood a marble statue of the abbey's namesake: Saint Vera, daughter of the esteemed Patriarch Saint Kato of Tiber, mentored by the Blessed Martyr Nadrine of Sydos. The stone mink towered over Lucille, paws clasped to her heart, eyes fixed longingly upon the heavens to which she had returned more than a millennium before the little weasel herself had been born. Vera had lived amidst the strife of the death of the Tiberian Republic, and the birth pangs of the empire that followed—an empire that had sought to use the blood of the faithful as its mortar, only for the work of the young saint and countless others like her to temper the hearts of its wicked rulers, and lead it gradually from heathen darkness to the light of the Kyrie.

Whenever she found herself on the cusp of despair, Lucille would come here to remind herself of the challenges God had called others to bear, and to draw on the same wellspring of strength in that shared suffering. This new home dulled the pain of the loss of her first, and yet the little weasel could not help but wonder at what beauty might be found in the world below, alongside and amidst the fruitless strife. Barely nineteen years of age, and with another year remaining before her ordination as a nun was confirmed, Lucille still had time to decide upon her path, but the way grew narrower with every passing day. The Church steadfastly maintained that those who would dedicate their lives to her service be thoroughly committed in heart and soul. With no family to encourage or pressure her, Lucille could, for the time being, set off in pursuit of the ordinary life she still sometimes dreamt of—but the question remained of whether that life could even be found, on her own, in these trying times. Often the weight of this decision drove her to the chapel, seeking solace. But with strange visitors nearing in the failing of the light, this was no time to be lost in thought.

She found the two priests in the study, an avios board between them. Father Anselm, the elderly marten, dragged a clawed pair of fingers through the silvery fur of his muzzle as he pondered his next move. His shadow, birthed by candlelight, danced upon the tapestry behind him. Across from the abbot sat Father Bastien, the mink's pure-white coat glistening as the flame flickered. His red eyes strayed to Lucille as he waited for the abbot's decision.

Lucille inched closer, peering down at the game, laid out upon a checkered battlefield of red and white. She had a passing familiarity with the rules. The pieces were carved from ivory, each in the shape of a different bird—from the lowly sparrow to the mighty eagle—and each with different options for moving and capturing an opponent's pieces. The object was to take the other's fledgling, the most valuable and vulnerable piece, while protecting one's own. She had often considered learning it herself, if only to aid in combating boredom, but perusing the library had always proved more suitable to that end.

The abbot reached a trembling paw out for a tiercel, then retracted it, selecting a raven, and moving it on the piece's strange, arcing path: two squares forward, one left. His opponent hummed in what might have been appreciation or consternation—with the younger priest, it was hard to tell. They were both of noble birth: The abbot was cousin to the Duke of Bayenne himself, while Bastien was the second son of some local baron, his life made an offering to God by virtue of having escaped the womb moments after his twin brother. Lucille, meanwhile, was of peasant breeding, delivered to the Church by parents too poor to feed another squalling cub, and yet too pious to leave her in the woods for the jackal-dogs.

"You know, Sister," Bastien began, keeping his voice level, "you really ought to set your mind to learning avios." His eyes scanned the board with all the intensity of the battlefield commander he might have been, possibilities sparkling in them. Seeking out openings, appraising vulnerabilities. Though always taciturn, he never seemed as alive as when engaged in some competition. "Game though it may be, this offers far more than mere amusement. For instance," he flexed his fingers over his left flank, then plucked an owl and swept it forward, capturing an enemy sparrow. "It proves most instructive on the roles each of us have been assigned in society, which in turn is reflected in God's ordering of creation."

"Ah, but you forget," Father Anselm said, a sly gleam coming over his face, "the sin of pride." He moved another sparrow forward, claiming Bastien's owl. "For even the humble sparrow is capable of besting the mightiest of birds in the right circumstances."

The younger priest furrowed his brow, and the elder went on. "The beautiful thing about this game is that if one pays close enough attention, he will be able to see every blow long before it lands."

Gently, Lucille padded forward. "Um?"

"Sister?" Bastien asked, keeping his voice level.

"Fathers," Lucille replied with a gentle bow, "I spotted a torch on the causeway. I couldn't make out their number, but it seemed to be two or three travellers, drawing near. They will likely be at the gates soon."

The abbot cleared his throat. "Did they seem dangerous, child?"

"No, Father. Er—I'm not sure. But with all that's been happening, I can't help but worry at the thought of unannounced guests arriving by night." She stopped, flexing her empty paws helplessly. "You don't think—you don't think they're pecheurs, or whatever those heretics call themselves, do you?"

Father Bastien waved a paw. "Oh, those lunatics have been dealt with by now, I'm quite sure."

The abbot rose from his stool slowly, clearing his throat. "Well, it appears you'll have plenty of time to ponder your next move, Bastien," he said with a wink.

The younger priest grumbled as he trailed the two down the worn stones of the hallway, the cracked walls drinking in the light of the torches guttering in the chill draughts. By the time the trio had made their way to the main courtyard, a new flame blazed on the periphery, drawing nearer. Lucille could make out four shadows half-coherent against the night's darkness beyond them.

"Well met, travellers," Father Anselm called out, in the voice normally reserved for intonations during the liturgia. The figures drew nearer, gaining substance in the glow of the flames.

"Hail," came the reply from a voice vigorous, and yet strained with the weariness of a long journey. The group stopped within the circle of light cast by the torch above the vestibule's archway. At its head stood a marten with a reddish-brown pelt, clothed in gambeson embroidered with the livery of a black eagle upon a verdant field. An arming sword hung sheathed at his side.

Giving a slight bow, he launched into what must have been a well-practiced introduction. "I am Sir Matthieu de Auvern, and I have the honor of presenting the Lady Delphine Langevin, wife to my liege-lord, who is under my charge." At this a mink, her coat a richer earthen shade, bowed her head, though in her gaze Lucille caught a glint of imperious expectation. Beneath her drab traveller's cloak she wore a dress of green to match the knight's livery.

Behind the highborn pair stood a frail polecat doe who kept her eyes fixed to the cobblestones, one paw loosely clutching at the lead of the party's pack animal. The roe deer stamped a hoof, but otherwise bore the burdens of its masters in stoic silence. In the distance, a mass of roiling grey was smothering the glow of the star-sprent sky, creeping nearer.

"We welcome you," Anselm told them, "though I'm afraid you may find our lodgings a tad austere."

"So be it," Lady Langevin muttered. At her nod, the knight sallied up the few steps and held the oaken door open, waiting dutifully as the doe stepped daintily past him before stopping beneath the arch. "Nina," she called, "have our things secured indoors. And I'm sure the Father Abbot has somewhere to stable the deer." Without awaiting an answer, she vanished into the relative warmth of the abbey.

Lucille felt an icy prickle on the fur of her muzzle, and glanced up to see a scattering of snowflakes, dancing gently downward. Clutching her shawl tighter, she hurried after the others.

The highborn pair's footfalls clattered like distant thunderclaps in the high reaches of the nave, causing the young Sister to wince, and share a grimace with the white-coated mink priest. "Is it...just you here, then?" Lady Langevin asked, sniffing delicately. She turned a curious eye to the abbot.

Anselm bowed his head slightly. "Er, yes, my lady. The servants have all gone home for the feast day tomorrow—of our namesake," he added, gesturing to the altar. The saint's serene countenance mirrored his own. "Apologies if this does not—"

He was silenced by a wave of the doe's paw. Lucille's eyes narrowed at the look that passed between the mink and her knight, though the young Sister stifled the question dancing on the tip of her tongue.

"I suppose this will suffice for a single night." The lady smoothed a section of her dress, then straightened, swishing her tail. "I pray the storm will not keep us here longer."

Father Bastien stepped forward, nodding gravely. "I pray so too, my lady." Lucille bit her lip to keep from smirking. Moments later, the creak of the door cut through the stillness, a bitter wind weaving its way over the pews. The polecat doe hurried inside, shaking a dusting of white from her fur.

"My lady, Father Abbot." Bowing, she drew a few quick breaths, then pointed limply to the doorway. "More visitors."

All eyes turned to the vestibule, and the sliver of snow-streaked night beneath the limestone arch. The world fell silent save for the muffled fury of the distant storm. Lucille clutched at her prayer beads by reflex. As the first hints of flame brightened the doorway, Sir Matthieu stepped forth, clasped a paw to the hilt and bared an inch of steel. Father Bastien looked half ready to join him, while the elderly abbot stood rigid, brows furrowed. "There's no need for—"

A tall, slender shadow thrust its way past the doors, and before anyone had dared to move the light of the sconces revealed it to be an otter, clad in a thick wolf's pelt trimmed with golden thread. "Apologies for the intrusion," he said cheerfully through chattering teeth, trotting forward with arms spread wide, as if he were the one welcoming guests.

Sir Matthieu let out a shuddering breath and dropped his blade back into its sheath, though his mistress kept her narrowed eyes on the otter. Father Anselm, however, warmed to the newcomer at once. "Kounavi or kisenos, kine or doe, highborn or low, all are welcome within our walls."

"Florian of Port-Caraix, merchant by trade," the otter said with a flourish. "My friends and I are most grateful for the hospitality, Father."

Lady Langevin quirked a brow. "...Friends?"

The merchant shrugged. "In truth, one is under contract, and the other a kine of the cloth I've known only a few days, but they've made for quite jovial company." He brushed a few stray flakes from his coat. "We're each of us heading for Korraine, though for quite different reasons," he added with a wink. As if summoned by his words, another figure appeared in the entrance: a second kisenos, though shorter and stouter than the otter merchant, and clad in far drabber attire. His ringed tail hung limply behind him.

The grey-furred kine clasped his paws reverently as he marched into the nave, then placed one above his heart before lifting it heavenward, attention fixed on the altar. His small, dark eyes, hidden in patches of equally black fur, scanned each of the people before him, only to settle on the clergy members. Lucille stared back, having never before seen a member of his kind in the flesh.

"God be with you, Fathers, and Sister," he added, nodding to Lucille. "I am Brother Corrin, of the Lucinian Rite." After the three introduced themselves, he retrieved a pair of spectacles, wiping them with the hem of his habit before donning them. "I have heard much spoken of the Abbey of Saint Vera, and to see it in person is truly a blessing. It is said some of the grandest hymns in the world were composed within these halls—and the library! Rumored to rival the royal collection in Auxenne." His gaze drifted up to the icons adorning the buttresses. "Oh, to have tread these stones in the prime of its glory."

"If it's music you're after, I'm afraid you'll be disappointed, Brother," Bastien said with a frown. He studied the prokyon with a focus that spoke to more than simple irritation over reminders of lost prestige. "This place hasn't seen a full choir for the better part of a century."

"Ah, a shame," the monk muttered, his eyes drifting to the floor. "But, the library is still intact, no? It would be a great honor to be allowed to peruse—"

The door groaned open once more, and the Brother's words were lost on the icy gust of wind that clawed its way into the nave. The swirling flakes dissipated to reveal a final figure, taller than all who had preceded him save the otter. He sauntered through the archway with a hilt clattering at his side, and the touch of torchlight turned his shadowed form to earthen brown with strange hints of silver that caught the fire's warmth. A stoat.

Lucille gasped. Truly, this was a night for peculiar visitations.

Beneath his cloak, the newcomer wore a battered surcoat much the same color as his fur, though the tabard, just shy of gaudiness, was orange and white. A crimson sash over one shoulder matched the feather in his wide-brimmed hat, which he doffed in a manner that suggested more boastfulness than proper deference. "The pack animals have been stabled," he said casually, his gaze cutting through the assembly to land upon the merchant. "And right cold work it was. So, what did I miss?"

Florian rolled his eyes. "You should have been an actor, Reynek." He quickly introduced each of the others to the stoat, concluding with a second, slight bow to the Lady Langevin. Reynek, however, seemed to take more note of Lucille than of the highborn mink.

"It's a pleasure to make your acquaintance," he said with another dip of his head, clutching the hat to his chest. "Rarely does a kine in my trade have a chance to converse with the clergy. Brother Corrin here has some rather...*interesting* ideas."

The monk shuffled back, slender fingers fiddling with his spectacles, but Sir Matthieu was quick to step forward. "A mercenary, then, I take it?"

Reynek flashed his needle-sharp teeth. "Indeed. Reynek of Saarenia, at your service." Lucille drew in a sharp breath, sharing much the same scowl as the knight, and at their shared indignation the stoat raised a brow. "I don't question our dear Sister's reproach, but I should think a knight would be no stranger to bloodletting."

Sir Matthieu straightened, his expression just shy of a sneer. "It is the lack of honor in the approach, not the thing itself, which I deplore. Soldiery is an art, and like any artform requires discipline and dedication, knowledge of what came before. You wouldn't go to a rye farmer for a coat of mail, or a sailing vessel, or a—a disputation on theology." He swept his paw, taking in the pair of priests. "But now any peasant with a pike or a crossbow, or one of those ghastly things at your hip, can fell a kine a hundred times his worth, with a pedigree stretching nearly back to the fall of Tiber!"

"Who knows what value may lie in the unassuming?" Steadily, Reynek drummed his claws on the leather pouch opposite his sword, and the curved wooden implement protruding from it. "But you would hardly be the first kine of high birth to quaver at finding the ground you stand upon less secure than once thought."

"When warfare becomes the domain of the commons, the suffering of war will become commonplace. You would make beasts of us all, sell-sword."

"I always did prefer that term. 'Mercenary' is so devoid of poetry, don't you think?" His sly gleam seemed to drink the very light of the torches, and Lucille found herself growing disconcertingly curious. Shaking the thoughts off, she turned her attention to the abbot, who had stepped between the pair.

"Please, sirs, there is no need to quarrel here. If you'd like, we can show you to your quarters, and then gather for supper in the dining chamber." He clasped his paws, looking from the knight to the mercenary. "And, er, please, I ask that you leave your weapons with your other belongings. Rest assured, you will have no need of them in this place."

"As you wish, Father Abbot," Reynek answered, just as Matthieu asked, "Might I retain my knife?" He glanced to the doe who had travelled at his side. "The Lady Delphine remains under my charge, and I would be remiss to leave my liege-lord's wife without proper protection."

The lady herself was quick to add, "He does have a point, Father Abbot. And feel free to have Nina assist with preparing the meal."

The abbot's eyes narrowed ever so slightly. "Very well. Bastien, escort our highborn guests to the visitor's chambers. Lucille, could you please show Florian and his companions to their quarters, and then join me in the kitchen?"

"Of course, Father." As the gathering dispersed, Lucille led the merchant and his retinue through a side door and down a hallway, stifling a tremble at the knowledge that the mercenary walked right behind her, and letting the merchant's prattle fade to a dull drone in her ears. She had almost no memory of her birthplace, nor of her first family, her blood family, but she did not have to see firsthand the destruction wrought by kines like Reynek and his ilk. It was they whose thirst for violence had laid waste to what should have been her home, who had kindled the flames that scoured a chance for a regular life from her fate. Only the knowledge that God did not approve of a soul harboring hatred prevented her from spitting where she stood at the mere thought.

And so, Sister Lucille kept her tone neutral as she beckoned the three into a pair of simple stone chambers, with all the necessary adornments and none superfluous. The monk, who she figured was accustomed to such accommodations, claimed the first room, while the merchant paused briefly from whatever subject he had been speaking on to remark upon the rustic qualities of their lodgings. Reynek, however, merely flashed a smile that made the weasel doe shiver.

Breathing out deeply, Lucille offered a silent prayer for strength, and for a quiet, quick-to-pass night. Though, even in her relative youth, she had lived long enough to know that God's plans were often inscrutable to the lowly mortals caught up within them.

After showing the three to their quarters, Lucille had gone straight to the dining chamber, helping to set the table at the abbot's direction while he and the polecat serving doe scrounged for enough to feed eight stomachs. Nearly an hour's work later, and the impromptu banquet had been readied: Baskets of rye loaves sat beside jars of quince jam, and rows of salted dace lay on simple wooden platters next to bowls of finely minced cabbage mixed with legumes and carrots, and dashed with hints of vinegar. The main course was a broth thickened with almond milk, containing small chunks of cooked leveret caught from the mountainside, with a number of cheeses rounding out the meal—and, of course, plenty of watery beer to wash it down.

Aside from holy days of the greatest import, Lucille had not seen such a feast since the bishop himself had visited, during her first week as a novitiate. As the others filed in, she guided them to their seats. Abbot Anselm would sit, naturally, at the head of the table, with Bastien and their highborn guests to his right, and Lucille and the others to his left. To her chagrin, the visiting monk was placed next to the abbot, while Lucille herself was seated between the mercenary and the serving doe, who, had she not spoken upon her party's arrival, the Sister might have assumed was a mute.

Lady Delphine objected to the arrangement almost as soon as she entered the room. "You intend for all of us to dine at once, Father?"

The abbot clasped his paws serenely. "Here in this house of God, we are all equals before Him." With a sniff, the mink took her seat, Father Bastien on her left, and the kine sworn to her husband's service on her right. The gleaming depths of the emerald clasped at her throat burned almost as bright as the torches whose light it caught. Lucille could not help but stare, even as she muttered along while the abbot said grace.

To the nun's left sat the servant, Nina. As the others dug in and dishes passed around the table, Lucille eyed the little polecat. She figured the other doe for around her own age, possibly a year or two younger. While technically kounavi, their kind were still generally considered distinctive from martens, minks and weasels, existing in a nebulous middle ground between the musteline races and the more divergent kisenos, such as otters or prokyons. Most polecats on the continent had, at least nominally, accepted the light of the Kyrie, though many still clung to old pagan beliefs, and their wandering clans almost universally held themselves apart from polite society. It was peculiar to see one in a noble's retinue, even as a lowly servant.

"So," the elderly marten asked tenderly, "what it is that brings each of you through the Avergne at this hour?" Grabbing a wooden knife, Lucille began to smear jam of ripened, mashed quince onto a loaf of day-old rye bread, gaze straying from one stranger to the next.

"My lady's business is her own," Sir Matthieu answered plainly. He raised a mug of beer to his muzzle, as if there were nothing more to possibly inquire after.

"I suppose you've already guessed our purpose," Brother Corrin offered with a sigh. "The merchant and I are bound for the council, in Korraine—though with very different purposes," he added with a sheepish chuckle.

Father Bastien, sitting across from him, cleared his throat with a near-growl, muttering, "Troubling times. And all because that deacon couldn't keep his mouth shut."

"Eh, well," the prokyon fiddled with his utensils, staring down into his soup. "There are...legitimate grievances, in need of redress."

Bastien waved his concerns away. "Of course, of course, but to make a show of it all? The Curia can handle these problems internally, as it always has."

"We are none of us free of sin," Corrin replied, straightening his spectacles. "Scripture is...quite clear on this point. No kine, not even those of the Church."

Bastien let his fork clatter to the dish, leaning in. "As *individuals* we are sinful. But the Curia speaks with the voice of God Himself, and God Himself through the Church." Lucille noticed Sir Matthieu nodding along gravely.

"Quoted well from the Catechism, but, er...well," Corrin ducked his head, sipping weakly from his mug. "It hasn't always been that simple. Or, to be more precise, the history of the doctrine is not so...readily established. As I see it, Scripture should be the final authority, where discernment of God's will is concerned." Seeing the glares across the table, the monk scratched at the fur of his chin. "Ah, are you familiar with the Pantherios controversy, from the seventh century?"

Bastien's eyes narrowed as if he were a battlefield commander appraising a potential ambush, but the abbot's expression was distant. "Vaguely," the former said, leaning back slightly. "A dispute on the nature of the Kyrie, concerning his bloodline."

The monk raised a slender, clawed finger. "Yes, specifically concerning whether, and to what extent, His incarnation had limited the priesthood along lines of race, as the Church and her offices were formally codified. Whether it was acceptable for Kisenos such as myself to take holy orders, or be inducted into the Curia." The prokyon paused to spoon up a mouthful of minced cabbage, glimmers of candlelight reflecting in the depths of his black eyes. "The Council of Asmyra, of course, concluded that though one of the kounavi, and specifically a weasel, in flesh, in spirit the Kyrie had constituted all of the higher beasts, as His life was offered that all might be saved."

"I don't see what that has to do with these notions of challenging the leadership of the Church," Bastien said flatly.

"Well," the monk replied, "while the details have been muddled by the passage of time, and direct records are sparse, it would appear that there was not one Council of Asmyra, but *two*. The first, in which the Curia had ruled to the contrary, and the second whereupon the present interpretation was recognized, after significant opposition, derived directly from Scripture, on the part of the lower clergy, and the general faithful."

"This all sounds rather far-fetched, Brother," the priest replied hesitantly, the white hairs of his coat beginning to bristle beneath his habit. "And besides, judging by your own words, it seems the Curia had not issued a final ruling. Merely...a preliminary interpretation, which upon further reflection was corrected by God making His will known in their hearts."

Sir Matthieu cleared his throat loudly, jutting his chin at the monk. "He sounds like that bloody sell-sword."

Reynek took the barb with a confident grin, though Brother Corrin blanched. "I—I merely suggest that the word of God makes for a stouter bedrock than our sinful hearts, is all. And this is not the only case in which such a thing has occurred: the Council of Sydros, the Tiberian Decrees of the 400s, the Sophrosunetos dispute, the Baptism of the Gailans," he ticked them off on his claws. "Firsthand accounts are hard to come by, which, er...as a matter of fact, is why I was hoping to peruse the monastery's library. From what I've gathered in my research in Trayes, some of the letters cited in the controversy's resolution were stored here. And with the storm, we won't be going anywhere..." he shrugged, then folded his paws. "God seems to have led me here, and I would be loath to forgo my part in helping to reconcile the members of His Church."

"Where would it stop, though?" The noise died away, and it took Lucille a moment to realize that she herself had spoken aloud. The eyes of the other eight fixed upon her, and she dabbed at her muzzle with a cloth. The doe shied from the sharp-eyed gaze of the mercenary, which seemed to cut harder than the others. "I—I only mean to ask..."

"She has a point," Bastien said, turning to stare down the monk once more. "Would you have every common kine emboldened to divine his own meaning from Holy Scripture?"

"I—er..." Brother Corrin stammered, a slice of cheese trembling in his paws. "I only seek the truth. Surely, God Himself calls us to this task?"

"And even the Devil can quote His words."

For the first time during the exchange, the abbot intervened. "I can't say for certain if there's anything worth finding—and to be honest, Sister Lucille has more familiarity with our collection than Father Bastien or I—but I don't see anything wrong with letting you sate your curiosity, Brother."

The monk's inscrutable eyes brightened at the words, but a dark look passed over the three figures across from him. Reynek, sitting by Corrin's side, likewise brooded in silence—the first time Lucille had seen him without a self-satisfied smirk.

Before any of them could interject, the merchant raised his mug with a cheery grin. "One of the many things I love about my trade is that you meet all sorts of folk, with all manner of interesting ideas."

"*Interesting.* That is...certainly *one way* of putting it," Reynek muttered. His smile was back, though it seemed less certain, now, like a flame guttering in a wintry gust. From across the table, Lucille saw Father Bastien lean over to whisper something to the abbot, but the words died in the silence of the empty hall well before they reached her ears. The only noise, save for the soft chewing of food and clinking of utensils, was of the wind, howling in the darkness beyond the walls.

Lucille woke to a draught in the cold silence of her quarters, shivering in her nightclothes beneath the ragged wool blanket. Straining her ears, she could catch faint hints of the storm, though her chattering teeth made it rather easy to picture the sheets of snow sailing down from the mountaintop. It drew from the depths of her memory what might have been her earliest, standing in a threadbare shift, quaking from more than the cold as the mother and Father whose names she had never learned picked through the blackened ruins of their barn. The livestock had all been driven off, and the sacks of grain that could not be carried away rent to spill their contents into the muddy snow. She had never known hunger to gnaw like the fangs of iron she had felt as a kit. A few members of the victorious company of soldiers had tossed the family pawfuls of stale bread as they carted the last of the dead from the carmine-stained field of white.

But those days were long behind her now, thanks be to God. Only He could temper the wickedness that dwelt in the hearts of lowly kines, and offer solace to those in need. And so, as she always did at times like these, Lucille rose, donned her plain brown habit, and headed to the chapel to pray.

To her surprise, she found the mercenary within, rising from the frontmost pew. He started much the same as she did, but quickly slipped back into the carefree demeanor that prickled her fur with unease.

"I heard you singing compline with the others, Sister," Reynek said as she brushed past him. "You have a beautiful voice, quite like a nightingale."

"And you have the tongue of a serpent," she hissed. Mock sorrow flashed across his features, but Lucille felt its true echo. Such behavior was not what she was called to. The doe muttered a quick prayer in the silence of her heart, then turned to the stoat and sighed. "Stay, if you must. There's room enough for plenty of supplicants." She gestured to the altar.

Reynek seated himself once more in the pew, then began a recitation. It took Lucille a moment to recognize the language of the liturgia, the harsh-yet-regal tones of a tongue that had long since died among the common folk. It was the prayer of Saint Kato, Father of the abbey's namesake.

"You know Tiberian?" she asked, to which he merely nodded. The weasel cocked her head. "I figured you for the type to hold nothing in reverence. To make mock of God and kine alike."

Reynek's gaze remained on the marbled face of the Savior, where His likeness stood between the father-and-daughter saints. Even the torchlight reflecting in the stoat's eyes seemed cold. Glancing to her, he said, "Humor is the blade that bites deepest, and every kine should know its sting." Then he turned back to the statue of the Kyrie. "But sully not the sacred things."

It was a line from Jeoralian, one of the Fathers of the early Church. From his treatise on the passions. Lucille's eyes widened slowly. "You're quite well read, for a sell-sword." This drew out the familiar grin.

"Oh, how you wound me, Sister." Reynek raised a hand to his heart, then turned his palm upwards before standing. Just as quickly the humor deserted his features once more. "You were right, to ask what you did, Sister. At supper. Far wiser kines than I have attempted to understand the will of God. But when I look to the coming days, I see only strife." He breathed out deeply, then gazed up at the statues in the altar's alcove. "Blessed are those too simple to know doubt."

Lucille repeated his gesture, then rose beside him, not quite sure what to think. Hesitantly, she trailed behind his imposing figure. At the doorway, the mercenary paused.

"Do I frighten you, Sister?"

Lucille fought off a shiver. "I'm not sure 'frighten' is the right word. 'Unsettle,' perhaps."

Reynek flashed a sliver of his needlelike teeth, then nodded softly. "Fair enough." He stepped into the hallway beyond. Despite her reservations, or perhaps because of them, Lucille followed. Their tandem footfalls echoed faintly down the darkened corridor, her eyes seeking out the melted contours of the stone walls. The two passed a window, offering a glimpse into the torrents of white blanketing the grounds. The mercenary approached first, silhouetted against the pallid backdrop of the world beyond the frosted glass.

"It almost seems peaceful, from in here," Lucille muttered. And yet some hint of the storm's fury still managed to worm its way through the halls. Shivering, she drew the worn cloth of her habit tighter about her. Her breath hung like a ghost in the stillness.

Lucille nearly jumped when she felt the touch on her shoulders. She spun to see the stoat offering his cloak, and shrugged it off. Her claws dug into the fur of her arms as she crossed them. "I'm quite fine," the doe stated brusquely.

She had just begun to march for the doorway to her quarters when a muffled thump echoed down the corridor. The rumble of quick footfalls followed before receding into silence.

Lucille shot Reynek an uncertain look, his face sterner than she had seen since his arrival. He gave a sharp nod, then slipped past her into the further darkness. The doe dithered for but a moment before hurrying after him.

She rounded the corner to find the mercenary halted, his tail rigid just above the cold floor. A few paces beyond, a torch hung burning in its sconce across from the open door to the abbot's chambers. "Father Abbot?" Lucille asked, her chest tightening. There was no reply. Together, she and Reynek entered.

A smoldering lantern cast the cluttered interior in sunset hues. Shaded against the light sat the form of the abbot, motionless, slumped in his chair, while papers littered the stones below. Lucille rushed forward, grasping her superior by the shoulder. He did not wake. Claws trembling, she placed an ear to his chest, then recoiled at the touch of wetness. She swiped a paw reflexively, and it came away stained crimson.

Fighting back the sting of tears, she looked up to see Reynek watching her solemnly. Lucille whispered a prayer, kissed the abbot's paw, and gently let it fall from her grasp. Here was the kine who had taken her in, who had offered her counsel in the midst of her despair, who had never failed to treat her with compassion and patience, even when she voiced doubts as to her vocation. She could still hear his words, echoing from the depths of her heart: *None can say for certain what paths God will call any of us to tread, but you must always remain watchful for the signs He sends.*

Doing her best to suppress the welling grief and fear, Lucille cast her gaze across the room. The mercenary had already begun leafing through the loose papers, and she followed suit: routine ledgers, correspondence with the local parishes, nothing of note. But then, her eyes strayed to the abbot's desk, and the open cabinets. Within the lowest, glinting faintly in the light of the dying torch, was a stack of leatherbound volumes.

"Whoever did this," Reynek said carefully, skimming through another sheaf of parchment before discarding it, "is still here."

"We need to warn the others," Lucille told him, though as soon as the words had passed her lips she tensed. Who would they tell? With Anselm dead, that would make Father Bastien the new abbot, and she could at least trust him...couldn't she?

The mercenary seemed to be of the same mind. "That may...complicate matters. But if we are quick, we may be able to catch the killer ourselves. Do you have any idea what he might have been looking for?"

At that, Lucille turned back to the cabinet, rummaging through the books, checking the symbols adorning the covers. Though she had rarely been entrusted with most of them herself, the abbot was rather open about the goings-on of the diocese he oversaw. She brushed a finger over the last, a ledger concerning the vineyards in the surrounding towns, before gasping, "The index—it's missing!"

"Index?"

"For the library," Lucille explained. "It contains information on all of the works stored within, as well as where to find them. Supposedly, at least. I often found it out of date, and even made a few corrections myself."

"Then it appears we know where to look next." Reynek beckoned her back into the hallway, then tenderly closed the door before hefting the torch from its sconce. He held his paw out, and a blackened mirror of his clawed fingers crawled down the shadowed cobblestones beneath the flickering flames. "Lead the way, Sister."

Suppressing a shudder, Lucille guided him down the twisting paths of the abbey, back towards the guest chambers, then right, then left. As they were nearing the library's entrance, a soft scuffing stopped the doe in her tracks. The mercenary halted a hair's breadth behind her, and Lucille had the sudden impression of a knife hovering over the small of her back, her companion's face contorting in vile glee.

But the noise ahead grew louder, and from the shadows emerged the slender, frail form of Nina, the serving doe. She had been shambling forward with her eyes cast earthward, and nearly stumbled upon noticing the two in her path.

"Oh! My—my apologies, Sister. And...monsieur. Sir? Uh, I, I—"

Reynek strode forth and laid a paw on her shoulder. "Calm down, it's all right. What are you doing up?"

The little polecat struggled to make eye contact with the towering soldier, which drew a flash of sympathy from Lucille. "Uh, just, just fetching more mulled wine, for Lady Delphine. She—she spilled hers. I didn't mean to bother you—"

"It's fine." Reynek shared a worried glance with Lucille. "Just be careful, understand? Hurry along now."

With a nod, Nina started down the hallway, but Lucille caught her by the arm. "Nina, have you seen anyone else, since everyone retired for the night?"

"Uh, er," the doe stammered, "the monk, Brother...Corrin, was it? I saw him, earlier. I don't remember where, my lady." She bowed. "I'm sorry, I must be off." With that, the polecat scampered down the corridor without waiting for a response.

"She'll be fine, won't she?" the mercenary muttered. "No one would care to kill a serving doe, would they?"

"I suppose that depends on the kine..." Lucille answered, glancing over her shoulder, in the direction the doe had vanished. "But the library is just around this corner."

They found the heavy, nondescript oaken door closed, but unbarred. As her paw gripped the handle, the doe turned back to Reynek. "You travelled with the monk. You don't think...you don't think he could do something like this, do you?"

"It's hard to say of anyone," the mercenary answered flatly. "I did not know him long, and I wouldn't have thought it of him...but I've been surprised before." He placed his paw over hers, and slowly cracked the door. "Regardless, whoever killed your abbot, it had something to do with this library." He sniffed at the musty air of the interior, then brushed past her. Drawing a deep breath, Lucille plunged after him.

The storied stacks of the abbey's library were lit by slender, opaque windows that would have fed moonlight to the eyes of any interloper, were it not for the blinding storm. As it was, Lucille could hardly see the tomes only a few paces from her snout.

"I suspect the good Brother is looking for the records he mentioned at supper," the mercenary whispered.

"Straight ahead, then left, then ahead once more," she answered. "The oldest archives are kept just beyond what looks to be an alcove, containing a recessed door. Though I've only been inside once or twice."

"Clever." He led the way, and it was all Lucille could do to avoid stumbling as she tagged along behind.

"I don't see how he could possibly find his way in this darkness."

"Then you've never spent much time with a ringtail before. Eyes like a nighthawk," he added with a chuckle. "Most only know them for their dexterous paws, but they make for damn fine scouts—"

The stoat froze as something clattered nearby, and Lucille bumped into him with a whispered apology. Turning, Reynek lowered himself to her height and placed a finger to his lips. She saw his paw go for the empty holster at his waist, then flex in frustration. The sounds of paper shifting were followed by a heavier thud.

Stay, her companion mouthed. Lucille nodded quickly, fearing that the mere thudding of her heart might betray their presence. She watched the stoat meld into the blackness, and pricked her ears for any signs of either his movements or their company. The rustling from beyond the closest stacks continued, then ceased abruptly at a louder creak from her other side. The doe clenched her teeth, blinking away the ghostly splotches swimming in her vision that she knew for tricks of the darkness.

"Reynek?" she whispered as softly as she could manage.

The library went even quieter than before, to the point where she could hear the rush of her own blood. The only warning she had was a faint click before a blaze of light and a crash of thunder sent her diving to the floor. She shrieked at the feel of another's paws grasping her waist, turning to claw her mysterious assailant, only to catch the mercenary's scent.

As he loomed over her in the darkness, both their ears caught the thud of retreating footfalls. The stacks ahead of them had fallen silent.

Reynek leapt from atop her in pursuit, and Lucille staggered after him. They reached the entrance to find the library door flung open, and their company gone.

Indistinct murmuring began to wash down the hallways, the ignition of distant torches carving flickering swathes from the shadows. Reynek leaned in and kept his voice low. "Go and usher the others to the main hall," he said. "I'll be just a moment." He turned to leave, but Lucille grasped his forearm.

"Where are you going?" she hissed.

"To fetch my weapons." His eyes shifted before settling once again on her. "I have a feeling they'll be needed before the night is done. Now hurry!" He dashed off towards his own quarters, and the doe huffed out a breath, then followed the voices.

As it turned out, the others had needed no shepherding to the dining hall, for Lucille was the second to last to join the gathering.

Bastien and the knight both scowled upon her entrance, while Lady Delphine sat near the latter, tail swishing back and forth over the stones. Nina stood behind her, hands folded and head bowed, barely daring to meet Lucille's gaze. Sitting across the table from them, Florian the merchant stifled a yawn, and Brother Corrin sat still as a stone, his beady, unreadable eyes darting between the faces of the others as if each were some rediscovered manuscript. His claws gripped the loose folds of his robe like dagger-points.

True to his word, the mercenary was not long in arriving. Passing through the double doors, Reynek wore his arming sword on one hip, though the firearm was noticeably absent from the leather pouch on the other. He sauntered past Lucille as if without a care in the world, then paused a pace ahead of her and craned his neck downward slightly. "As I suspected, someone took it," he muttered, patting the holster.

With trembling paws, Lucille closed the doors behind him.

"You!" Father Bastien thrust a clawed finger at the stoat. "Discharging that horrid thing in this place! Have you gone mad?"

Reynek strode to the center of the hall and clasped his paws. "I left it with my other belongings, at the abbot's request." He spread his arms wide. "And as you can see, someone took the opportunity to relieve me of it. But we have more...*pressing* matters to attend to. Though I cannot help but suspect they are linked." His eyes hardened, scanning the six figures before him, and Lucille swallowed the lump growing in her throat.

"What do you mean?" asked Sir Matthieu. "And where is the abbot?"

"Yes," Bastien coughed, "someone should go and fetch him." When they caught the torchlight, his red eyes almost matched the white of his fur.

"I'm afraid I have terrible news," Lucille said, raising her voice and stepping to the center of the gathering. The shock of her earlier encounter had begun to recede, leaving grief to rush once more into her heart. "Father Anselm..." She choked back a sob. "Father Anselm is dead. *Murdered.*"

Bastien scoffed. "Come now, Sister..." Just as quickly he trailed off, his disdain melting into uncertainty, tinged with what might have been despair. "Surely you must be mistaken?" he asked, but the conviction was gone from his voice. Seeing her expression, the priest half-stumbled into the nearest chair, his gaze going distant.

"The Sister does not lie," Reynek said, moving to stand beside her. "The abbot was stabbed through the heart, in his study."

Rising from the chair, the priest approached him slowly, until only a dagger's length separated their muzzles. "This had better not be some trick of yours, sell-sword," he hissed through bared teeth. Then Bastien turned to the others, waving his white-furred paw. "Come along, everyone. If what they say is true, then we are safest together."

"If there is a killer loose in your abbey, Father," Lady Delphine retorted, rising to stand, "I think it best that we leave. As it stands, I have—"

"Feel free to brave this mountain storm by nightfall, my lady," Reynek replied with a hint of a bow. "Father Bastien can perform the sacrament once we dig your corpse from the snow."

The highborn doe stared back with a gaze that smoldered fiercer than the torches, but held her tongue. "There's no need for such talk," the knight standing at her side interjected. "Let's do as the priest says."

In silence, the eight shuffled down the hallway, with Bastien leading what looked almost like a premature funeral procession. Lucille offered another prayer that Saint Vera herself might intervene on the fallen abbot's behalf before Almighty God.

Anselm's quarters, when the group arrived, were much as Lucille and the mercenary had left them. Bastien paused to steady himself before approaching the corpse, which had already begun to reek faintly of that ethereal quality which preceded the proper stench of decay. As the others shuffled into the room, Nina wept softly, while something more like fear lurked in Corrin's eyes. Sir Matthieu and Reynek shared the grim, stoic countenance of kines who had seen, and dealt, far worse.

"It is true, then," Bastien said, almost choking out the words. Lucille watched him carefully, searching for any telltale indications, of guilt or triumph or whatever else might pass through a murderer's heart, and in the same moment scolded herself for harboring such notions as to her companion's character. The priest sank slowly to his knees, one paw loosely grasping the sleeve of his former superior.

Steadily, his gaze sharpened, and he leaned forward to snatch something from beneath the chair. The object glinted in the light of the nearly dead lantern. Rising once more, Bastien turned the golden coin over in his clawed fingers. The others crowded closer, and Lucille noticed Lady Delphine's eyes flash with troubled recognition.

"A Saarenian coronet," the priest muttered. "That's the likeness of Prince Kaspran, and his heraldry. How did this—" He went silent as his attention fixed upon the mercenary, at whom several of the others were already staring.

"What is it?" Lucille asked.

"Foreign money," Sir Matthieu noted, "minted in the very land from which his folk hail."

Father Bastien seemed torn between a desire to flee the room and tackle the mercenary to the wall. His voice, when he spoke, was low and dangerous. "Heretics and murderers, making common cause. Was it *he* who bought you," the priest jutted his chin at the monk, "or someone else, then?"

"That's absurd!" Reynek growled back. "Lucille was with me when we found him. Tell them, Sister."

"It's true," Lucille nodded eagerly, her attention shifting to the ringtailed monk, who had backed against the wall, a trembling paw clamped around his spectacles. Nina still wept. By now, only the merchant possessed a semblance of calm. She went on, "We heard a commotion, and found the abbot...like this."

Bastien quirked a brow. "...What *were* you doing, at his side?"

"I had gone to the chapel to pray," Lucille nearly shouted back, feeling her face flush beneath her fur. "And—and met him there, by chance. We talked of matters of faith, and were interrupted by a noise from down the hall."

Sir Matthieu shook his head sadly, looking between her and the mercenary. "I've seen this before, with silver-tongued renegades of his ilk."

"And you were with him the *entire* time, Sister?" Bastien pressed.

"Well," Lucille thought back, prickling at the knight's insinuation. "No...but—"

"I think we've heard enough," Lady Delphine said tersely. She looked to the white-furred priest. "Well, you're the abbot now, aren't you?"

"Please," Florian broke in, raising his paws, "let's not be rash." But the otter's plea might as well have been in another tongue.

"Cast off your weapons, sell-sword," Bastien ordered. "If your claws are truly clean, now is the chance to prove it."

Sir Matthieu stepped over to his side. "Best do as he says," the knight added.

Lucille stood frozen as Reynek crept back, towards the door. Brother Corrin hurriedly made way. "Or what?" the stoat asked, his voice edged with violence. His paw hovered near the hilt of his slender blade.

"If you've done nothing wrong, you have nothing to fear from submitting yourself to justice." The knight mirrored his pose. "I think you know quite well how this ends otherwise, mercenary."

"Oh, I've seen what people will do when they've got a thirst for blood. But I swear, I had nothing to do with your abbot's death."

"Enough of this," Lady Delphine said. "Sir Matthieu, disarm him."

The two warriors' swords leapt from their scabbards in tandem, crashing together with a high clangor that made Lucille shudder. Before she could blink, Reynek caught the knight's blade with his own and thrust the marten back into the crowd of onlookers. A cry went through them, and by the time Matthieu had risen to his feet once more, the mercenary was gone from the room.

Father Bastien's face had darkened like a stormcloud. "To think, we welcomed a murderer within these hallowed halls."

"Father," Lucille said, rushing to his side and keeping her voice low, "Reynek could not have done this. He was with me when we heard someone in the abbot's chambers."

"For an innocent kine, he *was* quick to flee," Brother Corrin added meekly.

Sir Matthieu nodded somberly. "Pardon, my lady," he interjected, briefly turning to his noble charge, "but we all know how does can be. Her weak heart has let him beguile her."

"Silly thing," Delphine added, "trusting a vagabond like him. But what is to be done now?"

"He wouldn't dare brave the storm," Father Bastien said. "He's got to be somewhere on the abbey grounds. That should give us until at least sunrise to find him"

"And when we do?" asked the merchant.

Bastien clasped his paws before the body of his predecessor, and breathed out slowly. "We shall have to trust that God will see justice be done."

After Bastien said a brief requiem over the abbot's corpse, the seven had trod cautiously back to the dining hall, where the doors had been barred. Now, Lucille sat in their midst, running over what she knew, and what she was missing. But one thing was certain: one of the other six among them was a murderer.

The white-furred priest—was he the abbot, now?—paced up and down the length of the table, over which scents of the earlier meal still lingered. Every so often she caught him mouthing the words to some voiceless prayer. The merchant Florian had broken open another cask of ale, and was chattering away as if the group were attending a spring market, while Brother Corrin sat at his side contributing nothing more than the occasional shaky nod. The monk's trembling claws frequently darted to his spectacles, as if to wipe away a stain as indelible as it was invisible, while his small, black eyes fixed upon the shadowed corner.

On her other side sat the highborn party. The Lady Langevin was the very picture of imperious irritation, to the point that one might have thought her even more inconvenienced by the abbot's death than poor Anselm himself. Nina, the little polecat doe, waited unblinking and still as stone a few paces down the bench as Sir Matthieu, standing, discussed with his charge.

Lucille's focus flitted between the six. Father Bastien certainly stood to gain in rank from the death of his predecessor—but as bellicose as the younger priest might be, she couldn't see him breaking the most sacred bonds of their faith. To not only kill, but kill a friend, a *priest*, in a house of God? Then the mercenary's words cut through the assurance of innocence like a blade: *It's hard to say of anyone.*

Next there was Corrin, the mysterious monk in search of equally enigmatic apocrypha. He hardly seemed the type to even dream of drawing another's blood. Then again, Lucille had only known him for an evening. And whatever documents he sought might very well threaten the power of the Church that the abbot himself was sworn to serve. Were his timid mannerisms merely a nefarious façade?

She cast a glance at the prokyon, who was fiddling with his robes as the merchant blathered on. Florian seemed affable, but perhaps *that* was the subterfuge? A kine well versed in trade might deal in murder as readily as spices, after all, and the coronet found in the abbot's study could just as easily have passed through his paws. He was certainly strong enough to overpower the elderly abbot, as was Bastien—and the knight, for that matter. Sir Matthieu must have slain a dozen kines in the span of his service. And his mistress, the Lady Langevin, was rather eager to depart. For a highborn doe to travel in the company of only a single knight and servant surely hinted at some clandestine agenda.

Lastly was Nina herself, the frail peasant who seemed liable to jump at her own shadow. And a polecat, no less—what was one of their kind doing among ordinary kounavi? Unless this, too, was a ruse? Lucille thought back to sermons dealing with temptresses both mortal and demonic, who often assumed the guise of the helpless innocent. The death blow had come from the front, from a killer who had looked Father Anselm in the eye as the deed was done—but did that imply strength and boldness, or cunning and guile? Once more, she tried to imagine what Reynek, with all his experience of bloodshed, might think.

But another voice within her heart whispered that she was far too reliant on the mercenary's advice. She bristled at the memory of Bastien and Matthieu's admonitions. Lucille had sworn herself to God's service, was less than a year from her ordination being confirmed, and whatever rudimentary charms the stoat might have possessed paled in comparison to this higher calling. Besides, innocent or not of the abbot's murder, the kine still spilled blood for coin.

Shaking herself from the pointless, circling musings, the nun clasped her paws on her shift and glanced around. Bastien continued to pace, the hairs of his pelt almost bronze in the torchlight. Daring a peek at the trio to her left, Lucille leaned in furtively to eavesdrop.

"But how could it have gotten there?" Lady Delphine hissed.

The knight's nostrils flared as he drew a slow breath. "Who can say?" His attention seemed more on the pair at the far end of the table than on his mistress. At his response, the mink turned to him and thrust a finger.

"Need I remind you, my lord husband entrusted *you* to see me through safely. We don't have time to get entangled in these...petty ecclesiastical squabbles." She waved a paw.

"Pardon, but is that not what the Lord Langevin is doing?" Matthieu asked back.

Lucille shivered at the venom that crossed the noble's face. "This is no time for cheek, *sir*." Delphine swept her gaze around the room, and from the corner of her eye Lucille saw the doe's narrow momentarily on herself. The nun let her claws fiddle with the tip of her tail, draped over the bench, until Delphine's attention moved on.

"I suppose there's nothing to do but wait, now," she concluded with an exasperated sigh.

Pricking her ears, Lucille cautiously shifted her gaze back to the trio. Delphine was twisting an empty glass, watching it warp the torchlight. "Agh, I haven't had anything to drink since supper. Nina, run and fetch me some mulled wine."

It took a snap of her fingers to rouse the polecat from her torpor. The serving doe might as well have been one of the altar statues.

"Nina!" Delphine snapped once more.

The polecat shuddered, then stammered, "Ye-yes, my lady?" Seeing the glass, Nina took it from her mistress' paw and bowed. Turning her back on the pair, the little doe drew her own free paw up in what looked almost like a blessing, though none that Lucille herself was familiar with.

The weasel's gaze narrowed, but before she could grasp the thought firmly, her attention was drawn by a tap on the shoulder. She pivoted to see the monk standing before her, head hunched, his ringed tail swishing over the stones.

"Sister Lucille..." he began, then cleared his throat. "Er, may we have a word?" He nodded towards where the merchant was seated, one arm draped languidly over the edge of the table, the other hoisting a fresh glass of ale.

Lucille glanced back to the others, but Nina had already crossed the room to fetch more drink for her mistress. Huffing out a breath, she trotted over to join the merchant.

"Would...uh, would you be willing to help us, Sister?" Brother Corrin asked. Across the table, the merchant licked his lips with a wide grin, then set his mug down, leaned forward and steepled his claws.

"In what way?" Lucille asked back, trying her best to sound naïve. The monk fiddled with his spectacles, straining, and failing, to meet her eyes. After a stretch of uncomfortable silence, Florian cut in.

"Brother Corrin would like a chance to continue his investigation in the library, but..." The otter threw his paws wide, then shrugged towards the fastened doors, and the watchful, pallid form of Father Bastien pacing before them. "Quite the conundrum, you see."

"You would risk an encounter with the murderer?" Lucille asked innocently.

"I, er, am quite adept at passing unnoticed, Sister," the monk admitted.

"And we share your doubts as to Reynek's guilt," Florian added.

His admission left the doe pondering their words. "If that is the case, then why did you not add your protestations to my own, in the abbot's study? And why are *you* concerned with *his* research?" Lucille added, turning to the merchant.

Corrin drummed the claws of one paw over the back of the other. "Ah, well...you see..."

"Because I would have either been defending a guilty kine, or drawing the ire of the true culprit." Florian smiled apologetically. "In my line of work, you learn quickly when it pays to hold your tongue, Sister. And as to our dear Brother's quest..." he shrugged. "Call it 'professional curiosity.' Besides, I make friends easily—it comes with the trade." His smile broadened, flashing a sliver of spiny teeth.

Lucille struggled to keep the suspicions welling up within her breast from displaying on her face. However, the two did have a point: None of them would be learning anything cooped up in the dining hall. "I may be able to draw his attention," she said, nodding to Father Bastien, "if the merchant doesn't mind playing along." The white furred priest was still standing near the latched doors, occasionally striding past them only to turn and double back. "Just a moment."

Rising, Lucille did her best to appear timid as she approached her superior, whose back was turned. Stopping barely more than a tail's length from Father Bastien, she caught the last few words of a prayer for absolution, hastily mumbled. The little weasel swallowed against the stirrings of terror, once more assuring herself that the priest would never have done anyone harm, wishing that mere desire would make it so. "Excuse me, Father?"

Bastien jolted, then straightened himself and slowly turned to face her. His countenance was grave, and laden with distress. "Sister Lucille." He heaved out a breath, and brushed a stray lock of fur from his forehead. "I may have been...overly harsh, earlier. I shouldn't fault you too heavily for succumbing to the charms of that wicked kine. We are creatures of the flesh, after all, and even members of God's clergy have known such...desires. The important thing," he said, closing his eyes and raising a claw, feigning an easy smile, "is to steel oneself against them."

"Uh...I understand, Father." Lucille said. Despite her bristling irritation at their suggestions, and her desire to exonerate the mercenary, this was no time for argument. At least, not regarding *that*. "But I was speaking with some of the others, and a question arose regarding Scripture."

Bastien dropped into the nearest chair and rested his muzzle on a palm. "This is no time for philosophical discourse, Sister."

"Oh. It's just that the merchant was discussing the existence of the Ancient Ones."

The white-furred priest's head shot up at once. His nostrils flared. "Pagan nonsense."

Lucille shrugged. "He has some rather interesting things to say—isn't that right, Master Florian?" Striding towards where the merchant was seated, she glanced over her shoulder and saw that Bastien had risen to follow.

"About what?" the otter asked, watching the two approach, looking innocent as a newborn lamb.

"About the Ancient Ones." Lucille shot Brother Corrin a surreptitious glance. "You said you had reason to believe the tales were based in truth?"

Bastien waved an angry paw. "Baseless superstition, nothing more than primitive Tiberian myths. A race twice as tall as any kounavi, who built marvels beyond conception before vanishing from the earth entire?" He scoffed. "The tales have no basis in Scripture or creation."

"Go on," Lucille said, "tell Father Bastien what you told me."

"Ah, yes." The otter clapped his paws, grinning. "From what I've gathered, Scripture is rather silent on certain matters—and even certain passages from the earliest books may contain references to these figures. I'm sure you're well aware of the difficulties of translation. And I have seen—oh, let me find the sketches, in my journal—" He began patting his surcoat, then produced a small book. "In the hills outside of Kellstadt, you see, some kines came across the most peculiar remains in the bottom of a mineshaft, and I had a chance..."

The merchant's voice trailed from her awareness as Lucille watched Brother Corrin sneak up to the doorway. The knight and Lady Delphine seemed engaged in their own discussion, while Nina's dead-eyed gaze studied the blank wall as if it were the most magnificent tapestry in the world. With a few deft motions the prokyon slipped out from the chamber, so smoothly and silently that Lucille hardly would have believed it possible without some form of magic. Cautiously detaching herself from the escalating argument, the weasel skittered along the edges of the dining hall and followed suit.

From the corridor beyond, she could still make out the echo of oblivious voices, though the monk was nowhere to be found. Setting off in the direction of the library, Lucille cursed herself for allowing Corrin such a lead. What if he *had* been involved with the murder? Would he perhaps double back to the scene of the vile deed—or even worse, had he anticipated her pursuit? And why had the merchant been so quick to jump to his aid?

Then she caught sight of the Brother's ringed tail rounding a distant corner, flashing briefly in the torchlight, and the questions vanished like mist. He *was* returning to the library. Halting at the entrance to the archives, Lucille allowed her heaving lungs a moment of respite, and offered a prayer against the rising tension in her breast. She pricked her ears for any sign of being followed, and, hearing none, made her way once more into the darkness of the stacks.

This time, Corrin was making more of an effort at silence, but the weasel let memory guide her to the place where, a few hours prior, the abbot's killer had very nearly dealt the same fate to her. Listening for the telltale shuffling of paper, hardly louder than the flutter of a moth's wings in the prokyon's delicate fingers, she pressed on. Around the next corner sat the monk, facing away, skimming sheafs of crumbling parchment with eyes that seemed to need no sunlight.

Now came the question of what to do. If he *was* the killer, revealing herself here would be the greatest folly. But if—as Lucille had come to suspect—the abbot had in fact been murdered in an attempt to thwart the Brother's investigation, then he was in even more danger than the nun herself. The poisonous mixture of dread and doubt churning in her gut threatened to root her to the floor.

Lucille crept forth silent as she could manage, stalking towards the seated silhouette of the monk. When she was but an arm's length from his back, Corrin went rigid. Ears twitching, he craned his neck slowly to peer over his shoulder. When his eyes caught the shadowed form looming in the darkness, the prokyon toppled over and threw his paws up.

"P-please, mercy!" he shouted, burying his face in his trembling arms. After the silence had stretched uncomfortably, he risked a glance up at his company. "S-Sister Lucille?" He clasped a paw over his heart, breath clouding in the still air of the library.

Much of the tension drained from the nun's limbs, and she allowed herself to breathe again. Whatever his agenda, the kine before her hardly seemed capable of harming even a rodent. "Apologies, Brother, but I was...curious as to the nature of your inquiry. With all that has transpired tonight, it seemed connected to the abbot's murder."

"Ah, yes," Corrin said, rubbing his still-wracking paws over his muzzle. "Even before my arrival I feared my purpose might be challenged." He leaned back against the nearest stacks, gesturing to the tomes laid out before him. "The abbot was...refreshingly accommodating, though the younger priest had his objections. I half thought him ready to bar the doorway when Anselm handed me the library's index."

"Wait," Lucille asked, "Father Bastien was there when you spoke to the abbot?"

Corrin nodded, though Lucille herself could hardly see the motion in the darkness. "He imposed himself on our discussion, implored the abbot to consider the gravity of the situation—nothing I hadn't heard before, even in Auxenne. They were still arguing when I left. I'm surprised it didn't wake you."

Lucille let out a weary, somber sigh. "I hadn't wanted to believe Bastien capable of such a vile act, but..." she trailed off, struggling to even name the deed aloud. Corrin, however, cocked his head and arched a brow.

"You don't mean to suggest he murdered the abbot, do you?"

"But," Lucille stammered, "but you yourself just said—"

"I said I heard them *arguing*, Sister. As a matter of fact, I suspected Bastien might try to interfere—not to the point of *murder*, mind you, but..." the prokyon shrugged. "These disputes can grow rather heated, you must understand. Why, at my own monastery, I knew a monk who completely rearranged our own collection's categorization in a fortnight, when his superior was on pilgrimage." Corrin chuckled softly at the memory, then noticed Lucille watching him and cleared his throat.

"Er, anyway, I waited until their conversation had concluded, then followed the younger priest, to be sure he wouldn't try to obstruct my own work. After the abbot bid him an admittedly curt 'goodnight,' Bastien went straight to the chapel and began to pray. Satisfied, I headed to the library and began to delve through the stacks—and I was on the cusp of confirming my conjectures when I narrowly avoided being murdered myself!" He reached up to nervously brush the fur of his cheek.

"I was in here as well," Lucille said, "and the mercenary with me. We noticed the index to the library's contents missing from the abbot's quarters, and hoped to catch the killer."

"Oh. I assumed it was he who discharged the weapon." The ringtail frowned. "It belonged to him, after all, and while he seemed affable enough on our journey, who can truly say what a kine will do if there is enough coin behind the request?"

"When was it, that you saw Father Bastien enter the chapel?" Lucille asked.

Corrin scratched at his chin. "Hmm...not too long after compline, I'd say? And I was in the library for quite some time afterward."

Lucille wanted to believe in the innocence of her fellow cleric, but could not cast off a nagging doubt. "Could Bastien not have returned to the abbot and—I mean, wouldn't he have had plenty of time, then?"

Corrin shook his head emphatically. "He could have, but I caught a glimpse of the figure who fired the weapon. My kind see quite well in the absence of light, and the assailant's fur was too dark to belong to the priest. I assumed it was the mercenary—and the coin in the abbot's study all but confirmed this, until you voiced your own doubts."

"Why did you not mention any of this earlier, then?"

"Because whoever murdered the abbot came quite close to killing me shortly thereafter, and right as I had found what I was looking for! Hence why I was doubly eager to abscond from the dining hall."

Lucille mulled over all the monk had told her. "So, do you think—" Her words were cut off by the approach of heavy footfalls, echoing from the library's entrance. Icy terror flooded through her veins.

"Brother," she whispered urgently, "have you found what you need?"

Corrin's eyes darted over the documents before him. "Er—yes, I suppose."

"Good." She gathered up a few of the sheafs and pressed them into the monk's arms. "There's a hidden doorway in the alcove at the end of this corridor that leads to the vestry. You should be safe there."

"Safe from what?"

Lucille leaned in even closer, as the booted footfalls drew nearer. "Whoever killed the abbot meant to stop *you*, Brother, and I know my way through this section of the abbey well enough. Now go," she hissed, shooing him into the blackness. Gathering up the last of the tomes and sheafs, the monk melded into the shadows without a sound.

Steadying herself against the nearest stacks, Lucille laid a paw over her pounding heart, counting out the approaching footsteps. Whoever it was could hardly have been more than a dozen paces away. Hefting a nameless, dust-covered treatise, she offered a silent plea for forgiveness and then hurled it down the adjacent corridor.

The ancient book hit the stones with a thud, and the footfalls ceased at once. Straining to avoid drawing breath, her eyes shut tight against the danger stalking her, the weasel nearly sobbed with relief when she heard the stranger padding in the direction of the noise. Allowing a few more seconds, Lucille inched to a stand and crept for the entrance, taking care to scour the darkened floor for anything that might betray her passing.

Only when the arched entryway revealed itself in a glimmer of torchlight from the halls beyond did she allow herself a proper breath. Cursing the lack of a means to bar the entrance, she paused in the doorway to listen for sounds of pursuit. Her ears caught only distant steps from within the depths of the library.

Padding out into the corridor, Lucille turned to her remaining task: finding the fugitive mercenary. Fortunately, she had some idea of where to look.

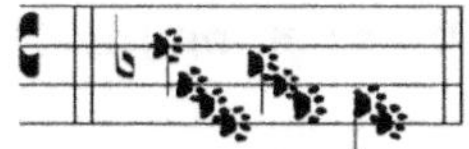

The cloister of the Abbey of Saint Vera sat nestled within an arcade built along the eastern wall, within which stood an oak tree possibly older than the monastery itself. It had been more than two centuries since resident monks had sequestered themselves away from the ever-changing currents of the material world to pray for its deliverance, but the abbey's current inhabitants were free to enjoy the quiet solitude of the courtyard whenever they wished, a luxury Lucille herself occasionally indulged in.

This wintry night, however, left little pleasure to be found in the open air of the cloister, even within the relative shelter of the arcade. But it did make for a sensible place to hide oneself away.

It took a few nudges for the door to give way, and Lucille's teeth began chattering at once as she stepped into the frigid, early morning air. The storm still blotted the sky, though the winds had all but abated, leaving a steady rain of thick white flakes to dance down beyond the covered walkway ringing the courtyard. At the center loomed the grand oak, its verdant branches wearing a fresh blanket of snow. Clutching her forearms, Lucille began a hunched circuit of the arcade, watching as her breath billowed out in plumes. Despite the bitter chill, the cloister retained the serenity it had always held. Here, even the storm seemed drained of its malevolence.

Though she was half-expecting it, Lucille barely contained a shriek when she felt a finger brush the fur of her neck.

"I was wondering when you would find me," Reynek whispered into her ear.

The weasel stifled a shiver and kept her back to him. "Was Father Bastien in the chapel?"

The stoat strode around to face her. "What?"

"Father Bastien. Was he in the chapel, when you arrived? Before I found you there?"

The stoat's eyes narrowed. "Yes, he was. He left almost as soon as I entered."

Lucille cupped a paw over her mouth. "Then the monk spoke the truth..."

Reynek shrugged off his cloak and draped it over her shoulders. "Come now, you'll catch your death out here."

Lucille begrudgingly accepted the furred cloak, leaning against the cold exterior as snow continued to drift beyond the walkway. She let the weight of the prior hours drag her down—the abbot's murder, her own brushes with death, the tensions in the Church and the world at large, even the memories of the life she might have lived that this night had dredged from the past—until she was seated on the ice-cold cobblestones. The tears came unbidden, then. The nun cursed herself for her weakness, but they would not stop.

Reynek crouched down beside her and reached a paw out, only to retract it. As Lucille shook gently with another wave of sobs, he said, "It's all right—you've been through a lot. I've known grown kines who can laugh through a dozen battles, only to break on the thirteenth." Eventually, he settled for patting her shoulder. For once, the weasel did not recoil at his touch.

Wiping her nose, she dabbed at her eyes with the hem of the cloak, then looked back to the mercenary, clothed as if he were enjoying summer in the dales below, his breath clouding as hers was.

"A-a-are you s-sure you don't need this?" Lucille asked.

"My people are used to the cold—many of our coats still turn white in the winter months." He leaned back and glanced to the sky with a grin. "Why, during the War of the Turangese Succession, Prince Garrik led an entire army through the dead of winter to surprise the League forces encamped—" Lucille's glare stopped him short. "Ah, the point being, I hardly feel it." The weasel sensed he was lying, but refrained from commenting.

Reynek seated himself beside her, leaving a few inches between them. "Tell me, Sister." His voice lost the boisterous charm it normally carried. "I sense your hatred for me runs deeper than an abstract disdain for violence. Why is that?"

Lucille drew the cloak tighter around her shivering form. "I never said I hated you." She glanced away, sniffling against the cold, and the threat of tears returning.

"You don't need to."

The weasel let out a slow, heavy breath. When she spoke, her voice was raw and fragile. "It was your kind, mercenaries, who sacked the village I was born in," Lucille said, brows furrowing, "during one of the many wars you waged for mere coin." She balled her paws into fists, sinking her claws into the thick fur wrapped around her. "I was the youngest, and my parents couldn't afford to feed us all, so I was handed off to the Church." She let her voice drop to a whisper, almost ashamed to admit the desire. "I will never know a normal life, because of people like *you*."

"War was here long before I took up arms, Sister," Reynek said with a shrug, though his voice was not lacking in remorse. "I merely meet a demand. You might just as soon blame a whore for the existence of lust."

Lucille sniffed and wiped her nose, then forced an uneasy smile. "So you're a prostitute?"

The stoat chuckled. "Well." He cleared his throat, then inched closer. Lucille shuddered at his nearness, but failed to move.

"You know, I wasn't always a mercenary. I was born to a burgher family in Rakovna—my Father was an armor-smith. Still is, I suppose, though God knows it's been some time." The stoat gave a wistful smile. "In my youth I thought to join the clergy, and began with the study of logic and rhetoric at the university of Arlés, intending to pursue a doctorate in theology." He sighed. "But I left before any of that could come to fruition."

"Why did you abandon it?" Lucille asked, the cold almost forgotten.

"The universities were rife with the children of nobles or wealthy burghers, come from bloodlines who had won their might through battlefield valor or tireless labor. And here their latest generations grew soft and pampered, given in to debauchery, detached from the world that had birthed them—and yet always chiseling merrily away at the rock upon which their luxury was erected. And there were always ever more questions..." The sell-sword's eyes went distant. "In truth...I dreaded becoming weak, like them." His paw found the hilt of his blade, and tightened. "Too much passive comfort kills the spirit, I fear." He glanced over to the nun, holding her gaze. "I suppose that's why I was drawn to you, Sister. I suppose...in your path, I see something of my own."

"I am grateful for all God has blessed me with," Lucille said. In truth this night had revealed the common brutality that she, through her role here, had been sheltered from. Perhaps her dreams of an ordinary life were merely a child's naïve illusion, especially as the real world teetered on the brink of further discord. "He has given me a new home, a new family, a new *purpose*. But I have always known the weight of wondering what might have been."

"Taken from the pages of my own heart."

Lucille paused, then risked a glance at the stoat. "You know, I still have another year before my status as a nun is confirmed."

Reynek nodded. "I suspected as much, given your youth." Rising, he shot a lingering look at the falling snow. "Now let's get you inside—after all, we still have a murderer to catch." He offered a paw down to her.

Studying it for a moment, Lucille clasped her own in his and rose to stand beside him. Taking a final look at the sturdy oak, she let the sell-sword lead her back inside.

Almost as soon as they had started down the hallway, heavy footfalls began to echo from around the corner. The two froze, and within the depths of her mind Lucille saw what she had until now been missing, as clearly as if dead tinder had suddenly flared to life. But the relief in her heart was half-formed, and tinged with new-found dread over what she needed to do.

"What is it?" Reynek asked.

The weasel turned to him. "I need you to trust me. Wait until I'm gone, then run and fetch Brother Corrin from the vestry. He's hiding there—left at this intersection, then right, and it'll be the second door on your right." As the footsteps grew louder and the fear coiled in her chest, she gripped his paws. "Tell him that I sent you—that your fur may not be white, but you weren't the one who fired. He'll know what it means."

"What are you—"

"Do you trust me?" Shrugging off the sell-sword's cloak, she handed it over.

Reynek held her gaze, then nodded and accepted it.

"Good. After you find the monk, send him to the dining hall at once." Standing on her tiptoes, Lucille drew to within an inch of the stoat's muzzle. This time, it was the mercenary whose words caught in his throat. "I trust you'll make your appearance when the time is right." Patting his paw, Lucille raced down the hallway.

She rounded the corner to find the shadowy figure of the marten knight blocking her path. The torches cut sharp angles over the raptor sigil, and Lucille gave the terror rising in her breast no time to dissuade her. "Sir Matthieu!" she shouted, clutching at his tabard as she struggled for breath. "I was wrong about the mercenary, and I know where he was hiding! If you see me safely back to the others, I think we can bring the murderer to justice."

The knight peered down at her, the torchlight casting his suspicious eyes in vengeful hues. Taking her arm in one paw, he easily moved her aside and glanced down the corridor from which she had just appeared. Not a figure stood amongst the darkened stones.

"That was foolish of you to venture out alone, Sister." He studied her for a moment before his gaze strayed elsewhere. "The monk is not with you, I take it?"

"No, sir," she replied, chest tightening. "I thought to prove the sell-sword's innocence, though now I realize my folly." She wiped the still-damp fur of her muzzle. "What a silly thing for a doe like me to do—but you'll protect me, won't you, sir knight?"

Matthieu's gaze returned to her, and in the depths of his eyes, beyond the cold determination, she saw the appeal to his honor take hold. The marten cocked his head, and offered what might have been his first genuine smile of the night. His paw, when it gripped her forearm once more, was firm but not brutish. "How could I refuse?"

As she trod the corridor with Sir Matthieu marching at her back, one of the knight's paws still grasping her forearm, Lucille felt as if another was slowly digging into the fur of her neck. Struggling to match the marten's martial gait, the nun sought the strength of will to not tremble or falter. In silence she pleaded fervently with Almighty God that her mind had puzzled out the culprit. At one and the same time she tried not to dwell on what her suspicions being proved would mean for her own safety.

The sounds of raised voices reached her ears as the two approached the dining hall. Praying that she had bought Reynek and the monk enough time, the little weasel steadied herself and pushed through the doors. To her relief, the ringtail was already present. Father Bastien had entrenched himself in a two-front argument, and was in the midst of berating the visiting Brother while fending off verbal barbs from Lady Delphine. As the otter merchant tried in vain to interject, she spotted Nina, the polecat doe, huddled away from the quarrel, staring blankly at the floor.

The moment the white-furred priest noticed Lucille's presence, he whirled on her. Gradually, the others' shouting fell away as they followed suit. "Sister Lucille!" Bastien gasped. "Where have you been? Running about while there's a murderer at large!"

The weasel freed herself from the knight's grip and stepped forward, feigning a calmness she could not hope to possess. "Begging your pardon, Father, but that's not exactly true." Seeing the doubt flare up in the priest's gaze, she huffed out a breath, straightened her tail, and raised her head high. "I know who killed Father Anselm. And I can prove it." The knight's brows furrowed, while even those who were only paying the little weasel half a mind now fixed their full attention on her.

Father Bastien stared, nostrils flaring subtly, before conceding the center of the room. Lucille let out a deeper breath of relief, strode into the midst of the group, and began. "I will admit—and I must ask your forgiveness, Father—that I was initially suspicious of you." She saw the look of hurt flash across the pallid mink's face and steeled herself to continue. "I had never thought you capable of murder before, but you had reason to quarrel with the abbot, announced at supper your desire to speak with him in private, and would have been poised to succeed him, in the event of his passing. It was you who plucked the coin from the floor, which directed our collective attention towards the mercenary. You also seemed burdened by guilt, and I caught you uttering what sounded like the closing lines of a prayer for absolution. I hope you will not hold it against me that I took the vigilance that Scripture requires to heart: 'Even the souls of the most devout harbor ever a spark of the flame of sin.' "

She met Bastien's gaze more directly than ever before, and the longer she held it, the more the irritation in his own eyes subsided, replaced by somber understanding. He nodded curtly, then lowered his head and folded his paws.

"My suspicions were split between you and our visiting monk— and here I must once again ask for forgiveness, Brother," Lucille added with a bow to the prokyon, who blinked in surprise. "The documents you admitted to seeking in our archives, and your intentions to employ them in the upcoming council in Korraine, could clearly threaten the authority of the Church, of which Father Anselm, however lenient he may have been, was still a representative. If perhaps the abbot had changed his mind and barred you from the library, I thought...well, I figured you might have resorted to violence."

Lucille paused, scratching at the back of her paw. "I surmised that your...meek demeanor might have been a ruse. It was not until I surprised you on your second visit to the library that I concluded it was not so." She shrugged apologetically, though the monk took it with a soft chuckle.

"In that moment, I thought my own death was upon me," Corrin said with an uneasy smile.

"Yes, well, you yourself confirmed, despite having no reason to exonerate him, that Father Bastien retired to the chapel after the abbot granted you access to the library. Where he remained until shortly before my own arrival, well before the murder occurred. I imagine," Lucille admitted, eyes straying back to the priest, "that your final exchange with Father Anselm was...unpleasant, which would explain your remorse, and your willingness to be gentler towards myself after you had learned of his passing."

"It is true," Father Bastien muttered, gaze dropping to the stone floor. "It pains me to think that our last words were...less than kind, and mostly on my part."

"Father Anselm knew that you loved him, and he loved us in turn," Lucille said with a strained, teary smile. "No minor squabble would change that. And, more importantly in terms of exculpation, Brother Corrin caught a glimpse of the murderer when the mercenary's stolen firearm was discharged. He sees better than any of us in the absence of light, and the assailant's fur was too dark to be yours."

Father Bastien sniffed. "Hmmm."

Lucille went on. "With my two primary suspects stricken from the list, I had to consider the others. Florian's readiness to aid Brother Corrin's endeavors certainly aroused suspicion, and he had both the strength to overpower the abbot, and the fur to match the figure the monk spotted in the library. And, as a merchant, the coin found in the abbot's study could very well have belonged to him." At this the otter quirked a brow, but Lucille did not let herself falter.

"However, the fact that Father Anselm willingly gave the library's index to Brother Corrin removed any motive to murder him. I suspect that our otter has had dealings with some of the dissidents, in the pursuit of financial gain, which gave him a passing interest in the success of the monk's quest. And, perhaps more importantly, he showed no distress over the misplaced coronet—something a kine in his trade would be quite concerned with, should it have belonged to him."

Florian merely shrugged, then flashed a knowing smirk.

"Speaking of the coin," Lucille said, turning to face the remaining trio, "that brings us to the Lady Delphine Langevin." The lady in question glowered back silently.

"A highborn doe travelling all but alone through the Avergne pass by nightfall naturally aroused my curiosity. References to a task your lord husband had entrusted you with, and your eagerness to depart the abbey, only heightened my suspicions. And, when Father Bastien retrieved the Saarenian coronet from the floor, it was *you* whose countenance revealed, albeit briefly, a look of surprise not shared by any of the others. You, whose destination was the very realm in which the coin was minted."

The Lady Langevin raised herself up and snorted out an angry breath, lashing her tail against the stone wall behind her. "Do you mean to accuse me of murder, then?"

"No," Lucille replied calmly, "as a matter of fact, I don't." She dared to venture slightly nearer to the trio. "Your eagerness to leave well preceded the abbot's murder, whose death in truth jeopardized your mission—especially when one of the relevant coins turned up beneath his corpse—and your single-minded focus on the Lord Langevin's task seemed nothing short of genuine." She paused, for confidence as well as breath. "Now, pardon my boldness, but based on the direction of your travel, and the unrest in the lands of your destination, is it wrong to assume that this mission involved a diplomatic entreaty to the Saarenian emperor, perhaps hoping to jointly crush the renegade princes who have embraced the clerical dissidents? An alliance many in your own kingdom might take issue with, given your longstanding rivalries?"

This elicited a rueful smile from the highborn doe. "How fortunate you were not born of nobler stock: You would either have lived far too long, or died far too early."

Lucille turned back to the others. "No matter. But it does beg the question: How did the coin get from her purse to the abbot's quarters?" The weasel let the question hang in the air a moment before drifting her attention over to the serving doe, Nina. The little polecat burst into tears almost as soon as her eyes met Lucille's.

"After discovering the abbot's body, Reynek and I encountered Nina traversing the halls alone. She offered the excuse of fetching more mulled wine for her mistress, which I thought little of, until I later overheard the lady herself mention that she had not had anything to drink since supper. But you weren't fetching drink, were you?" Lucille softened her voice. "You were planting the coin you had taken from your mistress' purse in the abbot's study."

Delphine whirled on her servant, who cringed away. "Nina, is this true?"

Lucille, however, was quick to interject. "Don't be too harsh, my lady. I hazard that she was coerced." The mink's face, already clouded with anger, grew perplexed.

"It seemed odd to me that a polecat would have found her way into service as a noble's handmaiden. After all," she turned to address the others, "they are an itinerant people, known for keeping to themselves." She saw several of them nodding along curiously.

The nun continued. "I myself was taken in by the Church, so I figured she must have been left in a similar situation, by parents who would, or *could*, no longer care for her. Parents who, might I venture, belonged to a group of heretics, and raised her in their rites—hence the poor doe's constant anxiety in this house of God, and her reflexively blessing herself in a peculiar manner?"

The little doe cringed further away from the overbearing eyes of the others. "It's—it's true," she stammered. "I—I was taken into my lady's household as a kit, but...but..." She broke off sobbing. "I was raised among heretics, and baptized by one. I thought if anyone learned..."

Lucille was about to offer words of comfort when, to her surprise, Father Bastien stepped in. "There's no need to fret, Nina." His voice was strangely tender. "Yesha Himself was quite clear that the sins of our forebearers do not damn us—that each is responsible for his own soul. Or hers, in your case," he added with a smile.

The little doe sniffed, dragging a paw across her muzzle, but for the first time since she had arrived, her face seemed to have lost some of the pall of fear.

"Which leaves us with only one suspect," Lucille concluded gravely. "Someone who might have discovered this secret of the servant's past, who likewise opposed the abbot's leniency to our dear Brother's investigation, who doubly benefitted from suspicion being cast on the reformist monk and the mercenary—and the only one of us to retain a weapon through supper, when even the sell-sword had the decency to abide by Father Anselm's request." She let her gaze settle on the knight, whose eyes blazed like coals within a countenance as cold and still as mountain rock. "Sir Matthieu."

A collective gasp escaped the others' lips as they too turned their attention to the marten.

"I'll grant you're fairly clever, for a doe," Matthieu said, the hint of a growl coloring his voice. His sword leapt from its sheath to level towards her.

Lady Delphine's eyes bulged, and she clutched a paw to her heart. "You dared to jeopardize the mission entrusted to you by your very liege lord?"

The knight spared her but a glance before shoving his mistress aside. The mink sprawled to the floor with a gasp, and Nina rushed in to attend her.

"And where is the stolen firearm?" Lucille mused, backing away slowly, doing her best to still her wracking limbs. "Ah, I take it you cast the thing into the night when you couldn't figure how to reload it."

"Bold, too." The marten took a step forward, and Lucille shuddered. "Not that either will save you."

"But why?" his mistress asked, cringing, half-risen from the floor. She looked torn between trying to reign in an unleashed beast and knowing her only hope was to flee its wrath.

"I am an *Auvern*," Matthieu snarled, "a warrior whose bloodline can be traced nearly back to the fall of Tiber! My very name is shared with the mountains from which this abbey was raised, stone by stone. And here I stand, master of a paltry estate that shrinks year by year, left to pick from third-rate countesses whose grandfathers were practically peasants themselves! Reduced to taking the orders of a soft-pawed court-fawning aristocrat too feeble to even run his own errands, who has his *wife* conduct his affairs with neighboring realms." The marten's blazing eyes narrowed, his voice lowering dangerously. "And when he does, he sends her to treat not with honor or duty or sacred custom, but with *coin*, like a common *whore!*"

Delphine opened her mouth to protest, only to snap her jaw shut when Matthieu's molten gaze passed over her.

"You all heard the monk with your own ears: He would make a priest of every kine, and a king, and a warrior—and therefore a slave. He would level the natural order ordained by God Himself. An honest farmer who knows his duty stands higher than a king who does not—but in his world, no kine would have any place appointed to him, and therefore nothing reserved." The knight gasped, as if even now he could not believe the sheer impudence. "And the abbot, entrusted to preserve the natural law, when given the opportunity to fulfil his own sacred oath, chose instead to abdicate. So say what you will of my bloodletting tonight, but God knows that it was not murder."

The marten took another step nearer, baring his steel at the nun's throat. "Though what He will think of *this*, I cannot say." He raised the blade. Choking down a scream, Lucille braced herself to dodge.

Then the doors to the dining hall flew open, and in strode Reynek. The sell-sword drew his own blade with practiced ease and sauntered up to stand before Lucille.

"Come, Sir Matthieu, I would hardly consider the dear Sister a worthy opponent." Even standing behind him, Lucille could picture the sly grin to match the bite of his words, and smiled through her own terror. "Then again, a valiant knight such as yourself should have no trouble besting a lowly sell-sword, either."

Sir Matthieu fell into a more proper stance, paw tightening over the hilt of his blade. "Worthless prattle is all I'd expect from you, stoat."

Reynek matched his posture. "So be it."

Their blades clashed together with a shriek faster than Lucille could blink. After the first blow, the two began to edge sideways in a rough circle as the rest of the onlookers gave ground. Bumping into the table behind her, Lucille clutched at one of the breadknives with a trembling paw. If the knight triumphed in this contest, she did not intend to follow her superior, or her newfound friend, quietly.

The stoat made a few cautious probes, dancing back out of reach after each thrust. It was on the fifth that Matthieu lunged. Taking a glancing blow on his gambeson, the marten slashed at the mercenary, who recoiled with a pained snarl. Lucille shuddered at the splash of warm blood on her forehead. Moments later she caught the reek of iron in her nostrils. The sell-sword still held his own blade, though his left paw clutched at a tear in his sleeve, just below the right shoulder.

"Not so boisterous now," his foe sneered.

Reynek gritted his teeth and held his tongue. Through labored breaths he moved in for another strike, parrying the knight's response and slashing his chest once more, to no avail. From what Lucille could tell, it would take a direct thrust to pierce the thick quilting. The mercenary, however, could rely on no such protection.

Their weapons leapt out to meet again, but this time Matthieu rushed in to follow through. Reynek barely brought his sword to meet the second strike in time. The blow sent him tumbling back, blade clattering to the floor beside him. The mercenary rolled upright and reached for his weapon, but the knight was already moving to cut him down. The other onlookers remained frozen.

With a shriek, Lucille sprang forth and plunged the breadknife into the marten's thigh, eliciting a vengeful roar. Twisting, he backhanded the weasel with his free paw. She sprawled into the bench, tasting blood as utensils clattered around her. Through the stabbing pain in her skull, Lucille watched Reynek's blade leap for the heart of his foe.

The knight gave a wordless gasp as the steel ran through his body. Trembling, he coughed up a mouthful of blood. "Honorless curs..."

Struggling to his feet, Reynek tore his weapon free and watched his opponent fall to the floor, then snorted. "You're one to speak." He staggered over to Lucille and helped her up, heedless of the blood trickling down his torn sleeve. She quickly shifted to prop his uninjured arm over her shoulder, though the stoat's weight was almost too much for her to bear.

Slowly, the others gathered around the dying kine with the morbid curiosity of vultures. Even the Lady Langevin, stricken silent, ventured to the side of her fallen knight. The defeated marten gazed up blankly, and sucked down a ragged breath. "Go on, then," he managed, lips flecked with blood-stained spittle. "Lay the tinder...for your own pyre..." With a shudder, his eyes dimmed to cold glass.

Tenderly, Lucille settled the victorious sell-sword down in one of the chairs, and set to work binding his wound with cloth torn from the hem of her habit. The white fabric was soon soaked through with carmine.

"It's my favor," she told him through a strained smile. Reynek laughed, then grimaced and clutched his chest.

"I shall wear it proudly, then," he told her. Lucille would have called it mock gravity, upon first meeting him—but now she sensed something genuine in his words. "Though, I may require a few more days' rest, after this night. I expect the sun will be rising any moment now."

"I could say the same," Florian chimed in. "No matter—the council isn't set to start for another two weeks. If it's all right with you, of course, Father Abbot."

Mention of Korraine cast a dark cloud over Father Bastien's face. "I am not the abbot. Not yet, at least. But we do still have one matter to resolve, I suppose," he said, staring another moment at the corpse, then wearily plopping down into one of the other chairs. The white-furred priest rubbed a paw over his face.

"Ah," Brother Corrin inched forward, "I take it you refer to me?"

"And the documents you discovered," Lucille added. She finished binding another strip of cloth to the stoat's wound. As far as she could tell, the bleeding was slowing, though it had not ceased.

Bastien blew out a long, heavy breath, then turned to the nun. "Well, what do you think, Sister?"

Lucille's head shot up. "Me?"

Bastien nodded, gnawing on his lip. "Yes, you. After all, it was you who uncovered all that was at play tonight, and deduced the identity of the murderer." He cleared his throat softly. "It appears...you have a keener mind than I gave you credit for. And to be quite candid, I am rather at a loss myself."

Lucille's eyes widened, and she felt a flutter of pride within her breast, though it was just as soon quelled by the burden now placed upon her. The documents Corrin discovered could very well shape the future of the continent, and the faith she had dedicated her life to—regardless of whether she saw her ordination through.

The weasel doe looked up to find the priest, the monk, and the mercenary all watching her in silence. "Well," she said, choosing her words carefully, "I think God would want us to seek the truth, wherever it may be found."

Brother Corrin's face brightened, while Bastien merely nodded again, his gaze elsewhere.

"What about me?" asked Lady Delphine.

"You are free to stay or go about your business as you please," Bastien said. "Perhaps the mercenary will allow you to travel under his protection," he added with a smirk.

Delphine scoffed at the suggestion, but Reynek, reclining in the chair, looked up. "Rest assured, I offer fair prices, my lady."

"I'm sure you'll need to stay another day, at any rate," Bastien went on. "No point setting out through the Avergne Pass with no sleep. And, that would allow plenty of time for a proper baptism," he said, turning to Nina. "Should you so desire." The little polecat beamed.

Sharing their smile, Lucille walked over to where Reynek was seated and traced a claw along the bandage. The sell-sword winced at her touch, though the blood had stopped seeping through.

"It will need further care, by someone more versed in medicine than I," Lucille observed, "but you should be fine."

"There is a good doctor in Korraine," Reynek replied. "Owes me a favor, as a matter of fact." He held out a paw. After a moment, Lucille laced her fingers through it.

"Swear to me that you will see Brother Corrin safely to the council?"

"I swear it," he said. Then, after a stretch of silence, the stoat added, "I take it we won't be seeing each other again?"

"I wouldn't say *that*. You are free to visit whenever your travels bring you by. I will certainly listen for word of the council's outcome." She shrugged, trying to appear at ease against the fluttering of her heart. Whether she remained in the clergy or opted for a secular life, Lucille has a sense that the days of her tranquil, if dull, existence in the abbey were waning. The dangers of this night had certainly given her much to consider. "And, if you are not too long in returning, I suppose I will have come to a decision of my own, by then."

Reynek's smile grew rueful, though it did not lose its sincerity. "Strange as it is to say, I've grown rather fond of your company. I have known many does, but you are without a doubt the most fascinating of the lot."

At this, the weasel leaned in, until their muzzles were nearly touching. The mercenary went rigid. "You're not entirely lacking in charm yourself," Lucille said. With a sly grin she darted in to kiss his cheek.

It took a moment for the stoat's surprise to melt into amusement. He licked his lips as his chuckle grew into an outright laugh, which Lucille joined.

"For the present, at least, my heart is sworn to God's service, sir—as yours is to warfare. Such differences would hardly make for a favorable courtship," she continued, "but I do not see why they must preclude friendship. And as to the future..." the weasel trailed off with a coy smile.

As every kine was called to bear their suffering, every age knew fresh strife, and none could truly say what the coming days might hold, for her own life, the Church, or the broader world. But regardless of her decision, Lucille had faith that the abbey, much as the everliving God to whose glory it was raised, would endure.

With a warm smile, she took the sell-sword's paw once more. "Well, only God can say for certain, right?"

Where His Side Was Pierced

Rose LaCroix

Author's note: The Black Death disrupted Europe so badly that the century after was one of the most violent in European history. A life of peace was a rare luxury that few people of any class enjoyed. But some, not content with that luxury, chose to make their own trouble. Death records of the era reveal a people so on edge that the smallest slight would lead to a fatal stabbing. And of course, there were plenty of judicial duels during this period. Trial By Combat is rather ancient, but in medieval Europe it reached its peak as a legal institution before falling into extralegal status in the modern era. So much so that by the end of the 15th century, German fight masters were publishing manuals on how to use every conceivable weapon. But the most celebrated and elegant weapon of the late medieval duel is the longsword, the two-handed evolution of the early medieval knightly sword.

Sir Alan bent over a simple breakfast of porridge with raisins, shoveling it in his mouth with a gilded spoon. The deer was never one to eat lightly when he was uneasy. If anything, lately he'd been putting on a little weight, and now his fine silk doublet embroidered blue and gold was straining at its buttons.

His wife, on the other hand, picked at her oats, her eyes downcast.

His servants stood at the ready, their faces gloomy and downcast.

Alan clenched his jaw and downed a measure of almond milk from a stoneware cup, wiping his mouth with the hem of his cloak.

"Well, no time to waste. Isabelle?" His tone was stern but calm, his face severe but stoic. No one was going to see him afraid.

Least of all, his brother.

He stood and extended his hand to the hind, who quietly, sullenly came along with him. Alan snapped his fingers. A young fox page came and fixed his longsword and scabbard to his belt with an array of highly polished buckles and bright red leather straps and stood by. It was a handsome sword, with a pommel inlaid with his blue and white coat of arms and the crossguard flared like a Maltese Cross, with cutouts of trefoils and rested in a sheath of deep blue leather.

Alan rested a hand on the pommel of the sword, giving the smooth metal and colored glass a reassuring stroke. A fine sword... but it had never tasted blood. The call to arms had passed over his house many times and the lords of the Five Woods lived easy lives.

Except his brother, who spoiled for war.

Out from the safety of Alan's hall they went, Alan, his wife, and a small retinue, down the Chemin des Renards to the town of Cinq-Bois-Sur-Lac where a church bell tolled, once for him and once for his brother.

Isabelle clutched his arm. "Please, forgive him! You've never fought a duel and he's fought so many! How many is it now?"

Alan kept his eyes straight ahead, straining not to show any emotion. "Six."

"Do you want to be number seven? Please! Drop your case and let's go home! You forgave me for falling for his charm. Why can't you forgive him?"

Alan stopped in his tracks. "Because he has no humility. And because every knight he's sent to God might have been a friend of mine." His voice cracked just a little. There was enough killing to go around these God-forsaken years since the Pest. Why should anyone want to make it worse?

Alan frowned as he and Jean walked to road that ran between a vineyard on a hill and the clear blue lake below.

"You don't have to do this," Alan muttered. "You were the one who called him a he-goat!"

Jean's jaw clenched, his eyes narrowed, and his ears flicked in silent agitation. "Well he's no wolf. I'd fear and respect a wolf!" he seethed, eyes black and intense.

Alan rested a hand on his brother's shoulder, stopping the elder stag in his tracks. "Remember what you said? Sometimes the chivalrous thing to do is to own your mistakes before they get out of hand?"

Jean never made eye contact. He roughly grabbed his brother's wrist and yanked it from his shoulder, shoving him aside. "You can talk to me about chivalry when you've got your spurs!"

"I'm not that much younger than you. And you only just got your spurs! He's said all he wants is a public apology. You're in the wrong and you know he could take you for much more than that. Why won't you settle?"

Jean clenched the hilt of his sword. "We're the lords of the Five Woods! A lord of the Five Woods never backs down!"

"You're being a fool with your life, Jean!" Alan insisted.

Jean smacked him in the face with the back of his hand. "Squires aren't paid for their opinions!"

They arrived at an old Roman milepost half-hidden in briers fat with berries, and waited there in the warm noon sun.

"Roland should have been here by now," Jean muttered, pacing and grinding his teeth.

A wolf dressed head to toe in silk and brocade of all colors and trimmed in silver buttons came strolling up the way, accompanied by a young marten who carried his sword.

"Am I late? Sorry. I had important things to attend to. And I've got supper with the count tonight so let's make this quick, shall we?"

The marten handed Roland his sword and Alan handed Jean his.

"You think you'll win so easily?" Jean taunted. "This fight is mine."

They squared off, but it was over in a moment. Jean gashed the wolf's right arm on his first strike, all the way to the bone. The sword fell from Roland's hand and he crumpled to his knees, howling in pain and clutching the badly-wounded arm.

"I'm out of the fight," the wolf sobbed. "Let's... Let's settle this another day."

The marten ran to him and tore the hem off his own tunic, using it to hastily bandage Roland's arm. But Roland was bleeding profusely, wheezing, the insides of his ears turning pale. "I... I don't feel so well," Roland muttered before pitching forward, gasping, eyes wide.

"Please! GET A DOCTOR!" Roland's marten squire begged.

Jean sheathed his sword. "He's done for. There's no saving him."

The marten was in tears now. "You'll hang for this!" he screamed.

Jean glowered, cold as ice. "They'll have to fight me first."

Alan fought back tears. *Maybe it's my fault.* After all, he could have pretended he didn't see. He could have had a gentlebeast's agreement with his brother to never speak of what he did. He'd already forgiven his wife. Jean was charming and a great singer after all (though most of his songs were about his other romantic conquests). Maybe he should forgive his brother too, and say it was all a misunderstanding, like so many other lords who'd wanted to avoid a scandal had undoubtedly done.

Alan clenched his fists. No. Jean's behavior went far, far beyond seducing other beasts' wives. Jean was a bully who always got what he wanted. Noble birth be damned; he had the heart of a burglar.

It was only right for Alan to meet his brother's challenge, even if it cost him his life. It was a matter of justice.

The town square was packed. The whole town had come to see this duel. Jean des Cinq-Boix' scandal could have stayed between the two of them, once upon a time. It made the stag's heart churn to see them, to air this awfulness to the gawking crowds, young and old, rich and poor, all here to see this poor cuckolded stag defend his honor to a six-time champion, and his brother!

Where was his brother, anyway?

The crowd parted as Comte Charles Fitz Richard, a fox dressed all in red accompanied by his court all in fine silk and velvet, strode solemnly over the paving stones. Alan knelt before the slight fox.

"Sir Alan, where is your brother?" Count Charles asked.

"Here I am."

Jean, dressed much like his brother in a short silk doublet and sleek hose, stepped forward from the crowd and knelt next to Alan.

Charles cast a stern gaze at the two stags kneeling before him. "Jean des Cinq-Boix, you have sought redress for the accusations brought to you by your brother that, on St. James' Day, the Year of our Lord Fourteen-Hundred and Five, you were found lying with your brother's wife. Here is your last chance to avoid a trial by combat. You may confess the sin of adultery now and I will let the church decide your penance. Otherwise it will be your brother's choice if we carry on. Do you confess your guilt and seek absolution before God?"

Jean's eyes were glued to the muddy ground. "Never," he muttered.

Charles gave a solemn nod as if expecting no less from Jean. "Alan des Cinq-Boix, you allege that your brother seduced your wife. Your brother has denied it. Here's your last chance to avoid a contest of honor. You may confess the sin of false witness now before God and apologize to your brother for accusing him of adultery. Otherwise you shall both face trial by combat, to fight each other even to the death. Do you confess to being a liar and pay your brother forty sous in recompense?"

It wasn't even a question of whether he forgave his brother, or his wife. Of course he forgave him. It was on Jean to walk right and he chose hubris instead.

And yet... this was his brother. They'd been squires together, fought together, hunted together. Wasn't forty sous a small price to pay to keep from having to cross blades with him?

Isabelle was nodding, mouthing the words "say yes." He wanted to. He yearned to put all this behind him.

But he remembered something Jean had told him years ago. "Never walk away from a challenge when reputations are at stake," the older stag had cautioned him. The faces of the knights and lords and magistrates assembled in the square were steely, cold, pitiless. They had come to see someone die and if he backed down now, they would never respect him.

He tossed his head in silent agitation. *A funny thing, respect. We put our lives on the line every day for it but we can lose it with a single word.*

"No," Alan said, standing with fists clenched, something vital breaking behind the stag's stoic eyes. "I told you the honest truth."

The fox saluted him. "Then the sentence of trial by combat shall proceed. You shall not leave this place til one of you has struck the other dead. May God have mercy on your souls."

Immediately a space was cleared for the two combatants. A rabbit priest mumbled their last rites to them as valets staked down a rope to form a ring only fifteen cubits on all sides.

When the priest had given them both communion, Gerard St. Maurice, a wolf magistrate carrying a wooden stave and wearing a great white ostrich plume fixed to the front of his bright green cap with a silver badge, ushered them into the ring.

"Combatants! Draw!" Gerard called.

Alan drew his sword, and with it a deep breath.

"Good, you remembered," said Jean, drawing his own weapon. "The biggest mistake a fighter can make is not breathing."

"You taught me everything I know," Alan said. "I didn't want to do this, Jean."

Jean managed a defiant smirk. "You'll do fine, brother."

The wolf placed the end of his staff between them, on the line. "Combatants! Salute!"

The stags raised their swords before their faces, tilting them forward and swinging them out and to the right.

Gerard lifted his staff and stepped back, walking out of the ring. "LAY ON!" he roared.

The stags took a fighting stance, upright with one leg forward and the other out to the side about shoulder-width. They held their swords close to their bodies and fully upright, masking their intended cuts.

Jean wasted no time. "I'm not going easy on you from here on," he warned, throwing a rapid series of diagonal cuts that forced Alan to parry. But in the confusion Alan saw the tip of Jean's sword leveled at his eye.

Alan compassed out of the way and threw a cut at Jean's left arm but missed as Jean side-stepped.

Now they were circling each other, each making tentative jabs and thrusts, trying to find an opening.

They kept each other at bay like this for some time, oblivious to the shouts and jeers from the crowd. Their focus was entirely on each other, watching every faint twitch of the other's muscles, timing their steps and their breathing just so.

This time it was Alan who went on the attack, squeezing to whip the cut, pushing out and forward with his left hand to wind for the next cut, one-two-one-two never missing a beat. But his brother parried or side-stepped his every move, matching him at every step.

Jean cast him a rueful smile. "I taught you well."

"One! Two! One! Two! Left! Right! Left! Right!"

Alan's arms were getting sore. His life as a page had ended three years ago, but his life as a squire was one of relentless training and service. Jean, himself a year from earning his spurs, was putting his younger brother through his paces. Hours and hours of cutting drills and, here and there, sparring with wooden wasters expertly carved in the shape of a longsword.

"Alright, get yourself a drink," said Jean. Alan grabbed a leather wineskin filled with a mix of vinegar, honey, new wine, and water. He downed greedy mouthfuls of the sweet drink. It was just strong enough to leave him slightly relaxed and it felt good when his tense shoulder muscles let go.

Jean picked up a waster and took a fighting stance. "Let's see what good a little practice did you."

Alan grabbed a waster and jumped in with the full confidence and gusto of a beginner. He slashed away wildly, his cuts and thrusts uncoordinated though not as bad as they had been. All at once he had the wind violently knocked out of him and he doubled over, sucking air and clutching his stomach. "What..." He wheezed as he caught his breath.

Jean stood over him, one hand resting a waster on his shoulder and his other hand on his hip, a big smirk on his snout. "You need to let the momentum carry the blade when you're doing multiple cuts of the same kind, You were stopping the blade. It threw off your rhythm and your alignment. Also, you need to breathe!"

Alan struggled to his feet, still clutching his belly. That stab hadn't penetrated at all but it had been worse than a punch. Breathing was hard. "Can we get back to this tomorrow?"

Jean chuckled. "That's the third worst place to get stabbed. If that was a sharp blade and it didn't make you bleed to death you'd die hours or days later, hot as hell with fever. I have rarely heard of doctors saving a beast who'd been stabbed in the stomach but most don't make it a week. But at least they have time to make their peace with God."

"What's the second worst?" Alan asked.

"The lung. You will die in minutes, it hurts every bit as much as the gut, but you'll probably die choking on your own blood. It's hard to pray with a mouthful of blood," Jean replied, casual as ever.

"And the very worst?"

Jean pointed to the crucified visage of a lion carved above a doorway. "That would be the heart, right where His side was pierced. It's quicker than the lungs but it's not immediate. You know it's pierced the heart when you see water coming out with the blood. You know you're going to die. And it's the most painful death of all though it comes fast. Too fast to say a prayer, sometimes."

Alan paused a moment in thought. "What if you've had your last rites? Is it the easiest death then?" he piped up.

Jean shook his head. "The only easy death by the sword is a blow that cleaves the head or the neck just enough. And it has to be a very hard blow, I've heard on the battlefield you might live long enough to cry out in pain if your head is cleft open. But if the blow is clean and forceful, death comes at once." He slapped the back of his hand into the palm of the other with some force to emphasize his point. "You will feel no pain if you died in grace... but every pain if you didn't."

Alan parried a blow and stepped out of measure, feet close together, sword leveled defensively. Alan circled him, Jean keeping his point on his brother's face at all times.

The tense silence was broken when someone shouted, "Are you fighting or courting?"

The rougher creatures in the crowd began to laugh and make lewd signs at them. And for once Alan saw, printed on Jean's face, the look of a creature who hadn't thought too carefully about what he wanted until it was too late.

Jean leveled his blade and made a long forward pass, aiming for Alan's chest but Alan closed the line, raising his sword and pushing his brother's blade out and toward the left, the tip cutting the side of Jean's face before the elder stag disengaged and began circling again, looking for an opening as blood poured from the side of his muzzle.

"Brother," Alan said, "If the Count would give you another chance to recant, would you take it?"

Jean's face hardened at the very suggestion. It was a hardness his brother never showed him before but a look he'd seen on the elder stag's face many times.

Jean and Alan's mother threw herself at Count Charles' feet. "Please! He's only a boy! He's only sixteen, Milord!" she sobbed.

"But he's earned his spurs, hasn't he?" Charles replied.

"It's this or the gallows," said Hubert St. Maurice, Count Charles' wolf magistrate. "My son's blood is on his hands! I demand justice!"

"Nobody saw him kill that boy!" Jean's mother screamed.

Jean cast a fearsome glare at Alan, and at Roland's squire, waiting for any sign they might dare give him away. But the fierceness in his eye when he looked at Alan was nothing compared to the cold contempt in his eyes when he gazed on Hubert.

"Then let God choose who will win," Count Charles commanded.

They hustled out to the bailey of the castle. Up in the galleries and on the ramparts dozens of knights, pages, ladies, and beasts at arms watched and cheered. A rabbit priest hurried through their last rites. Hubert held up his staff.

"Who will marshal this fight?" Hubert called. "I can't marshal my own duel."

"I will," said Hubert's younger brother, Gerard.

Hubert smiled. "thank you." He handed his staff to Gerard.

The younger wolf drew a line in the sand between Jean and Hubert, then lifted the staff.

"Lay on!" he called.

Hubert made the first move, stabbing with some force. But Jean parried and stepped out of measure.

His gambit worked. The more aggressive wolf threw a series of cuts at Jean but the stag parried each one until they were in a bind. They each worked to keep their point at the other's face, each struggling to lever themselves out of the bind first.

Jean was the first to break free and he wasted no time. The point of his sword went right into Hubert's eye and the wolf crumpled, never to rise again.

Jean sheathed his sword as Gerard and several members of the court ran to Hubert's side. It was no good. He'd died before he hit the ground, swift and clean as could be.

Nothing like the horrid way his son had died.

"Gerard St. Maurice, I hereby appoint you magistrate of these demesnes," Count Charles said, his ears pinned back, tail low, and eyes wet with tears.

Gerard squeezed his eyes shut and knelt before Charles, hands folded. "I will do my best, sire," he murmured, his voice barely suppressing a sob.

"Jean des Cinq-Bois, you are a free beast. You have proved your innocence before the court," Charles grumbled.

Jean saluted. His eyes were twin gemstones, bright but unfeeling. "I'm sorry it came to this. I take no joy in killing," he deadpanned.

Charles, a head shorter than Jean, reached up and put his hand on the stag's shoulder. "Don't get arrogant because you've won a duel. I've seen beasts like you become feckless. When you can get whatever you want by winning fights, you'll think you've been vindicated by God but one day, it's coming back to haunt you. Don't be like that, Jean. Quit while you're a winner."

"I will do whatever is needed of me, Sire," Jean mumbled, eyes fixed on some faraway point. "No exceptions."

"Recant!? NEVER!!" Jean bellowed, launching a ferocious attack that left a nasty gash on Alan's arm. It was serious enough that it would need immediate attention after the fight, but he could still lift his sword and he wasn't bleeding out; the duel had not been called.

Jean wasn't letting up either. He came on fast, so fast Alan found his parries striking late and his footwork barely quick enough to keep him out of measure.

Then Jean broke off the attack, standing narrow with his sword leveled at Alan's face, turning to face the younger stag as he circled, looking for an opening.

Alan stepped into measure and closed the line, his sword binding with his brother's sword as they struggled to get a clean jab in. Jean tried to step back out of measure. Alan saw his chance and thrust forward and upward, dealing a wound just below his brother's ribcage. Blood and water flowed down Alan's blade.

Jean's eyes went wide. "No..." he sobbed. Alan withdrew his sword and Jean des Cinq-Bois was dead before he hit the ground.

The priest prayed over him one last time, sprinkling his body with holy water and making the cross.

Alan knelt at his brother's side and pulled his limp form into his arms. "Why did you make me do it?" he pleaded to the silent husk, his brother's blood staining his fine clothes and tears streaming down his face. "Why did you make me do it!?"

The priest rested a hand on Alan's shoulders. "He that lives by the sword dies by the sword," the rabbit sighed, drying the stag's tears tenderly on his stole. "I only pray that he is not in purgatory long."

"Why did I have to be the one?" Alan sobbed.

The rabbit cleric's face twisted into pain. "Mysterious ways, son. Mysterious ways."

Gerard reached out a hand to help Alan to his feet. "There's nothing we can do for him now," the wolf mumbled. "Come on, Alan. Let's get you taken care of. Someone, please fetch me a measure each of vinegar, water, and honey and some clean linens!"

"I'll see to it your brother is buried honorably, at the altar of your family chapel in the cathedral," Count Charles said. "Don't worry about a thing."

Alan looked down at the body of the brother who had caused him so much grief and scowled, for once.

"No. A shroud and a hole, that's enough."

The Golden Son of Rahe Neer

Thomas "Faux" Steele

The fair cathedrals and grand plazas of Verona beckoned to Jai like the gentle strumming of a sitar as he gazed down at them from the bedroom of the Monegario estate's guesthouse. Set at one of the highest and most defensible points of the city, the compound gave him a stunning view of Venetian cogs sailing up the Adige, bearing fine glass from Hungary-Bohemia and luxurious wines from Naples.

Basking in the first rays of pearlescent dawn from the sun peeking over the horizon, Jai stretched out on a down-stuffed cushion stretching the full length of the windowsill. He sprinkled his fur with rosewater from a silver bottle before combing the tangles out with a boar bristle brush. Candles flickered gently in the breeze around him, ensuring he had light enough to carefully examine his skin for parasites.

"You're up early." Nonchalantly walking through the doorway despite Jai's lack of clothing, a fennec fox placed a tray of thick, crusty bread and golden-brown fig jam beside him. Amir was a handsome fennec fox with eyes like polished citrine and a wiry body adorned with hard-earned calluses. "I figured I'd bring you a snack. Would you care for coffee?"

"Please," Jai replied with a sigh, rubbing his eyes, still weary from spending several days evading bandits while hiking the old Roman road from Trento. Amir, ever the faithful servant, remained cheery, his natural rhythms less disrupted by the demands of keeping a night watch. "Have you had time to check out the Piazza delle Erbe?"

"Mrm...yes. I couldn't seem to catch a wink last night," Amir replied. He bent over a weathered mortar and pestle, using raw muscle to grind the coffee beans into a fine-grained powder. Rolling it between his paw pads, the fennec ensured it was smooth before pouring it into a copper pot with a deep blue-green patina.

"See anything of note?" Once Jai had restored his fur to its usual polished smoky quartz sheen, he stood up and padded over to a weather-beaten teak trunk, each dent and gash meticulously patched with sheets of hammered tin. Removing a stout key from a leather cord hanging between his toned pecs, Jai popped the lock of a strongbox inside.

"A merchant told me of a new brothel that's opened up near the Casa dei Mercanti. He said that it was the most exquisite establishment he'd seen on this side of the Po River," Amir replied with a sly smirk. "It's been a while since you've had *company*. Perhaps a visit is in—"

"*No*, thank you...at least not the kind of company you prefer," Jai replied with a chuckle. He gratefully accepted a steaming porcelain cup from Amir, savoring the fragrant vapors as they rose to meet the tip of his muzzle. "After that handsome tiger in Bergamo splintered the bed frame mid-coitus, I vowed that I would pursue more...genteel relations going forward."

"Fair enough, though I caught a glimpse of a striking courtesan whose company might be worth a measure of our profit from this trip." Amir winked as he turned toward the bed, smoothing the linen sheets down. "A warm body beside me does much to soothe my road-beaten muscles."

"I prefer a bed warmer stuffed with hot sand, personally." Jai took a sip of the bitter coffee as he surveyed the contents of the strongbox. Inside lay a medley of precious trinkets and treasures obtained during their travels, including a small golden scarab inlaid with lapis lazuli and a necklace of jade beads from distant Cathay. "Is there much in the city market worth buying?"

Amir shook his head, spreading a piece of bread with glistening jam before handing it off to the mongoose. Jai took a bite, the slight sweetness of the figs complementing the nuttiness of the acorn flour. "Not much; it's all the same old fabrics and baubles. Nothing really caught my eye there. Perhaps the specialty market on the Ponte Scaligero will have better pickings."

"How were the offers on spices?" Jai imbibed slowly, savoring the precious coffee as he let it swirl around his tongue. They were quickly depleting the cache they had acquired in Saba, and those in the Maritime Republics seemed to prefer wine and small beer above all else. He figured they would not be able to resupply until they reached Keşan on the return trip. "Do you think our cache will fetch a good price?"

"There's a handsome profit to be made," Amir replied with a sly smile, drawing a pawful of Venetian *zecchino* from the leather money purse on his belt. He placed a smattering of the heavy gold coins on the table, several bearing test cuts to verify their bullion content. "Still, we'll have to be careful. Remember last time?"

"Hey, I did get most of our treasure back," Jai said with a demure smirk.

Amir chuckled before taking a sip of his own coffee. Leaning over the strongbox, he selected a few pieces of gold jewelry for the mongoose from among a gleaming stack obtained through driving a hard bargain during an earlier trade in Venice. "Yes, but let's not tempt fate again. Next time we might lose more than just a few silver pieces."

"I only had to dangle the thief off the roof for what, half a *ghurry*?" Jai stood still to allow the fennec to drape a heavy choker around his throat. Rather than employing delicate prongs, a smattering of small rubies and sapphires were set directly into the gleaming metal. Crafted by an expert goldsmith, it fell perfectly around the muscular contours of the mongoose's neck. "I barely cracked a sweat."

"Your father did admonish you for that when he learned of it," Amir replied with a snort. After slipping an undershirt over Jai's head, he helped the mongoose don a loose-fitting *shalwar kameez*, a soft cotton tunic paired with baggy trousers. As Amir fastened his leather sandals, Jai couldn't help but feel a rush of excitement at the prospect of earning yet another handsome profit. "Don't forget, we have a meeting with a young noble of the House of Monegario this morning."

"Gah—I do hope he's at least entertaining. If I had to listen to another word from that blithering idiot in Florence, I think I would have burst." Amir adjusted Jai's tunic before adorning his wrists with a pair of gold bracers crafted in the Egyptian style and adorned with *khatt Islami* designs resembling lotus flowers.

Amir laughed, his melodious voice filling the room as he slotted pins through the bracers to secure them into place. "Fear not, my friend. The House of Monegario is known for their patronage of the arts and their love of all things extravagant. I'm sure you will find him to be a suitable conversationalist."

"Mrm...I hope you're right." Jai poured the last and most fragrant dregs of coffee into a pair of silver shot glasses before adding a dash of distilled spirits. The astringent aroma of the dark brew mingled with the sweetness of roses, creating a heady mélange that teased his nostrils. "Where are we heading?"

"The *seneschal* informed me that he'd be in the library," Amir replied. Glasses clinked like the striking of a gong before the dyad downed the rich contents in a single shot. A frenetic shiver raced from the tips of Amir's tall ears down to his tail, puffing his fur out as his pupils dilated. "There should be a small repast for us as well, if you're in the mood for more than a traveler's meal!" he said with gusto.

"Then let's go; I'm peckish already." Jai took a deep breath and stepped out into the verdant grounds of the stone-walled estate. The morning air was crisp, a refreshing change from the oppressive heat that had enveloped them back in Saba. Jai and Amir walked side-by-side down the path, the sound of their sandals on the rough-hewn slabs of marble punctuated only by the distant ringing of church bells. "Have you glimpsed him in the corridors?"

"Briefly, when he came out to discuss something with the *seneschal*. From what I overheard, he seemed a little naïve, but I chalk that up to his upbringing," Amir said, as they passed a bronze fountain that sparkled in the early morning light. Rising above the water, a figure of Artemis with a pair of feral wolves by her side gazed down at them with silent strength. "After all, nobles don't exactly experience all the highs and lows of the world as we do."

"I'm hardly a commoner myself," Jai replied, playfully punching the fennec on the shoulder. The Golden Son of Rahe Neer—as Jai styled himself—belonged to a noble family on the western coast of *Bhārata*, though not one of any particular importance. "Though I imagine my title carries little cachet around here. It's my place of origin that's of real interest."

"That may be so, but you're as august as the best of them." The library was situated in the left wing of the estate, overlooking a small vineyard where a few peasants were gathering grapes in a large wooden trough. "After you," the fennec said, parting a pair of French doors set with shimmering hand-blown glass.

The library was a truly grand room, packed with floor-to-ceiling shelves holding a variety of leather-bound tomes alongside racks of yellowed parchment scrolls. A large mahogany table was set up in the center of the room, adorned with a colorful runner embroidered with the red and white roses of the Monegario standard. Generous servings of fresh fruit, bread, cheese, and cured meats were clustered around two large silver candelabra in the center.

"Ah, you must be the *Bhārata* noble." A red fox gestured from the head of the table for them to take their seats. He was an angular vulpine in his early twenties with dark, inquisitive eyes and a muzzle whitened with powdered lead. An enormous cabochon ruby the size of a walnut hung below his throat, set in brilliant yellow gold. He shot them a welcoming smile from above the rim of a crystal goblet half-filled with wine. "You're a long way from home."

"I've gotten used to it. Traveling is in my blood, after all," Jai replied, settling into one of the high-backed chairs with a contented sigh. Upholstered in oxblood leather, it was more comfortable than expected. He broke off a piece of warm, fresh-baked bread and topped it with a hunk of firm Castelmagno cheese while Amir poured libations. "You have exquisite taste. It's very—"

"Different than what you've seen in other estates?" The fox softly chuckled. Jai couldn't help but notice the way his squid ink eyes looked at him with a mixture of curiosity and admiration before darting down to a thick Sanskrit volume beside his plate. "Yes, the House of Monegario favors more...refined forms of luxury. This library has the most comprehensive collection of Arabic scrolls from here to Córdoba."

"Most impressive, Your Grace." Jai couldn't help but feel a tingle run down his spine at the fox's intense gaze, almost as if the young noble was undressing him in a salacious fantasy. He quickly pushed the thought aside and cleared his throat, taking a sip of sweet, jammy wine. "I couldn't help but see a certain resemblance between your estate and the skeleton of the new basilica in Rome. Is that intentional?"

"You have a good eye. Cordiani redesigned the façade a few years ago, though parts of the interior date back to the time of Doge Gradenigo." The fox gestured behind him to a fireplace constructed of rough-hewn marble bonded into place with Roman concrete that had stood the test of centuries. "Like that, for instance."

"Remarkable. While I admit the finer points of architecture are beyond my sphere of wisdom, beauty is self-evident to those with an eye for it." Jai popped a succulent slice of prosciutto into his muzzle, washing it down with a quaff from a pewter tankard of refreshing Amalfi lemon juice. "This spread is delightful, Your Grace. Did your pantler send a servant to the market this morning?"

"Only for the meat. Everything else was grown right here," the fox replied, taking a bite of jam-slathered bread. He dabbed at his muzzle with a linen napkin after each bite, careful to ensure the white collar of his fitted waistcoat remained spotless. "I'm Luca of Monegario, by the way. It's my pleasure to be your host."

"I'm Thakur Jai al-Haddad...but most call me Jai," the mongoose replied. Jai shot Amir an authoritative look, prompting the fennec to pull out an airtight olivewood box from the inner pocket of his tunic. Amir slid it across the table like a stone skimming across an iced-over pond, Luca intercepting the package just before it flew off the edge. "Please, accept this token of my appreciation."

"Hrm..." Wriggling the manicured tip of his claw beneath the lid, Luca opened the vessel of intoxicating spice. His nostrils flared as the sensual aroma of saffron filled the air. Inside, exquisite threads shimmered like spun gold, tempting like the forbidden fruit of the Garden of Eden. Twirling a few delicate strands between his fingers, Luca marveled at how they stained his paw pads a vibrant shade of yellow. "It's beautiful, but what is it, exactly?"

"Saffron." Jai smiled, pleased that his gift had been well received. "It's a versatile spice which can be used in both sweet and savory dishes. My personal favorite is to use it to prepare chicken in the Berber style. Are you familiar?"

"I can't say I am, but my tastes are adventurous. You'll have to lend me a recipe...or perhaps show me how to prepare it yourself," Luca said, his eyes sparkling. Jai couldn't help but wonder if the fox's interest in him was purely culinary, or if there was something more lurking beneath the surface. "Are you as well-traveled as you seem, Jai?"

"I pride myself on my discerning palate, Your Grace," Jai replied. He leaned back in his chair, pouring himself a few fingers of burgundy port from a crystal decanter. A pleasing buzz radiated through the base of his skull, his paws feeling a tad heavier each time he reached for another morsel. "These days, there's a handsome profit to be made in catering to kindred souls."

"Luca, please," the fox playfully admonished. Jai couldn't help but admire the way that Luca's dark eyes swirled with amusement. His tight-fitting breeches hugged his legs, leaving little to the imagination while emphasizing his masculine figure. "Though aren't you concerned about the western route to Cathay? There are rumors swirling that the Spanish will soon reach it from the New World."

Jai interlaced his fingers, leaning forward with a hint of seriousness. "I've heard the rumors as well, but I'm not too worried. I have contacts that have assured me that the expansion of Devlet-i Aliyye will keep prices high. Those traders who lack knowledge of Mohammedan customs will soon find themselves strapped for inventory."

"Mrm...fascinating." Luca's gaze remained locked on Jai, warm curiosity evident in the gentle creases at the corners of his muzzle. "You're a refreshing contrast from many of the nobles here. They squabble amongst themselves, ignoring the clockwork ticking of events beyond the borders of our serene Republic."

"I think it's a shame to sap one's *joie de vivre* with such petty matters." Jai threw back the remainder of the port, warm and rich, with notes of dark berries and a hint of tobacco. Squinting to make out the finer details, Jai inspected the gilded spines of the novels that framed Luca's auburn headfur. "Though certainly not to enjoy a good book."

Luca nodded, the light thrown from the candelabras highlighting his sharp features. "I've always been fascinated by the outside world, but my father insists on keeping our family name untainted by the affairs of foreign luminaries. The written word has been my primary insight into what things are really like beyond the walls of this estate."

"Don't you venture into Verona?" Jai asked, thoughtfully interlacing his fingers.

Luca shrugged, his muzzle downturned. "Not alone. Even if I do go on a jaunt into the city, I travel by coach accompanied by a few *condottieri* in my father's service. Still...I am friendly with some of my servants. They bring oral apéritifs back with them, stories to help me paint a picture of the milieu of Verona in my mind's eye."

Jai shared a look with Amir that told him they were of one mind. Giving the fennec a subtle nod to authorize him to speak on his behalf, Jai turned his attention back to Luca.

"Perhaps, if I may make a bold request, Your Grace, would you honor us with your company?" Amir asked with the modesty of a faithful servant. "There is a seller of oriental specialties near the Ponte Scaligero who carries everything necessary for a chicken tagine. The lively air of the city is beneficial for the flow of blood and gives rise to a pleasing sanguinity."

"That would be marvelous," Luca said, eyes lighting up with unalloyed excitement. Pushing back from the table, he scrambled like an overeager mouser to grab a rapier from a *cabinet d'armes* set apart from the bookshelves. The mongoose watched with amusement as Luca buckled on his sword belt, his movements sloppy and amateurish. "You do know where you're going, right? If not, I can retrieve a map from—"

"Amir will know the way," Jai interjected. He nodded for the fennec to head back to the estate's fortified *campanile* to retrieve their weapons. While Jai preferred to use his wits to avoid conflict where possible, he'd never regretted having his trusty kirpan handy—just in case. "He'll meet us by the front gate. Shall we?"

"But of course." Luca grinned, the rapier bouncing against his hip as he lightly sauntered towards the door. Having crested the horizon, the sun cast a golden glow over the estate's verdant gardens. Blooming roses threw a rich, floral scent into the air, mingling with the aroma of fresh-baked bread wafting from the kitchen's ovens.

Making their way along a winding path that zig-zagged down the hillside, Jai couldn't help but admire the fox's lithe form, his fluffy tail swishing back and forth with excitement. He briefly wondered what it would be like to run his fingers through Luca's creamy fur and discover what laid beneath those tights. "What other passions swirl about in your mind?"

Luca grinned mischievously at Jai, a glint of something more than just friendly curiosity in his expression. "I am rather fond of *romantic adventure*." Emphasizing the last two words with just a hint of lust, Luca elicited a stirring in Jai's loins. "All in novels, of course."

"Is that so?" Jai waved to Amir, the fennec waiting by the gate with an iron strongbox held fast against his back in a frame of leather and sunbaked rattan. He took his elegant kirpan from the fennec, hilt wrapped in braided silver wire and blade forged from rare *wootz* steel produced by the finest alloyer in Rahe Neer. The scabbard was of sturdy leather, reinforced with brass studs that bore the blotchy patina of hard use. "Have any of those novels of yours taken place somewhere I might be familiar with?"

"Perhaps," Luca replied, cocking an eyebrow at Amir's dagger, the wicked blade of the *kris* like waves across a roiling ocean. The fennec winked before sliding it into a cloth-lined iron sheath on his thigh. "Are arms of this caliber really necessary? You're equipping yourselves for a Tenth Crusade."

"Better safe than sorry," Jai said, turning to allow the fennec to fit his tail with a nasty weapon modeled after the head of a *morgenstern*. Once the mongoose's fur was fluffed up around the blackened bronze spikes, they became almost imperceptible to the untrained eye. Jai then rolled his sleeves over his bracelets to conceal a measure of his wealth. "After all, what would Roland be without Durendal by his side?"

"Fair point...though I'd rather avoid experiencing the bloodier parts of those stories firsthand," Luca replied, nervously thumbing the hilt of the dagger strapped to his left thigh. With a handle made of ivory inlaid with gold filigree, it was far too ornate for base purposes. "Are you ready?" he asked, once Jai had finished inspecting his blade.

"Yes. Do try to avoid drawing too much attention to yourself," Jai murmured, walking beside Amir as the fennec led them onto the cobblestone streets of Verona proper. A pair of *condottiero* stationed at the front gate of the Monegario estate gave them a polite nod, wheel-lock rifles at the ready by their sides. They emerged into the wealthiest part of the city, where the crowds were thinner and the pockets of shoppers heavy with coin.

"I can't promise anything," Luca replied, awkwardly rubbing the back of his head. "But I'll try my best. May I inquire as to how far north you've ventured in your travels?"

"Only as far as the Duchy of Westphalia," the mongoose replied, keeping his head on a swivel as Luca lackadaisically wandered down the center of the street. While the young noble blended in at first glance, the elaborate Damascus steel scabbard of his rapier and the fine jewels he wore would make him an inviting target for a keen-eyed thief. "Why do you ask?"

Luca shrugged, his gaze transfixed by the bustling activity of the city. "Just curious, I suppose. The world is so vast and yet most of us confine ourselves to such little corners of it. I'm rather fond of *Bēowulf*, and I wondered if you'd ever had occasion to set foot in the *Tvillingerigerne*."

"I'm afraid not." Jai glanced over at Luca, admiring the way the morning sunlight danced across the fox's cloak, catching silver threads embroidered in the garment. His calf-leather boots stumbled on the uneven cobblestones, the pampered soles not yet worn enough to provide solid grip. "If I do ever find myself there, I'll be certain to regale you with every chromatic detail."

"If you'd have time for me on the return journey. You're from *Bhārata*, but I know that land is vast." Luca smoothed his starched collar down as a gust of wind threatened to carry it away. "Where exactly do you hail from in that distant expanse?"

"Rahe Neer. It's a rich and agreeable city, with wings spread wide to welcome trade from Malacca to Jingshi." Jai kept an eye on the crowd as it began to thicken, garments taking on a distinctly middle-class character with duller colors and an emphasis on practicality. "Being in close proximity to the Arabian Sea makes it relatively easy to reach as far south as the Kingdom of Mysore on a spartan sailing vessel. Even a simple fisherman can earn a mint when the winds are cooperative."

Luca nodded, narrowly avoiding bumping into a plump badger in a deep brown cowl as Jai commanded his full attention. "What is the weather like?"

"Usually hot during the dry season. The buildings are designed to promote the flow of fresh air and ensure there's plenty of shade to escape from the brutal sun." Jai gestured to one of the nearby buildings, a squat structure formed of bricks the color of low-grade rubies. "A structure built like that in Rahe Neer would bake you to death like you're inside a *tandoor*."

"That sounds...less than ideal," Luca mused.

"It's not so bad during the monsoon season. The rains can be quite heavy, but they bring with them a refreshing humidity that brings out the inner glow of one's fur and hydrates the sinuses." Jai grinned, lightly fluffing his cheek ruffs. "When I passed through Saba on my first trading run, I had a nosebleed for nearly a week."

While Jai and Luca chatted, they fell a few yards behind Amir while approaching the market square in front of the Ponte Scaligero. The smell of roast lamb and the sound of merchants hawking their wares permeated the air, greeting Jai like an old friend. "I imagine you don't get much snow, right?"

"No, I first saw snow during my travels in Europa," Jai replied, his tone wistful as he recalled the white-capped peaks of the Rhön Mountains. Though it had been bitterly cold, the hospitality of a family-run tavern dispensing an endless supply of fruit brandy had kept him in good spirits. "But I do have a fondness for the winters here. The frigid air is bracing and clear, and a thick blanket of snow carries with it an enrobing stillness that soothes my mind."

"I can see the appeal...curling up with a good book next to a roaring hearth is one of life's true delights." Luca chuckled, the sound light and melodic. He abruptly paused in front of a small stall filled with gleaming trinkets and baubles. The gilt acanthus leaves painstakingly carved into the pillars supporting the slate roof told Jai that the jeweler enjoyed a prosperous trade. "What sorts of precious stones are found in Rahe Neer's markets?"

"Ruby, sapphire, lapis lazuli, agate, carnelian, and many others," Jai replied, his love of precious jewels creeping across his muzzle despite his best attempt to appear disinterested in front of the jeweler. "The gemstone souk is an absolute treasure trove worthy of King Ravana himself. Merchants from all corners of *Bhārata* gather there to showcase their finest stones in fabulous and eye-catching cuts."

Luca's gaze wandered to a section of pendants set with precious coral, their vibrant red hue brought out in the form of polished cabochons. His fingertips lightly brushed across the smooth surface of a large oval-cut piece of coral set in intricate silver filigree to form a masculine pendant. "I doubt you have coral like in Rahe Neer. It's not the most precious of gemstones, but I find it incredible that a simple animal can produce an object of such magnificence."

"You're right," Jai murmured, cocking an eyebrow as he rotated the pendant in his palm to let the light dance across its surface. "I'm astonished that even after all I've seen, there are still treasures yet unknown to me lurking in the most ordinary of places."

A teasing grin curled at the edge of Luca's muzzle. "Ah, so even a well-traveled merchant like yourself can be surprised," he said, voice tinged with amusement. "Do allow me the pleasure of purchasing it on your behalf."

Jai's eyes widened in surprise at Luca's offer. He was taken aback by the fox's unprompted generosity. "That...that certainly isn't necessary, Luca," the mongoose protested, though a part of him was secretly delighted by the idea.

"Of course it isn't *necessary*," Luca chuckled, a hint of impishness in his eyes. "Consider it a token of munificence given freely to an esteemed guest."

"Do at least let me negotiate the price on your behalf," Jai insisted. "Even if you have coin to spare, a *bezzo* saved is a *bezzo* earned."

Luca grinned and nodded, handing the pendant back to the stall's owner, a wiry old ferret with a pair of glass lenses in an ivory frame perched on the tip of his muzzle. The jeweler wore a silver chain in the Byzantine style adorned with costly enamel in vibrant hues of green and red. "Very well, but don't go too easy on him. I want to see your mercantile skills in action."

"You've got it, Luca." Jai turned to the jeweler, his perked ears and subtle smile exuding confidence. "What is the price for this piece?" Jai asked, holding the pendant lightly by the bale.

The old ferret squinted at Jai, sizing him up with a shrewd gaze. He adjusted his spectacles before replying, his raspy voice evincing wisdom gleaned from decades spent in the market. "For a handsome gentleman like yourself, I would part with this pendant for ten *ducatello*. That is a fair price, is it not?"

Jai raised an eyebrow, feigning shock. "Ten *ducatello*? My friend, that seems rather steep for such a small trinket. Perhaps four *ducatello* would be a more reasonable sum."

"Ah, you drive a hard bargain," the jeweler said, stroking his chin thoughtfully. "But I cannot part with such a fine piece of coral so easily. My divers must go deeper every year to source it, and such expeditions come at great cost."

Jai leaned in closer, his eyes gleaming with determination. "Hrm, but look at the flaw here, my friend. There is a slight imperfection in the silver filigree. And do you not notice the faint scratch on the cabochon itself?" Jai asked, pointing out the subtle groove with expert precision.

The old ferret's lips curled into a wry smile. "You are a cunning one, I'll give you that," he conceded. "But I cannot go lower than six *ducatello*. This pendant is worth every bit of that price."

Jai allowed the corners of his muzzle to shift into a subtle smile, sensing victory was on the horizon. "Six *ducatello* and you throw in this little piece," the mongoose said, tapping a small brooch in the style of a rose window with a small coral cabochon set in the center.

The jeweler ran a clawed finger along the brooch, as his brow furrowed in thought. After a moment, he nodded in agreement. "Very well," he said, sliding the pendant and the brooch into a small velvet pouch along with a delicate silver chain. "I will accept six *ducatello* for the pair."

Luca deposited a few hefty coins in the merchant's paw with a diffident smile. "I would have happily paid full price," he said the moment they were out of earshot. "It would be a shame not to see this beautiful pendant adorning your neck."

Jai's cheeks heated at Luca's words, his heart fluttering with a mix of surprise and delight. "Thank you, Luca," Jai murmured with genuine appreciation, his cheeks glowing crimson beneath his fur. "I will cherish this gift dearly."

Luca's tail swished behind him as he mirrored Jai's subtle blush. "I'm...very glad that you like it," he replied, his breathing truncated as his scent became tinged with the pleasant sharpness of arousal. "Now, how about you showcase it on the Ponte Scaligero for me, hrm?"

"It would be a shame to simply slip it into my pocket." Jai paused, bringing the pendant up beneath his gold choker before awkwardly fiddling with the hook-and-eye clasp on the silver chain. After a few moments, Luca reached out, gently taking hold of Jai's paw and guiding it to secure the pendant.

"There we go," Luca said, his touch lingering for a moment longer than necessary. Jai struggled to catch his breath, his mind racing with a mix of anticipation and uncertainty. The air between them crackled with foretaste before Luca pulled away with a soft smile. "It suits you."

"T-thank you," Jai whispered, his voice barely audible. Reaching into the velvet pouch, he retrieved the Gothic brooch and fastened it onto Luca's cloak. "And here's a token of my appreciation."

"While I did technically buy my own gift...I do owe you my thanks," Luca murmured, his voice low and husky. His onyx eyes gleamed with mischief as he leaned in until their bodies were almost touching. The vulpine's warm breath ghosted over Jai's ears, sending a pleasurable shiver down his spine. Just before their lips touched, Luca pulled away with a smirk that seemed to promise more was to come. "Now, let's not keep Amir waiting."

"R-right." Heart still fluttering, Jai kept his guard up as they turned the corner onto the Ponte Scaligero. The air was thick with the scent of rich spices and potent incense, colorful stalls lining both sides of the weathered roadway in the center of the fortified bridge. Tall red-brick walls loomed over them on either side. The well-defended Castelvecchio was perched at the opposite end, a few footmen out front ensuring that the crowd didn't drift too close to the gate. "Amir, where are you!" Jai shouted.

"Over here, *tayir alhubi*," Amir teased. Walking over to join him, Jai's nose twitched as he breathed in the fragrant oils diffusing from an apothecary's stall. A moment later, the sharp, woody bite of herbal tinctures forced a sneeze from his snout. "Bless you."

"How much of that did you overhear?" Jai whispered to Amir while Luca sniffed curiously at different scents of *aqua mirabilis* in delicate, thin glass vessels.

"Enough to know you won't need the services of a courtesan tonight," Amir said with a playful smile, examining a clay bottle imprinted with a description of its contents in nigh-indecipherable Latin script. "Apparently this is supposed to help with...coital relations. Perhaps you'd like some for later?"

"I didn't know you could read Latin," Jai said, cocking an eyebrow. "And...yes. Get me some, just in case."

"I did have a life before I came to serve you and your father, you know," Amir said with a grin, tucking the bottle into the crook of his arm before inspecting a small jar filled with medicinal salve. It was a curious shade of red that recalled citrus fruit. "On the road, one finds all sorts who're willing to share their knowledge in exchange for a pint of ale."

Jai paused, paw sliding to his side as he caught sight of a pair of shifty figures eying Luca's jewelry covetously from near the farrier's stall where Luca was perusing. A moment after his gaze landed on them, they quickly faded back into the crowd. "Be careful. We're not entirely among friends," he muttered to Amir. "I don't think Ganymede over there will be of much value in a fight."

"I'd concur with your assessment," Amir said, dropping a small gold coin into the paw of the wizened badger running the stall. He tucked his purchases away in a leather wineskin he'd converted to serve as a cross-body bag before ensuring his dagger remained at the ready. "Good thing you've got me to back you up, right?"

"Yeah. Chew some khat. I need you alert," Jai murmured, sliding a tightly-packed ball of sweet-smelling leaves into the fennec's paw before taking a measure himself. After a few minutes of holding the astringent herbs against his tongue, the mongoose felt his senses sharpening. "Where was the trader you told us about at breakfast?"

"Just a few stalls ahead," Amir murmured, pausing at a covered cart dealing in traveling provisions to grab some salt pork to replenish their stores. The moment the fennec was distracted, the thieves made their move. A sharp pain cut through the nape of Jai's neck as one of the robbers slid his knife under the clasp of his gold chain in an attempt to pry it away.

"Gah, God damn you!" Jai snarled and rammed his elbow into the thief's muzzle while struggling to yank his kirpan from its scabbard. He wasn't a skilled swordsman, but he knew how to defend himself in a pinch—that is, if he could actually get a blade in his paws. "Amir!"

"I've got you!" Amir tackled the ferret with claws drawn, cutting through the meat of his shoulder like a slice from a *karambit*. The thief let out a cry of pain and attempted to scramble away, but Amir was stronger, holding him fast by the scruff of his neck before knocking him unconscious. "Go help Luca. I'll be right behind you as soon as I stash our assets."

Jai nodded, adrenaline pumping through him as he hastily wrested his kirpan free with the sharp screech of metal against metal. Blade glinting in the early morning sun, he rushed to where Luca stood, back pressed against a brick wall. The other thief, a wiry stoat with beady eyes, held a sharp dagger to Luca's throat while his free paw ripped the ruby pendant from his neck.

"Let him go," Jai growled, extending his sword beside his muzzle as he drew his arm back. There was fire in his gaze, a burning power that rolled down his muscular shoulders like licks of blue-white flame. "Take the gem and piss off or have your belly sliced open. Your choice."

The stoat sneered, dragging the tip of his dagger lightly across Luca's throat. A thin line of blood welled up from the wound as the vulpine let out an ear-splitting yowl of pain. His rapier clattered to the ground, bouncing once before rolling into the muck of a nearby gutter. "You better listen to him!" Luca snarled defiantly. "He's the First Sword of the Great Sultan him—"

"Drop the weapon, or I'll gut him like a fish," the thief hissed, pressure from the dagger cutting Luca off mid-sentence. Jai narrowed his eyes, studying him down to the subtlest of movements. He could tell from his awkward stance that the stoat was inexperienced with a blade, but that didn't make him any less of a threat with Luca in his grasp. With a deep breath, Jai slowly lowered his kirpan to the ground while pouring all the strength he could muster into his legs.

The stoat triumphantly smirked as his grip on Luca slackened. As soon as he shoved Luca to the ground and turned to make his retreat, Jai lashed out with his tail, his thick fur concealing the sharp and deadly spikes that now tore through the air. There was a sharp jolt as the tail-mace thudded against the meat of the stoat's thigh, spattering Jai's *shalwar kameez* with blood. "Now, Amir!"

Amir snatched Luca's dropped rapier before springing forward to drive the point into the thief's torso. Propelled with enormous force, the blade pierced through the visceral muscle of his chest with a sickening *squelch*. Staggering backward, he crumpled to the ground like a dropped flour sack, the tail-mace ripping free of his thigh.

"Gah...fuck. Why couldn't you have just been content with the pendant?" Jai asked, immediately knowing from experience that the stoat was beyond help. Blood spurted from the wound as his paws latched desperately onto the rapier, gasping for air as his life drained away into a nearby cesspool. After a few moments, the thief went still. "Are you okay, Luca?"

"Y-yeah...the wound isn't deep." Luca's voice quivered as he gingerly touched the shallow gash on his neck. The blood left a deep crimson stain on the white fur of his palm. "Though it still stings like an adder bite."

"Here." Amir disappeared for a few moments, returning with the jar of red ointment. The fennec quickly popped the lid and scooped a generous amount of the soothing balm onto his paw. Applying it with a practiced touch, he ensured every inch of the wound was protected. "This is an ointment of witch hazel and goldenseal which should stem the bleeding and prevent you from developing a fever."

"T-thank you..." The tension in Luca's shoulders eased as the ointment's analgesic effect kicked in. "Mrmph...that's good stuff. Were you trained in the art of the physicker?"

"No, but a servant does endeavor to soothe the pains of those he serves." Amir took a minute to finish dressing Luca's wound with a strip of soft cotton cloth before turning to Jai. "I imagine we don't want to be discovered when the city watch arrives. If they show up and find two greenhorns covered in blood next to a dead body, there's going to be a lot of uncomfortable accusations thrown our way."

Jai nodded, heart pounding in his chest as he tugged the rapier free and wiped the viscera onto a rag wrapped around the base of his scabbard. He managed to pry the pendant from the stoat's clenched paw before freezing up, muscles paying little heed to his commands. With a stout gaze, Amir grabbed the mongoose's paw and pulled him away, his demeanor betraying no fear. "C-can you...take..."

"Anything for you, my friend," Amir murmured, taking the rapier from Jai's paw and handing it back to Luca. An uncomfortable pressure seemed to squeeze around the mongoose's throat as he struggled for air. "Take slow, deep breaths for me."

"O-okay," Jai replied, taking comfort in Luca's presence as the vulpine wrapped a strong arm around his shoulder. Luca kept a firm grip on Jai, his reassuring touch grounding the mongoose's frazzled mind. The odor of the red ointment hung in Jai's nostrils, reminding him that Luca was very much alive thanks to their efforts.

"Just hang in there," Amir whispered, voice filled with concern as he guided them through the narrow alleyways of the city. The scent of damp earth mingled with the metallic tang of their blood-spattered clothes, only briefly disappearing beneath the pungent mélange of stale urine and equine manure that permeated the cobblestones. "Just a little further. I came across this seedy tavern while exploring last night. We can catch our breath there."

Approaching the flickering lantern that marked the entrance to La Tavola del Drago, Jai couldn't help but feel a surge of relief. The dimly-lit and crowded establishment looked like the perfect place to disappear, at least for a little while. While only half the panes remained in its glass windows, a roaring fire in the central hearth beat back the encroaching chill.

"Gah...that wasn't the kind of visit to the city that I had in mind." Jai sunk into the chair, ignoring the sensation of rough straw digging into his thighs as it poked through the weathered burlap seat. The acrid scent of burning wood rushed into his nostrils as an intense gust of wind kicked the smoke away from the ersatz chimney. He kept a wary eye on the door as Amir ordered them three tankards of ale from the flirtatious barmaid, a roe deer.

"So...is this a usual day for you two?" Luca asked, sagging down in his seat with a groan of discomfort.

"No, definitely not." Jai let out a dry chuckle tinged with exhaustion. He took a sip of the ale, relishing in the bitter warmth as it slid down his throat. "While we sometimes attract trouble, this was on another level entirely. Most street-level thieves usually aren't bold—or foolhardy—enough to attack their marks in broad daylight."

"It's best not to look for trouble, but sometimes it comes looking for you," Amir said, alternating sips of beer with candied coffee beans to keep himself alert. The fennec's ears remained ramrod-straight, twitching every time a chair scraped across the wood-plank floor. "Still...even I hadn't anticipated an attack like that."

"It's troubling. I'll request my father double the security patrols around the city." Luca chanced a glance at Jai, his gaze softening as the mongoose presented his ruby pendant back to him with a glowing smile. "It was fortunate that I had two trusty companions with me."

"Oh, did we earn a promotion? I thought we were merely your esteemed guests." Jai drained his tankard as a pleasant warmth rolled through his nether regions. Amir let out a hearty laugh, slapping his paw against the table with a resonant *thud*. "Though I'm not sure lowly traders such as us are worthy of such a distinguished title."

"Nonsense," Luca replied, leaning over to squeeze the mongoose's shoulder with aristocratic vigor. Jai's cheeks flushed as the vulpine's gaze lingered on him with a mixture of admiration and desire that sent a lascivious shiver down his spine. "Anyone brave enough to draw a weapon on my behalf is more than worthy. That goes for you too, Amir. Where did you both learn to fight with the vigor of Fiore Dei Liberi?"

"You flatter us," Jai replied, looking away with a demure smile. He filed the compliment away in his mind to be savored later like a bottle of rich Amontillado. "We've simply picked up a little knowledge from the wandering hedge-knights we've shared our hospitality with on lonely stretches of country road."

Amir snorted, setting his tankard down with a loud, resounding *thunk.* "You're being too modest. I imagine you know more about swordplay than half the knights of Frederick III," Amir quipped. "Even if you had to use your tail-mace this time."

"Perhaps"—Jai rose from his chair, lifting his heavy pewter tankard for a toast—"but, if it weren't for you, Amir, I'd be a pincushion fit for a noblewoman's sewing room right now. I propose a toast. To brave and loyal friends, both old and new!"

Luca raised his own tankard, a bright grin stretching across his muzzle. "Indeed! To brave and loyal friends," he echoed, clinking his tankard against Jai's. The vulpine looked utterly content as he took a small sip. "Still, I hope the remainder of your stay in Verona is far less exciting. I don't want you to get the wrong impression of this fair city."

"It's no different than anywhere else, believe me, and the city watch being on high alert should prevent another attack like that," Jai murmured, glancing towards a fence, a red squirrel, in a corner booth drooling over a gold chain clearly ripped from some unfortunate soul's neck. "It's a shame we didn't have an opportunity to pick up some olives. I can scrounge up everything else I would need for chicken tagine from the stores in our saddlebags."

"Fortunately, I had the foresight to pick up a jar while you two were lollygagging about in the plaza," Amir said with a smirk. "While

I still believe myself to be the superior cook, Jai does make a few recipes that I simply adore...chicken tagine among them."

Luca smiled as he finished his beer and left a few billon coins on the table to cover the tab. "Well, I can think of no better time than now for a cooking lesson. I suggest that we share a meal and some lively tales back at my estate, if you two are keen."

Jai and Amir exchanged glances before sharing a nod of agreement. While the chaos of the day had left them drained, the prospect of a warm meal and good company was exactly the *viaticum* they needed...

Jai stood over a tin-lined copper pot, vigorously stirring the fragrant concoction of chicken, spices, and olives. The air in Luca's bedroom was thick with the heady aroma wafting in from the balcony, which had been hastily converted into a barebones scullery. Lighting the mongoose with a lead-white halo, the moon hung low in the cloudless sky.

"So, there I was, cornered on the rooftop of the leather souk in Taiz," Jai said, the rhythmic stirring of the pot forming a soothing beat that flowed underneath his words. "At that point, I had only a loincloth and three silver *para* nestled up against my privates to my name."

Luca leaned forward, utterly captivated. "Incredible! How did you manage to get away?"

"I took a leap of faith," Jai said with a wink. "I vaulted off the edge of the rooftop and caught hold of a laundry line that was strung across the alley. With a bit of luck, I managed to swing down and land on a balcony three floors below. I gave a hapless washer-woman quite the fright as I landed!"

Luca's eyes went wide with awe, as though a character from one of his novels had been realized in flesh and blood in front of him. "But how did you end up in that situation in the first place? You left that bit out at the start."

Jai chuckled. "I had snuck into the hallowed halls of the Thieves' Guild in Cairo to fraternize and enjoy the bountiful refreshments. Just as I was about to take my leave, the Sheik of Thieves himself questioned my presence. I told him that I was a visiting journeyman thief from Zinjibar, and he challenged me to prove it by stripping down to nothing but my loincloth and taking a single *para* from three different vendors at the Khan el-Khalili market."

Luca stood up and joined Jai by the stewing pot, wrapping an affectionate arm around his shoulder. "God's hooks, Jai, you have the most outrageous stories! I can't decide if you're a masterful raconteur or truly the most audacious gentleman to ever grace this fine estate."

"A little bit of both, perhaps. But what's a good adventure story without a touch of exaggeration?" Jai responded, taking a small taste to ensure it was ready before dishing out a serving into one of the hand-carved ironwood bowls they used when traveling. "Here. It's been a while since I've prepared chicken tagine, so let me know if something's off."

Luca closed his eyes and inhaled the fragrant steam rising from the dish. Eagerly taking a bite, he let out a satisfied sigh while Jai enjoyed his handiwork by taking a spoonful straight from the pot. Jai squeaked with delight; the chicken was tender, the spices perfectly balanced, and the olives added a delightful tanginess to the dish.

"I take it that you approve?" Jai asked while serving Amir. After much objection from the estate's baker about the scandal of allowing a staple of the poor to disgrace a nobleman's oven, Jai had managed to bribe him into baking a batch of *piadina* smooth as a leaf and big as the moon. He slipped two beneath the bowl as he passed it to the fennec in exchange for a phial of herbal aphrodisiac. "Do try it with the flatbread. It's not quite naan, but it works in a pinch."

"I more than approve," Luca replied with unbridled delectation. A little cautiously, he used the *piadina* as a makeshift spoon to scoop up a generous portion of the flavorful sauce and a few hunks of chicken. "This is certainly different than using flatware...but not entirely bad."

"You get used to it," Amir said through a muzzleful of food. "Plus, using trenchers really cuts down on the amount of washing required when every drop of water counts."

Jai laughed heartily. He followed Luca back to the bed, taking a seat on the luxurious, feather-stuffed mattress. The room was filled with merriment and the warmth of the meal, and for a moment, all troubles seemed to fade away. "Ah, the joys of resourcefulness in times of scarcity. It brings out the creativity in all of us."

Luca nodded, eating slowly and savoring each bite. "It's during times like these that I'm reminded of the simple pleasures in life. *Alla fine del gioco, re e pedone finiscono nella stessa scatola.*"

"When the game ends, both the king and the pawn go into the same box," Jai replied, resting his head against the meat of Luca's shoulder. Their eyes met, unspoken desire simmering as it enrobed them like a layer of molten caramel. "I don't know much Italian, but I do know that proverb."

Luca reached out and brushed his fingers against Jai's cheek, tracing the contours of his muzzle with the delicate caress. Jai could feel the weight of Lucas's tender gaze upon him, a pressure like a calming quilt wrapped around his soul. "You continue to surprise me, Jai."

"Well, speaking of surprises...Amir, would you fetch a bottle of palm toddy from our stores?" Jai asked, using a coded message that conveyed his desire for a moment of privacy. "I believe libations are in order."

"Of course," Amir replied with a knowing wink. "I'll procure our finest bottle."

Jai watched the fennec gently shut the door behind him, leaving him alone with Luca. With the soft glow of candlelight dancing across their muzzles, they locked eyes. "You know," the mongoose whispered. "I may exaggerate some of my stories, but there's one thing I could never embellish."

"Oh?" Luca asked, Jai's sensual hunger mirrored in his eyes.

"My desire for you. I say verily that it burns my spirit like wildfire," Jai confessed. "Every word I've spoken, every story I've told, it all leads to this moment...the moment where I finally kiss you."

"Well? I'm waiting," Luca replied with an inviting smile. "Go on, Jai. Tonight, I am yours, and you are mine."

"*Aere perennius*," Jai replied, stealing one of Amir's romantic turns of phrase. With raw desire swirling between them like a tempest, their breath mingled as Jai leaned in to brush against Luca's muzzle. The kiss was tentative at first, yet it carried a smoldering intensity that soon ignited into an inferno of passion. Lithe bodies joining in a primal union, the Golden Son of Rahe Neer lost himself in a fervent kiss beneath the starlit sky of Verona...

The Bleak Tower

Cedric G! Bacon

t was said that when night fell upon the city of Howl-graves, that it was a fool's choice to be caught within its looming shadows. Behind the facade of safety could lurk a danger which could easily stain the cobblestoned streets from the cruel eyes of the scheming cutpurse and kidnapper, waiting to abscond with their latest victim across the borders and into waiting caravans for those same high-chinned nobles.

Between the infrequent lamps which broke up the major boroughs lay a part of the city known as the Desert. Passing through the Desert, a wayfarer would view the twisted, alien streets and garbage-blighted alleyways that were a haven for every thief, kidnapper, murderer, mercenary, and much more. Few of those furs who called the Desert home could be sure of the honesty of the fellow they dealt with; even the city watch, bribed with a few red-stained coins, could look the other way when it came to the Desert. And at night, it would seem as though a certain type of life would crawl from the hovels that called the square home, to congregate and hold carnival while the other furs of Howlgraves slumbered on.

Torches flared murkily on the revels in one such establishment. The furs could carouse and roar and howl as much as they liked, without fear of the disruption of their sport. The merriment thundered high to the low-hanging smoke-stained roof, where the rascals gathered in not just every stage of rags and tatters, but some wore the burnished steel and mail of some noblefur's army. As they congregated among the rogues where everyone wore steel of some fashion, from a poniard to the long broadsword, openly and without prejudice of using it.

But for the most part, despite coming from different walks and speaking different tongues, they eyed each other similarly. There were great northern sea pirates of Dane, bears with giant broadswords and axes strapped to their backs, turning their snouts to the lapping of the inky-blue ocean as though it were the call of the clarion. The shrill laughter of a gaggle of ewes from Scotland, one of whom sat on the lap of a gaunt-faced goat from further south, who fingered the ewe's dagger-strapped thigh with caution and calculated infatuation. Wandering mercenary soldiers of some defeated army or another, and bold-eyed tavern wenches serving beer and ale slop to the gross rogues who spun bawdy tales and sang bawdier songs, held court with these quick-hooved and swaggering bravos of a dozen or more countries.

And in a corner of this tavern, far from the eyes and ears of the dominant element, sat two occupants, both women. The first was the taller of the two, a lioness of late-middling years with dashes of gray swirling about the gold of her fur. Her head was turned down, with the graceful curve of practiced nobility, though the air about her was bereft of the sort of cadence that came with such titles. The chemise she wore almost enveloped her forelimbs, but it did not obscure the intricately woven bracelet which she fingered now and then while talking to her companion.

"It's not my purview to seek the assistance of a freebooter," she said. Though the words would appear nervous to burning ears, they were not: it was a statement of fact, lacking fear but also showing surety.

Her companion leaned back in her chair and laughed. "That would not be the first time such a thing has been uttered. Zounds, I'm sure I would have the king's purse for each moment I've heard it!"

"I'm sure," smirked the lioness. She cast a glance out the tavern window and heaved a sigh from her blunted maw as she looked among the stars which peppered the night sky. "I wish that I could achieve my goals myself, but these times are not like they were for me, when I lived in a land and a time long ago."

"Hence why you've sought the assistance of a freebooter," said the companion as she supped lightly at her tankard of ale. "But the task of your goal, it's…"

"Impossible?"

"Mad."

"And here my contact assured me of the courage that is imbued into each member of your guild of thieves and killers. Mayhaps I was a bit hasty in throwing in with such a lot."

The second shrugged her shoulders then folded her arms across her chest. Negotiations such as these were not made within the hour—it was a long game, strategic back and forth between parties, and from where the second woman sat, she knew it was her turn at the wheel of chance.

"By all means," she began, "seek another to take your proposal. We're in a location where you could just as easily ask any bravo for the task, should they be interested. Just don't expect them to be as polite about acknowledging the dangers they would undoubtedly encounter. Especially in matters concerning wizards."

"Ah, but there is where you are wrong," chuckled the lioness. "No one is asking you to slay a wizard. Were I, Fenella of the Isles, at the full of my strength, that task would gladly be my own responsibility. As such, there is no need to seek the help of a lout or oaf who'll completely bungle things and get themselves killed in the process."

"Such is my caution, for the risks you're asking me to undertake." The other who sat across from Fenella was young, but the lioness was not hasty to proclaim that due to her youth, her companion, a vixen, was naive. It was not lines of age which crossed that russet and white furred face, but scars which gave proof of some twenty hard seasons. The cloak of her hood was pulled back, and the lioness would nominally say she locked her eyes on those of the vixen, except that the vixen very visibly lacked the gaze of a right eyeball. Much of the dark scarring beneath her fur and around her head seemed centered on this crater, obscured behind a silken patch. Similarly congruent with the vixen's appearance was the presence of a long, light rapier nestled about her hip, around which was a belt that held twin dirks and a smaller poniard.

"You're very wise in your concerns, ah..."

"Raibyn," the vixen answered. "And caution and concern are what keeps the best of us alive."

Fenella laughed haughtily. "Wisdom I too live by, dear one." She reached underneath the sleeve of her left forelimb, producing a pouch that she laid with a heavy thud upon the table, too loud for the comfort of Raibyn. "There be your fee, upfront to allay worries and set you aside that you'll not be paid upon completion."

With the swiftness of the wind, Raibyn swooped the small fortune up and out of sight. She need not have opened it to feel its weight, far exceeding what the initial requirement for the task called for.

Fenella was amused by the vixen's reaction. "You betray your stoicism, Raibyn, and as such I believe you've said more than you intend to. Here is what I have asked of your guild and what I require of you." When Raibyn next looked up, she was surprised at the object in front of her. It appeared from nowhere, the little chest: it was nondescript in its appearance, with hasps of iron starting to sag to the rusts of age and its wood blackened and rotting. Raibyn moved to undo the lock when Fenella shouted, "NO!" and prompted the retreat of the vixen's paw.

"Open it not here," the lioness instructed, beneath hushed tones. "Only when you reach Connal, and only then will you open it, for he will not be in any position to do so himself."

"Wouldn't you rather have me abscond with your lover?" Raibyn asked. "No man deserves a fate as you have described, especially in the tower of Yudan."

Fenella shook her head, and the full weight of her age seemed to fall upon her all at once. "Nay," she replied. "Connal is lost to me. This I know to be true and that to which I accept."

"And you do not wish me to slay Yudan." When Fenella nodded, Raibyn heaved a sigh of relief. "Then all you ask of me..."

"Is for you to enter Yudan's tower, find Connal, and give him that chest."

"The task still seems paltry for the risk taken..."

"Are you implying that we haggle over the price?" Fenella sated amused.

"You've paid well in advance and it would not be a wise decision on my part to cross a sorceress that is right in front of me," chuckled Raibyn. "No matter how decrepit she claims her powers to be."

"Oh, you'll not come to any harm by my paws," said Fenella. "All I asked of your guild is that they send me a bravo they believed held the skill necessary for my request. The guild's quartermaster suggested you based on a past experience he said you had at sea. Given what I've heard about your voyage, I trusted his opinion."

At this Raibyn grinned, involuntarily touching the scars along her face. "You would know well had you been there. I had no interest in taking the assignment, if not for the pay, and even then the cost was too high."

"How so?"

Smirking, Raibyn lifted her patch. "I lost my eye, my opponent lost his life. And the companions I traveled with lost theirs."

"So perhaps you understand all too well that there are things we must do that are difficult but they must be done." She glanced at the chest that Raibyn held. "Contained within is something Connal has needed for a long time. Something that was separated from him when he was captured by Yudan. Something that took me a long time to retrieve from Yudan's clutches."

"Yudan is quite the adversary your lover made. What was the root of their dispute?"

"Connal did not make this enemy. It was myself, in my foolish pride, that set in motion these events. Yudan made an overture and

I rebuffed him, and so to punish me, he framed Connal for a crime he did not commit and for which he was swiftly arrested and adjudicated in a court not of his peers."

"Weren't there witnesses?"

"All terrified of Yudan, many of whom fear Yudan more than they fear death itself. The commander of the city watch, a fat rodent hight Duncan and paid most handsomely by Yudan, pursued the charges and Connal was found guilty. But, rather than remand Connal to the gallows, Yudan bought Connal's imprisonment, saying it was better for one wizard to jail another, and the last sight I had of him was his heavily chained hide being transported inside that damnable tower, never to be seen again."

Reclining in her seat, Raibyn found herself gazing out at the tower which seemed impossibly monolithic in the night. It sat in a great garden just beyond the city, surrounded by high walls and watched more keenly by city guards and soldiers than almost any quarter in Howlgraves. Much could be said of its form, which rose some hundred and fifty feet to the sky, with sides that appeared slicker than that of polished glass. More still was said of the dangers of crossing the walls into the tower grounds, where it were not the guards or soldiers that an enterprising rogue had to be wary of; rather, the dangers whispered beyond were never definitely ascertained, due to those who climbed over the walls and inside never climbing back out.

Those clouds of the unknown caused the hackles between Raibyn's shoulders to twitch in furtive anxiety.

Fenella recognized this and smiled. "I may be old and my strength dims with the seasons, but often when minds are open to me, their thoughts whisper out. Yours are muddled, Raibyn, but I do sense about you courage and confidence, and a wisdom not often gleaned by one so young. Your caution of magic and mages is understandable and not out of place, but be not afraid of the powers beyond your own. Trust in your abilities and means, and all will be..."

"Hearken here, my dear fellows! I believe we have two lonely wenches about us this evening!"

The two looked sharply up at the odious voice which broke through. The speaker was a warthog who smiled at them with broken, yellowing teeth; he snorted as he curled the tufts growing from the base of his tusks. Behind him were two others, a leopard and a jaguar, and all sported cruel and curved daggers at their hips and long, lethal swords were in their paws.

"Can we be of assistance to you gentlefurs?" queried Raibyn calmly.

"I think rather it is we that would be of assistance to ye ladies," answered the leopard. "My brothers-in-arms and myself heard you cackle about taking the tower of the wizard Yudan."

"It was just loose talk," said Fenella.

"Loose talk though it be, it burnished our interests. Ye'll need a few nimble-pawed figures to help you filch Yudan's treasure..."

"There is no need for a robbery," replied Fenella, standing upright. "I believe we've concluded our business, Raibyn, so..."

"But yeh've not concluded your business with us!" the warthog cajoled. He hooked his forelimb about her waist just as his two fellows began laughing. "Tell yeh what, give us a great kiss and we'll not spread word to Chief Duncan what you and the one-eyed wench are planning."

"That sounds like a far worse fate than what befell Connal!" hissed Fenella, writhing from his grip. "Release me at once!"

"You would be wise to do as she says," Raibyn stated, sipping the last of her drink. Finishing, she added, "There won't be another warning."

This caught the attention of the group of rogues who again burst into abject laughter.

"Look at the tiny slip of a whelp-bitch threatening the likes of us!" bellowed the leopard. "G'wan, get out of our sight before ye hurt yerself!"

"And just what will you do about it?" the warthog said. Then he eyed the small chest resting on the table. "Perhaps we'll just take yer gold as recompense for opening your maw against your betters!"

At this, a savage backpaw blow from Fenella cracked the warthog across the face. "Whoreson!" she spat. "Touch not what doesn't belong to you!"

Livid, eyes black with anger, a broadbladed dagger seemed to jump into the warthog's hooven paw, as he snarled, "You little slut, I think I'll cut your ears and nose off for that! Hearken fellows and hold her high!"

Raibyn appeared in one shadow stride and just before the steel flashed down on Fenella's face, her poniard parried the motion and clanged against the falling blade with the thunder of two anvils when met. Her next move saw her lithe paw curl into a fist as she rocked the warthog's face and sent him tumbling to the table with the ewes, spilling their ale over their customer and themselves. Almost at an instant he had sprung up again, and replaced his missing dagger with a sharper, longer blade.

"Heathen bitch, I'll have your heart for that!" he howled and lunged for the vixen.

Raibyn ducked low, the wind from his blade whistling past her ears and she took the wind from him when knocking the hilt of her rapier just under his ribs, doubling her opponent. The knee of her hindleg connected with his chin before he could rise again and he collapsed into a heap like tallow.

"Now, if you'll let us be on our way," Raibyn said, "nothing else needs to be said between us."

"Whelp of a whore!" barked the jaguar and he dove into the fray and took a chance on an awkward slash. Raibyn dropped to the right, just as the blade bit into the table she and Fenella had just been sitting at. A dark smile crept across her face as her rapier dashed out like lightning, just as the leopard marked the opportunity to deal a sneaky death-blow of his own with an overhand attack that the vixen parried off with her dirk, repelling the leopard.

The jaguar yanked his sword free and the clang and rasp of two blades punctuated the noise above the atmosphere. The jaguar was practiced, but his attack was built on power and brutality, as evidenced by his use of the bigger sword. But Raibyn's attack was an elemental—swift and fast moving, she dodged each awkward slash and parry shrewdly avoiding the lumbering steps made by the jaguar to close the gap for the killing blow, ignoring the waver in movements as fatigue slowly crept into the burning rage.

When the mistake happened, the jaguar could only possess seconds to process its occurrence: a backpawed cut slit the rim of the vixen's tunic, not quite touching fur and flesh, and the blade became embedded deep into a wineskin jerkin. A different type of death accented the preceeding as the jaguar's bulging eyes became filled with the knowledge of his death as Raibyn's rapier pierced the jaguar's chest, severing gristle, muscle, and bone until the fur's heart exploded like a melon and blood would cease to flow through those veins.

A scream brought the attention back on the leopard, maw bared in a savage snarl as he rushed at her with sword extended. Jerking and twisting her rapier free, Raibyn pivoted out just when the leopard's blade came down on his deceased companion and hewed him from neck to shoulder-bone. With her dirk-paw, Raibyn slashed at the leopard's neck, the return shredding the feline's throat. Blood spilled down his stained tunic as he tottered back, sword clattering from nerveless digits to the ground and eyes wide in disbelief as he pulled down a table with his death and extinguished a lamp.

Plunged into the darkness, confusion reigned. Howls and barks and shrieks mingled with the crowd—who had surged forward to watch the fracas—attempting to find their way out of the tavern. There was the crash of many upset chairs and tables, the thrum of footpaws in flight, shouts and oaths of furs tumbling over one another. By the time the torch had been relighted, most of the denizens had gone out by way of the doors or broken windows, the rest huddled behind stacks of wine-kegs or overturned tables. The two women—the lioness and the vixen—had vanished, but evidence of the vixen's work was left behind.

The lurid revelry of the tavern fell away quickly behind Raibyn. In the confusion she had discarded her torn and tattered hooded cloak, revealing the clothing of her profession: a snug fitting black tunic and matching breeks tucked into silken boots. The supple ease with which she moved about the night would have made the most seasoned of thieves blanch, but Raibyn was not of the mood to impress anyone.

She had parted from Fenella once they had made their way outside. The lioness imparted the chest into Raibyn's paws, with the final instructions of "Do not open until you see Connal!" echoing in her ears as the lioness disappeared into the night. Raibyn now entered the Garden District, a part of Howlgraves reserved for the aging temples hewn by the Romans and northern reivers many ages ago. Snowy-marble pillars and high domes depicted gods druidic and pagan who leered down upon her as she hugged the outer wall which divided Yudan's tower from the rest.

She looked up at the looming shaft of the tower. No lights ever shone forth from it, and there seemed to be no windows within—at least not to the eye level of this inner wall. Even against the backdrop of the night sky it seemed to exude an aura of great evil, and as Raibyn crept close and stood outside the dividing wall, she could feel a certain energy pulse and pass through her.

Placing an ear against the wall, she listened: there was the rustle of the thick shrubbery on the other side, and she heard no soldiers make their rounds just yet. But they would just portend mortal doom. It was the strange and unknown perils awaiting within that caused hesitation. She thought of Yudan, whom many furs said was very old and very powerful, who worked strange dooms from within and without. Raibyn's shoulders prickled at the memory of a drunken page of the court's tale of when Yudan laughed in the face of a naive lordling who attempted to eject the wizard from Howlgraves, and with but a wave of his paw the lordling was transformed into a withered and blackened beetle, which Yudan crunched with the heel of his foot, laughing maniacally as he did so.

These engrossing thoughts were broken when she heard the measured stride and clinking steel of the watch. Raibyn waited, expecting him to pass again on the next round, but silence reigned for many long moments. If she counted on the next pass, she would determine how much time there was in between to hop over and scurry to a hidden valley before being noticed. But that next pass never came, as long silence kept, with only the sound of the wind whistling through the garden walls. Finally, curiosity overcame the vixen: leaping lightly, she grasped the wall and swung herself up to the top and lay flat on the broad coping. Blending into the darkness, she darted her eye to her left and then to her right, waiting for the presence of the guard or a corps of soldiers. Satisfied that he may have been on the other side the grounds, she lowered herself cautiously and quietly, daring not to breathe until her feet touched the withered shrubbery.

She had only a few seconds to find cover; it was bad to stand beneath the naked starlight, and she moved swiftly about the curve of the wall, hugging to its shadowy edifices that divided it from the sward. As she crouched and moved below its apex, marking each and every cover of the darkness that she could, she stumbled over a lump that lay equally hidden near the edges of the bushes.

Raibyn bent low to investigate. Perhaps some bit of trash that the wizard or his guards had thrown off the side, she mused, until her keen sight showed her first the legs and finally the form a strongly built wolf in the silver jupon and crested helmet of the city guard. A sword and shield lay useless nearby. Raibyn judged by the wide maw and glassy, pop-eyed stare that was masked over the wolf's face, this fur had been strangled—a judgment of knowledge that left her wary as she stealthily removed her rapier and looked about uneasily.

This must have been the guard she had heard pass by the wall; but only a short amount of time, perhaps minutes, had elapsed from when she heard his steps and when she found him now. But somehow, in that interval, something nameless and unknown had struck out like a cobra and had choked out the guard's life.

The hint of motion in the overgrown sward from behind the guard caught her attention. Curious, Raibyn walked on the balls of her feet, gripping her blade and making no more noise than a ghost. Yet, the figure within the tall grass had heard and Raibyn caught a glimpse of a bulky form hugging closely to the wall. Two forelimbs, two hindlimbs, a head, and a tail—the knowledge left Raibyn with a sigh of relief that at least what she stalked was a fur. But then the stranger heard her and wheeled quickly with a gasp of panic, and made the first motion of a forward plunge, paws clutching some sort of rope but just as quickly recoiled as the sight of the vixen's blade winked in the starlight.

For a long tense space, neither spoke. Both stood ready for anything.

"Are you an assassin?" asked Raibyn with a suspicious whisper.

A low laugh rumbled from the stranger. "An assassin? Nay, though I've killed my share of furs, rarely for profit. I'm a thief, and judging by your dress, you're either like myself or a hired mercenary of the old wizard."

"Not a mercenary in the wizard's purse," hissed the vixen. "And I'm not a thief this night. I've a task within that I've been paid for, but it does not involve poaching what treasure lay inside, if the rumors be true."

"Aye, they are true indeed," replied the other. "Furs call me Basileus, but you can call me Basil."

Raibyn lowered her sword. "I've heard of you. Furs call you the greatest thief in all the land."

This elicited another chuckle from the stranger. Basil was a dormouse nearly as tall as the vixen; he was big-bellied and big-boned, yet his every movement betrayed a subtle ability to whisper in his strides. He was dressed in a simple dark tunic and wrapped around his shoulder was a thin, long strand of rope, knotted at irregular intervals. In the paws that had just moments before attempted to claim another strangling victim was a similar knotted cord. Belted around him was a short sword.

"It behooves me to brag about my successes," Basil stated. "Bad business when everyone knows who you are. Which leads me to question, who are you?"

"Raibyn, a freebooter," aswered the vixen. "And that's all you need to know. I simply wish to find my way into the dungeons and speak with a prisoner."

Raibyn sensed the large ears and belly of the dormouse shake in laughter, but it was not derisive.

"Well indeed!" he whispered. "And here I thought I was the only one mad enough in tempting the wheel of fate this night. The reward will far outweigh the risks, I believe!"

"So you killed the guard?"

Basil shrugged and said nonchalantly, "I slid over the wall when he was on the other side of the garden and I hid in the bushes. He heard me, or thought he might have heard something and came blundering over, making more noise than a newborn demanding milk from his mother's teat. It was no trick at all to get around and behind him, and grip his fool neck until he gave up the ghost."

Raibyn looked back at the body and then said, "However, you made one mistake."

"Impossible!" hissed Basil.

"You should have dragged him into the bushes so that no one would find him."

"Precisely why I didn't! There won't be another change of the guard until dawn when the soldiers awake from their slumber, and should anyone come searching for him now and find him, they would immediately flee at once to Yudan. That would give us enough time to make our escape, but if they were not able to find him and tore up these grounds searching for him, we would be captured like fish in a barrel. And while I've no doubt you're quite the swordsfur with that blade, you might not be able to overpower a score of heavily armed guards swarming upon you."

The vixen mused on this for a moment then nodded. Then her attention came to a word that the dormouse had uttered, and stated, "You said 'us'."

Basil grinned. "Aye. I've never shared an adventure with anyone, let alone one who is paid for madder tasks than I could fathom. I may not fully understand your purpose for being here but I like your grit that you still attempted to cross the wall where most would blanch and flee in terror." He held out a paw. "I propose that we unite and go as far as our destinations take us, and then part ways as friends and companions. Agreed?"

"Agreed," whispered Raibyn.

"So! Now that that's settled, we waste time in this discourse. There are no guards along the inner sanctum of the garden here. It's the tower itself we have to be wary of…"

"More guards?"

"Somewhat, my intelligence has determined that while there are a score or two of soldiers in the lower tower, there are sentinels of a different sort in the middle levels."

"What are they?"

"I don't know," admitted Basil. "I've not been able to ascertain as to what they are exactly. No matter, we enter from the upper floors and steal down from the top of the tower, and with a little luck it will be the same way we make our exit. With any further luck we avoid old Yudan as much as possible before he can weave any of his curses over us, if you are game."

"I'll go as far as any," Raibyn stated as she sheathed her rapier. "Lead the way."

They wove through the shrubbery to the foot of the tower, and there, with a motion quick and supple and belying his heft, Basil unwound his knotted cord. At the end was what appeared to be a strong steel hook, and immediately Raibyn saw his plan, musing to herself that she had not thought to do the same to avoid the guards on the lower floor. Asking no questions, she watched the dormouse swing it about his head and ears until he cast it far and wide, the hook curving and rippling until it vanished over the rimmed spire. A quick, cautious jerk of the cord did not result in any slack or give.

"Luck was with us," muttered Basil. "Can you climb?"

"If it will hold up to the stress," answered Raibyn. Casting wary glances about, she could not help but feel a strange nervousness come over her. The night wind blew with the same cadence as the two strangers, and that worried the vixen the most.

The dormouse gripped the rope and crooked a knee about it, beginning the ascent first. He moved like a feline, swift and quick, the cord swaying this way and that and turning on itself but there was no hindrance in his climb. Raibyn followed, just as silently, the dim lights of orange and red which dotted Howlgraves spreading further and further to her sight as she pulled herself up and over behind Basil over the grim tower's rim.

Flaming pits surrounded all four corners, but there was more: littered across the rooftops were the withered, skeletal remains of many different furs, some still bearing the shredded remains of their clothes. They were not intact—all appeared to be broken and shattered, jaws open as though the shock of their dooms before dying had left them unaware of just what it was that had killed them, perhaps evidence of some horrible, cannibalistic feast or something far more insidious. Various weapons were strewn all over the surface, from pikes to small daggers, all in various stages of rust and decay.

Raibyn looked sullenly at the chaos as Basil said, "Ignore the fools, they were not as practiced as we in making it further than most." Across the point from where they had entered there appeared to be a chamber built into the roof and made of the same stone as the rest of the structure. At inspection, the pair noted that it was adorned with designs which portrayed any of the pagan or Druidic gods and goddesses of the ancient times. These were effigies of abominations none had laid eyes on in many upon many seasons, the shadowy outlines of the half-forgotten Unknown Ones, with their many tentacles and bulbous shapes that could only be deigned as a "heads" leering out at the two intruders.

Like stalking shadows, they crept across the dark floor and halted outside the strange door. Perhaps what unnerved Raibyn the most was the center figure, which was of a giant serpent with its slavering fangs wide and dripping with venom. A warning, perhaps, for any who had come this far and not yet lost their lives to the guards below. She ran a paw over the surface, noting the peculiarly inlaid scales were made of gold; the door itself, should a thief have decided, would yield perhaps a fortune to equal that of a baron.

Basil tried the door first, with a cautious paw pulling and pushing with all the gingerness he could muster until it gave without further resistance. The pair looked in, tensed for anything; the fetid, loamy scent of decay and age smashed both in their face, as a torrent of dust rose and exited into the night air.

"This here will be the point of no return," hissed Basil, "at least until one or both of us completes the adventure they came here for."

Raibyn nodded. The vixen lifted the femur from a badger's skeleton and wrapped a piece of cloth around the joint and then dipped it within a nearby fire pit, creating a makeshift torch. Then she followed after Basil, who entered through the door first. Striding down the tower corridor, the pair were shown different remains which had been left as a warning to all trespassers.

The black darkness within felt treacherous. Despite the illumination gifted by the torchlight, it was a feeling that the evil which teemed inside seemed to animate and give life to the shadows. All the superstitious dread which had been borne and bred into her soul was aflame now, as her imagination of what lurked in the beyond left her uneasy, particularly at the jocular surety in which her companion stepped. Beneath each of their heels was the crunch and soft moans of the age-old remains, and Raibyn pondered if this would be her fate the deeper they descended.

"Hst!" whispered Basil, stopping them both short as he shot out a forelimb, shrinking both against the wall. Raibyn made a motion to say something when Basil hissed, "By all that is holy, keep quiet and look down!"

Raibyn followed the instructions, shining the torch where Basil indicated. A substance appeared where the bones ended, leading into and disappearing within a wall. The dormouse bent forward and touched it with his digits. It was thick and filmy, oozing off of him in peculiar rolls and leaving a peculiar pungency that neither could recognize. Whatever it was, the trail it left seemed incongruous to the two furs, dwarfing all sense of mass and weight that they could summon.

Basil returned his attention to the wall, running his paw along its surface until his digits uncovered the slits of a panel.

"Some sort of trick to opening this," he muttered as he eyed it up and down. "There's a riot of air seething from the other side here. There must be a way..."

"Here," Raibyn offered, and wedged her poniard through the indicated opening. It was narrow enough to pass through easily, and slightly moving the blade to and fro, she peered through.

"What do you see?" asked Basil anxiously.

Through the dimness within, there was the glitter of jewels, frost of ingots, and sparkle of gold eminating from the other side. Different gleams of colors from the rubies exploded in a ferocious riot, pulsating into a kaleidoscopic glare that shunted Raibyn away to preserve her own sight at the fabulous rainbow tints.

"Many things," the vixen answered, continuing to widen the aperture. "Wonderful things. I..."

She caught the smell before she saw it, and a moment's breath divided Raibyn from life and death as the curved scimitar crashed off the wall, the whistling arc parting her ears. She dropped backwards, tucked and rolled as the dormouse shrank behind her and unleashed her rapier.

It was a rat, but not one of the regular furs of Howlgraves. There was a demonic monstrous leer to its red eyes and hulking form; drool slavered from its jaws as it held the scimitar in its forepaws, looking at the two intruders with an intent Raibyn did not mistake.

Instinctively, Raibyn lifted one of her dirks from her belt and launched it at the rat's chest. It hit home, squarely where the heart would be, but to the shock of the vixen, the rat continued its advancement, raising its scimitar and bringing it back down just as Raibyn rolled out of the way of the killing blow.

"Move!" she shouted to the dormouse.

Basil nodded wordlessly, yelping just as the rat's blade whizzed past his backside. Quick as he was and nimble of limb, he could feel the breath of the horror at his heels and it almost overtook him, when another thing, just as quick and fast and deadly, careened into the rat and catapulted it off balance. The two combatants rushed up to their feet and stared at each other, one large and one small, though it was apparent that neither was aiming to give up to the other. It became apparent that one, and it was just a matter of which, would die this night.

Teeth bared and with a snarl, Raibyn stood and rushed at the foe, who whirled around and parried at her with its own blade. She drew back, prepared for the savage thrust that the rat unleashed, and caught the rim of steel with her own when the rat wheeled for a backpaw attack. That action flamed the blood in Raibyn's veins as she drew her other dirk at that same instant and drove it deep into the brutish back of the rat. It screamed, though not as a mortal fur would scream, piercing the veil of silence with a wail terrible enough to have risen the dead. It launched a brutal fist towards Raibyn, knocking the vixen off her feet and leaving her stunned for a moment as the nightmare charged once more, hurtling itself at her with frightening speed and agility.

Back and forth they moved, one whirling and darting and weaving to match the other, both knitting a net of death that would find a punctuation point. Her rapier was strong, but it was Raibyn's own skill that was keeping her alive now, as it seemed that whatever outer darkness had taken hold of this wretch, it was powering it past the point of exhaustion evident in most of her duels. But she was driving it away and back, allowing the dormouse to work the panel, which seemed to give way inch by inch.

The tip of the rat's scimitar kissed the ball of her shoulder and blood rushed to the surface, clotting at her fur. Raibyn hissed and fought the thunder of pain penetrating through her brain, but the injury provided her with the opening to knock the rat's blade out and shoot her rapier forward, piercing the rat's shoulder through flesh and bone and rendering it useless.

She was spurred now by the success. Doubling her efforts, Raibyn and rapier were like a blur of death, slashing and raining down blow after blow as the rat moved and tried to organize its attacks. It was clumsy in its movements, unable to make any effort with the scimitar in an unfamiliar paw, but its effort was not waning or in vain. If it was afraid of death, it gave no indication as such, and that worried Raibyn. Leaping as the rat swung its blade once again, it cut through the air and the vixen locked herself about its back, working to maintain a position as she parried the upperpaw slashes with her rapier and butchered the rat's neck with her dirk.

The combat was brutal, and in a whirlwind the rat's fur was awash in scarlet tatters, but despite the handicap that the blow to its swordarm had created, its brute strength held yet and inexorably it was bringing the vixen around to its front. Frantically, Raibyn sunk the dirk again and again into the torso, shoulders, and tree-trunk like neck; the wounds she had suffered bit terribly at her energy but she too did not know the meaning of yielding.

Then came a savage yell and she looked down. Basil had stopped his task and was now running his own short sword in and out of the rat's stomach and chest, blood streaming like water and splashing into the dormouse's face, until it shoved him away hard to the wall. Then, seeing an opening, as Raibyn continued fighting with all the madness she could muster, Basil grabbed a massive and heavy femur from a forlorn pile and swung at the rat's skull, just when it had bowed to staunch its torso wounds.

The attack stunned the rat, and momentarily took away its rending power. In that instant, Raibyn—gasping and streaming blood from her face, forelimbs, and hindlimbs—plunged to the ground and swung her rapier with all her strength. It created a silver line in the darkness as it cut through the rat.

Raibyn shook the blood drops from her face and sunk to the floor, catching her breath. "Are you hurt, Raibyn?" Basil asked, noting the blossoming bit of claret snaking on the vixen's shoulder.

"Aye, but they're not deep," admitted Raibyn. Blood trickled over her fur in rivulets, staining her tunic. "Little bit of time, little bit of wine, and all will be fine. What was that thing?"

"One of the dangers my intelligence spoke of, no doubt," said Basil as he went to assist her upright and through the now opened chamber. "Poor bastard may have been transmuted by the wizard into a sentinel, watching over where the others could not. Much sound may have been heard in that slaying and Yudan's other pets may have been alerted. Come, there is a passage just across the way here."

In the fracas outside, Raibyn had dropped the torch. But it seemed there was no need for it inside the jeweled room; a fortune of fabulous wealth was spread far and wide before the adventurers, casting its cold illumination upon them. There were no ornaments in the room, nor any furniture. Several silver-bound mahogany chests, sealed with heavy golden locks and inlaid with the same serpentine design as had been on the door at the roof entrance, were lined about them. Others were with their carven lids thrown back, revealing heaps of jewels in a careless frenzy of splendor to the vixen's amazed senses.

"You should help yourself at least to something for your troubles this night," Basil whispered.

"I've already been paid for my troubles," Raibyn countered, trying to push the temptation from her mind. She swore beneath her breath; already she had looked upon more wealth than she would ever spend lifetimes dreaming of, and dizzied at thinking that the value of such would be to the proper fence.

She stared ahead at the door across the marble floor. She did not know why, but it was as though something was pushing forward, imploring her to ignore the luster about her.

Basil stopped at a grouping, his ears wiggling as he lifted a chest open and the shine of the gold coins reflected in his eyes. "I owe you my life, friend Raibyn, for if you had not fought off that demon, I would not have gotten this far. And there's far too much for a simple thief like myself to loot and brag about."

Raibyn was standing in the center of the room, watching as Basil began filling his sack with gold from one of the chests. It was an intriguing proposition, and while she had said that they would part once reaching a certain point, the dormouse had been a reliable companion.

"Look to that corner over there," Basil instructed. "My intelligence noted that there's some Saracen rubies not seen since the days of Longshanks in there."

The vixen at first saw scant reasoning in this. She was perfectly capable of searching out her own treasures, if she so wished. But, she wondered, perhaps there was something to looking in that direction. Braced for just about anything, her brow raised in surprise that what she saw was what she least expected.

It was a large plant, colored crimson as blood and about the size of a tree stump. It was covered with many strangely pointed leaves, and similarly crimson blossoms that were—to the discomfort of the vixen—not the soft, satin red of natural petals, but livid, vivid, and unnatural to the sight, as though Raibyn were watching it teem with a perverse imitation of life. And perhaps it was a trick of her imagination, but was the thing...breathing?

She took one step back on her heel; no sooner had she done so that one of its vines darted out and snaked around her ankle, pulling her within its sphere. The vixen dropped her rapier with a clatter and within seconds, the blossom's clinging, pliant branches had wound about her body and limbs, holding her upside down as another vine seemed to caress itself along her shrinking form with a lustful avarice.

Basil ambled over, his sack weighted down with the gold he had scrounged for. He looked up at Raibyn and his whiskers bristled when he asked, "What happened?"

"Basil!" shouted Raibyn. "Take my sword and strike at the vines! Hurry, I can't breathe!"

"I know," stated Basil. The cadence of that statement and the way the dormouse said it sent a chill throughout the pit of Raibyn's stomach.

"You...know?"

"Aye. That's the demon root furs call the Devil's Sun. It would make sense that the old wizard would lift it up from hell, just to keep off any intruders in his home. But it can only hold one intruder at a time and while it's busy choking the life out of you, I can make my escape."

A red mist of fury exploded through Raibyn's vision. "You skamelar! I thought we were partners!"

"Only as far as the adventure went for either of us," grinned the dormouse. He bent low and lifted her rapier. "And I think the adventure ends here for us both. You cannot say you would not have done the same, were the roles reversed. Is that not your job to betray and slay?"

"That does not mean I have no honor!" shouted the vixen. The vines tightened like the coils of a snake. It was becoming harder to breathe as the air passed from her and her ribs constricted. "Were our roles reversed, I would have helped you!"

"And so you are, even without our roles being reversed. But it's as I said, without your help I would not have gotten this far, and so I'll offer you a boon." Basil dropped the sack of gold and gripped Raibyn's rapier. "It would be a damnation to leave you to the demons of Yudan like this, so I shall do what is only the right thing."

Raibyn seethed as she watched him line the blade along the ridges of her neck. Then, she saw him knot his hefty legs like Roman columns in preparation. Raibyn tensed, consciously straining against her bindings as the tiny black eyes glittered. But then her own sight darted just to the left, over the dormouse's shoulder, and became frozen by a greater horror as a vague, monstrously large form swayed about and lurked in wait.

"By the time that Yudan, or his buffoon guards, come and find you, I'll have long absconded and looted him right under his very nose!" Basil laughed. "But I'm sure you'll be nothing but bones by that point, your meat plucked off by Yudan's pets!"

Basil swung the rapier in both paws, his great muscles rolling and cracking against the cold, glittering frost of the jeweled treasure room. And at that instant, the titanic form which Raibyn had seen behind darted down and then out, the vaguely wedge-shaped head dropping its jaws down upon the dormouse with an impact that reverberated up and down the room. The action was so swift in its suddenness that Basil had but a moment to let go of a shout of agony as he disappeared into the shadows, the gigantic, sinewy shape's massive tail winding behind in a fiendish frenzy.

There followed the sickening sounds of snaps and splintering of bone, as well as the familiar copper scent of blood heavily filling the air. Raibyn could only wonder when it would be her turn when she looked just slightly to the trunk of the plant which held her: Basil had dropped her rapier into the plant when he was snatched. It was just a few feet away, and her heart leaped madly with renewed hope, just as the thing was completing its grisly meal.

Grunting and straining her tired muscles, she began motioning the vine to swing with her. It tightened, though not with the same ferocity as she struggled, and the thutter of her heart filled her ears with its panicked drumbeat. But she was moving, and with each swing, she was inching closer and closer to the hilt. When she was just within reach, she widened her jaw as much as she could to bite down hard upon it and yank it loose.

Maneuvering carefully, she brought the blade level with her torso and began cutting at the plant's tendrils. A low screaming moan echoed with each blow, but Raibyn could not think about that now as she worked. A few strikes were difficult and some clumsy; she almost dropped the blade back to the ground and she felt cold dread grip her when this happened. But furious exultation rose as she felt the slime from the plant's limb pour over her. In an instant the limbs unwound and she dropped to the floor, finally free.

She picked up the fallen blade. Instantly realizing its captive was free, the plant spread its giant petals, its hate glowing from it like the sun towards Raibyn. She knew, that this was not simply a plant of the natural world, but one with an incredibly evil intelligence, and that hate she felt came off in tangible ways as the whole plant shook and bloomed before her in a fit of rage. Marking the root stem, a stalk that pulsed like a blood-curdling vein thicker than a bear's thigh; she swung her rapier and cut through it like a heart.

The vine of the Devil's Sun lashed and spit and spun, knotting in on itself like a serpent and rolling into an irregular ball. The vines and tendrils thrashed and writhed, and the petals opened and closed, before the whole length straightened out limply, the colors of its life dimmed and reeking viscous liquid oozed from the stump.

Raibyn glared anxiously about, ears folded close to her skull and her long and bushy tail held high, waiting for more of the horrors to pass and threaten her with their dooms. But only empty darkness and glittering twilight of the treasures greeted her.

A moment's curiosity led her to follow the monster's slimy trail; if she killed it in its hovel, there may yet be a chance to survive this night with one less demon on her tail. She had not walked far into that darkened corner when she laid her eye on the travesty of a fur. It—and unfortunately that was the best description that Raibyn could manage—was a broken and shredded bloody heap that looked upward, maw wide in the rictus of death, forelimbs broken and twisted. It was missing everything below the torso.

Impelled by some strange sense of curiosity, Raibyn moved forward to it and stood looking down when the thing gave off a mighty, though gibbered and gnashed and ragged, breath. Crimson bubbles spilled from the broken nose and maw as it turned its head in Raibyn's direction, though she was unsure if it knew she was even there.

"Friend Raibyn..." it moaned weakly. "It appears...that fate has finally caught up to old Basil, the greatest thief in all the land." The thing that was the dormouse chuckled weakly. "Tell me, is...is it bad?"

"Could be worse," muttered Raibyn.

Basil lifted his head weakly, eyes glazed with agony and approaching death. "I did you...poorly, freebooter," he croaked. "Greed is a damnable thing. Let it...not be said that all that glitters...be not gold."

"Quit your tongue-wagging and make your peace before you go," Raibyn said.

"Peace?" Basil chuckled weakly as he moved a mangled paw southward down his body and the full weight of his impeding death came upon him. "Damned thing...didn't even have the good graces to finish me off, leaving me to suffer a thousand deaths...I am dying, but it will not be of the peace I would long for. Hence...a boon."

"I would've died if it weren't for you," growled Raibyn. "And you have the sand to ask of me a boon? Go on and die and go to hell already."

"Aye," said Basil, "and you do not have to...accept this boon, and care if I die. But...I implore you, please do not let me die like this."

Raibyn looked away, the same anger coming to the surface as common sense yelled at her to just walk away and leave the dormouse to the hell he had created for himself. But something touched at her as she brought the rapier up and gazed back down at the dying thief.

"Had our roles been different, I would have administered this strike in anger and vengeance, laughing about it later without a care in the world," she said. "But now, zounds knows why I feel that I must offer it instead as a blade of mercy. Fare thee well, thief-master. I shall tell your story in ballads in the seasons to come."

Basil closed his eyes; Raibyn brought her rapier down and it bit through muscle and bone and into the floor with a clanging rasp.

She wondered if the guards were now wise to her presence. Well, she was still high above their heads, and if the tales were true, then perhaps they were used to strange noises and sinister sounds in the tower above, an enclave of agony and horror that paled the imagination.

Yudan was on her mind, but so was Connal. The vixen's blood was up. No matter how sore and how tired she felt, she had not come this far into the adventure and overcome this much death and danger to simply lay down and submit to her fatigue. She wanted to see the adventure to its finish, no matter how grim the finale might be for any of them.

Careful of the slithering monster lurking about, Raibyn ran towards the door. Again she thought of Yudan, and hoped the old wizard did not dwell on the other side. She hesitated as she placed a paw on its surface, noting the strange and monstrous hieroglyphs which leered at her in their proud blasphemy. What dark and nameless paws had inscribed these had done so with a purpose, as the evil of the old ages stared at the vixen, and froze the marrow in her bones.

She opened it slowly, heart leaping to her throat and rapier held at the ready, and she looked. There was only a flight of silver steps leading downward, illuminated by means she did not know. Much like before, there was a psychical force urging her forward, taking light heed of her motion and inducing her to take one first step after another down the winding stairs. She listened, but heard nothing but the unearthly stillness call back to her.

At last, the coiling steps ended at a level floor, and an iron door greeted her. Raibyn paused to take in the scents and sounds; there was nothing, with more of the cold silence surrounding her yet again. But somehow she knew, and did understand why she knew, that the trail—the adventure—ended at this door and that she had to pass through.

And as she pressed the door open, she came away with the strange feeling that she was the last living soul in this tower, alone and shared with ghosts, phantoms, and—most frightening of all— the lurking unknown.

The door swung silently inward. The room was bathed in a faint glow, once more from a source that Raibyn could not pinpoint. She looked through the dim patch of darkness to see the iron bars and shackles which lined a stone wall. Manacles and rusty chains hung in revelatory tragedy, naked for all to see. So this then was Yudan's dungeon, Raibyn reasoned. That meant that the lone occupant must be...

She stood aghast at the unsavory detail which had made itself evident to her: laying in a crumpled heap in a far corner on the floor was a skeleton. What it had been, the vixen could not guess at—the fur and flesh had long been picked clean by time and parasites, the tattered remains of the clothes hanging from its dusty, ivory limbs.

A bony leg was shackled to a chain on the floor and as Raibyn looked closer upon the remains, she noticed shredded patterns in the skeleton's tunic that matched that of daggers, thrust into the torso many times when it was full of flesh and muscle.

And deep within the recesses of her mind, Raibyn realized that this had to be Connal, dead for who knew how long and shackled within this tower to rot and be forgotten.

She began to feel a sense of foolishness; yes, she had been well-paid for the adventure, but to give a moldy box to a moldier collection of bones? She could not understand the logic, and began to ruminate on if this was some sort of diabolical plan, and Fenella and Yudan were together planning to trap the wayward vixen within this cursed tower.

Raibyn sighed and shrugged her supple shoulders; trap or not, there was no further reason to be here. She had been told to find Connal and give the chest to him.

"I didn't know you, and I don't know who you were in life, Connal," she began. "Whether you were good or evil, it's not my burden to think on. But as someone who has known the mark of the rack and the sear of the torturer's flame, I do not wish this life upon even the worst of my enemies." Raibyn tossed the chest to the ground a few feet from the skeleton, half expecting the remains to rise and thank her for her efforts.

Instead, she heard the voice in her head.

The...chain...

She had turned on her heel and was preparing to make her way back up the stair when it came to her. She looked down at the skeleton; its jaws had not moved, nor had it made an indication of a motion itself. Perhaps it was the stress of the whole evening finally weighing down upon her, not a good sign for her profession, particularly if it meant hearing voices that were not there and listening to them while engaged in action.

Cut...the chain...please...

It had come through clearer that time, though weak and ragged in its cadences. Hellish though it sounded, the plea in that voice froze the blood coursing through her veins as she stepped towards the skeleton again. She looked at her blade and then back at the remains; what chance was there that this black sorcery would not result in her death if she cut the chain?

There would be no answer if she did not do something. Raibyn cut the chain with one strike at a link she deemed the weakest, where it joined the ring set deep into the floor. Then she hopped back, letting the bay of darkness sweep over the skeleton, the chest sitting at the arc of the light which separated the shadow. From beyond she heard the unmistakable rattle so familiar from watching the charnel house pour the rotted remains out across the floor and into the mass pits.

Was it insanity or had she really heard those old bones shuffle slightly?

As Raibyn looked on, she almost did not spy the thin, white forelimb reach out and grip the chest in its bony paws, opening it wide. The vixen became frozen at the sight; it was no trick of the light or her senses, it was a living thing and, she realized, she was trapped in its chamber.

That she did not explode instantly into one of two frenzies—babbling and murderous—spoke to the careful measure and calm, despite the paralyzing horror which held her firm to the ground. No longer in doubt of her senses, she knew that she was facing some curse of necromancy and began to instantly recall the tales of such demons, of their slavering jaws tearing out the throats and their claws ripping the flesh and fur from their victims.

Senses slowly returning, Raibyn resolved not to give this thing that satisfaction. She braced herself, faculties returning though tensed with fear as she watched the skeleton reach inside the chest, fumbling about with digits unused for far too long, until it let out what Raibyn could deem as a wheezy exultation of "Aha!" and lifted the object into the light.

It was something strange, which the skeleton held in its bony paws. A dust-ridden, hunk of something that had once dripped with the juices of life, but had now seen that same life flee and left in its wake was a meaty-looking husk withered and dank. The skeleton took this into the shadows and Raibyn heard the dull, thudding sounds akin to an object being pushed or hammered into place with extreme force. Then came the ragged breathing, or breathing as Raibyn herself understood and she took another step backwards, gripping the hilt of her rapier tightly.

"Be...at peace, freebooter," wheezed the thing in the shadows. "You've done...well, coming to this point."

"Tell me, monster, do you mean me harm or will you let me free?" Raibyn demanded.

"You will come to no harm from my paws," it replied. "Was...that not the bargain...made between yourself and...Fenella?"

The rapier lowered slightly. "Aye," Raibyn nodded. "So you are Connal."

The shuffle and rattle of the bones told Raibyn that the skeleton had nodded, or at least as she could understand the motion. "You need not...be afraid of me. Yudan pent me in this tower of his after he could not take the love of my life as his own. By fire and rack and strange tortures that you would not understand, he became my master, and when he tired of me, as he would of all things, he had me slain. But you have heard that you cannot properly kill a necromancer, have you not?"

"Aye," muttered Raibyn. "Any who thinks they can slay one easily must have a death-wish about them."

The skeleton wheezed a laugh. "And so even though my body was broken beyond the means of my spells, the final humiliation to be wrought was that cursed chain, keeping me tethered in limbo between this world and the next," huffed the skeleton. "But not even Yudan knew all the secrets, and my beloved Fenella was able to wrestle one away from the din of his knowledge. That chest you brought to me was my heart, preserved and blessed with the sorcery of one's true love, that could only be united with its owner through acts of blood and sacrifice."

Raibyn took a step forward. Fear still seized her, of what lay beyond those shadows, but somehow she was not as terrified as before. "The lady Fenella paid me for one task, but this is an allowance I make on my own." She held out her paw. "Come with me, Connal, so that I can lift you from this place. Your lover waits on you."

"Nay," the skeleton demurred. "My time is limited and already I feel the pull to the other side, strong as it is, wishing me beneath its blackened veil. Fenella will see me again when it is the end of her time, but no sooner, and you have already done the first part of the requested task. The second will ask of you to assist both Fenella and me in striking back at the dark wizard."

Raibyn listened to those ghostly tones which reverberated. A new power had seemed to take hold of its voice, a vitality that had replaced the ages-unused speech with command and control.

"But what do you request of me?" Raibyn asked, bewildered. "My blade is no more effective against a wizard as prey is to a butcher. What can I do?"

Something akin to a laugh came from the skeleton. "Did not Fenella say unto you that you must have faith in your abilities and your courage and caution? And so I turn to you, freebooter, to have that faith in your abilities and your courage, and to be my vessel in this final act of sorcery, a magic of blood and sacrifice the likes that not even Yudan ever knew and one that will wreak a vengeance the likes of which none have ever seen, or will ever see again."

The bones chattered together. Raibyn realized that it was moving, stepping on unsure limbs and moving forward towards the edge of the shadow and into the light. She caught sight beyond the dim shadow a form not altogether skeletal, but not altogether flesh and fur either. The trunk was mottled and rotten, and every shuffling movement was like wet and spoiled meat being dragged across the floor.

"You are the very paw which fate has placed in my sphere," the skeleton said. "And thus as you see, it is with your paws that you must do precisely as I ask, because it is through my life-blood that you will be absolved of this wretched place and I will have my revenge."

It stepped forward and revealed its bony chest. Raibyn could see beyond the ivory bars that were the rib cage something pulsing and teeming with animation, bright and throbbing and it was but a few moments that she recognized it for what it was: Connal's heart, placed back inside his chest and somehow through some sort of magic, had restored itself and given its former owner a semblance of life, if not the complete article. She could make out each nerve and ventricle, the veins rolling and pumping blood through nerveless tendons.

She had no time to contemplate the how as the skeleton lifted her sword and pointed at his chest. "Take your blade and cut out my heart. Let my shell leave this place as it entered, as little more than ash and dust. But take my heart and go back up those stairs and enter through an ebony door to a chamber. I can feel the black wizard's presence, he is lost in the dreams of the poppyseed lotus, dreaming of his next evil plots. Speak his name and awaken him, but be not afraid! Present my heart to him as a parting gift."

"Aye," said Raibyn.

"Upon completing that, get you from this tower as quickly as possible. And again, fear not, for as we speak I shall make your way clear. But hurry!"

Uncertain, Raibyn approached and the skeleton of Connal, sensing the doubt clouding the vixen's mind, stepped onto the rapier's point, shuddering as blood as black as the night began spilling out from the remains. The vixen understood and set her teeth to the task, driving the sword deep as thick blood flowed over the blade.

The skeleton convulsed once and shuddered, then fell backwards to the ground quite still and Raibyn was sure, as much as she did not understand it, that life had finally fled from Connal the wizard.

She set about her grim task and within moments had pulled forth the organ, surprised that it was still pulsing, despite its divorce from its owner.

Slinging it into her rucksack at her back, she moved away from the cell, unsure still at what was happening or had been promised by Connal, but she felt that she believed him, at some level, when the skeleton had promised to make Raibyn's way clear if she would complete the required task. She stepped out of the cell, and before closing the door behind cast one final glance backwards into the shadows. Rather than the cold ring of death which had permeated from this space, a new feeling pulsated, warming the entire room with a power that the vixen felt should not be seen by mortal eyes and she closed the cell door behind her tail.

Without hesitation, she followed the skeleton's directive, ascending the steps. It did not strike her to deviate from the instructions given. When she halted at a door, she took its presence in for a moment: at its center was a grinning skull, dripping wet with blood and muscle, a freshly slain foe it seemed. She pushed it open, and looked inside to a chamber awash in a soft, weird light that came from jewels set into the walls in many fantastic shapes.

Sprawled out upon a raised dais, she could make out the form of an antelope, his curling horns resting on an elevated pillow. His eyes were open and dilated with the fumes from the poppyseed blossom, as if fixed on dark gulfs and shadowy abysses that no mortal should have knowledge of.

Raibyn gulped and swallowed hard. Her heart pounded hard and fast in her ears. Instinct told her to run; the promise made her stay.

"Yudan!" she announced, voice booming with the command of a judge pronouncing doom on the condemned.

The eyes of the wizard cleared on instant and the elongated head declined, searching and finding the intruder. They then became cold and terrible as a fire, and the silken-clad form raised himself upright, towering mightily over the vixen.

"Bitch," he hissed. "What do you here, in the tower of Yudan?"

The air was charged and Raibyn intimated the wizard was preparing to pass a doom of his own. Coolly and without showing her fear, she unlatched her rucksack from her back and lifted the dripping heart from inside. "I've come to give you a final gift and a final farewell from the one who sent me. Connal offers to you his best regards."

"I've no idea who you are," Yudan sneered, "but those who cross this threshold uninvited do not live long to brag about their adventure to their mates. I shall have great pleasure inflicting torments the likes of which you have never known, and if I am merciful, instead of feeding you to my demons I may press you into the servitude of my bed. I..."

Raibyn held the heart before the wizard and for a moment, it appeared that nothing would happen. Then, as though some force from beyond space or the gulfs of life and death, Yudan gripped the heart in gnarled, trembling hooves, staring deep at it as one would a prized jewel and searching for some meaning inside its many chambers. Then, like a magnet, it began to be drawn towards him; the old wizard realized this too and attempted to throw the grisly thing away from him. But it was though his hooves had been clamped around it, and he tried to spring backwards to no avail, as it pulled his torso closer and closer until finally, with a gigantic burst of blood and bone, Connal's heart pierced through the wizard's chest in a ray of dazzling light.

Yudan screamed as he sank backwards onto his dais, and Raibyn watched on, transfixed at the transcosmic mutation taking place. The glare was awesome and too much, and she shielded her eye from its presence. When it was over, she looked to the dais, and saw Yudan laying on his backside. She pondered if she should offer assistance, when she heard, "Your task is complete, freebooter. You may go."

The voice was did not have the same, hard cruelty as before.

Nodding and without saying another word, Raibyn turned and fled from the chamber, down the stairs and past the cell where she had encountered Connal's skeleton. So amazed was she that it did not occur to her to make her escape the way she had entered. When she came to the foot of the gleaming stair, she realized she had come to a room of soldiers and guardsbeasts. She noticed the glitter of their jupons and sheen of their mail, and their blades which rested in their sheaths. All sat slumped in different areas of the room, in various stages of action before silent death had struck upon them.

The promise was made and the word was kept, by what means Raibyn would never know; questioning it further was not her place.

She saw the door which stood open and saw the portal to the world bathed in the splendor of its clean, fierce night as she knew it held out to her, with its riot of stars and the reality with which she was familiar. She almost dove headlong out of it and when she found herself back in the courtyard of the tower, she almost kissed the ground in gratitude, embracing the night wind of the weaving green garden and the cool perfume of the shrubbery as if she had entered a dreamland instead of a nightmare.

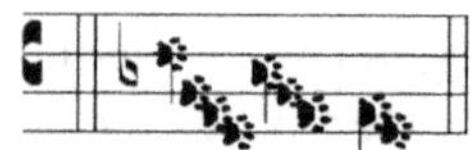

"What's this?"

"Consider it a bonus for a job well done."

"That was not in our initial agreement," Raibyn stated, looking upon the pouch of gold before her. "And you give me far too much for a simple bonus."

Fenella chuckled. "And yet you reach for it."

The vixen smirked. "And I didn't say I wouldn't take it, now, did I?"

The word had spread, as it does, quickly throughout Howlgraves of the events that had occurred at Yudan's tower. A score of furs dead inside, the bones of many more found strewn like harvested corn, and the congealed mass of something large and loathsome was discovered. But it was the treasure room, however, that piqued the interest of those who had long sought Yudan's chamber of splendors and to have it laid bare for the picking and plundering, it was a temptation few could resist. Many did, in fact, descend on the now seemingly defenseless tower before further word reached a cotillion of noblefurs who promptly sent a contingent of their best soldiers to deny access to all except royalty.

Raibyn was one of those few tempted by the prize within. "If there's anything left after the pilfering by sticky paws," she muttered, "it'll likely go and line the king's pockets to pay for another useless eastern campaign."

"I am surprised that you did not return to stake your share of the wizard's gold," said Fenella.

"I've had my fill of Yudan and anything to do with him," replied Raibyn as she sipped mightily of her wine. She was bandaged across her forelimbs and about her skull, many more wrapped underneath her tunic. The pain wracked her body with every breath, but she chose not to reveal it.

Rumors and news rippled through the Desert streets and were whispered about in the alleyways by the drunk and the scared. The gossiping mercenaries passed it about like water. They could speak freely, exchanging information that one would find useful, often for a price, or intelligence that could be used for the purposes of an enterprising partnership. Since that night, it was said, Yudan had gone mad. The wizard was always one step away from madness to be sure, but something pushed him over the edge to slaughter his guards and leave his tower unattended, bare of all his magic and enchantments. Stranger still was the action he committed before the soldiers struck him down with a rain of arrows, when he was found with his gnarled, wizened hooves in the gory throat of Duncan, captain of the city watch. Rumors passed that even as they shot shaft after shaft into the wizard, it seemed he would not stop until all the life had passed from the rodent and then, finally, he died, a smile upon his face more terrible and frightening than any scowl he had previously possessed.

"Word says that one of Duncan's lieutenants, upon hearing of the captain's death, ran to the magistrate and admitted that Duncan had been paid to execute innocent furs for a price," said Raibyn. "The lieutenant is preparing to name names on the morrow, so there likely will be a reckoning from the unjustly accused."

"Good," Fenella replied with a smile. "This will be mine," and laid down two copper pieces as she stood to leave. "I believe that will conclude our arrangements, Raibyn. Perhaps the next time we meet, the circumstances will be..."

"Hearken!"

The lioness and the vixen raised their heads. Raibyn smirked and said, "Oh, it's you."

Standing before them was the warthog, similarly bandaged and flanked with a small group of angry-eyed, swarthy furs all brandishing swords and daggers in their paws and hooves. "You bitches killed my mates and broke my head," he growled. "I demand satisfaction!"

"While I admit to doing nothing of the sort," Fenella said innocently, "I cannot lie and said that it was not warranted." She motioned to leave. A deer youth blocked her, standing in her path with his blade held in front of her face.

The warthog looked down at Raibyn and snarled, "You. Get your tail up."

"Impatient, aren't you?" said the vixen without glancing back at the warthog. She motioned to sip from her wine cask when the warthog smacked it out of her paws.

"Yudan's dead and you show up here looking like you went to war against the Saracens!" he bellowed. "Word is someone saw someone scale that wall that night, and you and this whorebitch cat were talking about the tower! Do you lie?"

"Can you prove that we were?" Fenella asked innocently.

"A word from me to the magistrate and I can have you both in irons!"

"You must ask yourself, friend," began Raibyn, "as to who the magistrate would believe more? Two women who haven't the faintest idea of what you're talking about, or a hog who likely has the bounty of five or six counties on his head and a reward more valuable than his fool life?"

The statement prompted a minor ripple of laughs from the bravos around the warthog. His ears turned hot and red as he snarled and pointed his scimitar at Raibyn's chest, "I want your head, bitch. I want your heart. I want your soul!"

Raibyn only nodded and stood. "I gave you a choice earlier, and you were lucky compared to your mates," the vixen said. "This will be your one and only warning to step away and leave."

"And how will ye make me? I've got you dead within my sights!" the warthog laughed. "Yeh've got no time to whirl or do any of your fancy sword work! And there's more of us and only one of you!"

"That's right," Raibyn answered.

"So, what will ye do for an encore? Let me answer for you: you'll die!"

"Maybe, maybe not," Raibyn agreed, as her paws fell behind her back. "What do you figure you'll be doing?"

The warthog snarled, "I figure I'll give you a chance before I kill you. Draw your blade on the count of three!"

He started. "One," followed by a drawling, "Two". He kept his eyes upon the vixen, who stood stock still before him. Perhaps it was her slim form that obscured what she was doing from him, as her left arm shifted gently behind her back and just above the nape of her tail, where paws gripped the tough yew handle and unlatched it from her belt.

"You asked what I will do for an encore, rogue," stated Raibyn.

"Aye, I did," replied the warthog.

"I believe I have your answer."

The warthog cracked an eyebrow as he looked upon the one-eyed vixen. "And what will you do for an encore?"

"Simple," Raibyn said. "I'll win."

The warthog smiled and shouted "Three!" as he dashed forward and made an arc for a slashing killing blow when he caught the thin, silvery glint of a blunted blade hurtling towards him, with the last thing the warthog would see in this life that of the hurlbat extinguishing the light of his existence.

Breathing hard, Raibyn walked carefully to the crimson caricature of the warthog's face. She bent down and wrenched the hurlbat from his crushed skull, tossing blood and brain to the side in an effort to clean it.

"Asshead," she muttered as she unsheathed her rapier and looked to the group before her. "Now, I believe there was business the rest of you gentlefurs had with me?"

The Course of the Reiver

Ziegenbock

ot vulpine breath misted on a cold autumn night. Fearghus glanced around, his fox-eyes glinting in the moonlight. Nearby, the gate of a sheepfold stood open, the sheep released and milling around. With crooks and snarls, the fox's gang kept the flock together.

Fearghus turned to the dog slumped beside his now-empty sheepfold: black and white, black and blue, bound and gagged. A smile tugged the corner of the fox's muzzle, cruel and carnivorous. Sharp night-vision let him see the contempt in the collie's eyes. He knelt down and leant in close to the sheepdog, a clear sneer on his slender vulpine muzzle.

"No hard feelings, my friend. We are all doing what we must to survive."

With a rough stroke of the collie's cheek, the fox swept away. The sheep were raising some commotion, bleating and jostling. The raiders paid no heed to their calls: such things happened when you roused a flock from sleep.

With the herd now gathered into some sort of order, three of the raiders mounted their hobblers, their sturdy moorland ponies. Fearghus took his lance in one paw, and with the other paw he took the withers of his hobbler, before he too mounted up. Keeping his voice low, but loud enough to carry, he addressed his band.

"All right, let's move out."

By the stars and the half-moon, the raiders left the hamlet in the valley, taking the stony road across the moorland. The old pony-track made for rough travel, with its steep climbs and rocks and loose boulders. The horses took a steady pace, and the riders clutched the reins a little tighter, thankful for the sturdiness and surefootedness of their trusty beasts. A cool and gentle breeze drifted across the moors, dispelling the musk of unwashed animals. A clear night in autumnal northern Britain also meant a cold night; Fearghus felt the chill on his nose, protruding from beneath his steel morion. He also felt it through his paws. Roughened though they were from many seasons of wrangling beasts and the manual tasks of Border life, they stiffened in the chill. Thank goodness for his quilted leather jack to augment his warm fur.

The journey home after a raid was always more treacherous. With livestock to guard and cajole and drive, their progress was slower than the outward ride. Not to mention the threat of being intercepted. Of course, should the situation become too dire, they could abandon the flock and scatter across the moorlands. However, that would mean an entire night's work wasted. *Still*, thought the fox, *the ride has been peaceful so far. Let us not expect disaster so soon.*

They followed the old reivers' road up braes and down slopes, stones crunching under horse-hoof and sheep-hoof, until they reached a high pass. From there, they struck out across the fells, guided by the stars and the fox's knowledge. The fells were still good and dry, the ground firm beneath hoof and paw, and the weather none too dreich. Therefore, the party made respectable progress. Fearghus rode at the front: few knew these lands as well as he. The fox even allowed himself a moment to smile. Who else, on either side of the Border, could rustle these beasts and disappear into the land without a trace?

The first bluish light of dawn appeared. The band were riding below a ridgeline when Fearghus pulled up his hobbler. The party stopped behind him, and a few of the sheep complained at the sudden stop. A vixen rode up beside him and whispered.

"Company?"

"Aye."

Fearghus pointed down the valley, behind them and to the right. A mobile patrol.

"I suggest we make ready the weapons," the dog-fox said. "Calan, you know what to do."

The only hare in the party nodded and slipped from view. The others readied their spears and polearms, while Fearghus and the vixen loaded their muskets. This was new weaponry on the Border; the gang had acquired two, and few questioned the lead tod and vixen carrying them. From pouches attached to their bandoliers, they poured powder into the barrel. From a pouch at their side, they added the shot. Then, taking their ramrods, they tamped everything down. Stowing the rods, they each took a spanner, and turned their wheel-locks a quarter-turn, before priming the pans with more powder. They caught each other's eyes with a smile. Good and ready.

Fearghus trained his sharp yellow eyes on the approaching group. A scant band of three on horseback with dented and rusted armour, along with eight or nine miserable sorts traipsing beside, shepherds or labourers most likely, carrying spears or farm implements, protected by light jackets or just the rags on their backs. They wore white armbands adorned with a red cross. Fearghus sneered at the symbol, stolen from a God-fearing Turk and co-opted by these heretical bitches. Were there no worthy beasts south of the Wall? And what a wretched life for these folk, duty-bound to answer any hue and cry and to pursue any raider. Was this really the best that the wee sheepdog could muster?

With muskets aimed dead ahead, the raiders watched their pursuers approach. The newcomers must have noticed the firearms, because they brought their horses to a halt out of range. One horse rider, a terrier, carried a polearm and wore a livery badge of a rampant badger—maybe the dog was a magistrate of some sort? He spoke up first.

"By order of His Majesty, and of his Warden the Lord Ragnar of Northumbria, you are hereby ordered to surrender these beasts and to go about your lawful business."

Fearghus broke into full-throated laughter, gums and yellowed teeth on full display. His clanmates joined in.

"And a fine morrow to you too! How delightful that some crowned head, once again, sees fit to impose his way of life upon us, and to press us into being his subjects. I ask ye, sir, what does your 'Majesty' truly think of us Borderers? Does he care for us? I tell you, he only cares when we are useful to him. He calls himself 'king', ruler among animals. Ha. Get him to overwinter here, see how this fringe of his kingdom chills his heart, and makes his very bones shiver. And as for that badger...a pompous, overstuffed lord if ever I saw one, playing the fief in his wee riverside hame. Neither of them deserve our loyalty and we owe them none. Our loyalty is to our clan, our foxes and our allies, who trod these lands before the invaders raised the Wall. We played our part in that resistance too: side by side with hare and otter we fought. This is our land, the reason we live and prosper, and we have fought for it, and defended it, from every pretender and every invader for centuries."

The terrier spat sideways from his horse. "Spare me your fancy words. Why don't you bugger off to Oxford and find some schoolboys to play with. And give those sheep back while you're at it."

"Ye really fancy your chances against us? A band of farmers and wet-eared cubs, clinging to your notions of 'law' and 'justice' like they're worth a sheep's shit? Then venture another hoof forward and face my weapon."

The two leaders stared each other down, patrolman and outlaw. Nobody spoke or moved. The patrol leader felt the burn of his own men's stares, hotter than any musket-fire. They wanted action. He gripped his polearm tight.

"A rat's piss on your little weapon."

With a kick of the spurs, the rider and horse closed in. Fearghus waited until they were in range before he pulled the trigger. The wheel struck the fool's gold and the powder caught light, throwing off heat and sparks before a sudden final surge of flame led to...nothing. Nothing but smoke. The fox sighed.

"Fenrir's balls."

Only a last-second yank of the reins pulled Fearghus away from the polearm-point. Amidst the smoke, the hobblers collided, and the fox, already off-balance, fell from his mount. His pony reared up and fled through the smoke. On seeing the first action, a cry went up from all beasts, raider and interceptor alike, while Fearghus slipped to a nearby lea with a twinge in his leg. He heard the melee ensue, with the clash of weapon on weapon starting mere seconds later. Sheep bleated, horses whinnied, and Borderers of all stripes surged into the battle with gusto, until a wet gurgle shocked the pursuers and sent shouts and cries through their number.

"Archer!"

"Do you spy him?"

There was the crack of the second musket, and a second rider fell from his whinnying horse. The remnants of the force must have decided the poor collie's sheep weren't worth risking their pelts for, because the terrier gave the call to retreat. Back down the slope they fled, while the raiders cheered their good fortune, weapons and even helmets aloft. Fearghus rejoined them—clutching his side, a limp to his walk, but still in one fox-shaped piece. His companions slapped his back, and Fearghus grinned and gestured to their spoils.

"Well done, my friends. We shall eat well after all."

The excited sheep took a moment or two to calm. Once the raiders had returned to some semblance of order, and Calan the hare rejoined them from his hiding place, the party continued crossing the rough country. The vixen Melrose, still astride her hobbler, took over lookout duties from Fearghus, who walked with his companions. Though he limped, he declined all offers of help. No injury, not even the loss of his bolted horse, could take the grin from his fox-maw that day.

The reivers entered the forest where their encampment lay concealed. By now, the sun sat low in the western sky, its golden light shining through the trees. Up ahead in a clearing stood a few houses, cobbled together with any material to paws. The walls consisted of clay, spare timber, turf sod, and a few good stones in some instances. The roofs were topped with thatch or more turf.

Muzzles appeared from doorways on hearing the calls of sheep. Foxes in the main, though some dogs and a cat and other, wilder species made up their number. Back at the safety of camp, Fearghus slipped his steel helmet off. He shook his head, and twitched the one intact ear atop his head. Where his other ear once stood, the tatters of fur and cartilage twitched in sympathy.

The chatter and scamper of little paws provided welcome distraction. Fearghus and Melrose's four kits rushed from their home and surrounded their father. Ignoring his injury, he regaled his litter with the tale of the raid, sparing the more macabre details. The kits listened, transfixed, excited, and Fearghus couldn't help but smile.

I cannae wait to take ye hunting.

By the time the sheep were safely corralled in their new pen, the light had faded. The raiders, weary from their excursion, decided to toast their fortune the next morning. No sense in lighting a fire and attracting attention. Though they could high-tail from their hideout and raise new houses somewhere else in a matter of hours, they wanted some rest. However, they still shared a few words of congratulation.

Melrose took the kits off Fearghus's paws. Finally, a quiet moment. Fearghus took his musket and slipped a short way into the forest, where he found a boulder upon which to perch. He inspected his weapon, turning it around in his paws and tutting.

"You cost me quite severely today. Now, why'd you refuse to work?"

The fox knocked the barrel with the pommel of a knife, emptying the weapon of burnt powder and clogged shot. With his rod, he cleaned out what residue he could, and he blew out some more, peering down the barrel with one open eye.

"Why do you waste any more time with that contraption?"

Fearghus twitched his intact ear towards the newcomer, keeping focused on his weapon, but baring his sharp yellow teeth into a grin.

"Because...my prey...it works as a deterrent."

The fox cocked a sideways glance. Calan the hare stood a short way off, tapping his foot-paw on the ground. *Just outside of firing range*, Fearghus observed. The fox continued cleaning his weapon. "If you aim one of these at a fellow's face, it will always give him pause."

"So would a bow. Which is quicker to use, easier to maintain, and more reliable."

The fox rose to his paws, standing taller than the jumpy herbivore. If one discounted the ears.

"And when this *does* work, well, you saw the effect. As for reliability..." The fox tossed the weapon into the air, caught the barrel, and brandished it stock-first at the hare. "I could always club ye wi' it. Then we shall see how reliable it is."

The leporine closed in, all hare-lip and toothy grin. "There is another weapon I would far rather you wielded. A reliable weapon, at that, even given its size."

He groped Fearghus through his trews, and the fox stifled a yip. The fox grabbed the hare's paw and pulled it away. "Goodness, you horny bugger of a hare. There might be kits watching. Let me finish seeing to this."

The hare watched the fox inspect his firearm. A moment or two later, the fox lowered the weapon with a grumble.

"Well?" asked the hare.

"It seems fine. Barrel is clean an' straight, the arm isn't jammed... I cannae fathom it out. Ah, it's getting dark. I'll gi' it another look the morrow, and maybe take a test shot too."

With the musket attended to, Fearghus and Calan closed in. They held paws, their noses and whiskers close. The hare grinned wider still.

"I still hope to celebrate a successful raid with you. Personally."

Fearghus licked that twitching nose. "Soon, my long-eared friend. Tonight, I lie with my vixen."

Fearghus turned his brush-tail to the hare and took a few steps, before suddenly turning back to his companion.

"Although, bunny, if my darling Melrose wishes for some rest, don' be surprised to find a fox sniffing at yer back door. No guarantees, though."

Darkness did not cover the hare, grinning like a leveret with honey on his paws. Such details did not escape the sharp-eyed fox.

The new day brought light back to the world, though the sun did little to alleviate the chill. Fearghus lay nestled in his home, beneath a heavy woollen blanket, curled up and snoring softly. The fox glowed with satisfaction; hopefully Melrose would forgive him the scratches from the night before, and his companions the yowls.

A smoky scent reached the fox's nose. Warming, meaty, enough to make his stomach growl. Grumbling and muttering at being aroused, he stretched out where he lay, feeling his joints click into place. His side twinged and he yipped and bit his lip. Yet, when he rose to his paws, he could walk, albeit with some stiffness. Emerging from his home, he found a fire in full flame, with a sheep on a spit roasting above. Some folk milled about, tending to the horses or the newly acquired sheep. Others prepared the meal, or else warmed their fur by the fire. Though the growls of a score of stomachs filled the air, every beast kept their counsel. The food would be ready when it was ready.

And before long, it was. The foxes removed the carcass from the flames, carved it, and shared it among the band. The kits ate first, while Fearghus waited until last, though they were kind enough to save him a shank. The outlaws sat around the fire, letting it die down, conversing and savouring their first red meat in days. No more digging up root vegetables or shooting little game-birds—for the time being.

Fearghus had taken his first bite when a familiar voice reached his one-and-a-bit ears.

"You know something, Fearghus? I envy you."

The burly fox chewed his mouthful of mutton, before gulping down the tough meat. "And why is that?"

The hare took a seat, crossing his long legs, and nibbling a handful of dock leaves. "Because nothing ever gets you down. We live in the wilderness, we prey on our fellow animal, a war-badger is determined to have your head, you lost your horse last night…"

"There are plenty of good horses hereabouts. I shall simply acquire another."

"Uh-huh. With all the coin we carry. Unless…" The hare stopped his rapid chewing, his big herbivore eyes growing wide. "You're licking your maw, Fearghus. That always makes me nervous."

"Why ever so, my tasty wee rabbit?"

Calan had long ago given up correcting the fox about his species. "Are you seriously suggesting…stealing a horse?"

The fox said nothing, only grinned, just enough to show a hint of his sharp yellow teeth.

"Please tell me you're not. You're already wanted for all the sheep and cattle you have lifted. And now you want to take horses as well? How much more of the badger's wrath do you want to face? Forget all your bluster yesterday. You know as well as I how ruthlessly he patrols his watch. Fifteen he has killed with his own sword, they say. And he has fought for both sides as occasion called for."

"Many of us have. Though you make a fair point, my friend. However…" The fox gestured with a paw. "Look to our paddock. How many horses do you see?"

"Three. I see three."

"Aye. A paltry number, which only diminishes. It pains me to remember how many horses we have lost to sickness, injury and battle. And yet, are they not also essential to our way of life? If we lose any more, how shall we provide for ourselves? Or for my kits, for Tod and Holly and Jed and Kelsie? Even if our stallion covered both mares this minute, the foals would need time to grow. And even if I had the money, I can hardly stroll to market when every soldier and guard is lookin' for my brush. Now, there has to be someone who wouldn't miss a nag or two. None of the big Families, o' course: we hardly need to make enemies with them. Any more than we have already. Hmm... I wonder if they ever refilled the stables at Black Middens?"

The hare blinked. "As in...the Warden station?"

"Pff, 'Warden station.' It's an outpost. A faraway pile of crumbling old stones, surrounded by miles of open country. When do you suppose that badger last visited? The station lies some twenty miles from Featherstone. And if you had a castle with a roarin' fire and a larder of vittles and a detail of fawning woodland critters, would *you* ever leave it?"

"It is still under the Warden's purview. Are you seriously suggesting we steal from him?"

"Oh, I dinnae doubt there are easier targets. But I could not, in good consciousness, strand some poor shepherd by depriving him of his only horse. Not when that overgrown weasel has horses going spare. And like I said, it's not like the stripe-dog will be personally leading drills at that outpost. The only folk who accept that wretched commission are the ones too weak to stand up to the badger. We stand every chance of succeeding, the same as when we face his more capable beasts."

Calan spoke softer. "Some folk might call this plan harebrained."

Fearghus cracked open the sheep bone. "And those folk should remember that shy kits get nowt. However, we still ought to find out what's on offer, and what we're up against. No sense in a wasted journey, after all. So, my leporine friend, how would you feel about a little reconnaissance?"

The next day, when Calan set out to survey the land, Fearghus practised with his musket. And of course, the blasted thing fired first time, shattering a wooden log with a satisfying splintering *crack*. The fox thought about testing a second time, but decided he would rather not tempt fate nor waste what little shot he had. When the hare returned to Fearghus that evening, he reported that, yes, the house at Black Middens had a brace of strong horses, ripe for the taking. Fearghus could not contain his grin. With the sun dipping low, he gathered the hare, Melrose, and three other foxes. Together, the six of them formulated their plan.

That night, through the cover of darkness, they struck out with two of their horses. A gamble, yes, but at least two of them could make a quicker escape on horseback. Fearghus and Calan went on foot with two dog-foxes, while Melrose and another vixen rode beside. The dewy grass sprang under paws and hooves, the dampness seeping through Fearghus's worn leather boots. Yet all the same, the fox kept his muzzle raised. He smiled with a growl at the chill in the air, at the silent and rough and barren moorland devoid even of birdcall, and of course at the promise of plunder.

As the first strand of light appeared on the misty, jagged horizon, they reached a gully with a patch of woodland at its centre. Though they could not see the tower, Fearghus and Calan both knew it lay nearby. The party tied their horses by some trees on the woodland edge. They checked their equipment, and from there, they set off through the grass, creeping low as their four-legged ancestors once did.

Soon, the pele tower came into view: a squat watchtower rising above a cluster of outbuildings. The whole compound was surrounded by an outer barmkin wall. Two of the foxes stayed outside to keep watch and to help their companions over the wall. After Calan kicked out of the leg-up, Fearghus followed. He vaulted onto the wall-top, before lowering himself down. The scent of nearby stables, horses and muck, reached the fox's nose. He heard the beasts rustling inside, and he felt his muzzle water. Soon, they would be his.

But first, they had to wait. And so they waited, three foxes and one hare, hidden behind the walls, silent.

And eventually, the door to the tower opened. A weasel in a cloak stepped into the yard, yawning with a show of carnivorous teeth before scratching his neck fur. He looked around, and seeing that all was quiet, he went to check the outer buildings. He walked right past Fearghus and Melrose, who had hidden behind opposite walls. Fearghus grinned, trying hard not to swish his tail. He nodded to his partner, who drew a dirk from her belt. The vixen crept behind the weasel, silent on her bare paws, before she pounced, clasping a leather-gloved paw over the mustelid's maw and pressing the dirk to his neck.

"The keys to the stable, and be quick about it."

The weasel struggled, but before he could writhe, Melrose held him tighter. Outmatched in strength, and a single knife-swipe from bleeding to death, the mustelid relented, reaching a paw inside his cloak. Melrose pressed the blade closer, in case the weasel fancied himself a hero and pulled out a weapon. Even when the vixen heard a metallic jangle, and eventually saw the keys, she did not release the weasel.

"Drop them."

The weasel did so. Fearghus bounded in and swept them up. While Melrose and the other fox restrained the weasel and stuffed his maw, Fearghus unlocked the stables. Calan joined him at the stable and, together, they opened the doors.

"All right, my friend, pick your mount and hope it's a quick one."

The door swung open with barely a squeak: Fearghus smelled the beef-fat on the hinges. The horses whickered at the strangers, but with some strokes of the muzzle and mane, and a few handfuls of oats, they soon calmed. Fearghas and Calan fetched a saddle each and led their ponies outside, before saddling and mounting them. The ponies kicked up some fuss and held unsteady beneath the strange riders, but the raiders' spurs soon brought them into line. With Melrose standing guard over the watchman, the other fox opened the outer gates, and the party prepared to make their escape.

"Halt! All of you! Stop right there!"

Fearghus scoffed. *As if that ever worked.* Spurring their new mounts, Fearghus and Calan made for the open gates. The whistle of an arrow, and the shaft clattered into the stone paving of the court-yard, harmless. *Weren't squirrels supposed to be skilful archers?*

The riders cantered through the gates and into the open moor. Their companions followed in their wake, and scattered across the land to throw off any pursuers. Their assistants outside the walls had also left their positions: Fearghus spied the flash of russet fur, stealing away through the long grass. Now in the open, the riders pressed their knees in, kicking backwards in the stirrups while keeping the reins slack. The trained horses recognised the signal and, gradually, picked up speed. Before long, they were galloping across the rough grassland. Fearghus's legs burned with the effort of the ride. From steep hillocks to sudden soft earth, the terrain presented challenge after challenge, and only the ruggedness of the ponies and skill of their new riders kept them on an even keel.

Soon, the clamour of guards faded to the distance. Thanks to their choice of horses, their swiftness of escape, or simple dumb luck, no pursuit followed. Maybe the captain decided an early-morning jaunt over the moors wasn't worth it for two nags. Or he just wanted some extra time in bed. All the same, Fearghus focused on the ride, not taking any chances despite their apparent success. Too many young foxes—kits—had celebrated their escape too soon, only to be caught and left dangling from a rope. If Fearghus hoped to see his twenty-fifth summer, he could ill afford such hubris.

And so they rode, a mile or two or more, furlongs flying under hoof as fast as the terrain would allow. They crested a ridge into a gently sloping meadow. Hare glanced to fox, the fox nodded, and they dropped into their saddles, letting their horse's speed ease off. The party stopped by a burn, a narrow stream running beside a forest. All animals slaked their thirst, two-legged and four, and there in the glade they rested. Fearghus stroked his horse's muzzle and got to know his new steed.

Suddenly, a rustle in the trees caught everyone's attention.

"Company again?" asked the hare.

"Could be."

Baying and barking rang through the woods, as a canine in a leather coat broke cover, closing in on the pair.

"Sleuth-hound!" Fearghus called. "Take the horses and ride!"

Fearghus bundled the reins into Calan's paws. Yet rather than scatter, the fox ran *towards* the hound.

"Fearghus? What are you doing?"

"Buying us some time. Move!"

Calan did so, tethering the horses together before mounting one and spurring through the meadow. Fearghus, meanwhile, took a deep breath and stepped forward to face the bloodhound, who called beyond the fox's ears.

"Stop! Hold those horses! In the name of His Majesty!"

Fearghus stepped forward to face the puppy. "You really think he'll listen to you?"

The hound tried to circle around Fearghus, but the fox dashed to block his path.

"Move aside, sir. You are impeding official business."

"Bugger your business. We simply go about ours."

A flash of recognition did bring the bloodhound to a stop. His keen eyes focused a short way upwards, widened, and his muzzle lifted into a sharp canine smile which sent a shiver down the fox's spine.

He'd forgotten his helmet, hadn't he? So now the hound could see...

"Well, well, if it isn't the famous Fearghus of Leaderfoot, the one-eared outlaw himself. It will be my pleasure to finally bring you to justice."

"Who, me? You'd rather have some tick-bitten fox than those braw and fine-bred steeds?"

"We have other men on your tails. Let one of them wrangle the ponies. You are mine."

Even now, Fearghus could hear shouts and calls, over the horizon towards the north. While he tilted his ear to the sound, his eyes locked on the pistol now aimed at his muzzle. The fox rolled his eyes.

"My friend, I have stared down more muskets and blades than you could imagine. And none of you ever attack. You know why? Because you want me alive. You want to haul me before the goodbeasts of these twa' realms, the soldiers and wardens and maybe even the Kings themselves, that they may howl and caterwaul and curse the very ground I tread. It's nowhere near as cathartic to curse a dead fox."

Whatever the hound's original plan, to shoot or not to shoot, Fearghus's words gave him reason to stall. The fox watched the ropes and pulleys working in the dog's mind.

"I warn you, *goupil*, this weapon is loaded."

The fox scoffed. "Spare me your airs and pretentious French. You are no beast of the court, cur. Neither of us are. We're just normal men."

Fearghus stared the bloodhound down, eye to eye. Then, with a wink, he dropped to all fours and scarpered through the long grass, leaping and weaving before the hound could aim his single shot. He heard the dog curse, and glancing over his shoulder, he saw the dog stow his firearm and set off in pursuit of the fleeing fox.

All right, puppy. Let's see how good you are.

Grass and tussock and heather—the lithe fleet fox bounded over them all, tail streaming behind him, almost in taunt. *Look how close I am. Catch me.* Fearghus ran for his freedom, yes, maybe for his life. Yet he rose to the challenge. To run was to live, to be alive. So let the dog chase. Whatever the terrain, however many miles, Fearghus had outrun the hound before, and he would do so again. He knew which way to leap, which ground would carry an animal and which would snare him deep.

Up ahead lay some woods, and Fearghus dashed straight in. He twisted and skipped and dodged around rocks and branches, his every step landing true. He heard the laboured pant of the hound behind him, slipping into the distance. Perhaps if he were lucky, one of these branches might snare his pursuer?

Or luck and fate would play a cruel game on him.

A sharp hit on his shin and the fox tumbled, tripping over a fallen branch. He scrambled down a muddy bank, with no purchase for paw or claw, until he landed in a pile. He groaned, and his hip twinged afresh. The bark of the hound made his heart jump. He tried to get to his paws, but the hound was upon him. The first bite landed true on his neck; Fearghus yelped and sank to his knees, trying to shake the dog off, but the bloodhound's bite was too firm. He tried to roll, tried to scratch, and the pressure of that bite ratcheted up. Enough to hold him, but with enough in reserve to bite deeper if needed. Fearghus tried to reach with his claws, fore or hind, to swipe at the dog, who held the fox's arms and kicked the fox's shins and kept biting anyway. And with the commotion, the men of Black Middens soon found them. They swapped the dog's jaws for stout rope, and when Fearghus tried to pull away, they pulled the rope tighter like a noose, making the fox yipe and fall to the wet ground, breath heaving but body otherwise still. The bloodhound sneered down at the gasping vulpine.

"He weren't kidding about the tick-bites. Oh, and don't even think about biting me. Or we'll see how your muzzle stands up to my boot."

"So," asked a squirrel soldier, "back to the Middens with him, I suppose?"

"No," replied the hound, "I say we take him to Featherstone. Let His Lordship decide his fate."

"What, lead this scrap a day's ride away? Let's just feed him to the ravens and have done. That brock ain't gonna care about some petty raider."

"Oh, His Lordship will care about *this* raider. Count his ears."

The fox's remaining ear swivelled back. A few seconds later, and the soldier gasped.

"Bugger my tup. Is that...?"

"The very same. So if you want to sit around the Middens all day cuddling yer ram, you go right ahead. I will hand him over to His Lordship's court personally. I caught him, after all."

The hound reached for the rope, and the squirrel pulled it away.

"Not so fast, glory hound. We'll prepare a little detail to escort him. Wouldn't want him giving you the slip again."

Fearghus gave a laughing snort and the hound kicked him.

The badger's men hauled Fearghus to his feet by the neck-rope. They decided amongst themselves who would accompany the fox to the southern fortress. The bloodhound, naturally, volunteered. He spared a moment to catch the fox's eye.

"No hard feelings, hey? You may think you're playing Reynard but, well, life isn't always a folk tale, is it?"

Fearghus raised his middle claw. Whether that provoked them to bind his hand-paws, it still made the fox smile.

With no further words, they led the fox away. They marched south, across the rugged hills, two guards on each side of the fox. *Sensible,* he thought. *They know they underestimate me at their peril.* All the same, he kept silent. Why trouble the good beasts of the badger's watch with futile yelping and greeting? None would assist him. The rope bit into his neck, and he felt the fur rub away. He hoped it would grow back. The rope around his wrists also bit like a dog. As for his feet-paws, they ached. His boots were already wearing through, and the leather only deteriorated further over that boggy terrain. And yet, in that moment, Fearghus felt more alive, more alert, more in tune with the land he called home.

So, he was to be a prisoner. Kept at the pleasure of some distant 'majesty', who neither knew nor cared for nor understood this land. Who knew when those agents of that distant crown, the brock and his men, would let him cast his yellow eyes on these braes again? And so, he took in the land around him. The scents of heather and rich peat and fresh grass drifted to his nose. Beyond the traipse of hooves, and the chatter of soldiers, nature came alive with its sounds. Birds called over the chilly moors—blackbirds, thrushes, robin-redbreasts. He twitched his ear, and he cast his eyes skywards. Skeins of geese, thirty apiece or more, flew in arrowheads towards the south. The party passed a hedge, and a kestrel emerged, flying a casual flight before them all, before she wheeled higher and glided towards a thicket.

The early mists and clouds had lifted. Now, a pattern of autumn colours spread out like patchwork over the hills which rose and fell gently, far towards the horizon. They still wore green, but straw and brown blended their way in. Above the jagged horizon, the grimness of the morning gave way to a brilliant pale blue, while a smattering array of light-grey-dark-grey cloud drifted in from the south.

They reached a north-south road, and they followed it towards the sun—no need for legitimate forces on official duty to conceal themselves. After crossing miles of open and bleak and windswept country, the rough path dipped down a bank into woodland. At the bottom of the bank, they found some late apples, which they crunched on to sustain their strength. Fearghus sat watching his captors, his paws still bound behind his back, his stomach growling. One of the dogs dangled an apple-core before the fox. Though mostly cleaned, the sharp crisp scent of the fruit filled the fox's nose. All the same, he declined the soldier's taunting offer with a shake of the head. When the soldier asked if Fearghus was sure, and the fox shook his head again, the dog pitched the apple core far into the trees.

"Suit yourself, tod. It may be a very long time before His Lordship fills your plate."

Soon after they resumed their journey, Fearghus heard the rush of water. Across a meadow, he saw a river, rushing in rapids in places. Soon the path reached the river, both of them passing in parallel through patches of trees. And moments later, up ahead, from among the fields and the trees, a stone edifice emerged. Set back from the river, nestled beneath a bank, its flint-flecked and crenellated walls lay low along the meadow, except for its southern corner where it rose to form a tower. Folk across the Borders and beyond knew of Featherstone Castle, a fortification which the Lord of Northumbria had kept following his promotion to Warden of the English Middle March. A place of refuge, a sanctuary, which centuries later would still bring joy to beasts. Yet Fearghus felt no affinity for its stones: he doubted his stay as the badger's guest would be particularly comfortable.

Up the castle track they marched, to be greeted by the castle guards. They exchanged words, exchanged the fox, and the guards led Fearghus through a side entrance. A hare led the way: similar fur to Calan, Fearghus noted, similar age and height too, yet fuller-built, a well-fed animal: how his leporine companion may have looked in another life. He could not let his thoughts wander too much: he needed some way to save his own pelt, then eventually return to his hare. Oh, and to his vixen. Mustn't forget his vixen.

At the bottom of a spiral staircase, in a dim and narrow passageway, the guards stripped the fox of his clothes and weapons. Without another word, they pushed him through an open door into a cold, stone dungeon cell. They slammed the heavy door shut, locked it with a key, and left the fox alone.

The fox huddled in a corner, shivering, yet grateful for the insulation of his fur. Though there was no combatting all the chill of this cell. Up high, a tiny crack of a window gave a glimpse of the night sky. The drudge of the walk had left the fox's mind hazy, and he rested his head and his good ear on the cold floor, staring at the high window, thinking of the outside world as he drifted to sleep.

As dawn rose, so did the urge to piss. Sure, he had a bucket nearby him. But then he would be forced to endure its scent, for goodness-knew-how-long. The fox fought the growing urge, while he tracked the shaft of sunlight swinging clockwise around the cell. Morning, afternoon, evening again...why did he drink so deeply of that burn? He ignored the twinges, squirming, until a sudden sharp one made him yip. Rising to his paws, he trotted to the bucket to answer his call of nature.

For untold hours more, the fox sat, boredom gnawing at his mind. The rank, sour odour of his urine filled the room, its warmth and its scent filling his nostrils with every breath. How he wished for a drain, or gutter, or anything to sluice the brackish liquid away. Sometimes, a fox's nose could be too sensitive.

And after all this, what business would Lord Ragnar have with him? And how soon would the badger deal with him? Doubtless the brock had other matters he would consider more pressing: marching young cadets up and down the riverbank, counting the pennies he wrung in tax from citizens, licking the arses of the King's advisers...maybe even the King himself? How long would it be before Ragnar even remembered the fox, or someone reminded the badger that Fearghus was down here? And did he even want an audience with the badger? Folk had hung for lesser crimes than stealing a horse. And to be caught stealing from a Warden's own stock... At least he hadn't stolen from Lord Corbier, the Warden of the Scottish March. A wildcat in name and nature, he would have made Fearghus food for the crows in an instant!

And yet...this was Lord Ragnar's watch, so the badger had the final say. How cruel or lenient would the Lord be? Fearghus would find out in time. No sense in worrying without reason at this stage.

Simpler matters preoccupied the fox's mind: hunger, and thirst. No guard had furnished him yet, not so much as a burnt oven-bottom crust. *Okay, Fearghus, don't think about food.* If anything, the urge to drink was stronger. Yet the only liquid around was...

The bucket sat in the corner of his cell, its contents marinating. Fearghus felt his stomach burble at the very thought of drinking from it. But like all animals, he needed to drink. Did he dare? Surely, any liquid was better than none at all...surely! He tried not to pant, desperately aware of how parched and dry his maw was.

A wooden door opening down the corridor made the fox perk his single ear. The sound of quick and heavy boot-steps drew closer. Probably that bunny again. But maybe...he had some drink? Or even food? Fearghus tried not to think of such: best to temper one's expectations.

"Hey! Dog-fox!" The guard rapped the door hard, probably with the butt of his spear or something. The sharp sound made the fox shudder, close his eyes tight, and grumble.

"Oh, quit yer worrying. I have a message from His Lordship. He requests an audience with you."

"With me?"

"Well, he won't wanna talk to the piss bucket."

"So let me clarify. I have an audience with Ragnar?"

"That's *Lord* Ragnar to you, you cur. So mind your manners, groom your fur, and try and look presentable."

Fearghus scrambled to his paws. He ran his claws through his pelt, smoothing it down as best he could and working some of the tangles free. The dungeon door unlocked, and the built hare tossed him a rough woven cloak. The cloak covered his bare fur and his lack of modesty. When ready, the hare escorted him from the dungeon. They climbed the stone spiral stairs, before they twisted and turned through a series of passageways and corridors, all built with solid stone walls. The hare had not bound Fearghus, not even by his wrists, and the fox's mind clicked, eyes and ear scanning for any slight opening, some doorway or walkway he could sneak through. But he saw nothing. And even if he gave the overgrown bunny the slip, could he really find a way to escape this labyrinth, filled with beasts, many of them armed? Unlikely.

And so they walked on, until they came to a stop before some solid wooden double-doors. A broad ash-tree was carved into the wood, with a squirrel resting in its boughs. *The World Tree. At least the badger still honours the Old Ways.*

The hare banged the door four times with his spear, and Fearghus grimaced at the sound barrelling through the corridor. *Your paw works as well, young pup.* There followed silence. And more silence.

"Enter."

The reply came from within, deep and grizzled, making the fur on Fearghus's neck bristle. Fearghus could guess who had replied, and that knowledge made his fur bristle all the more. The uniformed hare pushed open one of the solid doors, and tilted his head, ears tipping to the side, signalling for the fox to enter first. He did so, the hare at his back. They entered a stone hall, with a long oak table at its centre, running away from the door. And at the head of the table, seated in a carved wooden chair, was the largest animal the fox had ever seen.

The fox tried to read the great badger, yet he drew a blank. How many seasons of experience, intrigue, politics, and bluff had weathered that striped and scarred muzzle? And just what did Lord Ragnar, Warden of Northumbria, want with a mere cutpurse fox?

Two hedgehogs emerged from a side door, each carrying a tray with a bowl and tankard atop. A few paces from the table, they slowed their approach, their eyes on His Lordship. The badger tap-tapped the table with a digging claw, and the hedgehogs placed the food and drink before the badger.

"Thank you, Merrin, that will be all."

The older of the two 'hogs gave a slight bow, before both prickly beasts scurried from the hall. Once the side door closed, the big brock turned his attention to the fox.

"Please, take a seat." He gestured with his claws. "And help yourself to the repast. You must be hungry."

The fox kept his pointed snout low and stepped forward. He slipped into one of the chairs, two spaces along from the badger's end. He reached for a tray, licking his lips before he could stop himself: mutton stew, with a hearty hunk of oat bread on the side.

He took the spoon from the tray, and took a chunk of the roasted sheep. The tough meat, stewed and softened, took a few chews for the fox to manage. Yet eat he did, savouring the meaty flavour and the rich gravy sauce. At least he remembered to chew with his maw closed.

Swallowing the meat, he reached a dirty paw for the tankard; the badger pushed it closer with his claws. Fearghus reached to snatch the handle, before he remembered his manners and grasped it more delicately. He lifted the tankard, letting the scent rise to his slender muzzle. Ale: dark and strong, not the weak watery small beer he usually encountered. Judging from the crisp, malty, hoppy aroma, two or three of these could knock a fox out for a day. Given the size of Lord Ragnar, though, he would probably barely feel it. While the fox brought the tankard to his lips, the big badger took his own ale, lifted his head, and with four audible, visible gulps, he drained his tankard of most of its contents. Setting his drink down, he turned to the fox.

"Fearghus of Leaderfoot. An infamous name on both sides of the Border. Very brave of your kin, first of all, to bear the name of that bridge, long after your compatriots broke your toll gates."

"We took pride in the service we offered. Safe passage across rapid waters and a treacherous land."

"An extortion scheme, some would call it. Yet that is in the past, and it is not only your surname which arouses fear in your enemies. Your reputation is well-earned, I might add. When animals speak your name, they do so with a good deal of admiration. Even the enemies you chose to make."

The fox gulped down his mouthful of bread. "I didnae choose them. What was a fox to do? Especially looking like this?" Fearghus jabbed a claw, pointing at the remnants of his left ear. The tattered and part-furred ear twitched. "Surname or no, every Family and Clan from the Solway to the Tyne would recognise me in the fur, and cast me out like scum-water, to float aimlessly from field to farmstead. If they didn' introduce my innards to a spear-point first. Or a rusty knife." Another spoonful of stew, which almost burned the fox's mouth. "And at least my associates and I are honest about our station. How many seasons have folk professed to be upright, said their Credos and Ave Marias like good wee puppies, only to turn their cheeks the very next day to raiding and feuding and watering the fields with each other's blood? These cycles began well before living memory. When, great brock, do you foresee them ending?"

"All the same, you made a fair success of your lifestyle. Picking your targets, striking when your quarry was most vulnerable. And never did my northern counterpart sniff you out. Though I am sure that Lord Corbier tried, wily wildcat that he is. To the best of his ability." The badger took a languorous drink from the remnants of his beer. "And yet, even the most optimistic of us would acknowledge that you rode your luck. The going must have gotten tougher, which in turn drove you to more desperate measures. Not only are you now a cattle-raider and a sheep-rustler, but also a horse thief? And raiding so deep into the English March, no less. Yet somehow, again, you almost slipped away. I know you have escaped the slew-hound before, and were I a gambling beast, I would not have bet against you sneaking free again. And yet, what should undo the notorious Fearghus of Leaderfoot but some simple dead wood?"

In such situations, Fearghus would have normally retorted to the person. Normally, however, they would speak with sneering, mockery, or pride in besting their fellow animal. Lord Ragnar spoke with no such disdain. That was the reason the fox kept quiet...of course. It had nothing to do with the badger's size, of course not. Nor because the fox was intimidated, most *certainly* not.

"You are a wanted animal, Fearghus. You know full well how many folk would gladly see you dangle from a gibbet. And yet, if you were to ask me...that would be a waste of a good fox."

An intriguing turn of phrase. Fearghus lifted his eyes, meeting the badger's deep brown hues for the first time. "A...good fox?" And he added, "Sir?"

The badger nodded. Small, subtle, confirmatory. "I have been pondering, discussing with my advisers. And I reckon your skills could be put to better employ. Your knowledge of the land, I mean, and how an outlaw might use it to avoid detection."

Here we go. Doubtless the badger intends to use me for one of his *raids.*

"I talk of lawful employ," continued the badger, "under my watch, and among my forces. And I offer your fellow outlaws the chance to live within these walls."

Fearghus gave a little snarl. "I knew it. You are blackmailing me."

"Far from it. You are free to leave whenever you want, and to live however you want. I know as well as anybody the strife of this land, caught between two kingdoms in perpetual conflict. You have kits now, I understand. They would have the chance at a safer life."

The fox lifted his muzzle-corner and huffed, yet did not reply. The badger continued.

"And as for yourself, you would have a mount of your own, and the chance to ride under the protection of the Middle March—of Northumbria itself. No beast could trouble you while riding under my badge. Not even Lord Corbier. Much as he would love to."

The fox pondered all that the badger said. How would things change for his companions? Could he even trust the badger? He tried to gauge the expression on the brock's face, yet beyond severity, he read nothing. Certainly nothing that looked like duplicity.

"And I would no longer be a prisoner?" asked the fox. "What of my alleged past crimes?"

"They would all be discounted. After all, if one were to trace the myriad feuds and skirmishes and blood-lettings, through every Family and every generation, there would not be an innocent creature among us. Holding onto past grudges will get us nowhere."

Fearghus stroked his tufted-furred chin. "You ken, badger? Ever since you took your seat as Warden, rumours began to spread. How you would cleave an animal with that claymore, and only ask questions when both halves stopped twitching."

The badger smiled. "Our reputations go before us. And perhaps we both encourage those reputations. After all, sharp claws and fierce weaponry strike a certain instinct in an animal."

"You speak the truth, sir. Very well, then. I accept."

"Excellent. Lieutenant Bramblebush will show you to the guards' quarters. Make yourself proper, then ride out and find your men. We shall take you in."

The hare, Bramblebush, looked ready to hop in protest. Maybe before a lesser beast, he would have. But something unspoken passed between the Lord and his officer. Fearghus's yellow eyes darted from buck to brock and back, and the leporine's ears dipped. He nodded, and turned to make his departure.

"Come, tod," said the hare. "This way."

Fearghus felt he should acknowledge the badger in some way. So he bowed to the badger, who dipped his head in return. He turned to follow the long-ear, two paces behind. Even as he left the badger's court, a spark flickered in the fox's mind: how to slip the bunny, rustle a stout horse from the stables, and canter ahead to his gang's hideout in that dreary wood. He felt the foxy grin rise on his muzzle, but he snuffed out the spark before it ignited the dry tinder of his scheming mind. And anyway, whichever horse they gave him would likely have no part in such a scheme, however much spur the fox gave. No, instead, he composed a speech, a pitch to sell the badger's offer as an opportunity. A chance for him and Melrose to raise their kits in warmth and safety. The kits could learn trades, or maybe even learn to read and write? As for Calan, the victuals in these walls alone would be persuasion enough. Plus, good bowmen were hard to come by. Doubtless His Lordship would find space for the long-ear among the ranks. Though of course Fearghus would have to sneak him out of the soldiers' quarters from time to time.

And it would be a chance for all his fellow outlaws—or should that be 'former outlaws'?—to set aside their troubles and start afresh. A pardon for alleged past misdemeanours.

And if things didn't work out...well, there were miles more Borderland where a fox could go to ground.

One Book to Burn

Faolan

artinus de Vries?"

"Yes, that's me?"

"Excellent. You're coming with us."

The small roe deer who had answered the door looked up at the two tall wolves in guard uniforms with an expression of confusion mixed in with fear. "O-okay, but eh...why?" he asked with the smallest of voices. He adjusted his glasses and swallowed hard.

The older of the two wolves shrugged and looked bored. "Mayor's orders." Martinus could tell he was the oldest, for he clearly had more white fur around his muzzle than his fellow guardsman.

"Okay. Uhm...now?"

"Now."

They led him from his home and through the city's many stone streets, past one of the various harbours, the Church of Our Lady, which was the biggest church in Dordrecht, and the crowded market where people mainly sold fish. The smell of fresh fish was strong in the air, and a whole plethora of different merchants shouted from the tops of their lungs to get people to browse and sample their wares. Despite his current confusion and anticipation, Martinus loved watching the people go from stall to stall like bees gathering honey from fresh spring flowers.

Dordrecht was surrounded by rivers and turned into an island ever since the St. Elizabeth's flood in 1421. It was a disastrous event that ate up a large chunk of the land, along with no less than sixteen villages, and turned Dordrecht into an island. Now, all naval traffic that wanted to travel from Rotterdam to places further inland had to pass by Dordrecht first, making it a perfect trade hub. This happened before Martinus was born, but older people still spoke of it regularly.

The mayor's home was an impressive building in the middle of Dordrecht. The building was an interesting mix of classical pillars and a pediment reminiscent of Roman times and Dutch architecture. It was topped by a small clock tower that showed the time on all sides. The place radiated power. Between the two centre pillars stood an imposing grey wolf in an equally intimidating uniform. He could be called classically handsome, but it was ruined by the permanent scowl on his face. Everybody in the city knew his name: Mark Koudstaal. The captain of the guard looked down at Martinus and nodded at the guards.

"I'll take it from here, boys. Well done."

His voice was low enough to make bones vibrate, and his tone was as unyielding as steel. The guards bowed their heads in respect and went on their way. Captain Koudstaal opened the door to the house and motioned for Martinus to get inside. Unable to refuse, and frankly too nervous to do so, Martinus did as he was told. He climbed the stone steps and passed between the two lion statues lazily keeping guard from where they lay on low walls. He swallowed hard again when he looked up and saw the wolf's steel gaze on him. He hurried inside as if whipped.

His hooves sounded louder than he liked on the polished wooden floor, and his eyes needed a moment to adjust to the dark interior that was a polar opposite to the bright outside of the house. He was led to an anteroom and invited to sit on a beautifully carved wooden bench.

"The mayor will be with you soon," the wolf spoke before knocking on a door next to a beautiful painting depicting a typical scene of Dutch countryside, windmill included.

"Enter," a booming voice answered from inside.

The wolf left the room and closed the door behind him. Martinus was left to wait alone in the small dark wooden room. He fidgeted nervously with his paws and crossed his legs. He looked around the room to take in any interesting details, while his ears swerved to the door in a futile attempt to catch whatever the two men were talking about in the next room. He stood up and walked over to the painting. It had clearly been done by a talented artist, as the attention to detail was immaculate. He could almost see the reeds waving on the wind simulated by the rotating mill and the ripples on the water. The sun was slowly setting in the painted world, as told by the slight hints of orange and pink in the sky. It was a masterpiece for sure.

Martinus tore himself away from the painting and wrapped his arms around himself. He still had no inclination of why he was there. He hadn't broken any laws he was aware of, and the books he wrote were far from controversial. Maybe the mayor was a fan of his work and wanted an autograph? The thought brought a smile to his face, as well as a light chuckle as he shook his head. It was highly unlikely that the mayor had read his books. Surely, a man of his calibre had more important things to do than to read his romantic fiction. He sat down again and tried to come up with other reasons.

Martinus had no time to ponder the question further as the door opened and the wolf showed his signature glower. "Inside, please." His tone made clear that the 'please' was only there for show.

The small deer stood up and dusted off his moss green coat before entering the room, his fingers intertwined to stop himself from fidgeting. He was not in any trouble, was he?

The room he walked into was nothing short of breathtaking. Beautiful paintings and sculptures decorated the large room, and there were multiple bookcases filled with a fortune of tomes of all colours along one of the walls. The sound of his walking was muffled by an elaborate rug covering most of the floor. He had to compose himself for a moment, but the clearing of one's throat drew him to a stately desk, behind which sat an enormous brown bear, the man of the house.

Mayor Barend Bijkerk was a powerful baron before he became the mayor of Dordrecht. His strong connections with the various noble houses and important merchants made him a powerful man. Becoming the sole person who ruled the city was a piece of cake for this man.

The door closed behind him and was blocked off by the captain. The mayor folded his ringed fingers together and rested his chin on them as he looked down at Martinus. Even seated, the bear towered over him.

"So," said the bear, drawing the deer's full attention with just that one word. The dark timbre of his voice vibrated his bones. "You are Martinus de Vries, the famous writer?" His voice carried a hint of disappointment.

"W-well, I wouldn't necessarily call myself famous just yet, Mr. Mayor," Martinus answered in a manner that was less strong than he would have liked. Way to make a first impression.

"No, no, you are the famous writer," the baron said, stressing the word famous and holding up his paw. "After all, my darling wife, Nel, would never read the words of one who is merely mediocre. Therefore, you must be a famous writer."

Martinus still didn't agree with the mayor but figured that arguing with him would lead nowhere good. He just nodded along with the man and stayed focused on him.

"My wife is a big fan of yours, you know? Positively devours any of your books she comes across."

The small deer shuddered at the word 'devours' and glimpsed the bear's sharp fangs for a moment. "Th-thank you."

"However, she is always...What to call it? Left hungry for more. You tease your audience with your characters and their romances a little too much, Martinus, and yet you never give them what they so desperately desire. You throw out the bait, but never let it be caught." He had gotten up from his luxurious chair and paced around the room. Each step caused the wooden planks to creak and complain below the carpet.

The writer wasn't sure where the mayor was going with this. He followed the bear with only his eyes. "I am s-sorry your wife feels that way a-about my work, though I am not q-quite certain about what you would like me to d-d-do with this information." He started fidgeting with his hands again. "What would your w-wife like to see in my stories?"

The large bear moved surprisingly quickly and slapped his heavy paws on Martinus' shoulders, straining the frail deer's bones. "Sex, my boy. Pure, uncensored rutting," he spoke in his ear, sending shivers all the way down to Martinus' tailbone. "The ploughing of fair maidens by rugged men!"

"B-b-but Mr. Mayor, surely you wouldn't want your wife to read stories of such a d-d-deviant and p-perverse nature?" Martinus squeaked.

The bear's boisterous, booming laughter filled the room. "Do you think my wife frail and prudish, boy? I have yet to meet a bigger deviant! Oh, the things she can do!" he said before clearing his throat and stopping himself from revealing too much private information. He walked up to the door and bent over to look Martinus in the eye. The bear's were such a dark brown that they almost appeared black. Martinus couldn't look away and was faced with his own reflection in those dark pools.

"I will cut to the chase here, boy. I want you to write my wife a personal book that will never be published anywhere else. It will be my special gift for her birthday. You will make this the raunchiest and most perverted story ever written. Do you understand me, boy?"

His eyes nearly doubled in size. "B-b-but sir! I could never-"

"You can and you will if you know what's good for you! I will not take no for an answer. This is non-negotiable. You will be adequately compensated when you're done. Mark will show you your room." He took a seat behind his desk again and waved his paw to indicate they were done.

Martinus was absolutely flabbergasted by the mayor's words. "S-sir, you cannot do this! What do you mean by 'my room'? I always write from home! What about my wife?!"

"*Silence!*" the bear roared as he slammed his massive fist on the wooden desk and stared the deer down. "You will be my guest until you finish the book to my satisfaction. Your wife will be notified of your absence. Good luck, little writer. Mark."

The wolf was already right behind Martinus. "Follow me." When Martinus didn't immediately obey his command, the captain of the guard pulled him by the arm and dragged him from the room. Martinus was led upstairs to a small guest room. It was furnished with a small bed and a writing desk, as well as a small wardrobe. A quill and ink pot were waiting for him next to a stack of paper.

"This will be your room until the mayor is satisfied. You will be assigned a maid to see to any needs you may have. She is currently on her way to your wife with the news of your assignment and residency here. Good luck," Koudstaal said without the slightest hint of emotion before leaving the room and locking the heavy oak door.

Martinus flung himself against the door and watched the wolf disappear through the glass of the small window in the door. He collapsed on the bed and took off his glasses before burying his face in his hands. He rubbed his eyes and let out a shuddering sigh. What was going on? He could not believe that he had just been pressured into doing the mayor's bidding. The bear had called him a guest, but he was just a prisoner now. He could not even leave this room. He sobbed into his hands as the reality of it all sank in. "Oh, Agnes...What am I to do?" He curled up and let the reality of his predicament wash over him.

After a moment of wallowing in self-pity, the roe deer put his glasses back on, got back on his hooves, and walked over to the windows, to see if they could offer a means of escape. He had a gorgeous view of the Church of Our Lady, which was tilted to the right as usual. Unfortunately, there was no balcony to climb to, not that he was brave or athletic enough to pull that off, nor was there a set of stairs or even a canal to jump into. He sighed and looked out over the town square, where people happily went about their day. None of them had any inkling of what was going on with him. He dejectedly sat down at the desk and checked the many little drawers for anything he could use. All he could find were more quills, ink pots, and paper.

He looked at the windows again in frustration. There was no possibility of opening it, so he couldn't even try to get messages out that way. He could break the window, but that would alert the mayor or Koudstaal and leave him with a draughty room. Martinus leaned back in the chair, which was unexpectedly comfortable, and took the quill between his fingers. There was only one thing he could do. He racked his brain and tried to come up with various ways to describe what the baron wanted of him more crudely than he normally would, but he just couldn't think of anything. He had never used vulgar language like this before, and it didn't match his usual writing style at all. He lowered his glasses and pinched the bridge of his nose. "Lord, give me strength."

He had no way of telling how long he'd been staring at that blank page when something familiar appeared in the corner of his eye, drawing his attention back to the window. It was Agnes! His beautiful wife, a fellow roe deer, was in the worst of moods, judging from her expression, and was walking so fast that her beautiful blue dress couldn't keep up with her. She was accompanied by the fluffiest dog Martinus had ever seen. He figured that she must be a Keeshond. She was wearing servant clothes, from which he deduced that she was probably the one who informed Agnes of his current predicament and would be tending to him. She was doing her best to keep up with the marching Agnes, hoisting up her skirt to walk faster.

Martinus was overjoyed to see his wife, and he jumped up from the chair to walk over to the door, eager for it to swing open. There was a commotion downstairs, and he could clearly hear Agnes shouting as he put his ear to the door. He couldn't hear her exact words, however. He could make out both Mark and Mayor Bijkerk arguing with her, followed by the slamming of a heavy door.

He rushed over to the window to see his wife storming off, fists clenched. He desperately knocked on the window to let her know he was there, but she must not have heard him. He lowered his hand and head and sighed in defeat. If anyone could've gotten him out somehow, it was Agnes. He lay down on the bed and looked up at the ceiling as if the answer to all his problems was written there.

A knock on the door alerted him to a visitor. Whoever it was unlocked the door and walked in. Martin quickly sat up and brushed off his jacket. "Good afternoon. I brought you some tea," the grey Keeshond he had seen earlier said with a careful smile.

"Oh, eh...Could you put it on the desk, please?"

"Of course, sir. Is there anything else I could help you with?" She asked as she placed his tea on the desk. She then moved her paws behind her back and smiled kindly at him.

"I don't suppose you could let me out?" he tried.

"I'm afraid not, sir. Mayor Bijkerk would not allow it. He has guards stationed downstairs to prevent your escape," she said with a look of pity in her eyes.

"What is your name, miss?"

"Hildegard, sir, but please call me Hilde," she said with a small curtsy.

"Pleased to meet you, Hilde, though I wish we had met in different circumstances. There is something I would like your help with."

"I'm all ears, sir," she said with a polite smile.

"I'm sure you have heard of my current situation, yes?"

"I am afraid I do not know the specifics, sir."

"Oh, well eh...The mayor would like me to write a book so perverted that even the devil would think twice about touching it."

"Oh heavens!"

"Heavens indeed. The problem is, Hilde, that I have no experience writing such stories whatsoever. Have you read my work?"

"I am afraid I cannot read, sir."

"Oh, that's most unfortunate. Anyway, I need your help in procuring books of a more...exotic...nature, so I have some sort of reference to work with. Is that something you can do?"

"I will ask the mayor for permission and funds first. I think I know someone who might be able to help you," Hilde said. "A merchant friend of mine. He and I go back many years. He specialises in jewellery and antiques, but always boasts that he can get his paws on anything if the price is right."

"Thank you, Hilde. That would be a great help. Thank you for the tea," he said as he smiled at her.

Taking that as her cue to leave, the Keeshond bowed her head and left the room, locking it behind her curly tail.

Not much later, the door was opened again, and Mayor Bijkerk walked into the room. "Here he is, Nel! I told you I would get him to write for you!" he stated proudly as he puffed up his barrel of a chest.

A massively overweight female bear squealed in delight and clapped her massive paws together as she entered the room and saw the tiny writer sitting at the wooden desk. "Oh, I can't believe it! He's really here! In our house!" She bounced up and down a couple of times, causing the chair Martinus was sitting on to bounce with her. The deer held onto the desk as he stared up at the humongous woman.

"Uhm...h-hi?"

"HI! By God, you are so cute! I am so honoured that you decided to write a story for me! I am your biggest fan!"

"I...don't doubt it," Martinus said with a polite smile as his eyes moved over her. He bit his tongue before he argued about how he had not decided anything of his own free will. He doubted it would do him any good. "So uhm...Would you like to star as the main character, or should I make someone up?" he asked, trying to sound professional. He had never written on commission before, but he figured it would go something like this.

"Oh! I would simply die of joy if I could be the main character!" she said as she moved closer and pressed her colossal bosom against him as she looked over his shoulder, trapping him in her cleavage. "Oh...You haven't written anything down yet."

"I...wanted to get the specifics right before I tried anything," the deer lied.

Both bears nodded as it somehow made sense to them. "Hilde is off getting those books you wanted. You had better make it worth our time, little writer. Disappointment is not an option," Barend spoke with a threatening undertone.

"Don't speak to him like that, Barend, please. I am sure he will do a great job! Won't you, Mr. de Vries?" she asked sweetly after reprimanding her husband. She squeezed him between her knockers even more.

Martinus, having trouble breathing at this point, squeaked out a "yes", before Nel moved away and hugged her husband.

"Wonderful! Remember, my birthday is in two months' time!" the woman said with a big smile on her round face. "I'm so excited!"

Barend shot him an intimidating look before leading his wife out of the room and locking the door behind him again.

Martinus slumped in the chair and rubbed his forehead with a sigh. His paw trailed off towards his small antlers and gently let his fingers follow the modest branches. He sincerely hoped that Hilde would be able to procure the books he needed, or he might end up as the bears' dinner the next month, to ease their disappointment.

Hilde returned somewhat later and informed him that it would take a few days to get the desired books. She checked the hallway and turned around before reaching into her chest fluff and pulling out a folded piece of paper, which she held out to Martinus with a slight blush colouring the insides of her ears. "Your wife asked me to give you this."

He eagerly accepted the letter from her and unfolded the paper.

My love,

I cannot believe what is happening to you right now. The mayor has clearly lost his mind. I have instructed Hilde to come visit me every other day, so she can deliver letters and fresh clothes. She seems like a trustworthy girl, so be kind to her.

I will come up with a plan for you to escape your prison. You can count on that. For now, sit tight and do your best to please the mayor to the best of your abilities. Do not let him suspect anything.

Love,

Agnes

Martinus sighed in relief at the letter and hugged it to his chest as if she were there with him. Her words gave him strength and filled him with hope. If anyone could get him out of there, it would be his brilliant Agnes. "Thank you, Hilde," he said as he looked at the servant girl. "Do you think you could get me something to eat? And would you ask the mayor if it is okay if I go on a short walk to stretch my legs?"

The girl curtsied with a smile and left the room, leaving him alone with the spirit of his wife. As soon as she left, Martinus started writing a letter to his Agnes.

Hilde returned with some food, after which the captive writer was allowed out for a short walk, flanked by two menacing-looking guards. He figured the mayor would not have fallen for such a cheap attempt at escape, but it was a shame, nonetheless. The deer looked up at the reddening evening sky and hoped he would soon get to enjoy this view as a free man again, together with his wife.

Hilde walked along Dordrecht's paved streets and bridges a few days later. She had received word from her friend that the ordered books had arrived. The Keeshond looked down into the small canals and smiled as young kids rowed small boats along its waters. How peaceful life seemed for them. She waited patiently at a nearby crossing for some horses and wagons to pass her by. She was on an errand run, which included getting some more wine and cheese, and paying a short visit to Agnes. She was carrying a bag of clean clothes, another letter for the roe deer's husband, as well as one from Anges for the merchant friend she was about to visit. Strange. Agnes didn't even know the man.

Reinier Donkersloot's shop was located near one of the smaller harbours. Hilde always enjoyed watching boats and ships of various sizes flying flags of all colours pass by on her way to her childhood friend. His shop was not very popular but attracted the right clientele for his business. Reinier specialised in wooden furniture, trinkets, and expensive jewels, but he sometimes branched out into other areas if he could get a profitable deal somewhere.

The black rat was standing outside his shop, watching a horse and a ram carry an expensive-looking table out of his shop. "Don't you dare drop this one, or I will deduct it from your pay! I mean it this time!" he said, threateningly shaking his silver-topped cane at them. He righted his top hat and huffed. The scowl on his face melted like snow in summer when he spotted Hilde. "Hilde, darling! So nice to see you again! I have the books you ordered, come, come!" he said with the brightest of smiles as he ushered her into his shop.

The place was absolutely packed with intricately carved wooden furniture and display cases filled with all manner of bracelets, necklaces, and the like. There were a few women browsing the glittering gems and happily cackling amongst each other. "Mister Donkersloot?" one of them, a chicken, asked. "Could my friend perhaps try on this magnificent blue pendant?"

The rat left Hilde's side immediately and smiled at the women. "Of course, ladies, of course. You have excellent taste for spotting that one, m'lady," he said with a practised voice meant to instil a sense of importance in his customers. He opened the cabinet and took out the pendant. He gently moved the chicken's friend, a magpie, in front of a mirror and hung the silver chain around her neck. "This sapphire pendant will draw the eye of many an onlooker, especially since it compliments your feathers so beautifully. You will turn heads wherever you go," he said with that same silky voice as he looked over her shoulder, at her reflection.

Hilde smiled and leaned back against a large bookcase while Reinier did his thing. It was always a joy to see him subtly manipulate his customers into buying things. The rat never lied though, which was probably why it came so naturally to him. He genuinely believed the sapphire would look great on her.

The magpie ended up buying the pendant after having been persuaded by the combined convincing by Reinier and her friends. The shop owner bid them farewell and turned his attention back to Hilde. "Sorry about that. Business called. I've been trying to sell the pendant for weeks. As beautiful as it was, I am happy to see it go." He chuckled and straightened his lavish coat. "Now then, where were we? Ah, yes! The book chest!"

He led Hilde to the back of his shop, where a large wooden chest decorated with carved flowers waited for them. He opened it and showed the dog that it was filled to the brim with books. "The book chest was easy to get, but these books were harder to come by. I had to talk to a lot of people to find all of these. I read one of them, and I had to say a few extra Hail Marys after that!" he joked as he fanned himself for emphasis.

"I just hope they will be of help to Mr. de Vries. The poor fellow is locked in his room until he comes up with something. It really is quite cruel," Hilde said, her ears down. "Oh! I have a letter from his wife for you."

"I made sure to charge that corrupt bastard extra for these books," Reinier said with a judgmental air. "More money out of his pockets means there's less chance he'd pull something like this again." He held out his paw for the letter and looked at it in confusion. "Why would she write to me? We've never met, so it can't be a declaration of her undying love for me."

Hilde shrugged at this question and just pointed at the letter.

He used one of his sharp claws as a letter opener and pulled the paper out of the envelope. He unfolded it and started reading. He looked up to make sure nobody could hear them from where they stood, before whispering to Hilde. "She wants to break him out. You told her about the book chest, and she thinks it could be a way to smuggle him out. I need to procure a small ship with a trustworthy captain. She promises to pay me handsomely for my help."

"Do you think it can be done?" Hilde asked, her wagging tail and raised ears betraying her eagerness to help.

"Sure. It sounds easy enough. The difficult part is getting him out in the chest. I assume the guards will check the chest, so there is no way he would get out that way unseen."

"We'll figure something out. Let's just get the book chest back to the mayor's house for now."

"Of course. I'll get someone to put it on a cart and walk with you. Let me just write a response to this letter," he said as he walked over to his desk and quickly scribbled a letter to Agnes. Hilde could tell that his handwriting was a lot sloppier than the refined hand of Mrs. de Vries. Reinier put the letter in an envelope and stamped it shut with some wax and his personal seal. "Hand this to her at your earliest convenience."

Hilde nodded and stuffed the letter in her chest fluff to keep it safe. "Thank you. I'm sure we'll meet again soon," she said with a smile.

"It's always a pleasure, my dear friend."

The two embraced and parted ways. Hilde waited outside until a strong bull with a wooden cart loaded with the book chest showed up. "Miss Hilde?"

She nodded. "That's me. Follow me to the mayor's house, please."

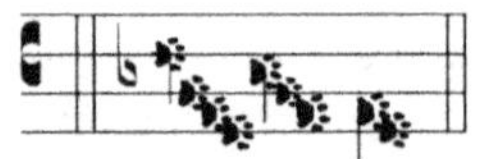

The two guards stationed outside the place called for Captain Koudstaal, who came outside with his usual sunny disposition. He opened the chest and removed all the books to check for any hidden items. All without saying anything. He even flipped through a few of the books before nodding. He placed everything back in the chest and closed it. "All clear," he said to the bull. The wolf called the two guards over and had them carry the heavy chest all the way upstairs. The bull was dismissed. Mark nodded at Hilde and disappeared inside.

Hilde bit her lip and exhaled through her nose. This escape plan was doomed to fail without a distraction.

The supplied books helped Martinus out tremendously, and he spent most of his days reading them and taking notes. When he wasn't reading, he went on escorted walks, ate his meals, or worked on the story for Bijkerk. He was forced to spend his dinners with the bears, which was a most awkward affair. He was still allowed to go to church on Sundays, where he could sit with his wife. Mark would sit next to him, though, so he could not discuss any plans with Agnes. Nevertheless, it was great to hold her paw in his and be physically close to her. It sustained him in a way he had never realised before.

Barend and Nel checked on him regularly, Nel more so than her husband. Getting to know her helped him portray her better in his story, but he almost couldn't fathom how deviant this woman was. He found that she was a creative spirit in her own way. She had even tried to undress and make a move towards him. For the purpose of improving her portrayal in the story, she claimed, after which she was banned from entering his room by her jealous husband. He could hear his revenge through the walls later that night.

Whenever Martinus finished reading one of the books, and was done taking notes, it was given to the mayor's wife to appease her. Before the month was out, Martinus had gone through all the books. He had to admit that, against all of his expectations, reading all of these books had improved his writing in certain areas. Perhaps, once this was all over, he'd try writing a more...daring...book than before. Of his own free will. He also knew exactly how many tiny cracks were in the ceiling, which floorboards creaked and which didn't, and had even named a fly as though it were a pet. It flew out of the window to enjoy the freedom Martinus could only dream of now. "Bye Willem."

Hilde had him practise lying in the book chest, as per Agnes' instructions, but his antlers proved to be a problem. They wouldn't fall off until October at the earliest. It was the first week of June now, and Nel's birthday would be in July, so that wouldn't happen in time.

Hilde took the book chest to Reinier's repeatedly, after which it was always checked by Koudstaal. The rat had not been able to fill the chest since the first time, and there were fewer and fewer books left to fill it. This didn't mean that the mayor paid any less, for Reinier was driving up the prices. "It's a question of supply and demand, sir. Your demand is higher than what can possibly be supplied!"

Hilde excitedly went up Martinus' room with a letter from Agnes. "The plan is here! Your wife prays that you trust her," she whispered as she handed it to the roe deer.

"Of course. I always do," he said with a smile as he opened the letter.

> My Love,
>
> Everything is ready. Reinier has procured a means of escape. We will get you out during the next big festival, to be held on the first of July, a few days before Nel Bijkerk's birthday. The guards will hopefully be too busy with all the extra merchants and folks coming to the city to pay attention to you. We have yet to come up with a distraction big enough, but you can trust us to think of something in time. At least Bijkerk will not be home, as he will be holding a speech as usual. You will travel in the chest as planned. Please, keep acting as if nothing is wrong. Hilde assured me that you are doing splendidly.
>
> I cannot wait for us to be together again.
>
> Love,
>
> Agnes
>
> P.S. I found a solution to your antler problem. I am sorry.

Martinus stared at the letter in both elation and confusion. "What does she mean by saying she has a solution for my antlers and that she is sorry?" He looked up at Hilde, who nervously revealed the small bone saw she had been hiding behind her back.

"...oh."

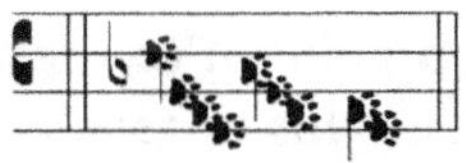

Loud banging on his door woke Martinus up so abruptly that he fell out of the bed in panic, entangling himself in his sheets. He yelled and pulled them hard, ripping the fabric with his sharp antlers. Having freed himself, he stood up and huffed to see Hilde had let herself in. He screamed and covered himself up even though he was wearing his pyjamas. "I'm not decent!"

"We have no time for decorum!" she said as she closed the door behind her and walked to the window. "Look! The city is on fire!"

He ran to the window and gasped as his eyes beheld what could only be described as a scene directly from the circles of Hell itself. The overcast sky was painted bright orange, and the flames rose so high that they seemed to be licking the clouds, turning night to day. People were running through the streets, some with buckets of water, and others with as many of their belongings as possible.

"What happened?! Did you do this?!" he asked as he turned to look at Hilde.

"Of course not! Nobody knows what caused it, but this is our chance! We must go now!" Hilde said as she took the bone saw from under the mattress and walked up to him.

Martinus let out a less-than-manly scream as the fires outside cast the Keeshond servant in a most devilish glow. His knees trembled, and he held on to the window as she advanced on him, her eyes never leaving his.

She pulled out the desk chair. "Sit."

The deer complied and trembled as he sat down at the desk, his hands clutching the underside of the chair as Hilde took hold of one of his antlers. "This won't hurt you, right?" she asked.

"I-I-It should not, n-no. My antlers are f-f-fully grown!"

She hesitated no longer and got to work on his antlers with determination. She grunted and growled as she sawed away at them, first one, then the other. Agnes had warned her that antlers are stronger than bone, but she hadn't expected it to be this difficult. Martinus whimpered and held on to the chair so tightly that he squeezed all the blood out of his fingers. After what seemed like an eternity, both antlers had dropped onto the desk. Hilde dropped the saw and massaged her sore arm.

"The book chest, quickly!" the dog said as she dragged it towards the door. "No, get out!" she yelled as Martinus had tried stepping into it.

"I thought that was the plan?"

"The plan was to have someone here to carry the whole chest downstairs, but I cannot lift you on my own."

"What about the guards and the mayor? They'll see us!"

"They are all off to fight the fire! They can't have it reach this place."

"Can't we just make a run for it then?"

"You wish to risk the chance of anyone spotting you and alerting the mayor or Koudstaal? We don't know who else is involved in this!"

"Where's the help you planned for then?"

"I don't know, but we're on our own now."

The deer nodded, understanding the situation, and carried the chest downstairs with Hilde. Martinus climbed into the chest, which was then closed by the Keeshond. "Wait here! I'll try to find them!" As if he had any other choice.

Hilde returned with Agnes, Reinier, and the bull who had carried the chest from Reinier's to the mayor's multiple times already. Agnes and Reinier wore cloaks to hide their faces, to be as inconspicuous as possible. They loaded the chest onto the cart and hurried through the streets, using the panic unfolding before them as cover. Martinus lifted the lid just a smidge, so he could see what was happening. He couldn't allow himself to miss this. He'd never forgive himself.

The warm scent of burning wood filled his nostrils. It was a scent he would normally associate with good company, good wine, and song. However, at this moment, people were running around like headless chickens, screaming and carrying whatever belongings they could save. His eyes watered as smoke stung them, and he was forced to narrow his eyes to see. Various wagons were leaving for the city gates, while other people stayed to fight the fire. The city guards tried to retain a certain level of order, but it was all for naught. Chaos reigned in Dordrecht now.

Reinier did his best to clear the way for the cart, but it was difficult to clear the way enough for them to push through the thick crowd. Several streets could no longer be used, due to the fire spreading, which only made the journey longer. Martinus gasped as he witnessed flames licking the tower of the Church of Our Lady. Surely such a strong stone building would not be torn asunder by mere fire! He could not believe what was happening to his beloved city. He had lived here all his life. He had never imagined himself fleeing from it, but the devil had laid his claim tonight. Martinus' heart wept.

"We're almost there!" Reinier shouted.

"Hear that, love? Almost there!" Agnes spoke loudly to Martinus, her face close to the chest as she stroked it lovingly. She pulled back her hood and kept walking briskly beside the cart.

Just a few streets further lay one of the smaller harbours, where a small boat lay in wait. An old stocky male beaver stood at the helm, smoking a pipe. He narrowed his eyes at the party and grinned. "There they are, boys! Help them onto the ship, post-haste!" He shouted at his loyal otter crew. Two otters readied the gangplank and held it steady, while three more jumped off the ship and helped push the cart from behind. "That's it, lads!" the captain shouted.

Reinier pulled back his hood and ran up to the captain to shake his paw. "Leendert, am I glad to see you!"

"You were lucky I was in port today, lad. If your messenger hadn't found me just now, I would have been gone already! Can't risk my lovely girl catching fire, after all!" Captain Leendert laughed and slapped the rat on his shoulder, causing him to wince.

"Yes, well, I'm glad he found you. This moves our plan up a few weeks. I trust that it is no problem?"

"Eh, I guess I could charge you a fee for it. It would only be fair, after all," the beaver grinned.

Reinier sighed and leaned on his cane. "You drive a hard bargain." He reached into his pocket and handed the man a small bag of coins. "That should cover it all."

The bull and the otters had moved the book chest below deck, to the cargo area. Agnes opened the chest and let her husband out. She hugged him tightly and kissed him repeatedly. "It worked! You're free!" she said.

"I couldn't have done it without you, my love. Thank you. Thank you thousandfold."

"And I couldn't have done it without dear Hilde," Agnes said as she walked up to the Keeshond and hugged the girl. "My husband would still be trapped by that awful bear if not for you. I hope this didn't ruin things for you."

Hilde smiled and returned the embrace. "I guess I could always start anew somewhere else. Working for Mayor Bijkerk was far from ideal anyway."

One of the otters poked his head downstairs. "People, your friend is leaving!"

They hurried upstairs to see Reinier Donkersloot and his employee standing on solid ground, away from the boat. "Reinier! Thank you so much for everything! I hope we meet again!" Hilde called as she waved at him.

"No worries, Hilde! I am sure we'll see each other before long! May the wind be in your sails!"

Agnes turned to the captain. "Where are we headed, sir?"

"'s-Hertogenbosch, and then to Maastricht!"

They untied the ropes, raised the anchor, and sailed away on the river Merwede, which flowed into the Maas. Martinus and Agnes de Vries, along with Hilde, watched their once beloved city burn. Martinus clutched the book he had been writing for Nel Bijkerk in his hands, and flung it overboard, into the raging inferno of one of the many wooden houses that lay abandoned now. As he watched it catch fire, a special feeling of satisfaction washed over him. He kept his eyes on the burning church tower until the last flames disappeared from view.

Heaven Will Weigh the Heart of Stone

Pascal Farful

The gate opened. There, alongside a tall badger, stood Walther. in immaculate leather armour and tights, with a sheathed broadsword strapped to his waist and a trailing cloak, the fox stepped out and towards a ruffed lemur in a tatty tunic.

Wolfgang gazed into Walther's jade eyes. The taller fox looked down at him with a firm stare. A stare that was calculating, focused and very male. It was all the lemur could do to keep his own gaze at the fox's eyeline.

"Is it you?" The fox asked abruptly.

"Yes, me." The lemur replied.

Walther's stare moved down over the lemur's physique, then to his blade. Wolfgang's tunic was cheap, and his sword was cheaper.

"Very well." Walther turned his head towards the river. "Come. Let us put you out of your misery."

The lemur nodded and followed, the badger in tow. Wolfgang noted all the extra swords that the badger was carrying, along with a small bag of medical supplies. It finally dawned on him just how woefully ill-equipped he was.

In a small clearing just off from the river, the fox threw down his cape and drew his blade. The lemur had nothing to discard, not in an honourable fight anyway. With the badger stood to the side, Wolfgang entered the clearing and drew his cutlass.

A harsh wind blew through the trees, carrying the echoing voice of the lemur's father; "Come back a real man, or don't come back at all."

When the wind died down, the fox lifted a cry of his own: "For honour!"

As the swords met, it was immediately apparent that where Wolfgang was determined and brave, Walther was skilled and expertly trained.

The lemur swung quickly, but he could never strike the fox. The blows were parried effortlessly. And Wolfgang couldn't bring himself to take the vicious opportunities when they arose. Walther's strikes and slashes found no equal. Unstoppable and unable to be intercepted by Wolfgang's less trained hand.

Quickly, the blade found flesh. The lemur was unprepared to handle the pain of being struck. Once the fox made his first successful strike, Wolfgang was soon consumed by the flash of the blade. As more strikes came, the lemur could barely swing to defend. Bloodied, tunic torn, the pain consumed him.

Wolfgang was defeated.

Falling to his knees, the lemur was kept from slamming into the ground completely by the fox's blade resting against his throat.

The ruffed lemur's pain gave way to thought. He thought of the failure of it all. What his mother and father had said. Realising the only option he had left, he began to weep. "I have been crushed. Let me have my honour." The lemur whispered, staring deeply into Walther's eyes. "Kill me."

The wind surged through the clearing again. It's bloodthirsty voice rushed through the leaves, letting Wolfgang's plea echo and ring. With a twitch of the wrist, Walther seemed to consider it.

"No." the fox whispered at last, withdrawing the sword. Wolfgang's body crumpled to the ground, the hard grass battering against his bones. He tilted his head just enough to see Walther pick up his cheap cutlass. "Instead, I will take this. I can see it's more valuable to you than your life is anyway." He swung it in the air before the lemur. Wolfgang tried to beg for it to be returned, but his lungs were dry and empty.

"This is the true mercy, I hope you understand." Walther grunted. "Today, I take your blade. If you're foolish enough to return, I won't hesitate to take your life." The fox turned heel and walked back towards the city, the badger in tow.

"I hope you understand that he will be back?" The lemur overheard the badger say.

"What makes you say that?"

"I am observant of things Sire otherwise misses."

The woodland had been calm on Wolfgang's walk to the city. Where indecision and fear fought to sway him from his path, he turned to what he trusted most; he followed the river. In his twenty years, he'd learned that the river was never wrong. But the river had given a kinder request; to turn back, that he didn't need to do this.

But Wolfgang wanted honour, wanted the right to have pride. Because that was what the lemur was to be. And in that, he had ignored the river's words and paid the price.

Wolfgang had long heard tales of the fox, the master swordsman from the city. A year ago, Walther and his army had been summoned to Wolfgang's village to ward off an invading force. The lemur, hiding behind the wooden palisade and gazing through the cracks in the wall, had seen the brave, strong, *male* fox in combat and was enamoured ever since.

Whether he was allowed to be so smitten, well, that depended. If Walther could beat Wolfgang sufficiently that he would realise what a real man was, and buck his ideas up to become it, his mother and father had reasoned that perhaps his infatuation with a man was acceptable. They did remind him that submission to such a man would be punished severely, though when Wolfgang had taken up the old sword and set out to duel him, they were thrilled.

Either he'd become a real man, or he'd die.

A different, less bloodthirsty wind swirled.

Air finally filled the lemur's lungs.

Blood stained the grass.

To live or to die; the decision must be made.

Wolfgang staggered to his feet.

Live.

He hobbled his way to the river, to begin cleaning his cuts and scars. The river did not scorn him for his foolishness, nor reject him. Once again, it sought to help. And it cleaned Wolfgang's wounds as best it could.

The ruffed lemur's red-tinged reflection gazed back at him. To be a real man or to die in the course.

He'd achieved neither.

Perhaps he could fight again. Avenge his loss. Nowhere was he told that to be a man you had to win in your first attempt. Though there were never specifics. Just nebulous concepts.

With his cuts as clean as he could make them, he turned heel to head back towards his village. Clean wounds were good, but bandaged ones were essential. With haste alone, he began to limp home.

On the path, a few miles outside of the village, the river guided him past a small blacksmith's hut. It was the abode of a crocodile named Gianfranco. Wolfgang had only spoken to him a handful of times, after all he'd only picked up a sword for the first time a matter of days ago.

As he passed, he considered asking there for help with his wounds. But he reasoned that a blacksmith likely wouldn't have bandages. So he wandered onwards.

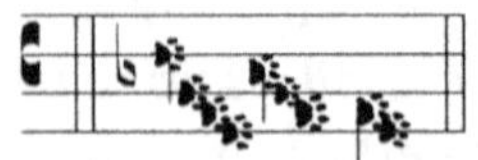

"You still haven't told me what happened." The priest whispered, wrapping the last of the bandages around the ruffed lemur's arm.

"I did." Wolfgang grunted. "I had a duel."

The badger sat back on the pew. "Wolfgang, if you've been attacked and are worried that I would mock you, I promise I-"

"I'm not lying" Wolfgang grunted. "I got in a duel with Walther, from the city."

Father Franco's brow furrowed. "You went to Vanguard to duel Walther?" His disbelief soon became displeasure. "How much training have you had?"

"None." The lemur grunted. "I was just given the blade and told to manifest manhood."

"You could have died!" The priest protested.

"Unfortunately I didn't."

Franco growled and dismissed Wolfgang's words with his paw. "Your lips drip of poison. Your family put you up to this, didn't they?"

"My family requested preparations for its next patriarch." Wolfgang said. "My father is ill, when he dies, who is to lead it?"

"Oh and this is how one is created, is it? Hand a young man a sword and send him to die?" The badger continued. "I've seen the grave of your brother. I have accepted that the Lord sees fit for me to see your father's grave next, but do not let me see yours before my fur goes completely grey."

"Then what am I to do?" The lemur asked. "What is my purpose, if not to fulfil destiny as patriarch when the time comes?"

"Who will be your wife, Wolfgang?" The badger asked.

The question brought silence to the room. Wolfgang turned his head. "The question is irrelevant."

"The question is completely relevant. Once you return, drenched in the blood of your foes, you must marry a wife and make children. I may have my vows of celibacy, but I know precisely how it is meant to work." Father Franco nodded. "And I know one thing about Wolfgang; He seeks not a wife."

"I have said no such thing!" The lemur snarled. "Do not deceive me into a false confession!"

The badger took a calm breath. "The Church and the Word of Jesus Christ. What makes you think the two have much in common?"

Wolfgang narrowed his gaze and Franco smiled.

"I have often heard confessions from women who are fearful, for they have found that great magic that is love within another woman. And of men, shivering and shaking, terrified to discover that they have found that very same love within another man. I have seen how direly they all feared damnation for it." The badger said. "The only thing 'false' about their confessions was that they felt the need to confess at all." Franco took another breath and his voice softened again. "That being said, anything you must say, I will hold under the seal of confession, even if it needs no forgiveness."

"What would you know about the way of the man?" Wolfgang grunted. "To whom is to say that the path of meekness and scripture is that of truth and glory?"

Franco snorted and folded his arms. "Am I not male? Male like you? Male like Walther?" He gave the ruffed lemur a weary gaze. "Wolfgang will do anything to earn the love and respect of powerful men, for it is this love and respect that fuels his every move. His father may shout, but his heart doth scream." Franco continued. "But who is to say that a man respects and loves a man who answers aggression with aggression?"

Wolfgang fumbled back and glared. "I will not sit here and be deceived into sin." Abruptly, and slightly shakily, he stood up. "I thank you for your healing, and I bid you good day."

And with that, the lemur stormed out.

With his tunic in tatters, Wolfgang set off for the one person he believed could help him; Gianfranco.

With no money on him, he departed back through the woods. The river was cautious as ever about what Wolfgang had planned. But it acquiesced and led the lemur to Gianfranco's hut.

"I wish to earn a sword from you" The lemur requested.

The crocodile blinked. "...earn?" He grunted. "I know of your father, you have no need to "earn"..." he dismissed.

"My father bestows me no gifts, nor love until I earn it." Wolfgang said. "Please, I'll do anything you need, anything you desire."

Gianfranco paused. "You would clean and sweep? For that is what I would ask of you. The jobs that someone in your position has never had to consider doing."

"My mother and father had punished me with them many times before." Wolfgang said. "I do not fear it, as it will not be a punishment, but a chance at victory."

The crocodile nodded. "Very well. I agree."

And so, Wolfgang brushed and swept, cleaned and kept. The days were long and dirty, dusty and rough, but the lemur was working out of want rather than punishment. After long days, he would depart back to the river to wash, this time soot and dirt, not blood, from his fur. Then the walk back home. Before long, however, Gianfranco would let the lemur share the sleeping quarters within the hut.

In breaks from the heat of the furnace, Wolfgang would be allowed to take up one of the blemished blades that had defected in the forge, and practice using it. It helped him twofold, to be better equipped when he met Walther again, but also to distract from the conflict he felt over Gianfranco. For while he was not the model "real man" that his mother and father had so wished for him to become, there was no denying that he found the strong-yet-quiet masculinity of the crocodile appealing in its own right.

"Who taught you to duel?" Gianfranco asked.

The lemur blinked, snapping out of his cleaning and wiping his brow. "Nobody did." Wolfgang replied. "I'm learning as I go."

The crocodile grumbled and lit the forge. "Most people don't survive long that way."

"Well I don't have much of a choice." The lemur replied. "Who else is going to teach me?"

The crocodile stopped and the room hung in an uncomfortable silence.

"How much would it cost-"

"I'm not teaching you." Gianfranco said firmly. "Every man at one point in their life feels the need to take up the blade. Or so they say. I learned how to use one, in the hope of never needing to. And I focus so much on crafting swords as to ensure that I would be more useful with a hammer in my hand." The crocodile picked up the tongs and withdrew a glowing rod from the furnace. "And besides... by now you've likely learned more than I could teach you."

"What makes you say that?" Wolfgang asked, but as the words left his lips, Gianfranco's hammer met the steel and the lemur's voice was lost in the violence.

By week's end, the crocodile handed Wolfgang a longsword.

The lemur took it and thanked the crocodile who simply stared sadly at him.

"Why are you doing this?" The crocodile asked at last.

"Because I must."

"Why?"

Wolfgang grumbled. "Because... because it's my duty, to my family and to my kin. To become the new patriarch. To be a real man."

The crocodile rubbed his head. "That's not really why you're doing this though, is it?"

Wolfgang once again got impatient. "I told you no mistruth!"

"But that's not the real truth either." He insisted. "If you were doing it for other people, you wouldn't have spent the past month cleaning my courtyard just to earn a sword to go and fight Walther again."

"You saw the last duel?"

"I saw what the man did to you. What do you think you will gain from fighting him again?"

"It's not about what I gain."

"You lie again." Gianfranco grumbled. "Before I let you have this sword," The crocodile said, snatching the blade back. "You will tell me the truth. Why do you keep fighting Walther?"

The wind blew once again. That bloodthirsty wind.

"I want to be loved!" Wolfgang barked at last. "That's all I've ever wanted!"

Gianfranco's arms drooped at his side in disbelief.

"Is that good enough for you?!" The lemur pulsed with rage. "If people's love wasn't conditional on me being a warrior, a swordsman, a soldier of fortune, then maybe I wouldn't throw everything I have at achieving it!" He snarled again, snatching the sword back from the crocodile's hands. "If I die in the quest for love, then I will die with dignity and honour!"

With blade in hand, Wolfgang stormed off towards the city.

Gianfranco watched him go. "If you want to be loved, all you have to do is ask." The crocodile whispered into the wind.

The river objected. It objected with all its might. It wove Wolfgang in circles through the forest to try and make him stop. But it was just a river, and Wolfgang was a fool in love. The ruffed lemur reached the clearing once again, where he found the fox stood waiting for him.

"Walther, I'm delighted to hear you've accepted my challenge again." The lemur smiled, drawing his new sword.

The fox glared at Wolfgang's ripped tunic. "I see your priorities are unchanging. You still wear rags and ignore my warnings. You've wasted your money on another sword such that you can waste what remains of your life upon my blade." The fox replied bitterly, drawing his sword. "Very well. A mercy killing it shall be." The two began to slowly circle each other.

"I spend my money and my time where it is of value." Wolfgang grinned. "I don't need expensive leather and alluring tights to win a duel and claim my glory."

"Glory? That's what you want?" Walther snarled, becoming far angrier than the lemur anticipated.

The lemur laughed. "You doubt my sincerity still? Perhaps you are the fool." He gave the fox a look that wiser men would understand, but it seemed Walther did not. "I ask for my sword. And I wish to meddle with those stronger than I. It is the way, is it not?"

The fox grunted. "You are wise at least enough to know that I am stronger than you. That you cannot even equal me. But indeed, that ever since I spared you, I wanted to fight you again."

"To the death?" The lemur asked with a raised eyebrow and a smile.

Walther faltered. Not fear, it seemed, but that perhaps he was finally understanding what the lemur was actually saying.

"On your guard." Walther announced.

Wolfgang stepped forth and immediately, their blades met.

Instantaneously, the lemur outpaced his former self.

Walther seemed to assume that his old tricks would be enough. They were not.

The quickfooted lemur dodged a slash of the blade, before striking the slower fox across the chest.

Wolfgang was astonished for a split second as Walther lost concentration.

He was doing it.

The fox made a heavy strike, but the lemur ducked aside.

Another quick slash.

Parried, but barely.

Incoming strike.

Parried too, but Wolfgang could feel it was his weakness if Walther could get through.

Quick slash.

Contact.

The fox's thick tunic ripped and the blade had made its mark.

Walther snarled, and Wolfgang got another strike in while the fox was unsettled.

But then Walther swung again and this time Wolfgang was not able to parry perfectly.

The blade got to the lemur, but not as harshly as before.

The world began to swirl a little, but Wolfgang's focus was stronger now.

The wind roared, overjoyed for it was going to drink the blood of two this day.

Another strike.

Another hit.

The fox was furious.

Pained.

Angry.

Concentration slipping.

But Wolfgang was still not as agile as he hoped.

And still the fox's blade could and did cut deep.

Finally, Walther landed a blow across Wolfgang's chest.

It cut the primate's flesh, yet also snagged the remains of the tunic, ripping it clean off above the waist and knocking the lemur off his feet and leaving him in what amounted to a loincloth.

The fox moved in to strike the fallen Wolfgang, to finish him once and for all.

But as the fox brought his blade down, the lemur raised his again, blocking him at the pass.

"Not so easy this time, is it?" Wolfgang teased.

"You have lost!" Walther bellowed "I will slaughter you!"

"Then do." The lemur kicked the fox firmly in the gut, knocking him back.

While Walther regained his footing, the lemur sprung back up and swung for him again.

Again, the fox underestimated his foe. He was struck to the side and at the shoulder, where a hole was poked through the leather, the blade able do more damage in the area it had made for itself.

"You still don't believe I am deserving, do you? You really are the fool. The one who underestimates his foe. Blinded by the arrogance of the very manliness that I am drawn to you by." Wolfgang grinned, bleeding but too full of adrenalin to notice. "If in death I may at least teach you not to underestimate those around you, perhaps it will be worth it. I may have failed in my quest, but it might not be in vain."

"You are nothing! A deranged rat! I should have slaughtered you while I had the chance! I don't know what worth you think you deserve, but you deserve none! For victory is the decider of worth, and I will be the victor!" Walther shouted, still oblivious to the obvious. "I shall not be dishonoured by some pathetic, gutless knave!"

The lemur took a deep breath. The fox's tongue cut him far deeper than any sword could.

The wind shook the trees impatiently. It's poison words begged for the ultimate feast; to claim the lives of both of them.

The pair raised their blades again and swung.

The two clattered.

And shattered.

Two severed blades swung off into the red grass, leaving both wielding little more than stubs.

"Jacob! Get me my broadsword!" Walther called to an aide.

There was no aide. Where the badger had stood in the last duel, there was now nobody. Now Walther too was one man, all alone.

Wolfgang threw down the sword's handle. It had only lasted one battle, but it was the one that mattered.

The wind retreated, humiliated and defeated, leaving just the sound of the river's wise waters.

It seemed the Lord had found him worthy, at last. That finally, their masculinity was assured, strong, equal and noble. That finally, Wolfgang was a real man, deserving of Walther's love. And with this masculinity, Wolfgang would be able to assert the validity of this homosexual love over the whims of his mother and father. That with this masculinity alone, all life would fall into place at last.

And most foolishly of all, Wolfgang thought he could now convince the fox of his worth too.

"Perhaps we shall call that a draw." The lemur smiled, holding out his paw. "It has been a pleasure fighting you again." He said, closing the distance between himself and Walther and staring deeply into the fox's eyes.

What he found inside the fox's eyes was not love.

Wolfgang could see the moment Walther finally realised, finally understood what the lemur was hoping to gain.

The fox staggered back. "God's Blood! That's what you want? You think I'd stoop to such a thing? You insult me! Pah!" He growled. "I shall get forth another blade and make good my promise to kill you! I will not be bested! I will not be defeated and sodomised by some half-naked godless savage!" He snarled, turning heel and storming back to the town.

Wolfgang stood numb as the fox's figure limped back towards the city, a trail of blood following him. The wind swirled again, but Wolfgang ignored it's cheap poison.

As Walther disappeared out of sight, the lemur's feet found purchase and he retreated to the river.

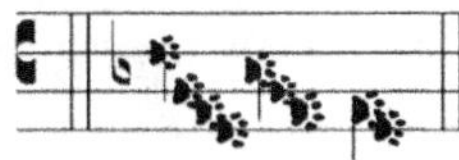

The river once again cleaned Wolfgang's wounds. The ruffed lemur pondered what he really saw in Walther.

But more than that, he realised that Walther, the masculine one, the template of the male identity, had given into rage, demanding the right to kill him, over little more than a handshake. Little more than respect. Little more than love. And even worse, Wolfgang had deemed that perfectly acceptable.

Paradoxically, the realisation that all of this was in vain didn't cut at him. Not at all. The idea freed him. He realised that the things he had been told, that his father had demanded of him, that his gut believed to be lies, were truly thus; lies.

As he climbed from the river, his only worry was of being caught duelling again. But he knew his wounds needed to be bandaged and soon. Perhaps he could earn favour by telling Father Franco that this was his last duel? That he was right? Wolfgang gathered his strength and made his way back up the road.

"You survived?"

The lemur stumbled.

Gianfranco was staring over at him, stood on the riverbank in his tunic.

"I did."

"I'm glad." The crocodile said, closing the distance between them. "Come, your cuts need bandages and quickly."

The crocodile and badger sat either side of Wolfgang, the former watching and helping as the latter made busy with the water and bandages.

"Have you made peace with the futility of your father's dreams yet, Wolfgang?" Father Franco asked, a slight sternness to his tone.

"Yes." Wolfgang said, cheeks growing wet "This will be the last time".

"Forgive me the transgression of disbelief." The badger grunted. "It's a good thing Gainfranco brought you back here, otherwise I doubt they'd let a man in a loincloth covered in cuts through the gate."

Before Wolfgang could repost, there was a cry from the gate-house.

"I am Walther of Vanguard!" The words rang throughout the village. "Bring me the one named Wolfgang! The impotent duelist, the rat of your town, such that I may avenge the slight on my honour!"

"It seems the man you love seeks you." Gianfranco whispered.

Wolfgang wiped his eyes. "I love him no more."

"What do we do?" The crocodile asked the badger.

"Vanguard is mighty and so is Walther's seat at its court. If his anger is left to fester, he could take out his vengeance over the entire town, and cause the city to no longer protect us." He looked back to Wolfgang. "Do you believe you could talk him down?"

The lemur shook his head. "If I believed I could, I might still be in love with him."

Father Franco sighed. "Then... I fear you might be forced to take up the blade again."

"Very well." Wolfgang whispered. "I will need another sword, mine was destroyed along with his in the duel."

Reluctantly, Gianfranco handed Wolfgang his own blade. Then, the crocodile kissed him. "Good luck."

The gate opened. There, alongside the crocodile, stood Wolfgang.

What once was a tunic, torn down to just a breechcloth. His body adorned with scars, of flesh and of mind. He clutched Gianfranco's sword in his hand. He stepped out towards the fox, a shoddy patchwork of bandages beneath Walther's damaged armour and a new sword in his paw.

Wolfgang stared Walther down. The fox's eyes of fire glared back at him. His glare pulsed with rage, discordant and even more male than before. But the lemur was calm, for at last, there was nothing for him to prove.

"Onward to the clearing." Wolfgang said calmly.

"No!" Walther growled. "I want you to suffer here, in front of those you call family."

The crowd murmured and grunted.

"Not here." The lemur said softly, but firmly. "I refuse to bring bloodshed into my home."

The fox scoffed. "A true man would fi-"

"Is that all you think about?!" Wolfgang snapped. "Is that all life is to you? Is a man just an arrogant, angry, impatient, immoral war machine? Is that all your vision permits? Is your destiny written in blood, Walther?"

"It was you who started this! You who came to duel me twice already! And you did it for pride, for glory and for your disgusting perversions!" Walther growled back. "I am many things, but a hypocrite I am not!"

"We don't have to fight. You can just walk back to Vanguard and we can forget all about this." Wolfgang said.

"No, it's too late for that. I want you dead. That's all I want." The fox snarled and slowly backed up.

Uneasily, the pair departed the village. Wolfgang tried to calm himself. His outburst felt justified, but in battle, focus and calm was the lifeblood. To let anger get to you would be your undoing.

The river didn't impede them. And the wind encouraged them on.

They walked until they stood in the clearing again. The wind picked up and rustled the red grass. People hid between trees to watch.

"I have pride. I have dignity. I have the love and adoration of my city and my people." Walther said. "I have ascended to court. The swordsman of the king. You have some vulgar rags around your waist and a perverted mind. We are not equals. Fight me such that I may rid you of your sin."

"Very well." Wolfgang whispered. "Anything to please you."

The fox snarled and charged the lemur.

Wolfgang stayed perfectly still, until Walther was barely feet away, before dodging the fox's overhead blow and slashing him across the chest.

The lemur expected the blow to only temporarily slow the fox. But it did not. Walther tumbled and fell into the grass.

In this moment, Wolfgang could have taken Walther's life. The wind ordered him to do so.

He did not.

The lemur stepped back and prepared, while Walther slowly staggered to his feet, turned, then charged again.

Quick, angry strikes were parried effortlessly by the silent lemur. Focus never waning. Never underestimating his combatant. The fox snarled, growled, cursed and roared. Wolfgang concentrated in silence. The anger and rage was predictable. Imprecise and instinctual. Not strategic. Easy to outsmart.

Their swords caught and their tempo stalled.

The lemur kicked the fox square in the chest.

Walther's grip failed.

His blade soared into the air, where Wolfgang caught its handle.

The fox staggered and slammed back, falling to his knees against a tree, where the lemur stepped forth, crossed both blades and held them against Walther's throat.

"Kill him." The wind seemed to say. "The path to manhood is paved in blood, don't you see?"

In a moment that seemed to last for decades. Wolfgang let his adrenalin subside. Let the sounds of the river return. Let the grace of The Lord dilute his instincts. He drew a long, slow breath, then released it.

Walther looked up at his conqueror in shock and pain.

"You have lost." Wolfgang whispered. "Why?"

The fox blubbered and whimpered.

"Was it worth it, Walther?" The lemur asked.

"W-what?"

"You spent all your worth, all your time, to be the best warrior, best duellist in the land." Wolfgang continued. "And what has it got you?"

The fox only stammered and whined.

"It's got you nowhere." The lemur concluded. He spat in the grass, as if to try and wash some of the blood out of it. "I loved you." He admitted. "For ages I thought you were all I ever wanted. The brave, noble swordsman. A real man. What I was expected to be and to become. And even if I failed to become one, I could love one, or at least die honourably to one."

The pair's eyes met.

What could have been.

"I can't believe I saw anything in you." Wolfgang growled. "I can't believe I wanted your love. I can't believe I wanted to be like you. I can't believe you're what I was told I had to be. I wonder what it might have been like. When you spared my life, I thought you knew what I wanted and was willing to entertain my advance. And that I just wasn't good enough with a sword to earn your love just yet." The lemur let his anger show itself, then breathed it slowly back out. "But I realised when I disarmed you that you care only about being a man. Only about being the best. Honour. Pride. That's all you are."

Walther coughed and whispered. "End this. Kill me."

The wind tried to pressure him again, but the ruffed lemur didn't let it in. Wolfgang drew a long, deep, slow breath. As if he was breathing in their very lives, before exhaling and whispering. "No."

He uncrossed the swords and stepped back, letting Walther fall to the floor, just as Walther had done to him.

"Your life is nothing to me. I only want a man who's worthy of my love. And you are not." The lemur said.

Walther was gathered up and placed in a small narrow boat on the river. Wolfgang and Father Franco went along with the ship's small crew. The river's grace guided the group slowly downstream towards Vanguard.

Wolfgang stared up at the trees as they passed. Walther's whimperings of pain having grown quiet, the fox's wounds being cleaned and dressed by the vicar.

Victory was of no comfort to Wolfgang. None at all.

"What happens now?" Walther asked nervously.

The lemur sat up in the boat "We are taking you back to Vanguard. And then your fate is your own."

"I'm a free man?"

"What use do I have for a man without love in his heart?" Wolfgang replied. "I was invested in you for admiration and love. And I no longer admire you, nor can I love you." The lemur lay back again "So you shall be returned to Vanguard and they can deal with you."

Walther lay silent for a moment, interrupted only by the soft splashes of water wafting up the sides of the narrowboat.

"I can learn to love." Walther said.

Wolfgang laughed. "It is a great tragedy that you should need to learn. That it not be core to your being. It is perhaps a greater tragedy that those who should have taught did not." He shrugged. "Foolish was I, to have assumed that through the act of becoming the king's swordsman and hiring a stout male assistant, you'd have become experienced at interpreting the male gaze."

The fox grunted. "Jacob... I don't know where he is."

"You don't?"

"No, they left me."

"And for why?"

Walther sighed and looked away from the lemur "I drove them away."

Wolfgang snorted. "Perhaps they will accept your grovelling apology where I will not."

"Or I will return to the king's court and bring forth a great army to your city." Walther snarled.

"So that I may make husbands of your entire army?" The lemur laughed and lay back in the boat again. "Walther, Walther, please. Learn. Learn something that doesn't require your swordarm."

The boat arrived at the dock of Vanguard. They moored the ship and Walther was raised out of the boat.

"I'll win you back." Walther snarled.

The lemur's cackle filled the air. "How your priorities change! But I am not yours to win! I feel flattered to be a man's prize, but you can no longer win me." He grinned at the furious fox. "Though, if you wished to impress me, you might be able to learn my respect, though never my love, if you brought me a knitted scarf. Or a sewn shirt. Perhaps a carved statue. Something to show that Walther of Vanguard is capable of more than violence."

The fox spat into the boat as he was carried ashore. "What will you do without me!?"

"Your sword." Wolfgang said, offering the blade back to the crocodile.

Gianfranco nodded and took the blade back. "Thank you."

"While I appreciate your craftsmanship to no end, I hope you take no offence that I will never ask for, nor buy a sword again."

The crocodile smiled. "I take none at all." He said. "I only hope that you find comfort and purpose without a swordarm."

Wolfgang chuckled and stepped closer still. "Perhaps I will learn to sew and knit."

"Perhaps then you will wear more than a loincloth?" The crocodile teased with a raise of the eyebrow.

"Perhaps." The ruffed lemur said.

"You kissed me in the church." Wolfgang continued, placing a paw on Gianfranco's chest.

"I did." The crocodile said with a blush. "I was worried The Lord would damn me for it."

"But it seems, as Father Franco predicted, He did not." Wolfgang said. "You have convinced me well to lay down the sword. Could I convince you to lay down yours too, and instead..." The lemur leaned close and kissed the Gianfranco on the lips. "Lay your love upon me?"

"I'm afraid you cannot." The crocodile put his hands on Wolfgang's shoulders. "For I am already convinced." Gianfranco eased his lips against the lemur's own, and the two kissed and embraced. Finally comfortable and confident that, whatever they were seen as, by Walther, by Father Franco, by Wolfgang's mother or father, they would be seen first as lovers.

NightEyes DaySpring

NightEyes DaySpring is a known troublemaker who is rumored to have a penchant for coffee and an interest in dead, ancient civilizations. He has been writing furry fiction for over twenty years, and over thirty-five of his short stories have been published. His work has appeared in various anthologies, including Werewolves vs. Fascism, Heat, and FANG. He also has contributed multiple stories to The Voice of Dog podcast, and he recently published his first novel, Scars of the Golden Dancer. Currently, NightEyes resides in Florida with his fiancé, where in his spare time he masquerades as an IT professional, plays board games, and doodles. Visit his website, nighteyes-dayspring.com, for more about his writing, or find out where he is on social media at nighteyes.carrd.co.

J.F.R. Coates

J.F.R. Coates is a speculative fiction author living in Australia, though originally from the picturesque West Country of England. Her stories tend to focus away from human characters, instead giving life to the creatures that dwell alongside the familiar. She has been the Furry Writers' Guild president since 2021.

Alex T. Dragonson

Alex T. Dragonson lives in the Pacific Northwest and spins cozy hopeful yarns from atop a hoard of cozy yarn. You can find more of their work on the Voice of Dog podcast.

Fopfox

Fop is a furry writer and IT worker from Vancouver, Canada. Most of his stories deal with fantasy or science fiction and can be found on https://fopfox.sofurry.com/.

Erik

Erik is a Furry Writer on Sofurry, under the username Erik2000.
Writer of the ongoing series A Biorgaphy of a Human, and a General History lover with a paticular affinity for Sinology, Egyptology
and Ottoman studies.

Televassi

Televassi's stories have been previously published in a number of
anthologies and publications in the furry fandom. They write in a
number of genres, but mostly fantasy, science fiction, and speculative fiction. You can find more about them and their writing on the
usual furry places, including televassi.sofurry.com/.

Valduin

Valerie "Valduin" Gershman is an artist, propmaker, and author
lurking in the cold forests of Canada. She loves all things fantasy and
science fiction. When not running dragonstormstudios.ca, she can
be found managing construction projects and screaming at paper
until art appears.

Rob MacWolf

Rob MacWolf lives somewhere in North America waiting for the
world to end. In the meantime he practices neo-pagan sunset worship, writes poetry, and hosts the audiofiction podcast The Voice of
Dog, at thevoice.dog.

Domus Vocis

Nathan "Domus Vocis" Hopp is an author, writer, storyteller, and
dedicated lover of literature and learning history. His debut novel is
a historic coming-of-age fantasy set in 1890s New York titled "The

Adventures of Peter Gray", and he's been published in anthologies such as "Furries Hate Nazis", "The Haunted Den", and others. If you can't find him writing in a quiet café or reading in a library, he can be found on https://domus-vocis.sofurry.com, as well as on Twitter @HoppNate

J.S. Hawthorne

J.S. Hawthorne was raised in New England, but now lives in exile on Long Island, where she pretends to be a lawyer by day. She is almost definitely not three mice in a trenchcoat, probably. She requests if you enjoy her story to leave a large hunk of cheddar underneath the fedora, and to ignore the squeaking.

Utunu

Utunu has been a video game developer since the mythical early '90s, and is fond of worldbuilding, linguistics, ancient history, fantasy, and Oxford commas. He's written a few short stories, two of which have received both a Cóyotl and Leo Award. His recently published first novel, 'Rafts', is now available at his website, mapakuvillage.com.

Casimir Laski

Casimir Laski is a writer, YouTuber, and literary critic from Virginia. He is the author of Winter Without End, a post-apocalyptic survival story told from the perspective of a dog, inspired by the animal stories he grew up reading. Additionally, he writes for Furry Book Review, and operates the YouTube channel Cardinal West, primarily devoted to discussion of literary xenofiction and western animation.

Rose LaCroix

Rose LaCroix, sometimes known as Threetails or The Sword Vixen, has been writing furry fiction for 20 years. Her first published novel, Basecraft Cirrostratus, has been in print since 2010. She has a long-time interest in medieval history. Some of her medieval history research has been published on Brittanica.com. She is also a medieval reenactor and historic European martial artist, specializing in Italian longsword. She lives in the Portland area with her husband Kobi and their cat Venus, and is interested in working as a historical consultant for film and television.

Thomas "Faux" Steele

Thomas "Faux" Steele is an author and attorney who has been creating short stories since 2015. He enjoys writing in many genres, including horror, science-fiction, fantasy, and adult contemporary. He specializes in descriptive stories with rich world-building whose written words render a painting in the reader's mind. His work has been printed in many anthologies, including FANG Vol. 7, Exploring New Places, and Beast Vol. 1 as well as many 'zines including #OhMurr. In his free time, he's an avid coin collector and fancier of antiquities and fine art, almost all thrifted or picked from estate sales.

Cedric G! Bacon

Ziegenbock

Ziegenbock is a goat from the United Kingdon who wields both pen and sword (though rarely at the same time). He was the winner of the 2021 Sofurry Short Story Contest, and his work has been featured by Thurston Howl Publications and The Voice of Dog podcast. He has upcoming work with Fenris Publishing and Oak Paw Publications.

Faolan

Faolan is a writer and dancer living in the Netherlands. He spends his days trying to teach kids the beautiful English language, and his nights gaming, watching series or films, writing, reading, buying things he absolutely doesn't need, and hoarding gems and jewellery. You can read more of his work in publications by Thurston Howl Publications and Weasel Press, such as Infurno, Purrgatorio, Slashers, Dogpile, BEAST, and the Howling Dead.

Pascal Farful

Pascal Farful is an author, musician, fursuiter, railway enthusiast and photographer. At one point almost all of these occoured at once. He lives in a hollowed out volcano on the outskirts of the UK where Angels Pizza Company fear to tread.

www.ingramcontent.com/pod-product-compliance
Lightning Source LLC
Chambersburg PA
CBHW050009070726
47598CB00015B/2254